LOVE'S AWAKENING

"Open your eyes, Sarah," Nick whispered. His breath fanned her face even as his fingers outlined the contours of her mouth. "You're so beautiful," he whispered, his breath warm against her face. "You have eyes that can look beyond and capture a man's soul."

For an instant, panic filled her. She didn't want to capture anyone's soul. But her body was mesmerized by his touch and his eyes refused to let her look away. "Please," she whispered.

"Please what?" he teased. "Please stop?" His finger moved over her lips. "Or please continue?" He captured her lips in a first gentle kiss.

Sarah's eyes fluttered closed.

He took possession then, his lips moving over hers. She tasted of wine, and passion, and madness. A small sound, perhaps a sigh, escaped their lips as Nick took the kiss deeper. Like a starving man presented with a banquet, like a pauper presented with untold wealth, there was a strange desperation stirring within him. And suddenly he realized that no matter how much he took, he would never have enough of her.

SURRENDER TO THE PASSION

LOVE'S SWEET BOUNTY   (3313, $4.50)
by Colleen Faulkner

Jessica Landon swore revenge of the masked bandits who robbed the train and stole all the money she had in the world. She set out after the thieves without consulting the handsome railroad detective, Adam Stern. When he finally caught up with her, she admitted she needed his assistance. She never imagined that she would also begin to need his scorching kisses and tender caresses.

WILD WESTERN BRIDE   (3140, $4.50)
by Rosalyn Alsobrook

Anna Thomas loved riding the Orphan Train and finding loving homes for her young charges. But when a judge tried to separate two brothers, the dedicated beauty went beyond the call of duty. She proposed to the handsome, blue-eyed Mark Gates, planning to adopt the boys herself! Of course the marriage would be in name only, but yet as time went on, Anna found herself dreaming of being a loving wife in every sense of the word . . .

QUICKSILVER PASSION   (3117, $4.50)
by Georgina Gentry

Beautiful Silver Jones had been called every name in the book, and now that she owned her own tavern in Buckskin Joe, Colorado, the independent didn't care what the townsfolk thought of her. She never let a man touch her and she earned her money fair and square. Then one night handsome Cherokee Evans swaggered up to her bar and destroyed the peace she'd made with herself. For the irresistible miner made her yearn for the melting kisses and satin caresses she had sworn she could live without!

MISSISSIPPI MISTRESS   (3118, $4.50)
by Gina Robins

Cori Pierce was outraged at her father's murder and the loss of her inheritance. She swore revenge and vowed to get her independence back, even if it meant singing as an entertainer on a Mississippi steamboat. But she hadn't reckoned on the swarthy giant in tight buckskins who turned out to be her boss. Jacob Wolf was, after all, the giant of the man Cori vowed to destroy. Though she swore not to forget her mission for even a moment, she was powerfully tempted to submit to Jake's fiery caresses and have one night of passion in his irresistible embrace.

Available wherever paperbacks are sold, or order direct from the Publisher. Send cover price plus 50¢ per copy for mailing and handling to Zebra Books, Dept. 3435, 475 Park Avenue South, New York, N.Y. 10016. Residents of New York, New Jersey and Pennsylvania must include sales tax. DO NOT SEND CASH.

RAINY KIRKLAND

BEWITCHING KISSES

ZEBRA BOOKS
KENSINGTON PUBLISHING CORP.

To Bob, Nancy, Jerry, and Lois who
Produced Mike, Chrissie,
Jimmy, Lindsay, and Ashley.
Now That's *Creativity*

Special thanks to Maryjane Nauss of Venice, Florida, for research and to Bev, Bernadette, Bernice, and Lee of Rhapps for their support

ZEBRA BOOKS

are published by

Kensington Publishing Corp.
475 Park Avenue South
New York, NY 10016

First printing: June, 1991

Printed in the United States of America

Chapter One

Salem, Massachusetts

The last rays of the full moon danced in eerie splendor on the snow-covered Massachusetts countryside. Snowcapped pines and ancient oaks with their stark gray branches encased in ice stood at attention as the cock crowed. The bitter wind answered in kind. But as it raced through the tiny village of Salem touching every household with its frigid bite, it left fear and apprehension in its wake.

Samuel Wittfield hung the milking stool away, then turned to face the sleek black cat that sat silently watching him. The cat had arrived at the barn two days ago, and with it had come the idea; just a vague notion at first, without form or substance. But this morning, as he milked during the cold gray hour before dawn, Samuel felt the idea germinate and begin to grow. Before him sat the devil's familiar and the answer to his prayers.

Carefully, he poured some treasured cream into a cracked dish and gently nudged it toward the cat with the toe of his boot. He'd have to be very careful that no one saw the beast until his scheme could be put into motion. Mesmerized, he watched the pink

5

tongue reach out again and again until the dish was empty. The cat sat back and looked up at Samuel expectantly.

"You keep yourself hidden for the next few days and don't go wandering off," he ordered. The cat's ear twitched. "You do this for me and there'll be more cream than you can drink."

The cat stretched lazily, then picked out a patch of ground where the sun's first rays poured in between two cracked boards. She circled twice, then curled into a tight black ball to sleep.

"Just see that you stay there." Turning, Samuel stumbled over the milk pails and hit the ground hard. "Damnation," he swore, watching the milk spread over the frozen earth. But as he rubbed the sting from his knee and thigh, a slow smile covered his weathered face. He would use this, too, for his advantage. Giving up cream for his morning porridge would be a small enough price to pay for five hundred of the best acres in Salem Village. Gingerly he stood and brushed off his clothing. Then with the side of his boot, he pushed straw and dirt over the puddle of milk.

Samuel walked softly to the barn door with an empty milk pail in his hand. These were dangerous times in Salem, and they would suit his purpose well. Massachusetts was without a charter, a colony adrift without direction. Old feuds had begun to surface and three townsfolk had already been arrested as witches. Samuel smiled at the sight of the sleeping cat.

"You just stay there where it's warm," he whispered, "and when the hour is at hand, you'll travel with me to visit little Sarah." Taking no chances, Samuel carefully latched the barn door behind him. The wind stung his cheeks as he stomped over the snow-covered path to the house.

"Elizabeth," Samuel bellowed, allowing the door to snap open with the wind.

"There is no need to shout, Samuel, and do close the door." Elizabeth Wittfield bent near the fireplace and lifted the porridge pot from its cradle in the coals. "Come, your breakfast is ready."

Samuel pulled off his coat and hung it on the wooden peg behind the door. "Sarah was here yesterday, wasn't she?"

Elizabeth brought the heavy cast iron pot to the table and gave her husband a puzzled look. "You know she was, Samuel, you sat and argued with her at this very table."

Samuel reached down for the milk bucket, held it over the table, and deliberately turned it upside down. Elizabeth gasped as only two large drops ran out to splash on her plate.

"The cow's gone dry."

Elizabeth's eyes grew wide. "Samuel, what are you saying?"

"Witchcraft."

Elizabeth pressed her hand against her heart. "Samuel, no."

Silently, he nodded. "And there be two in Salem Jail that carry her name."

"Sarah Good and Sarah Osborne," Elizabeth whispered, as if saying the names aloud might call forth evil. "Oh, Samuel, no. This can't be happening to us."

Samuel sat down at the table, and propped his head in his hands. "I don't know what to think, Elizabeth. But what I know is that my sister comes to our house and the next day our cows are dry."

Elizabeth took her place at the table and reached for her husband's hand. "Sarah is your sister by marriage only, husband. Forget not that you carry none of the same blood. Besides, you are a good man, Samuel Wittfield. Surely God would not cast another burden upon your shoulders. You've lost your parents and half our land in the same month. So if the cows be dry, then 'tis witchcraft to be sure."

"I fear the Lord is testing me, Elizabeth." Samuel struggled to keep his voice tone weary. "Mayhap Sarah is not the guilty party."

"But she must be." Elizabeth's eyes narrowed with thought. "Sarah is headstrong and willful just like her father. How your mother, God rest her soul, could have fallen in love with that penniless dreamer is beyond me."

A dark scowl covered Samuel's face. "Jon Townsend may have acted the dreamer, but he succeeded in getting half of our family's land to be left to his daughter as a dowry." Samuel reached for the porridge. "Lord forgive me, but I never liked that man."

"Little Sarah." Elizabeth glanced toward the empty bucket then back to her husband. "Samuel, the others accused are old and feeble. Sarah's just a child."

"Now listen, wife." Samuel's voice went soft and menacing. "For the last time, Sarah's no child. With that midnight hair and those flashing eyes, 'tis no wonder the devil took a fancy to her. She's the most comely female in all of Massachusetts, and I'd challenge any man to say different. But facts are facts and now is not the time to ignore them."

Elizabeth dropped her gaze, her hands clasped tightly in her lap. "What shall we do, husband? I cringe at the thought that one in our very family would consort with the devil."

Samuel laid a comforting hand on his wife's shoulder as his plot became clearer. "Mayhap it would do you good to go over to the Widow Tate's and ask her to pray with you for Sarah. I have business that will take me into Salem Port this morning and I shall not be home till evening." Samuel placed a fleeting kiss on the top of his wife's head. "I would not have you be alone this day."

Elizabeth looked up at her husband with troubled eyes. "Do you really think that Ann Tate can be trusted? You know how she likes to carry tales, and well . . ."

Samuel sat back in his chair and hastily began to eat. "I am sure that you can press her into your confidence, my dear. If you stress how important it is for none to know the circumstances that prevail, I believe she will truly help us to do the right thing." Samuel offered the porridge, but Elizabeth just shook her head.

"I shall spend every hour in prayer," she stated quietly.

Samuel rose from the table and reached for his coat. "You just finish your chores and then spend the day with Ann. And Elizabeth . . ." His voice grew hard. "On no account are you to go into the barn today. We know not what other madness might be afflicting those animals, and I'll not have you placed in danger while I am away. I want your word that you'll not open the barn door for any reason."

Elizabeth looked up. How like Samuel to think of her safety at a time such as this. "Have a safe trip, husband." She smiled weakly. "You have my word."

Sarah Townsend clutched her cape more securely around her as she stood in the Salem graveyard. The March wind stung her eyes, bringing tears that were already too close to the surface.

"I miss you both so much." She reached down and pushed some dead leaves away from the marker that carried the names of her parents. "The snow was bad last Sunday," Sarah whispered against the wind. "And I attended services at the meeting house instead of traveling over to Topsfield. You would never have stood for such goings-on, Papa." Sarah shivered. "Some children disrupted the services and the Reverend Mr. Parris did nothing to stop them. I understand now why you disliked the man so intensely." Sarah rubbed her hands against the cold. "Evil is in the air." She took a shallow breath. "You can almost taste it." Her fingers again traced over the cold gray stone. "And Mama . . ." she whispered. "Did you have any premonition of the turmoil you would cause?" A sad smile touched her face. "I didn't need all that land to know that you loved me. And now Samuel feels that you have betrayed him." Heedless of the snow, Sarah knelt at the gravestone. "What am I to do, Mama? Samuel will barely speak to me he is so angry, and now George Porter has asked me to marry him. You know that he and Samuel have always been rivals. What am I to do?"

The clouds moved across the sun and the wind took on a sharper bite. Sarah ran her fingers across the stone's rough surface one last time, then rose and shook the snow from her cape. With the wind at her back her steps quickened as she moved between the carved gray stones. Reaching the gate, she was surprised to find Elizabeth and the Widow Tate huddled near the entrance.

"Whatever are you doing here, sister?" Sarah took Elizabeth's hand and found it stiff from cold. " 'Tis too bitter a day for you to visit the graves. Come, both of you, I will see you warm."

"Actually, Sarah, we were coming to visit you."

10

Ann's voice held a curious tone as they walked briskly back toward Sarah's house.

Once inside, Sarah quickly built up the fire and put her kettle on. She pulled the high-backed settle close to the hearth to trap the heat and carefully positioned a corn-husk mat for her guests to warm their feet. With a practiced hand she measured spices into the cider, then moved to the dresser to gather her mother's best earthenware cups. Slowly the warmth of the fire began to invade the room.

"Tell me, Sarah . . ." Ann's voice was sharp. "Do you spend much time in the graveyard?"

Sarah smiled and reached for the kettle. "Sometimes, when I need answers. I find it a restful place to think."

"So you like doing your thinking in the graveyard?"

Sarah turned a quizzical glance back toward her guest. "My parents are buried there. You know that. And these days," she thought of the feud between George Porter and her brother, "I find I miss them more than I can bear."

"And what did you think of Reverend Parris's text last Sunday?" Ann gave a curious sniff at her steaming cup.

" 'Tis fresh cider, Ann," Sarah said softly. "I drew it just this morning."

Ann sniffed again. "But 'tis not plain. What did you put in here?"

Sarah gave the widow a patient smile. "It's chamomile flowers and sassafras root with a touch of maple syrup." She handed a cup to Elizabeth. "Your favorite."

"Darling . . ." Elizabeth's voice quivered with uncertainty. "You know how much I enjoy your special brews, but perhaps today," she glanced nervously toward her companion, "if you have it, plain would be more welcomed."

Stunned, Sarah reached for their cups. Elizabeth was always after her to share her special herb mixtures. What had happened to change her so? She watched her guests watching her as she emptied the kettle and poured in fresh cider.

"You didn't answer my question, Sarah," Ann commanded. "I wish to know your feelings on Sunday's service. You and your parents always went to Topsfield and now suddenly you decide to attend our own meeting house. I would know why."

Sarah sat on a low stool at Elizabeth's feet. " 'Tis no great mystery, Ann. The snow was heavy last week, and rather than miss Sacrament Sunday, I decided to stay in Salem."

"And how did you find the service?"

Anger flashed in Sarah's violet eyes. "Most distressing. Never have I seen such a spectacle. You were there." She looked up at Elizabeth. "You saw the way those children were allowed to behave. And not one word of admonishment was uttered."

"Dear . . ." Elizabeth's hand trembled as she hesitantly touched Sarah's shoulder. "The children are afflicted. They're not responsible. Surely you could see that."

"What I saw were five little girls rolling about on the floor, and not even the Reverend Mr. Parris gave reprimand."

" 'Tis said that they are the victims of witches," Ann announced with authority. "Surely you've heard the news about Goodwife Nurse."

Sarah turned a puzzled look to her brother's wife. "Has something happened to Rebecca?"

"She was arrested yesterday afternoon." Ann looked down her thin nose. "The children named her as their tormentor."

Sarah jerked to her feet and began to pace. "That is the most ridiculous thing I have ever heard. I went to visit Rebecca just two days ago and found her too poorly to leave her bed." She poured fresh cider and handed them the steaming cups.

"It was her specter that did the mischief," Ann stated as she reached for her drink.

"Darling, I didn't know you were spending time with Goody Nurse." Elizabeth's face grew pale.

Sarah sat back on her stool and took a deep drink of the hot mixture. "I visit Rebecca often. She's an interesting woman and has much to teach. Besides, I love listening to her stories." She gave Ann an irritated glance. "But I don't believe for a minute that those children are bewitched. And certainly not by Rebecca."

Elizabeth's hand visibly trembled as she set her cup back on the table. "But Sarah, Dr. Gribbs stated it himself."

"Bah." Sarah pulled her legs up before her and balanced her cup on her knee. "The good Dr. Gribbs is a kindly man to be sure, but he knows only what is written in his book. Those children are no more afflicted than I am." Filled with righteous anger, Sarah missed the nervous glance exchanged by her guests.

"So you would challenge both the good doctor and a holy man of God?" Ann's voice rose in indignation. "Then just who, pray tell, has gifted you with this wondrous knowledge? I would know your source."

Elizabeth jerked from her chair before Sarah could speak. "I have completely forgotten the time, Sarah dear. Come, Ann, I must see you home before darkness falls. Samuel will be most distressed if he returns home to find an empty house."

Sarah looked to the clock and frowned. Sunset was more than an hour away. "But, Elizabeth . . ."

Elizabeth silenced her with a look. "Thank you for a lovely afternoon, dear." Snatching her cape from the peg, she ushered Ann out the door and into the winter wind.

"Will you wait just a minute," Ann snapped as Elizabeth closed the door behind them. "I am not walking home until my cape is fastened. And why did you insist we leave?"

Elizabeth stomped down the yard leaving the widow to hasten her step or walk alone. When Sarah's front gate was no longer in view she turned to her breathless companion. "Whatever possessed you to question her in that awful manner?" She struggled to keep her voice even. "Do you not realize what could have happened?"

"But we got our answers, didn't we?" Ann challenged.

Elizabeth slowed her step and wiped at her eyes. "Ann, if what we suspect is true, then we would do our cause well not to antagonize Sarah."

"Bah, Sarah would not dare to harm us. We are good Christian women."

Elizabeth paused, despite the bitter cold that urged her onward. "Ann, what if all you say is not true. What if Sarah has already done her damage."

Ann reached for Elizabeth's arm, alarmed by the lack of color in her friend's face. "Elizabeth, what are you saying?"

Elizabeth shuddered, then turned her haunted eyes to her companion. "Did you never think it odd that I have reached my thirty-second year and I have no babies? Every child. I conceived came into this world dead. Does that not tell you something?"

14

Ann's eyes grew wide with confusion.

"Think, Ann. Surely you remember. The year that I married Samuel is the same year Jonathan Townsend came to Salem with his daughter." Elizabeth's voice took on a wistful tone. "How I envied Samuel's mother. With her husband long dead and her only son married off, along came Jonathan Townsend with little Sarah for Prudence to care for."

Ann's eyes grew wide as realization set in. "But after Townsend came, neither you nor Prudence had any more children that lived."

"Exactly." Elizabeth's voice shook with fear. "Now Sarah holds in dowry as much land as Samuel, the rightful heir. If Prudence had had more children, the land would have been divided differently. Or if Samuel and I had children, Prudence surely would have bequeathed land to them in her will. But Sarah is the only child."

"And Sarah can now lay claim to half the land that should have belonged to Samuel alone." Ann Tate straightened her bony shoulders. "If what you say is true, Elizabeth Wittfield, then your husband's sister is indeed a witch. And I must admit that I am not surprised. Sarah is entirely too pretty for her own good. She admits to spending time with an accused witch, and she challenges both the doctor and the good reverend. I think she must commune with the devil."

Elizabeth swayed on her feet. "Samuel does not deserve this. He is a good man. How will he stand the humiliation of having a stepsister who is a witch?"

"Well, if you ask me . . ." Ann paused at the gate to her yard, "I would beg Samuel to speak with the good reverend as soon as possible. If Sarah can make the cows go dry and keep you from having babies, then who knows what else she is capable of doing." With her declaration hanging on the bitter wind, Ann turned and snapped the gate on her friend.

Sarah shivered under the covers. Nights were the hardest. Every evening when she pulled in the latch string and raked the fire, a melancholy would fall like a damp cloak about her shoulders, chilling her bones and surrounding her with fear. The wind rattled the shutters, the boards creaked, and her heart pounded. For two weeks after her parents had died she had not slept at all. The sudden silence of the night had become more than she could bear.

Tonight, even though the hour was well past midnight, she lay awake in her bed. Moonlight streamed through her window but brought no comfort, for the corners of the room were filled with shadows that played with her mind. The wind howled and cold shivers ran down her spine. *I'm such a coward,* she thought, rolling over to bury her face in the pillow. *Mayhap I should just accept George Porter and put an end to this.* But even as the thought surged forth, Sarah knew it was not the answer. Flopping onto her back, she straightened the covers and clasped her hands as if in prayer. *I want a husband,* she whispered to the ceiling. *But I want someone who wants me, not the land I carry.* Warming to the thought, her fantasy bloomed. *I want a man to look at me with the love in his eyes that Papa showed Prudence. He should be kind, and gentle, and caring.* She ticked the list off on her fingers. *And I would not find it amiss if he had a pleasant face. And babies.* She sighed. *He would give me lots and lots of babies.*

A smile touched her lips as she hugged the thought to herself. The face of George Porter surged

16

into her dream and she jerked herself back to reality. *You have no care for me, George Porter,* she thought with sudden clarity, *and I'll not betray my brother.* She thought of the hurt she witnessed on Samuel's face each time he looked at her. *You were wrong, Prudence, to place me equal to Samuel. I know in your heart you meant well, but your death has bequeathed your only son with bitterness.* The wind howled, and Sarah frowned. In the night's stillness she heard horses. Shaking her head, she chided her imagination that would place a body out at midnight. *I could gift Samuel with the land,* she thought suddenly. *Then George Porter would no longer desire me and Samuel would smile again.* But even as she whispered the words to the ceiling, she knew her prospects of marriage would dwindle to naught if she carried no dowry. *'Tis not right to think of myself first,* she decided. *The land belongs to Samuel and I shall learn to be content.*

Reluctantly, she sat up and rubbed her hands over her eyes. Her body ached for sleep, but her mind raced on. Perhaps if she read some verses . . . But she dismissed the notion, knowing full well it was only a ruse to light the taper. And once lit, she would never be able to extinguish it this night.

Taking a deep breath to strengthen her resolve, Sarah flopped back against her pillows and squeezed her eyes tightly shut.

"I am sleepy," she chanted softly. "My eyes are closed and I will sleep." But over and over she thought of the distressing events of the afternoon as Ann Tate's disagreeable words echoed in her mind. She had not meant to speak ill of Dr. Gribbs. He was a kindly old man and she often enjoyed conversing with him. But why, she wondered, did he spout such nonsense as witchcraft? He knew his book did

17

not contain all the secrets. Why, her mother's special salve and herb teas weren't in that volume and he knew it. Had he forgotten all the hours he had spent with Prudence discussing the merits of this potion or that? It simply made no sense.

She rolled over on her side and pulled the covers higher about her. And dear Rebecca. Sarah shivered. If she was cold safe within her bed, how did Rebecca fare in Salem Jail? *I shall go and see for myself tomorrow,* she vowed, mentally listing what blankets and other essentials she might spare. Sarah shifted her pillow. Those children needed a few well chosen words, she thought, and then they'd stop that nonsense soon enough. She turned onto her back and straightened the covers. *I shall speak to their parents myself. Mayhap they are too distressed to know what to do. Mayhap* . . .

Sarah's heart froze in her chest and, despite her fear, she jerked upright. The creak stopped as suddenly as it had started, but it was one she knew well. It sounded every time she opened the front door. Her hands, trembling with terror, reached for the candle and flint. But when her fingers touched the waxed taper, her haste knocked it to the floor.

Sarah scrambled out of the bed as if it were aflame and frantically felt along the frozen boards for the slender taper. Her heart pounded so loudly in her ears that thinking became impossible. She found the candle under the bed and fought back the desire to simply crawl under and hide there until morning came.

The beating of her heart slowed only a fraction as the candle sprang to life. The warm light touched the room, but left too many shadowy corners for comfort.

Her feet felt like blocks of ice as she inched her way to the open doorway of her room. "Is anyone there?" Her voice trembled, and hearing the question aloud only added to her terror. Cautiously, she inched down the hallway and stepped into the main room. The outside door was shut and the coals in the fire still glowed with warmth. Feeling utterly foolish, Sarah took a deep breath and relaxed. *I am a goose,* she thought, giddy with relief. *At ten and nine I should not be afraid of the dark.* But as she stepped further into the room, a shadow from the corner moved toward her.

Sarah's cry of terror was short-lived. She was caught from behind as a sack was roughly pulled over her head and down her shoulders. She could feel two sets of hands as her arms were pressed to her body and tied. She lunged, trying to escape her nightmare, but only succeeded in falling to the floor. Her head struck hard and pain filled her being. Her ankles were bound; then she was pulled to her feet again and propped against the table.

Refusing to admit defeat, Sarah sucked in her breath and began to scream. There was a moment of searing pain along her jaw, then, mercifully, darkness consumed her.

Chapter Two

Middle Plantation, Virginia

Lightning streaked across the midnight sky, its deathly glow illuminating a path for the bellowing rolls of thunder that crashed on its wake. Fierce winds shrieked with demonic glee and raced about in search of sport. Trees bent in protest and houses shivered as the turbulence grew. Unable to stand the assault, the sky rent open, releasing torrents of rain to mix with the wind in its fury. Shutters were ripped from their moorings and glass windows rattled with ominous sounds. But even as the storm reached its zenith, it found its rival in Nicholas Beaumont's foul mood.

Like a caged cat, Nick paced the length of his study. Frustration marred his classic features, turning his dark-sapphire eyes cold. Waiting was not one of his virtues, and he made a practice to do it as seldom as possible. But tonight fate had left him no choice. He reached for his gold timepiece to find the hour only a quarter past the last time he had checked. Why tonight? he thought with irritation. For a fortnight he had awaited word that his ship, the *Lady May,* had been sighted. But when the message finally arrived, it came on the heels of one of the worst storms of the season. Nick paused in his pacing to peer out the window. He had dined with the governor, and as the minutes had ticked slowly by, he'd concluded his business, forced polite conversation, and chaffed at not being down on the docks himself. Now, as the hour grew late, his patience was completely at its end.

He shrugged out of his jacket, then, out of habit, folded it neatly over the chair. A wry smile touched his lips as the memories rushed forth. He had been with Gran for less than a week when she had found his discarded jacket and breeches tossed carelessly on the floor of his room. It mattered not to her that he had yet to reach his sixth year, or that the tonguelashing she delivered had lasted even longer than the sting of her switch. His fingers smoothed the lapel of his jacket and he shook his head with the thought. She was a tough old bird even then and he had taken his meals standing for two days. Nick moved to the side table, poured himself a generous brandy, and forced himself to sit before the fire as he reviewed the events of the evening.

The governor had been most receptive to his ideas, and the promise of government contracts would do much to maintain Beaumont Shipping's status as the leader in the colonies. Nick took a healthy drink and leaned back in his chair. His business was thriving, so why then was he not content? Lightning flashed and he scowled at the window. Only a fool would wish to be down on the docks on a night such as this, he thought, rising to pace again. But as he thought of Captain Riggins, his hand tightened on his glass. *Be calm, man,* he chided himself. *Beckett is the best agent on the pay ledgers of Beaumont Shipping. And if what you suspect of Captain Riggins is true, Beckett will find the proof.*

Nick stopped at the window to watch the fury of the storm. Lightning crackled, casting the grounds in an eerie blue-white light, and his eyes narrowed as he spied the open carriage slowly make its way up the lane. He waited by the window until the carriage stopped and he saw the driver descend. Stemming his desire to rush forth, Nick turned and moved to perch on the corner of his desk as the clock in the hallway struck the hour past midnight. Before the solitary chime had ceased, the door to his study edged open.

"Excuse me, sir, Master Beckett is here. Shall I show him in?" Nick nodded. Wadsworth swung the door wide, gave a slight bow, and formally announced the rain-soaked agent. Peter Beckett stepped inside the doorway and hastily pulled his knit cap from his balding head.

"Sorry I be so late, sir, but the rain . . ." Lightning flashed and the thunder roared, drowning out the agent's words.

Nick motioned the man to the fire. "Were you successful?"

Beckett's boots squished on the Persian carpet as he gratefully accepted the invitation. "Aye, sir." He took only a moment to warm his hands before turning back to face his employer. "I rowed out as soon as the *Lady May* dropped anchor and searched her good just like ye said. And Captain Riggins be as crooked as a corkscrew." Heedless of the puddle that had begun to grow on the floor before him, Beckett continued to

22

nervously twist his cap.

"What did you find?"

Beckett reached into his coat pocket and retrieved a wadded manifest from its depths. His anxiety grew as he realized the paper was soaked through, and his hand trembled from more than cold as he handed the limp document to Nick.

Nick spread the sodden paper across his desk and scanned the faded contents. His eyes widened first with surprise then disbelief. "The man would risk his reputation and his employment for a few extra barrels of fish?"

Beckett nodded anxiously. "But I checked everything good, just like ye said, and those barrels hold more than just fish. Riggins had himself quite a stash. Brandy, rum, brocade . . ."

Nick's eyes hardened as he rose from the desk and began to stalk. "If Riggins thinks to deceive me with his wit, he had better be ready to pay the price. The man is either a fool or a scoundrel, and I've room on my pay ledger for neither. Why didn't the harbormaster notice the irregularities in the manifest?"

Beckett nervously shifted from foot to foot. "There be two manifests, sir. That one," he gestured toward the desk, "matched the cargo Riggins truly carried, so the harbormaster had no cause for alarm. But I found a second manifest that matched the cargo that ye had commissioned him for. That would have been the one Riggins would have presented if ye had not found him out."

"I see." Nick fought to keep his anger from exploding. "Mark this day, Beckett, for it is the last one that sees Riggins as the captain of one of my ships."

Beckett shuddered at the quiet tone of his employer's voice. He had worked for Beaumont Shipping for years and knew firsthand that the tales of Nick's foul temper carried more truth than most realized. The man might dress like a gentleman, with his fine white breeches and costly silk jackets, but none on the docks dared to challenge him. And those who were foolish enough to miss the steely determination in his eyes never had the opportunity to repeat the mistake. Eager to be gone lest he feel the backlash of Nick's anger, Beckett edged toward the door.

"Will ye be wishing any more of me tonight, sir?"

Nick reached for a small leather pouch that rested on his desk and gave it a toss. The agent caught it with practiced ease, but his eyes grew round as his palm expertly calculated its value.

"You will find there is more than the usual amount. Despite the elements, you stayed with the task at hand. You've done well, Peter."

"Thank ye, sir," Beckett's head bobbed up and down as he stammered with pleasure. The master had never called him by his given name before. He backed toward the door, only to bump into it as Wadsworth pushed it open.

The butler stood stiffly in the doorway, his pale face wrinkled with confusion. "I beg pardon for the intrusion, sir," he looked to Nick, "but am I to do something with Master Beckett's sack? It's already stained the floor and now it is starting to move about."

Beckett slapped his palm to his forehead and his eyes rolled upward. "Lord have mercy, sir, I completely forgot. What do ye want me to do with the girl?"

"Girl?"

At the tone of Nick's voice both men took a hasty step backward. "Wait, I'll fetch her." Beckett scrambled past the butler and into the foyer. He returned a moment later, carrying a heap of drenched sackcloth. Uncertain what to do, he dumped the bundle in the center of the floor and pulled back the cloth to reveal an unconscious girl.

Nick looked from Beckett to the girl, then back to his agent again. "Why bring her here? Does she belong to you?" His brow arched down in a curious scowl.

"Lordy no, sir," Beckett stammered, fearful he had fallen out of favor. "I found her unconscious in the cargo hold. Captain Riggins claims she's indentured to him." Beckett scratched his ear. "But then the man also claims he's innocent of any wrongful deeds. I didn't think ye would jest want me to leave her, so I brought her with me." He watched Nick's eyes darken. "Did I do wrong, sir?" he asked, his anxiety mounting.

Fascinated, Nick watched the girl struggle into consciousness. Her dark hair was soaked and matted, and beneath the sackcloth carelessly wrapped around her, she wore a thin tattered gown that curiously reminded him of his grandmother's nightdresses. Her hands were bound before her with rags and her feet were bare. She was too thin for his taste, and filthy as a guttersnipe, but he found he couldn't take his eyes from her. "Does Riggins have papers for her?"

Beckett nodded and twisted his cap in trepidation. "He said he put them away for safekeeping but couldn't remember where." The agent halted and looked nervously down at his feet.

"And then?" Nick prompted in a harsh clip.

Beckett took a deep breath and gathered his courage. "Then Captain Riggins offered to sell her to me, sir."

"Damn the bloody bastard." Nick's temper exploded. "I'll see the man rot for this. Why is she bound?"

Beckett shrugged helplessly. "Riggins said she tried to attack him."

Nick snorted in disgust. "She can't even hold her head up." He took a step toward the girl only to watch her frantically try to scoot from his path. But with her hands bound and the tattered gown twisted about her legs, her movements were futile.

Irritated with both her fear and his own fascination, Nick struggled to keep his voice calm. "Easy now, I'll not hurt you." His tone was gentle, but when she flinched from his outstretched hand, he paused. "Wadsworth," his words were soft but deliberate, "I think some hot coffee would be in order."

"As you wish, sir."

Nick continued his silent study of the girl, then he tipped her chin up with his forefinger and felt the breath leave his body. She had the most haunting violet eyes he had ever seen. *You've become too jaded, Beaumont,* he thought to himself. *Tonight you turned down the finest ladies the great colony of Virginia has to offer and now look at you, lusting after a guttersnipe who's wearing more dirt than the bottom of your boots.*

Lightning flashed, thunder exploded, and the house trembled from the aftermath. He caught a fleeting glimpse of terror as the girl's violet eyes grew wide with fear before her face was buried against her arms. " 'Tis just the storm," he said softly, not understanding why it was suddenly so important to stem her fear. "If I take the bindings off, will you behave?" He watched the emotions play across her face before she slowly nodded her head. As gently as he could, he removed the rough rag bindings. Her hands felt frozen within his own and, once free, her arms immediately wrapped about herself.

Beckett edged a step closer. "I'd be careful, sir, if I was you," he stammered. "Captain Riggins may be a thief, but he carries her claw marks down his cheek as proof of his story."

Sarah blinked rapidly, trying to keep her fear at bay. She knew she was no longer in the belly of the ship, yet she found the man before her more terrifying. His dark eyes were hard and cold, and she felt naked beneath his stare. She shivered and shifted her arms to block his view, but his sardonic smile told her that her efforts were wasted. "Where am I?" Her voice came as a husky whisper.

Nick frowned as the sound of her words sent a curious jolt deep within. "For the moment, you're safe," he stated quietly. "My name is Nicholas Beaumont and you are in my home."

"Where?" she persisted as her eyes darted about the well-furnished study.

Nick watched gooseflesh rise along her arms, and his scowl darkened. "You're in the grand province called Virginia. But before you ask any more questions, I think we need to see you warm." He pulled her to her feet carefully, then edged her back until her legs bumped the chair and she sat.

27

Wadsworth entered the study to set a pewter coffee set on the sideboard. "Do you wish me to see to anything more, sir?"

Tearing his eyes away from the girl, Nick tried to clear his mind. "Yes, though the hour be late, I feel the need to bathe. See to that, then you may retire for the evening. The water can be emptied in the morning."

Wadsworth bowed. "As you wish, sir."

Nick turned back and realized the girl was almost blue with cold. "Beckett," he snapped. "Bring me a mug of coffee, then help yourself if you've a mind to." Stifling a curse, he grabbed a lap robe from the corner chair and placed it over the girl's trembling shoulders, not realizing that his very presence was adding to her distress. Her eyes filled with panic, and Nick watched as she quickly scanned the room like a trapped animal seeking means of escape. Kneeling beside her chair, he pulled the wet sackcloth from about her legs to reveal a slender calf and fine-turned ankle. His stomach muscles knotted and, despite the filth that covered her, his hand ached to touch.

"Please be careful, sir," Beckett pleaded, handing him a mug. "Your grandmother would take her cane to me if anything was to happen to you."

Dismissing the warning, Nick took her stiff fingers and wrapped them around the mug, then urged the drink to her mouth. He chuckled at her grimace as the first of the brew passed her lips. "I don't think our little stowaway is fond of coffee." But he persisted with his efforts until she had downed half the contents.

"Now," he said gently, setting the mug aside, "I can tell from your speech that you're from the

North, so why don't you tell us who you are and how you came to be aboard my ship?"

"Your ship?" The last scrap of color drained from her face. "If that was *your* ship, then you know, sir, that my name is Sarah Townsend and that I was kidnapped."

Nick jerked back as if she had slapped him, and his scowl darkened. "I would be careful, my little miss, just who you accuse of kidnapping—"

"She might speak the truth, sir," Beckett interrupted. "Captain Riggins being the scoundrel that he is." But at Nick's glare the agent edged back again toward the door. "Of course there is always the chance that the captain paid good coin for her. Even though she be a bit on the slight side."

Nick watched as tears welled in her eyes and wondered why they should move him. He cared not a whit about the girl, he only wanted answers. "You say you were abducted, yet Riggins has papers for you. Was he the one who took you from your home?" His voice grew hard with his impatience.

A single tear traced a path through the grime on her cheek. "I don't know. I only know that two men came to my house in the middle of the night and then I was on that ship." A violent shudder consumed her. "I've got to get back. My family must be frantic by now." She tried to rise, but her legs refused to support her.

"Do ye want me to take her back to the wharf, sir?" Beckett asked.

Nick held her panicked gaze with his and suddenly realized his mind was settled. "No, I'll keep her here tonight."

Beckett nodded. His employer's manner didn't allow for further questions and he struggled to keep his surprise from showing. "Kind" was not a word he would ever have used to describe Nick Beaumont.

"I want you at the wharf at sunrise," Nick continued. "Stress to Captain Riggins how important it is for him to find those papers, if, indeed, they really exist. Then have the crew remove that scum from my ship. Put word out that Riggins is a thief and no longer works for Beaumont Shipping."

"Ye know if I do that, sir, Riggins will be hard pressed to find work as a mate, let alone a captain."

Nick turned and cast a dark look in Beckett's direction. "I'll expect to hear from you before noon."

Beckett saluted. "Consider it done, sir."

As the door clicked from Beckett's departure, Nick watched the sound snap Sarah back to reality. "I can't stay here," she declared, panic edging her voice, and this time when she jerked upright, she managed to stand.

Nick caught her arms as she began to sway. "I don't really think you have much choice in the matter, my dear."

Her eyes, wide and frightened, darted about the room in confusion. Frantically she pulled herself from Nick's grasp. "I've got to get home. Which way is Salem?" She took less than a step before spinning back in his direction. "I have to . . ." But her words never came as her body failed her and she fainted.

Catching her before she hit the floor, Nick swung her high into his arms, surprised at how light and fragile she felt. Her head rolled to rest on his shoulder and for a moment he stood silent before the fire, angered by the desires that clamored throughout his body. The hall clock struck the half hour, its deep chime ringing through the house. Sarah never moved. Not when Nick slowly climbed the stairs or later when he laid her on his bed.

Undaunted by the storm that continued to rage outside his window, Nicholas Beaumont sat in his study, lost in thought. The fire crackled warmly in the hearth, casting a golden glow. Books of every description filled the floor-to-ceiling shelves that flanked the fireplace, and an imported tapestry cloaked the opposite wall with its splendor. As the rain pelted the windows, Nick studied the indenture papers that Beckett had delivered.

They certainly looked official, but then so had the duplicate manifest. Nick reread the contents for the third time. Sarah Townsend, of Salem Village in the Massachusetts Bay Colony, had been sold into bondage for a period to last not less than ten years. And the grand sum that had been placed on her worth was five shillings. Nick steepled his fingers as he contemplated the document. Who was Samuel Wittfield and why had the man sold one as comely as Sarah for only five shillings? Had she already been in service to Wittfield and deemed a troublemaker? She claimed to have been kidnapped, but her hands were not those of a well-bred lady. She had labored somewhere, for her palms bore the calluses of steady toil. His brows knit in thought. Never had he imagined that under all that filth he would find skin the color of ivory. A smile tugged at the corners of his mouth. Never had he imagined that such a simple experience

31

would touch him so deeply. He had only to close his eyes and the image of her sensual body sprang to mind. She was tiny, but the memory of the gentle curve of her breast made his loins tighten with anticipation. He could still feel the softness of her hair as it swirled in the water about her head, caressing his hand and wrist, enticing him to touch. It was the blue-black color of midnight and it felt like the finest of silks as it slipped through his fingers. His smile vanished as he carefully folded the indenture papers and fought back his desires. He would have her, of that he had no doubt. But first he would have his answers . . .

"I don't care what your orders are. I said, get out of my way and let me pass."

Hearing the commotion outside his study door, Nick slipped the documents into his desk and locked the drawer. Tucking the tiny gold key into his vest pocket he leaned back in his chair to wait. Within moments the door flew open and a disheveled Wadsworth stepped inside.

"I beg your pardon, sir, but . . ."

"Get out of my way, you old fool."

Nick stood as two burly men carrying an invalid's chair brushed past his butler. Drenched from the pouring rain, their boots left a trail of wet footprints across his carpet.

"Over by the fire." Agatha Beaumont whacked her porter on the shoulder with her cane. "And don't you dare drop me." She gave a grunt of dissatisfaction as they lowered her chair and unhooked the poles that allowed them to carry it. "Hurry up," she snapped. "Be gone with you now. I have business to see to."

Careful to stay clear of her cane, the two men

gave the old lady a hasty nod and fled toward the door. "Don't go too far," she cautioned, "I may want to go home soon."

Nick folded his arms across his chest and leaned back against his desk. "I thought we decided that on days with weather such as this, you would stay home and I would come to you."

"We decided no such thing. Besides, if I waited for you to fit me into your ridiculous schedule, I would be cold in my grave."

Nick crossed the room and placed a kiss on the old woman's cheek, inhaling the strong rose scent that clung to her clothing. "I broke fast with you just yesterday, Gran."

Agatha shrugged and pulled off her gloves from fingers bent with age. "If you're too busy to spare a moment and a nip of sherry for your last living relative, then I shall just leave."

Nick rolled his eyes and moved to the side table. "Don't work yourself into a tizzy, Gran. You know I am always glad to see you." He handed her a small crystal glass filled with amber liquid. "Except when you foolishly venture out in the worst storm of the season." Punctuating his words lightning streaked the sky and thunder cracked on its wake. "See, the hem of your gown is wet."

Agatha frowned. "You watch your mouth, young man, and mind who you call foolish." She downed her sherry in a single gulp and extended the glass for a refill.

Nick cocked a brow as he reached for her glass. " 'Tis not yet noon, Gran."

"I can tell time, Nicholas. It's my legs that don't work, not my mind. And at my age, if I feel a want for sherry, I don't need you or the clock to grant

33

me permission." Snatching the filled glass from his hand, she again downed its contents. "And don't go sending that wicked scowl of yours in my direction, young man, or I'll send you out to cut a hickory switch, and don't think I won't."

Shaking his head and forcing the smile from his lips, Nick bent to stoke the fire. "What pressing business can I help you with, Madame Beaumont?"

Agatha smiled and relaxed back in her chair. "Come to supper tonight. Cook is going to make your favorite, fried clams and oyster stew."

Nick sat on the chair before her, took the empty glass from her fingers and kept her hand firmly within his own. He felt the tremors that she tried so hard to hide. "I can't today, Gran. I already have an engagement."

Agatha sent a shrewd glance in his direction. "And is it that prissy Marigold Thermont that you'll be bedding tonight?"

Nick's laughter filled the room as he flopped back in his chair to stare at his grandmother. She was wizened and bent with age, wisps of white hair stuck out in all directions from a scrap of lace she wore on her head, and at two and seventy she was still sharp as a tack. "I can't tell you that. You raised me to be a gentleman."

Agatha gave a snort. "I did nothing of the kind. You have no one to blame that on but yourself. Marigold, that's a stupid name, but then she's a stupid girl. Marigold. Ha, makes me want to sneeze each time I say it." She waved her handkerchief before her face. "I'm too warm here, Nick, you made the fire too hot."

Nick rose and gently eased her chair away from the hearth. But before he could guess her intentions, Agatha's hand shot out and scooped up the stack of invitations that rested on the corner of his desk. "Gran." Nick reached for the correspondence, but she handed him only the empty envelopes as she quickly scanned several invitations before he could rescue those too.

"Why does Mrs. Hawkins want to see you tomorrow?"

Nick stacked the papers together and pointedly placed them in one of the desk drawers. "I won't discuss that, either."

Agatha cocked her head as she watched him return to his chair near the fire. He was too handsome, she thought. Despite the fact that he refused to follow fashion and wear a wig, he had only to smile and the ladies swooned at his feet. "You're up to no good, Nicky. You'd just better be careful that Master Hawkins doesn't come home and take offense to what you're planning. He's liable to shoot you."

Nick returned her level stare. "For having tea with his wife?"

"Ha!" Agatha cackled. "I never heard it called *that* before. But if you want to go and get yourself shot, that's fine with me. The shock of it will probably kill me, but that's fine, too. Just tell me why Beckett was all over the *Lady May* like a fly on a fresh pile."

Nick folded his arms across his chest. So now we finally come to the point of the visit, he thought. "How do you know that?" he challenged.

"Don't change the subject, Nicholas. We're in this business together and don't you forget it. More than half of the ships in Beaumont Shipping belong to me, at least until I die. And I

35

want to know what is wrong."

Nick thought of Sarah, still sleeping in his bed. "And what makes you think that something is amiss?"

Agatha's fingers thumped against the wooden arm of her chair with impatience. "You always wait to hear that the ship has docked before you send an agent down. Suddenly, you have your best agent waiting in the rain for a ship that is not due in for days. That's not coincidence, Nicky, that's careful planning, and I want to know why."

Nick leaned back in his chair and wondered what she would make of Sarah's story. Her body might be failing, but her shrewd insight to business constantly amazed him. "The last few trips I've had an uneasy feeling about Captain Riggins."

Agatha rubbed her hands together, her eyes narrowing. "I never did like that man." She gave a shrug at Nick's startled expression. "Oh, he's a good enough captain. But he always gave me the feeling that he was looking for ways to make a quick fortune. Is he taking cargo?"

Nick shook his head and rubbed his hand across his jaw. "I thought he might have been dealing with slaves."

"What!" Nick watched his grandmother's pale face turn a sickly white before blooming a fiery red. "I won't have it, Nicky," Her cane thumped hard on the floor. "I don't care how much money there's to be made in that. I simply won't have it."

"Gran, many people don't carry the same beliefs that you do. And besides—"

Agatha's stunned expression fixed on her grandson in horror. "If you are going to tell me, Nicholas Beaumont," she interrupted, "that you don't share my feelings in this matter, then I am going to march out and get that hickory stick myself. You always did pick the puny branches anyway."

Nick reached for her hand and found it cold to the touch. "You know better than that, Gran. After all you've taught me, do you really think I would sanction such an act?"

"Slaves." Agatha shuddered. "What would the good Lord think if he were to look down and see slaves on a Beaumont ship? Why, I'd die from the shame of it." Despite the heavy layer of rice powder she wore, her cheeks kept the fiery glow of her indignation.

"You get down to that dock yourself, Nicholas, and you drag that blackheart Riggins back to me by his ear. I'll give that man a healthy piece of my mind and then see him hung."

Nick struggled not to laugh at the thoughts of his frail grandmother trying to thrash a man who easily outweighed her three times over. "Gran, Riggins wasn't carrying slaves. If you'd hush a moment I'll tell you."

Agatha frowned. If her legs were working, she'd go down to that dock and see for herself, rain or no rain. She drew herself upright in her chair. "I'm still the head of this business, Nicholas, so if you know what's good for you, you'll give me a straight story."

Nick smiled. Some things never changed. "Beckett found that Riggins had a duplicate manifest. He wasn't taking any of our cargo. He was simply using our ship to transport some of his own."

Agatha's eyes narrowed in thought. "I never did like that scum. Too shifty, if you ask me. You relieved him of his position?" Nick nodded. "Good, I want to go home now. "Luuuttherrr, OOOOscarrr." Her shrill voice filled the room, and Nick winced from the sound.

Stepping to the hearth, he reached for the bell-pull. "Gran, you don't have to yell." But his words were lost as the door to the study again crashed open and his grandmother's two porters scurried in. Within moments they had secured their poles to her chair while Wadsworth stood uneasily in the doorway holding her cape. Nick took the cape, settled it securely around her frail shoulders, and pulled up the hood, before dropping a kiss on her wrinkled cheek. "Next time, wait for me to visit you," he challenged. "I've got a five-pound note that says you can't."

Agatha looked up at his classic features and gave his cheek a sharp pat. "Never bet on something unless you're sure you can win, Nicky. Otherwise it's a waste of money." She pulled her cape more firmly about her. "Oh, I almost forgot. You can't come for supper tonight, I've made other plans. What are you two waiting for?" she snapped. "The good Lord is going to call me to my grave before you even get me home. And if you don't like carrying me about, think how you'll feel carrying a corpse."

Nick laughed, then gave the porters a sympathetic wink as Wadsworth closed the door behind them.

Chapter Three

Squaring her shoulders as much as her borrowed shift would allow, Sarah stood at the top of the massive staircase and looked down at the lavish foyer below. Huge paintings broke the starkness of the pristine white walls and a bouquet of fresh flowers graced a highly polished table near the door. The fierce rains had ceased and sunlight now poured through the tall windows to bounce off the crystal chandelier and scatter in all directions.

The sudden brightness stung her eyes, and Sarah felt her head grow light. Desperately, she clutched the banister and sank to the steps offering up a fervent prayer.

"Please let this be a dream," she whispered, willing the queasiness in her stomach to pass. The rocking motion of the ship washed over her, and her hand rubbed absently on the smooth oaken banister for reassurance. Her memory of the night before seemed as scattered as dandelion fluff tossed by the wind. There had been a man. She remembered his silhouette illuminated by the firelight, but no face came to mind. Then she remembered waking to the smell of hot cider. A young girl, no more than nine years in age, had gently bade her to rise and bathe. Sarah smiled. The luxury of a pitcher of hot water had done much to restore her spirits and push the clouds from her mind, but as she donned the offered garments, she could not help but wonder as to their owner. Carefully, she had tried to glean information from the girl. She had smiled shyly but offered no answers. By the time Sarah was dressed she knew only that she was to make her way to the master's study as soon as she was fit. The master waited for her and would she please not dawdle.

Sitting on the top step, leaning against the newel post, Sarah rubbed her temples. Her mind raced with confusion. Where was she and in whose bed had she slept? A score of questions tumbled one over the other for her attention until her head ached.

Sarah opened her eyes. "Have you forsaken me, Lord?"

The sunlight intensified, bathing her in a golden glow, and she reveled in its healing warmth. Relieved that the steps before her no longer rocked to and fro, Sarah slowly rose to her feet. Gathering what was left of her dignity, she smoothed the borrowed skirt and pushed the shift back onto her shoulder. But as she soundlessly made her way down the carpeted stairs, her hands turned clammy and her anxiety grew.

She tapped firmly on the study door, then taking a deep breath, turned the latch and stepped inside.

"Mistress Townsend, do please come in."

Sarah paused just inside the doorway and blinked with confusion. Something was amiss. Despite the sun that poured in through the deep windows, a hearty fire crackled in the hearth. The massive oak furniture that filled the room carried not a speck of dust and the air smelled faintly of beeswax and lemons. But as Sarah stared at the short, wiry gentleman who rose to greet her, her brow wrinkled. His thinning blond hair had been combed across a wide forehead in a futile effort to disguise a balding pate, and glasses rode low on his thin nose. His nasal voice bid her enter and sit.

"Mr. Beaumont?" she hesitated, using the name the child had spoken.

"What? Oh, my, no, I am Michael Danvers, Mistress Townsend. I am an attorney." His chest puffed with pride. "I represent Beaumont Shipping. I . . . aaaaachoooo."

Sarah waited impatiently as Danvers sneezed several times, then made a grand show of blowing his nose into a white handkerchief the size of a small table covering. The man wiped his tearing eyes and tried to settle his glasses.

"I have no quarrel with Beaumont Shipping, sir," Sarah said quietly. "And the only recompense I seek is a passage back to my home."

"Recompense," Danvers stammered as his watery eyes grew wide. "Surely, madam, you misunderstand. As a bondswoman, you are hardly eligible for recompense. Oh, no, madam," Danvers stuffed his handkerchief into a bulging side pocket and then made a grand show of stacking the papers before him into a neater pile. "I am here to inquire about your previous owner for Mr. Beaumont."

"You think that I am a bondswoman?" Sarah struggled to make sense of the attorney's words.

Danvers looked down his nose and his voice filled with censure. "You obviously gained passage on the *Lady May* without purchase of fare, and . . ."

"Purchase of fare!" Sarah leaned forward in her chair. Her hands grabbed the edge of the desk and her eyes flashed with anger. "I was kidnapped, sir. I had no wish to leave Salem and travel here." She glanced about at the book-lined walls. "I'm not even sure where here is! But what I do know is that I was taken against my will and thrown into the belly of a ship that belongs to your employer. I was bound and half starved for days on end while rats larger than your foot were my constant companions." Sarah suppressed a shudder. "And now you say that I deserve nothing? I deserve more than recompense, sir. I deserve the most humble of apologies. If Beaumont is the owner, then perhaps 'twould be best if I speak directly with him. Where can I find the man?"

"Directly behind you, my dear." The voice was a rich baritone that had Sarah leaping to her feet and spinning about in the same motion. Her heart quickened as she stared at the tall, well-dressed gentleman. He moved around her with careless ease to stand before the desk. Sarah took in the costly brocade of his coat and the muscles that flexed beneath the garment's fine stitching. Unlike the attorney, his complexion wasn't a pasty white, but a rich golden hue that spoke of hours in the sun.

"Mr. Beaumont?" she stammered, wondering if he could hear the pounding of her heart from where he stood.

"Nicholas Beaumont, your servant, madam." He gave a mocking bow.

Sarah took a deep, steadying breath and clasped her hands tightly together. "I believe there has been a hideous misunderstanding and we are now left to deal with a most grievous problem."

Nick waited patiently until his silence caused her to look directly at him. He caught and held her gaze with ease. "*We* have a problem . . . ?" His thick brow arched in silent amusement.

Sarah stared in wonder. His was a most handsome face, framed with thick dark hair pulled back in a queue at the nape of his neck. His jaw was firm, taking on an almost stubborn tilt, but as her gaze locked with his, the devilish twinkle of his eye brought the memory of the night before crashing down on her with painful clarity.

He had been the one to free her bonds and wrap her gently in a blanket. Then she had floated in a sea of warmth. Resting against his strong arm, she had watched through a cloudy haze as he washed the filth from her body. He had seen her as no man ever had and she hadn't possessed the strength or the will to stop him. But now, in the light of the afternoon sun, her cheeks flamed with the memory and the shame it brought. Mortified, she watched as his smile deepened and knew he read her thoughts with ease.

Unaware of the ever-growing tension, Danvers flipped the papers down on the desk before him and impatiently cleared his throat. "Mistress Townsend, please, if you would sit, we could continue."

Sarah tore her eyes away and gratefully sank back on her chair. She tried to concentrate on the attorney's words, but her thoughts kept returning to the night before. A soothing voice, more dream than real, had banished her nightmares and bid her rest in peace. She remembered the softness of a fine feather pillow beneath her cheek, and blessed warmth, then nothing more. She stole a glance from the corner of her eye to find Nick Beaumont watching her with unwavering persistence.

"So it would seem, Mistress Townsend, that you are not telling the truth."

"What?" Sarah snapped back to the present and stared at the attorney in confusion. Had the man just called her a liar? "I beg pardon, sir." She strove to keep her voice calm and her fear from showing. "I have been through an ordeal and beseech your indulgence. What are you saying?"

Danvers propped his elbows on the desk and glared. "Madam, the charade is up. Captain Riggins produced the papers that prove your bondage. Why not ease yourself and tell . . ."

"Charade!" Sarah flew to her feet, every delicate feature filled with rage. "Sir, I am a God-fearing woman. And I do not lie! I tell you I was kidnapped. My family must be frantic by this time."

"You are married?" Nick's eyes narrowed. The thought of her with another man was less than pleasing, and he found it irritating he should care.

Sarah shook her head. What agonies Elizabeth and Samuel must be facing not knowing what had become of her. "I must be returned to Salem," she demanded.

"Mistress Townsend, calm yourself," Danvers snapped. "I have checked the documents carefully and they are completely in order. They state very clearly that you are bound into service for an additional ten years."

Sarah felt the blood in her veins turn to ice as a dreadful premonition washed over her. "I'm not going back on that ship." Her voice quivered and she struggled not to scream her frustration. She had

44

only to close her eyes to see the pockmarked face of Captain Riggins with his leering smile. The terrors of her voyage were too fresh to be easily forgotten: the bleak darkness with its constant dip and sway, the stench of human waste and rotting fish, and the scurry of rats as they brushed against her feet ready to challenge her for the bits of food that were tossed down. Bitter acid rose in the back of her throat and Sarah struggled to fight it back.

Nick watched the color drain from her face and wondered if she would faint. Damn, but she was a fine actress. She actually had him believing her story, feeling sympathy for her plight. The drooping shift and oversize skirt should have made her a comical sight, yet she only appeared more fragile. Her thick midnight hair was pulled severely from her face, but it only served to heighten the perfection of her delicate features, the soft curve of her cheekbone, and the sweet fullness of her lips.

Danvers cast a fleeting look in his employer's direction and received a scowl that hastened him on again. "We at Beaumont Shipping can understand your distress, Mistress Townsend. And I am happy to be able to tell you that returning to Captain Riggins is completely out of the question." He waited for her smile or word of thanks, but when none came, Danvers rolled his eyes. "Mr. Beaumont has bought your papers," he explained.

Sarah turned to stare at Nick. "You bought the papers?" His look of indifference baffled her.

Irritated by the intensity of his reaction to her, Nick cocked a brow. "Does the situation not please you? Did you want to go back to the ship?" He watched her ivory skin grow paler, saw Danvers smile, and felt instant disgust for what he had just

45

done. "You say you were kidnapped," he continued, "yet we have no proof."

"You have my word, sir," Sarah snapped as color surged back into her cheeks.

Nick stared, suddenly pleased that she met his gaze with conviction. "As I was saying, we have no proof. But I do intend to get to the bottom of this." He straightened and moved to stand beside the desk. "Beaumont Shipping has a vessel that leaves in a few days for the Bay Colony, and arrangements have been made for one of my agents to go along. Beckett will make inquiries of this family you speak of and bring back the answers we need."

"Let me travel with him." Sarah turned back to Danvers. "Surely that is possible in a situation such as this. That way when the truth is known, I will be almost home." Again she watched him glance in Nick's direction.

"I am afraid that will not be possible, Mistress Townsend. Mr. Beaumont has papers that indenture you to him for the next ten years and—"

"I'm sure my family will gladly reimburse Mr. Beaumont for any expense he has incurred," Sarah interrupted. "Don't you see how much sense it would make for me to accompany the agent back to Salem?"

"Two thousand pounds."

"What?" Sarah turned to watch Nick Beaumont perch on the corner of his desk.

"You may buy the indenture papers for two thousand pounds."

Sarah felt her world begin to spin out of control. "You spent two thousand pounds to purchase me?"

Nick gave her a sardonic smile. "If you want to

46

buy the papers, then you may do so for two thousand pounds."

Without thinking, Sarah jerked from her chair and snatched the document from the desk. Her eyes scanned the contents before looking up at Nick. "But you only paid Riggins ten."

Nick's smile deepened. "I'm a businessman, my dear. And you can read. That's a rare accomplishment. Now if you can also guarantee that your family will be willing to pay, then we can settle the matter here and now. But tell me first, just who is this Samuel Wittfield who got you into this predicament."

Sarah's eyes dropped to the bottom of the document where her brother's signature stood, bold and clear. Her hands began to tremble and her knees turned to jelly as she sank back into her chair. "It can't be true." Her voice was the barest whisper as she stared at the signature.

"So you do know the man?" Nick prodded, annoyed with himself for almost believing her story. He watched her violet eyes fill with pain and wondered if the cause was justified or just part of her charade.

Sarah laid the document back on the desk. "Samuel Wittfield is my stepbrother." The back of her eyes felt stingy and hot. She clasped her hands again in her lap and struggled to remain composed. *Samuel wouldn't do this,* she argued silently. *No matter how dear the land was to him he would never sacrifice family.*

Surprised by his reaction, Nick reached to take her hand. "Have heart," he said slowly as his thumb caressed the inside of her wrist. "The signature could be a forgery." She looked up, and Nick

47

felt desire surge through his veins as he watched the seed of hope flicker in her eyes.

"That must be what happened." Her words were slow in coming, and her brow wrinkled as she tried to puzzle it through. "But how would Riggins know that Samuel was my brother?" She shook her head. "Salem Village is a half day's ride from Salem Harbor. I was there only once and that was as a child."

Nick shrugged. "Men will do strange things for wealth."

An ironic smile touched her lips. "I would hardly call ten pounds wealth. In fact, I think I should be insulted."

Nick grinned. "Then I am happy to restore your feeling of confidence in yourself. You may purchase the papers, and your freedom, for two thousand pounds."

Sarah felt her thoughts scatter in all directions. The papers had to be a forgery. "Wait," she gasped. "I own five hundred acres of land in Salem Village. I would deed them to you in exchange for the papers and passage home."

"Mistress Townsend . . ." Danvers peered over his glasses. "Think about what you are saying. We have papers that prove your bondage, yet you expect Mr. Beaumont to accept your word that you own property? You are more to be pitied than censured if you think to match wits with us."

Sarah felt the last of her control begin to slip away. "I have only the land with which to bargain. That is my dowry and all I own."

Nick smiled with satisfaction. "Then we shall go back to our original plan. You will stay here until Beckett has determined just what happened. If it becomes evident that these papers are a forgery, then I will return you to your home in the Bay Colony with the utmost speed and give recompense of five hundred pounds for your inconvenience."

"Mr. Beaumont . . ." Danvers stuttered. "Surely you don't mean to offer such a grand amount. I'm sure Miss Townsend would be more than satisfied with passage home."

"Five hundred pounds." Nick's quiet voice allowed for no argument, and Danvers pulled off his spectacles and hastily began to clean the lenses.

"Yes, sir," he stammered, turning to Sarah. "Surely you can see the generosity of this arrangement, Mistress Townsend."

Sarah watched Danvers wipe the perspiration from his brow. What manner of man was this Nick Beaumont that he could offer sums of five hundred pounds without a thought? "Have I no other choice?"

"Legally, it would appear not. And as I said, Mr. Beaumont is being more than generous."

Sarah nodded and turned to look at her host. "Then I am to stay here as your servant until the matter is settled?" She watched his eyes darken.

"The title is not necessary. You may consider yourself a guest in my home if you wish."

Sarah felt her cheeks grow red. "Sir, I am unmarried. What you suggest is most inappropriate."

Nick's laughter rang out, and his dark eyes took on a devilish light. "Then consider yourself my . . . housekeeper if you will."

Sarah nodded slowly. She would consider herself employed. That was something she could deal with. "One month," she stated firmly. "I shall keep your house for one month."

49

"Mistress Townsend!" Danvers rose from his chair.

Nick felt the corners of his mouth ache to smile but held his ground. The mouse wants to bargain with the cat, he thought, watching her stand before him.

"Two months—" he countered.

"This is most irregular." Danvers tried to interrupt.

"Six weeks and you carry a letter to my family that tells them I am safe and well." Sarah crossed her arms over her chest and gave her sternest look.

Nick's laughter rang out. He held all the cards and she knew it, yet still she stood her ground. It would be a most interesting six weeks. "Done," he declared.

Sarah tried to smile, but her stomach was tied in such knots she marveled that she stood. "And you'll let your agent carry my letter?"

Nick nodded. "I realize that if your tale be true, then 'tis a most uncomfortable situation you find yourself in. But you have my word, Sarah . . ." He hesitated, tasting her name on his tongue, "that I shall do all in my power to make your stay a pleasant one."

Sarah felt a shiver race down her spine, then settle deep within her. And as they stood facing each other, she couldn't help but wonder if she had just made a pact with the devil.

"Then if you will excuse me, I shall go and see where I can best be of use." The neckline of her shift slipped as she moved, and a deep blush stained her cheeks as she pulled the gown back over her shoulder.

Nick watched her pause in the doorway. "I have

arranged with the dressmaker to arrive shortly, Sarah. Order anything you need." He waited for her smile, but none came.

Mortified that he would speak of something as intimate as her clothing, especially before his attorney, made her burn hotter still. "Thank you," she whispered just before the door closed behind her.

"That is a beautiful lady," Michael Danvers sighed. "No wonder you want to keep her here." He began to stack the papers that covered the desk. "But I think you are making a mistake to offer her so much money."

Nick's smile faded and his eyes grew hard. "Really?"

Danvers nodded, peering over his glasses. "You saw her hands. She is beautiful, but she is not gentry."

"Your advice in this matter is completely uncalled for and unwanted," Nick counseled.

Involved in the sorting of his papers, Danvers missed the dangerous light that touched Nick's eyes as he continued. "I just think you are being very foolhardy. Marigold Thermont is much better suited. Her features may be a bit rough, but her father is nearly as wealthy as you are." Danvers chuckled. "In fact, if you play your cards right, you could probably get her father to pay you five hundred pounds."

Nick motioned Danvers from his desk and plucked Sarah's indenture paper from the stack to set it aside. Taking his quill, he scratched a few terse words on a clean sheet of parchment, then handed it to the attorney.

Danvers frowned as he looked down at the paper. "What's this?"

51

A dark smile touched Nick's face. "Consider it your severance pay. Your services are no longer needed at Beaumont Shipping."

"What?" Danvers sputtered. "You can't do this. I've worked for Beaumont Shipping for over two years."

Nick's face grew hard. "I *am* Beaumont Shipping," he said, his voice carrying a dangerous tone. "Therefore you work for me. I have no use for employees who speculate about my private life or spread tales like gossiping old women." He watched Danvers's pale face turn a fiery red and knew he had hit the mark. "Consider yourself well paid and get out of my house."

Danvers glanced down to the amount recorded. It was more than generous, but his reputation was threatened. "Surely you don't mean this, Nick. Your thinking is confused because of that girl. Those violet eyes of hers can make a man's mouth water. But think of all the service I have been to you and your grandmother."

Nick's gaze locked with Danvers, and in that instant he saw guilt. The man wasn't even wise enough to pretend indignation as Sarah had done. Instinctively Nick knew he would believe Sarah's story before he would ever trust Danvers again with his business matters. He retrieved the paper from the attorney's trembling fingers and ripped it in two. "You're right," he said quietly. Again his quill scratched across a paper, then he handed the new note back.

Danvers looked down and his eyes grew wide. "But this is half the amount."

Nick stood. "That's right, and if I think on the matter further, I might change my mind again. I

52

believe you will find it in your best interest to leave immediately."

Danvers bit back his words of protest as he clumsily gathered his belongings. There were others, he thought bitterly, who would pay for the information that he already carried about Beaumont Shipping. But first, he was going to pay a timely visit to Mrs. Agatha Beaumont. Once he hinted about the nature of his information, the old lady would pay dearly to find out what her grandson was up to. And when she learned he had taken a common bondswoman to his bed . . .

"Danvers." The menacing quiet of Nick's voice stopped the man in the doorway. "Stay away from my grandmother. If you should try to drag her into this in any way, know here and now that I will consider it a personal insult and deal with the matter accordingly."

Danvers felt the sweat trickle down his back and tried to swallow, but his heart filled his throat. He had watched Nick Beaumont's ruthlessness in business for months but never had he thought to be on the receiving end. Knowing the threat not to be an idle one, he nodded and hastily left the study.

In the foyer, Wadsworth stood ready with his cape and hat. Danvers glanced about the hallway with envy in his eyes. An imported vase filled with fresh flowers stood on a table by the wall and he knew its cost would have paid his expenses for a year.

Stepping outside, Danvers squinted in the sunlight. The month was only April but already the spring heat was growing. He watched an open carriage stop and Madame Rousseau, the dressmaker, descend. So Nick intended to dress up his new plaything, Danvers thought, tipping his hat as the Frenchwoman passed. She was certainly going to have her work cut out for her. The girl might look beautiful, but blood would always tell.

Danvers took several steps and felt his heart quicken as a new thought prevailed. Agatha Beaumont had many spies; maybe he could work a deal. If he played his cards close to his chest and distributed bits to several different sources, Agatha would get her information, he would get his money, and Nicholas Beaumont would have no one on whom to lay the blame.

Whistling a tune as he left the mansion, Danvers felt his head grow light as his plan began to take form.

Chapter Four

Nick rose as the French couturiere entered his study. "Ah, Madame Rousseau, how good of you to come."

"But of course, monsieur." Charlotte Rousseau smiled as Nick executed a courtly bow, then kissed the back of her hand. "You know you have only to send for me and I am at your service." She didn't mention the two customers she had shooed from her shop or the appointment she had canceled. If Nick Beaumont wished her presence she would be there, for there was a debt between them that had nothing to do with money.

Charlotte accepted the julep Nick offered. "Ah, my favorite," she sighed, taking a sip of the sweetened rum drink. "And what can I do for you, *mon ami?*"

Nick set his own glass aside and wondered exactly where to begin. "I have a guest in my home, Madame, who is in dire need of clothing." He watched Charlotte's pale gray eyes grow wide as he quickly shared the story of Sarah's kidnapping. "So you see," he concluded, "in order to protect her reputation, she needs a—"

"She needs a wardrobe worthy of a guest in the

Beaumont household, does she not?" Charlotte interrupted. "I can certainly do that. But Nicholas, what of your grandmama? Surely you do not think to fool her with this crazy plan of yours. She would certainly remember if she had met your Sarah's family and with but one false word all would be lost."

Nick rose and began to pace, uncomfortable with the easy way Charlotte had labeled Sarah as his. "I shall handle my grandmother. I need only know if you can provide the necessary garments in a timely fashion."

Charlotte nodded and rose to stand before him, wishing, not for the first time, that she was ten years younger. "I shall help you, *mon ami,* but your grandmama is going to make your life living misery when she finds out that you have deceived her."

Nick dropped a kiss of gratitude on Charlotte's forehead. "I am thirty and three, madame. I love Gran dearly for all that she has done for me, but my gratitude does not run so deep that I can allow her to dictate my life. The price is simply too high. Besides," he winked, "if all were calm, she would have nothing to complain about."

Charlotte shook her head and reached for her sketchpad. "Enough," she chided, "or you'll have me believing you are doing this for your grandmama's benefit. Now where can I find this *petite enfante* who you have rescued?"

"Madame, you are a dear friend." Nick smiled as he opened the door to his study.

Charlotte Rousseau looked back over her shoulder. "You won't think so, *cher ami,* when you get my bill."

* * *

Less than half an hour later Charlotte again found Nick in his study. "She is indeed enchanting, Nicholas, but I fear we have a small problem."

Reluctantly, Nick pulled himself from his work. He had lost too much time already, and his patience was beginning to wear thin. "Madame, I am up to my ears, as you can see." He gestured to his cluttered desk. "If you fear the cost is a problem, best put it from your mind. Sarah may choose, with my blessing, anything you can create for her. Does that satisfy you?"

Charlotte nodded. "Then you mean to purchase an entire wardrobe?"

"Of course. The only clothing she has is the absurd garment that Mrs. Killingham was kind enough to lend to her."

Charlotte's eyes narrowed with thought. *"Mon ami,* 'tis not that I don't appreciate your business, but the offer seems a bit extravagant for a girl who will only be staying several weeks at best. Why not—"

"Enough," Nick interrupted. "Madame, I want her to be outfitted completely from the skin out and with a variety of gowns. The cost matters not, so let your conscience be at ease."

The smile faded from her lips. *He's in love,* she thought, watching Nick's dark head bend again over the column of figures. Charlotte felt the last dream of her youth begin to crumble. She was respected and successful, but Nick would never turn to her in wonder and declare his love. She would never feel his strong arms gather her close, except in friendship. *He's in love and he hasn't even real-*

ized it yet, she thought. Her eyes pressed closed from the painful reality.

Nearly fifteen years had passed since the night she had gathered her courage and approached Nicholas Beaumont in the Blue Horse Tavern. She had offered her body for his pleasure, knowing the pocket change he carried would pay her rent for more than a year, and although she had approached him privately, Nick's friends had accurately interpreted her intentions. They publicly laughed and scorned her offer. Nick was legendary with the ladies, they touted. He didn't have to pay for pleasure. And what would he want with an old hag like herself? Charlotte shuddered from the memory. She had been only six years his senior, but in that moment she had felt as ancient and desirable as Medusa. Desperation had given her a stubborn streak, and with her pride shattered, she had asked young Nicholas for a loan.

Charlotte opened her eyes and smiled sadly as she watched Nick tally his last column of figures. He had known her only as the widow who did mending for his grandmother, but he had not laughed at her that night as his friends had done. He bought her a drink and a meal, listened intently to her needs, and then turned her down flat. He would not loan her the money, he had stated, but he would consider a partnership. And thus their unlikely friendship had been formed.

With the burden of keeping a roof over her head lifted from her shoulders, she was free to do what she did best—design clothing. Nick arranged for her fabric to be imported at his expense, and within months she had had more orders than she could fill. Now, fifteen years later, she owned her own home and her own business. Her daughter lived in France studying the latest fashions and her son attended university in England. Five girls now worked for her, and everyone of station wore clothing made by Madame Rousseau. The pain in her chest caused her to gasp and Nick looked up, piercing her with the crystal-clear sapphire eyes that always caused her heart to flutter.

"I understand your intent, *mon ami*," Charlotte struggled to keep her voice even and her smile in place. "But are you sure you wish to leave the choices to Sarah?"

"I see no reason not to." Nick made a final notation and set down his quill. "How soon can you have something ready?"

Charlotte rose, feeling each of her thirty-nine years, and silently cursed the circumstances that had tossed Sarah onto Nick's doorstep. "I shall send something around before the evening meal, *mon ami*." Donning her cape, she paused at the door. "Just remember that I bow to your judgment in this matter and am doing as you wish."

Sarah smoothed the gentle folds of the new gown and surveyed herself in the tall looking glass. Vanity had never held a place in her upbringing, and now she wasn't exactly sure how she felt about seeing so much in herself. She reached out to touch and felt the cold, hard surface beneath the warmth of her fingers. Prudence Thompson had owned a looking glass once, she remembered. But it had been a small one. Sarah smiled, thinking back to that first time. She had seen her nose and mouth and then her eyes, but the glass fit into the palm of Prudence's hand and didn't allow one to view both mouth and eyes at the same time. Now, as she gazed before her, she could see the top of her head and the toe of her shoe all at once.

Sarah shook her head in wonder. Madame Rousseau had done such a beautiful job and so quickly. Had she herself made the gown it would have taken two days at least. It would have mattered not that the cut was simple and the style plain. She turned up the hem of the skirt and ran her finger over the smooth, even stitches, each perfect in its placement. The lady was truly a marvel. Carefully, she smoothed the skirt back into place as her fingers gently brushed back and forth over the fabric's soft nap. Never had she owned a gown so fine.

Sarah combed her hair back from her face and secured it with the pins Madame Rousseau had lent her. *'Tis still too fancy to do housework in,* she thought, looking at her reflection, *but mayhap if I'm careful* . . . Sarah smiled, realizing that for the first time since she had been taken from her home, she was beginning to feel like her own self again. And for that she owed thanks to Nicholas Beaumont. Indulging in one final look, her smile deepened at the image she presented. *I am going to be the best housekeeper Nicholas Beaumont has ever encountered,* she declared solemnly. And with her determination firmly in place, Sarah went to seek her chores.

The hall clock struck the hour of seven as Nick entered the dining room. A frown marred his features when he saw that three places had been set at the large oaken table. He was in no mood for company, and, try as he would, he couldn't remember extending an invitation for anyone to join him. Determined to get an answer, he reached for the small golden bell that sat beside his place. Wadsworth entered immediately bearing a silver platter, and set it on the sideboard. But before Nick could voice his question, Sarah entered and added the covered dish she carried to those already displayed. The butler turned and was gone as silently as he had come, but Sarah remained.

She reached for Nick's plate, meaning to serve him, but his angry words halted her actions.

"What in the devil are you wearing?" he challenged.

Stunned, Sarah felt all sanity flee from her body as she silently stood before him. Nick paced completely around her frozen form.

"What is this?" His fingers ran down the long, fitted sleeve of her black velvet gown.

Sarah clutched her hands tightly together. "I'm so sorry," she whispered to the ground before looking up to face Nick's displeasure. "I know I should not have chosen such a costly garment, but Madame Rousseau insisted that it be made in this fabric. I'll take it back at daybreak tomorrow and ask her to exchange it for one less expensive."

"Less expensive?" Nick's eyes narrowed. "I can't even imagine this gown coming from her shop."

Sarah gave a weak smile, understanding his distress. "It is beautiful, is it not?" she sighed. "Still," she straightened her shoulders, "it is much too fancy for a housekeeper and I shall return it as soon as possible. But you must admit, Madame Rousseau is most talented."

Nick's frown deepened. "You mean to tell me that that gown is one of Charlotte's designs?"

Sarah grimaced, wishing his scowl wasn't quite

so fierce. "I did ask her to make several changes," she stammered. "But Madame Rousseau assured me that the added fabric at the neck and sleeves would not alter the cost."

Nick stared and wondered how in such a scant amount of time Sarah could have charmed the most stubborn dressmaker in Virginia into creating a garment so plain that even his cook would have refused to wear it. The neckline reached her throat and had no collar to decorate. The sleeves were long and fitted, but they, too, sported no cuff. The black velvet was indeed a fine choice of fabric, but not a sprig of lace or a single bead graced the gentle folds of its skirt. Nick shook his head. Sarah looked magnificent.

"I'm very sorry to have caused you such distress," Sarah whispered, suddenly close to tears.

Nick felt his anger drain as he watched her eyes grow bright. "Forgive me." He spoke gently and moved to the chair on his right. "You look lovely. I would not think of asking you to return something that brings you such pleasure."

Sarah blinked back her tears, raised her eyes to his, and felt her breath leave her body. He was the most handsome man she had ever encountered. The skin on his face was smooth and tanned, and the blue of his eyes startled her with its brilliance. She watched him pull back a chair and motion for her to sit. "But I thought—"

"Hush," Nick interrupted. "It was the plain style of the gown that startled me, not the cost. I had expected to see you in something more grand."

Sarah's eyes grew wide in confusion. "Grander than this?" Her tone clearly carried disbelief. As Nick smiled, Sarah felt her heart begin to thump loudly in her chest.

"You are beautiful," Nick continued, realizing that she had not an inkling of how comely she appeared. And if a simple gown could give her such elegance, what a vision she would make in one of Charlotte's special creations. Nick made a mental note to visit Madame Rousseau first thing in the morning. He reached for the platter of meat that rested on the table before them and passed it to Sarah only to notice her brow wrinkled in thought. "Is there something amiss?" he questioned.

Sarah swallowed hard. It was not her way to instruct others or to point out their faults, but her upbringing would not allow the Lord to be slighted. "In the confusion I have caused with the new gown, I fear we have forgotten to give thanks," she replied softly, praying her response would not bring him embarrassment.

Nick's puzzled look returned. "Thank who for what?" He watched Sarah's violet eyes grow round with amazement. Then she smiled. That mouth, he thought, watching the edges curl gently upward. Had he ever seen anything so deliciously sensuous?

"You are teasing me, aren't you?" Still smiling, she bowed her head.

For several seconds Nick stared at her bent head and folded hands until it dawned on him she was waiting for him to offer a prayer of thanks for their meal. How was it possible, he wondered for her to appear both captivating and innocent at the same time? Shaking his head, he mumbled words he hoped would be appropriate. She was a paradox to be sure, and silently he vowed to find the answer.

When Sarah raised her head and unclasped her

hands, Nick reached for the meat platter and again Sarah frowned. Setting it down with an impatient thump, he directed his full gaze upon her.

"Is there something else I have forgotten?" he questioned, noting the blush that stained the porcelain of her cheeks.

Sarah heard the impatience in his voice and knew she was the cause. "Should we not wait for Wadsworth to join us?" She looked pointedly at the third place set across from her.

Nick stared in amazement and wondered where she had gotten such a ridiculous idea. "Madame," he said slowly, "I consider myself a fair employer, but I do not eat with my servants."

Sarah's face bloomed a bright scarlet as she jumped from her chair. "Oh, I'm so sorry," she stammered, trying to maneuver the gown's full skirt from between the table and chair. "I didn't realize. I thought . . ." She looked down at the place she had assumed would be hers and realized the magnitude of her error. It had never occurred to her that they would not eat together.

Sarah struggled to keep her composure, but in her haste her chair tipped precariously. She turned to grab for the falling chair, but the velvet nap of her gown caught on the tablecloth, and as Sarah moved, the table covering moved with her.

In the blink of an eye, Nick was on his feet to rescue both the chair and his dinner. Catching Sarah by the arms, he stilled her motion. "Stop," he commanded. The tone of his voice left no room for argument, and he felt Sarah turn to stone under his hands. His fingers gentled and slowly kneaded the stiffness from her flesh. "Look at me." When she refused to raise her head, Nick released one arm and, using only the arc of his fore-finger, lifted her chin until their eyes locked. "I've embarrassed you," his voice was warm and sooth-ing, "and for that I apologize."

Sarah shook her head. This was all wrong. She was the one who had committed the error. "But I . . ." Nick's finger touched her lips, halting her words.

"I am the master of this household, and if I say that I was wrong, then you shall not contradict me. Do you understand?" Sarah nodded, and beneath the touch of his hands, her body was assaulted with fiery sensations she did not understand. What was it about this man that made her feel both safe and threatened at the same time?

"Now, I would like to eat my dinner in the com-pany of a beautiful lady. Do you mind?"

Sarah shook her head slowly and wondered if he could hear the disappointment that pounded through her flesh. But before she could turn to leave, he was setting her chair to right and gently guiding her back to her place at the table. Had he meant then that *she* was beautiful? Numbed with confusion, she silently allowed him to seat her and watched as he returned to his place at the head of the table.

They ate in silence. Sarah had no memory of what passed her lips as, fascinated, she watched Nick sample each of the dishes presented. Never in her life had she beheld such an abundance of food. Even at the grandest of occasions, her Salem neighbors would have considered the meal extrava-gant and wasteful. Even her father, who had dearly loved his meat, would have frowned at the serving of four different kinds of fowl at the same meal.

And such quantity! she thought, watching Wadsworth clear the platters from the table and sideboard. Why, a score of neighbors could have joined them and still the dishes would not have been emptied. Wadsworth returned with a tray of sweets, and Sarah could contain her amazement no longer.

"How ever do you eat so much and stay so fit?" Even as the words left her mouth she regretted them.

Nick smiled, liking the way her cheeks bloomed with color. "So you think I look fit?" His brow wriggled and his smile became a comical leer.

Refusing to be cowed, Sarah gave him a long, appraising look. "I think that if you consume many more meals of that magnitude, you'll not retain your trim figure. Your breeches are already . . ." As his smile deepened, Sarah felt the words lock in her throat. Again her skin grew hot. What had she been thinking of to mention something so personal? If Nicholas Beaumont wished to wear breeches that fit like a second skin, it was his choice to do so. But it was certainly not her place to mention it. Stealing a glance in his direction, she watched his eyes turn a darker shade of blue. What was it about this man that caused her to say the first thing that popped into her head? She wasn't normally flighty and indiscreet, yet he had only to look in her direction and she felt as if her feet no longer touched the ground.

"I think you need a sweet, little Sarah." Nick winked. "Your disposition is growing tart." Nick offered a fluted crystal glass the likes of which Sarah had never seen. He placed the confection before her and dipped her spoon into the creamy top.

" 'Tis called syllabub," he said, lifting the spoon to her lips. "A lemon cream mixture that sits on brandy." Captivated by his smile and the soothing sound of his voice, Sarah obediently opened her mouth and felt the tart cream melt on her tongue. Their eyes locked as Nick slowly pulled the spoon from her lips.

The spell was broken as Wadsworth chose that moment to enter the room. Sarah immediately jerked back in her chair and wiped her lips with her napkin.

"I beg pardon, sir, but I thought you would want to know that Miss Ruby was at the door with a note from Mrs. Beaumont."

Nick scowled and reached for the folded paper that Wadsworth offered on a small silver tray. He recognized the delicate scrawl of his grandmother's hand and knew the contents before he even read the words.

Alarmed by the look on Nick's face, Sarah could not contain her curiosity. "Is something amiss?"

Nick's smile was tolerant at best as he refolded the note and tossed it onto the table. " 'Tis from my grandmother," he explained, then turned to Wadsworth. "Is Ruby still waiting?" he asked.

The butler nodded. "She's in the kitchen. Cook gave her a glass of buttermilk while I brought you the message."

Nick rose from his chair, his jovial mood shattered. "Have Ruby tell my grandmother that I am already committed for the evening. I shall call upon her tomorrow at two as originally planned." He turned toward Sarah. "Business matters demand my attention. But stay and finish your dessert. I've no doubt I shall see you on the morrow."

As the door closed behind her host and his butler, Sarah reached for the discarded note. Her eyes grew wide as she scanned the contents. Jumping from her seat with the paper still clutched in her fingers, she turned first one way and then the other in utter panic. Wadsworth returned and his brow lifted, but Sarah was too distressed to care that he had caught her reading the master's correspondence.

"Did he leave yet? Quick, tell him to wait, I can accompany him. I have some skills . . ."

The butler calmly began to set the dishes onto a tray he carried. "I believe Mr. Beaumont has gone to his study to resume his correspondence."

Sarah jerked backward as if the words had been a physical blow. "But his grandmother is dying!" She offered the note in fingers that trembled.

Wadsworth set several more dishes on the tray.

"What can I do to help?" she pleaded. "Does Mrs. Beaumont live nearby? Has the doctor been summoned?"

Wadsworth straightened and gave her an appraising look. He had been with the Beaumont family for most of his life. And much of his success was based on his unwavering loyalty and his ability to understand people. He took in Sarah's pale features, the tremor in her voice.

"It would be best, Miss Townsend if you were to return to your room. I'm sure that all will look brighter in the morning."

Sarah squared her shoulders and took a deep, calming breath. "Wadsworth," she said quietly, "I am not a child to be protected from the tragedies of the world. I might be only ten and nine, but I have already tasted death. I have buried both of my parents. Now, you must trust me when I say that my presence will not be a nuisance. I possess some skills of healing and I wish to give assistance. So, will you help me or shall I leave and ask the first person on the road how to find the property of Mrs. Beaumont?"

Wadsworth returned to stacking the dishes. "The master's grandmother lives about two miles down the road. 'Tis a grand white house with pecan trees in the front yard. But you'll not find the master there tonight. He'll be in his study attending to his business."

The note dropped from Sarah's fingers as disbelief clashed with her confusion. "Mr. Beaumont has just received a letter saying his grandmother will not live out the night and you want me to believe that he has gone to his study to deal with business?" Her eyes narrowed in challenge. "Sir, the man who was kind enough to offer me shelter until my family could be contacted is not a man to sit idly by and wait for death to claim a member of his family."

Wadsworth set down his tray and made his decision. "Miss Sarah . . ." He said her name gently. "I have worked with Mr. Beaumont since before we came to this house, so you know my word is good. Trust me when I say that all is well with Mr. Beaumont's grandmother."

Sarah shook her head and reached for the note, smoothing it flat against the table. "But the letter says . . ."

Wadsworth slowly picked up his tray. "Mr. Beaumont has received that note or one like it at least once a month for the past ten years."

Sarah flopped back down on her chair like a

marionette with no strings. "Who would commit such a cruel act to say that a loved one was dying?" she shuddered. "Does his grandmother know of this horrible mischief?"

For the briefest moment Wadsworth's face sank into a sad smile. "Mrs. Beaumont is the culprit."

Sarah's gasp echoed her disbelief. "Nick's mother?"

Wadsworth quickly shook his head. "Oh, no, miss, the master's mother and father both passed on when he was just a little tyke."

"How horrible!"

Wadsworth glanced toward the door that led to the hallway. " 'Twas no great loss, miss. The master's parents had no time for him anyway. They were both killed in a carriage accident and that's when the master went to live with Miss Agatha."

Sarah had no trouble picturing Nick a child, but when she tried to imagine her own childhood without the love and support of her father and stepmother, an aching void filled her chest. "Was she good to him?" she whispered, feeling the pain of Nick's loss.

The butler nodded enthusiastically. "The old lady loved him dearly. But Miss Agatha, well, she's a tyrant of sorts and them being two cut from the same cloth, there was bound to be trouble. When the time came for the master to move out on his own, Miss Agatha, she wouldn't hear of it. She tried holding the family business over his head to make him move back, but, like I said, the master is just as stubborn. He took his half of Beaumont Shipping and expanded it more than three times over." Wadsworth looked at Sarah in wonder. "Do you know in all these years, I've never heard him complain that half of everything he makes goes directly to his grandmother. I think he's pleased that he's found a way to give her things without her realizing it."

"But the note . . ." Sarah prompted.

The smile faded completely from Wadsworth's pale face. "Miss Agatha suffers greatly from old age and can no longer get about on her own. The first time she sent a note, why, the young master dropped everything and rushed right over. There he finds his grandmother, fit as a fiddle and sitting up in bed. She was lonesome, she said, and felt poorly. The master, he didn't say anything until it happened again about a week later. Now he just doesn't go at all."

"He never sees her at all?"

Wadsworth picked up his tray and turned toward the door. "The master sees his grandmother several times a week. In fact, she was here just this morning."

Sarah rubbed her temples in confusion. "But if that is true, then why would she send such a note?"

Wadsworth pushed open the door. "Control," he said quietly. "Miss Agatha just can't give up the control."

For several minutes, Sarah sat alone in the dining room trying to understand a woman who would go to such lengths. Her fingers smoothed over the delicate penmanship as she searched for her answers. *You are making a mistake, Mrs. Agatha Beaumont,* she whispered to the empty room. She remembered the story her father had once told her about a young shepherd boy tending his sheep. When the lad had grown lonely on his mountainside he had called wolf, and the townsfolk had rushed to his aid. But there had been no wolf and it hadn't taken long before the villagers began to ignore the boy completely. Sarah shuddered, remembering the tragic ending to the tale.

Quietly, she stood and smoothed her gown. On the morrow she would pay a visit to Mrs. Agatha Beaumont and tell her how distressing her notes were for Nick. Then again, she thought, what if the woman was truly ill? Filled with doubt and confusion, Sarah returned to her room.

I don't understand these people, she thought, lying down upon the soft mattress of her bed and pulling her knees up to rest her chin upon them. *I need to be home.* Tears swelled but, staring at the ornate ceiling, she blinked them back. *Samuel,* she sighed as her throat grew tight, *if only I had a way to let you know that I am safe.* Silently, she rocked back and forth. *I'll never forgive myself for the anguish I'm causing you, dear brother.*

Chapter Five

Salem, Massachusetts

Ann Tate shifted anxiously on her wooden stool, her eyes never leaving Samuel Wittfield's back as he hung his coat on the peg by the door.

"Well, Samuel, are you going to take all afternoon, or are you going to tell us what happened?"

Samuel fought back the grin that hovered at the corners of his mouth. Stone-faced he turned to his wife and their neighbor. "I presented the evidence to the Reverend Mr. Noyse, the Reverend Mr. Parris, and the magistrates." Slowly Samuel pulled out his chair and wearily sat at his place at the head of the table.

Feeling a sudden chill, Elizabeth wrapped her shawl more tightly about her shoulders. "Samuel, 'tis unkind to keep us in suspense. Tell us what they said. What was their verdict about Sarah?"

Samuel folded his rough hands as if in prayer. "Reverend Parris said that under the circumstances we witnessed, Sarah must be considered a witch. We are to notify the magistrate immediately if her human form appears again."

"Dear Lord in heaven." Elizabeth flopped back in her chair, her face pale as parchment.

"Well, what did you expect?" Ann demanded shrilly. "Did we not see Sarah turn into a cat with our very eyes?"

Elizabeth rubbed her temples with fingers that felt like ice. "I did see the cat in her bed," she whispered. "Samuel?"

Samuel Wittfield shook his head. "I was standing in the hallway when I heard your cries. By the time I reached you . . ." His voice choked, and Samuel looked away.

"Well, I saw it all," Ann declared emphatically. "One minute Sarah was sitting in her bed, then within a blink she's gone and a black cat is standing on her nightdress. You might as well face it, Samuel Wittfield . . ." She paused for effect. "Your sister is a witch."

"Stepsister," Elizabeth snapped, reaching for her husband's hands. "They carry none of the same blood."

Ann pulled her chair closer to the table. "Why do you think Sarah's name was missing from Tituba's list?"

Samuel shrugged his shoulders. "Tituba is but a slave. I'm sure the Reverend Mr. Parris has tried to instruct her, but we must remember, she's been influenced by the devil. Today at the trials, she spoke of riding between Sarah Good and Sarah Osborne as their specters flew through the sky in search of mischief."

"They flew through the sky?" Elizabeth's voice quivered with apprehension.

Samuel nodded solemnly. "Tituba said she stood at the reverend's back door when they appeared and bid her to join them on their broom. She said she refused at first, but they pinched her and struck her with a stick until she agreed. Her back is covered with fresh welts, so her story must be so—"

"But what of Sarah?" Ann interrupted. "She turned into the devil's familiar before our very eyes." The widow's voice was tinged with awe. "Why would she show herself to us in that way?"

"I can't say I'm completely surprised." Anxiously, Elizabeth's eyes darted to the shadowy corners of the room. "Jonathan always encouraged Sarah to speak her mind. And they always went way over to Topsfield for services."

Ann's eyes narrowed as her imagination took hold. "Yes, but did you never wonder why Jonathan Townsend did not get on with the Reverend Mr. Parris? Somehow he must have suspected that if they prayed in Salem, the good minister would route out the evil that he and Sarah harbored." Ann stood up and reached for her cloak. "I think we should attend the trials tomorrow. We should leave early in the morning to get good seats before the magistrates arrive at noon. I'm a God-fearing woman, but I would see for myself those whom Tituba spoke of." For in fact, no matter how she tried, Ann couldn't imagine the hefty Sarah Osborne seated on a broom.

"But what of Sarah now?" Elizabeth shivered with anxiety and fear. "Should not the good people of Salem be warned that she stalks as a cat?"

"The reverend will announce it from the pulpit on Sunday." Samuel shook his head sadly. "All will be warned to beware of a sleek black cat that could be Sarah."

Elizabeth shuddered. "I shall never forgive her." Her voice was low and full of venom. Samuel turned to his wife. In the firelight her eyes were hard and glittered with hatred. "I shall never forgive Sarah for the disgrace she has brought upon this family." She squeezed Samuel's hand. "And I shall never forgive her for the injury she has caused you, dear husband."

Samuel patted his wife's hand, and for the first time that evening, he allowed a contented smile to touch his lips.

Chapter Six

Middle Plantation, Virginia

Nick Beaumont paused at the top of the stairs and smiled at the sunshine that poured in through the foyer's tall windows. Mornings were his favorite time, with the air crisp and washed clean with sunlight. Energy filled him, and he eagerly embraced the new day. Turning back, he looked over at the door of Sarah's room. Would she smile if he slipped open the door and kissed her into waking? The clock in the hall struck half past the hour of six, and Nick continued down the stairs whistling softly between his teeth. He'd let her sleep. *In fact,* he thought, *I'll have Mrs. Killingham fix a tray that I shall take up myself.* He remembered the last time he had brought breakfast to a woman in bed and his smile grew deeper. Sarah would taste delicious.

Wadsworth greeted him in the study with a fresh pot of coffee and a dower expression.

" 'Tis a beautiful day, Wadsworth, is it not?"

Wadsworth nodded silently. He understood all the master's quirks except this one. Rousing from his warm bed when the sun had just touched the sky with its light had never brought him joy, and he'd often thought that had the situations been reversed, and he the master, he'd stay snuggled beneath the covers until he was called to the midday meal. Wadsworth struggled to keep his eyes open as he poured coffee into a pewter mug.

"I'd like you to instruct Mrs. Killingham to prepare a tray for our guest," Nick continued as he began to shift through his papers. "I'll take it up to her myself in about an hour."

Wadsworth paused in the doorway, his brow wrinkled in a frown. "For Miss Sarah?"

Nick sipped the hot brew. "Yes, and ask Mrs. Killingham if any of our strawberries are ripe. I have a taste for them this morning."

Wadsworth took a step back into the study. "But Miss Sarah is already up."

"She's what?"

Wadsworth watched Nick's eyes narrow as he pulled out his gold timepiece, and for the first time that morning he felt a grin tug at his mouth. "Miss Sarah was already in the cookhouse when Mrs. Killingham arrived this morning. Gave both of them a good start, I must say." Wadsworth struggled not to smile openly at the stunned look that covered the master's face. "Now I believe she is in the herb bed . . . pulling weeds," he declared solemnly.

Nick flopped back in his chair. "She's pulling weeds?"

Wadsworth nodded, and turned back to the door. "And from the look of it, sir, the lady knows what she is about."

Nick stared blindly at the correspondence before him. Why on earth had she risen so early? Had she slept badly? Was she not comfortable? Did her room not suit her? With quick, efficient motions he gathered his papers and tucked them back into his desk

78

and locked the drawer. *What I need,* he thought, *is a good brisk walk in the garden.*

Nick found Sarah kneeling on the brick walk that edged the herb garden. Her hair was completely covered by a white cloth and although she wore the same black dress from the night before, much of the skirt was hidden by a large white apron. At first glance she could have been any servant tending to morning chores. But on closer look, one noticed the delicate wrist and the long, slender fingers as they competently attended their task. Sarah hummed an unfamiliar tune and seemed completely at ease with her chore. Nick thought of Marigold and shuddered.

In his mind he could hear her breathy whisper as she hinted for another piece of jewelry, preferably a betrothal ring. He tried to imagine her tending a garden, but the image refused to come.

A sharp breeze whisked through the garden, and Nick looked up at the sky in surprise. The sun had vanished and a heavy gray cloud now hung overhead. Deciding they were in for another unpredictable spring storm, he took but a single step in Sarah's direction before his feet refused to move any farther. There, on the path directly before him where Sarah was working, a single beam of sun broke through the clouds. Startling in its brightness, it illuminated Sarah with its intensity. Nick watched as she paused and brushed the dirt from her fingers. She tipped her head back and smiled toward the heavens. The sunbeam began to grow brighter as it expanded to encompass the surrounding gardens. Nick looked up at the sky in amazement. The clouds had vanished. Turning back to Sarah, he found her again tugging at the weeds. Nick looked at the glowing sun until his eyes hurt from the brightness. Blinking, he rubbed his hands against the spots that still burned from behind his closed lids. Had he imagined it? Shaking his head, he wiped the moisture from his eyes and took a step toward Sarah. Surely she had noticed the strange event.

"Sarah . . ." His voice sounded harsh even to his own ears, and Nick suppressed a smile as she jumped.

"My word, Mr. Beaumont." She pressed a hand to her heart. "You've given me quite a fright. 'Tis most impolite to sneak up on someone like that."

Now he did smile. "Forgive me," he said quietly, not adding that he wasn't in the habit of announcing himself in his own garden. He watched her hastily brush the dirt from her fingers and extended his hand to help her rise. But when she stood, Nick found himself reluctant to let her go. The bright violet of her eyes rivaled the deep purple of the pansies that bordered the walkway and her thick, dark lashes were in sharp contrast to the milky whiteness of her skin. Nick felt his heart quicken as he glanced down at their linked hands, hers delicate and pale, his large and dark. He smiled again as he watched her nervously tug her fingers from his.

"Did you wish to speak with me?" Sarah struggled to keep her voice even. Her heart pounded in her ears, and she wondered if its loudness was the reason for his smile.

Nick gave her a curious stare and made no comment when she took a hasty step backward. "Did you notice anything peculiar about the weather just a moment ago?"

Whatever she had been expecting, it was not for him to comment about the weather. Sarah cleared her throat and wondered why he had to smell so fresh. Shading her eyes, she looked up at the clear blue of the sky. "I think 'twill be a beautiful day."

Nick's brow wrinkled and his eyes narrowed. "But just a moment ago, did you not see anything strange?" Sarah answered with a puzzled look, and Nick shook his head, convinced that his mind had taken to playing tricks. "Why did you leave your bed so early? Did you not sleep well? Is your room not comfortable?"

Sarah's eyes widened with amazement. "The room is lovely."

Fascinated with the soft fullness of her lips, Nick took a step closer. "Then why aren't you still there?"

"You wish me to remain in my room? Have I done something to displease you?"

Nick shook his head and wondered why nothing was making sense. "You please me fine," he whispered, snaking an arm around her waist. "In fact, better than most." Her eyes were wary; still, he was unable to resist. His lips brushed feather-light across hers. Just a taste, he told himself. But Nick wasn't prepared for the rush of desire that had him tightening his arms, pulling her close, then closer still. He had expected a cool reserve, not heat that seared the last of his reasoning. Again and again his lips pressed in gentle persuasion against hers until her lips parted on a moan and his tongue gained access. Like a man dying of thirst, he drank of her sweetness.

Sarah felt the heat of his body and her bones melted. The dream that she had never dared to linger on now bloomed into reality. She met passion with passion and gave more than he would have willingly taken, stunning them both in the process.

Gasping, with her hand pressed to her heart, Sarah pulled from Nick's embrace. Her breathing

81

came hard and labored, but it silently pleased her that his was just as unsteady.

"Forgive me," she whispered. "I shouldn't have done that."

Stunned that she had uttered the very words on his tongue, Nick wondered if things with Sarah would ever be what he expected. "There is nothing to be sorry for," he said quietly, trying not to frown when she stepped back as he stepped forward. "I was only going to suggest that we return to the house for a more private interlude."

Sarah felt her fist clench, though she knew she had no right to be angry. After what they had just shared, he had just cause to think the worst of her. Guilty in her own mind, she squared her shoulders and prepared to take her punishment.

" 'Twas most unseemly for me to have . . ." She searched to find the proper words. "To have done that." Her voice wavered as she struggled to find control. "I pray that you will not think harshly of me."

Nick frowned at the picture she presented. They had shared a moment of bliss unlike any he had known, yet now she stood as a schoolchild ready to extend her hand for the rod of correction.

"Sarah . . ." He groped for the words that might make it right for her. "We are two adults and we shared a moment of pleasure. Surely there is no sin in that."

Her eyes looked doubtful. "The sins of the flesh are many. But I've never . . ." Her cheeks blossomed with color as she looked down at their feet.

"You've never what?" he prompted, fascinated with her.

Her eyes lifted to his then quickly darted away. "I've never felt that way before. Not that I've been kissed by many."

Nick grinned, and stepped back to lean against the thick base of the pecan tree. "How many?"

Her face snapped back to glare at him as her eyes grew wide. "I must not speak of such things with you."

His grin deepened, and his dimples winked at her distress. "How many? Ten, twenty . . . How many men have you kissed?"

Horrified that he could even think such of her, Sarah pulled her shoulders erect and gave him her coldest glare. "You insult me with your assumptions. If you must know, 'twas only one."

"You've only kissed one man or you've only been kissed once?"

Sarah closed her eyes and silently prayed for salvation. "George Porter kissed me once behind the barn. I was feeding the chickens."

Nick struggled not to laugh. Her stiff posture and fiery cheeks told him she was already in completely over her head. "I see," he said solemnly. "And just how did you find that kiss?"

Sarah suppressed a shudder at the memory. " 'Twas wet." Her eyes lifted to his, and she wondered why his gaze could make her knees go weak. "But just now . . ."

"Go on," Nick prompted.

Sarah took a deep, cleansing breath. "I think I have discovered the true meaning of temptation." Nick's smile turned to heat before her eyes.

"Then you liked what we shared?" He stepped forward, but this time she didn't retreat.

"Never would I have believed such feelings could exist," she admitted in innocence. She took a deep breath to strengthen her resolve. "But 'tis something that cannot be allowed to happen again.

Without the sanctity of marriage, the pleasures we shared are unholy and foul."

Nick's smile vanished. "Ha!" he snapped. "So you want marriage, just like the others." He watched a sad smile cross her face.

"No, Mr. Beaumont," she said quietly. "What I want is to go back to my family."

Nick watched in stunned silence as she turned and steadily walked back to the house.

Chapter Seven

Filled with frustration and armed with lemon oil and a soft rag, Sarah flopped down on the chair behind Nick's desk. For the past hour she had searched the house for dust and found none. Each room contained treasures the likes of which she had never seen, but there wasn't a speck of lint to be whisked away or a single smudge to be polished. Nicholas Beaumont kept his house as he did himself, she thought — in fastidious order.

She had tried to lend a hand turning the spit in the cook house, but Mrs. Killingham would not hear of it. And when she had offered to aid little Annabelle in peeling the vegetables, she was politely ushered out the door. Wadsworth had proved no more helpful when she offered to aid him in polishing the silver.

" 'Tis my task, madam, and one that I am proud to attend to."

Leaving him busy at work in the dining room, Sarah had gone off on her own in search of ways to be useful. Now, as she sat in the study, the clean rag dangling idly from her fingers, she considered her situation. *Nicholas Beaumont needs a housekeeper about as much as a man needs to wear two hats,* she thought, tossing the rag onto the desk. Her eyes scanned the book-lined walls and she fought back the urge to choose a title and lose herself within the written words.

"I will find a way to be of use," she declared to the empty room. "There must be a dozen tasks that need attending. I am simply not looking hard enough." With renewed determination, Sarah reached for her discarded rag, noticing for the first time the crumpled note on the desk before her. Immediately she recognized the hand and the stationery. The clock had yet to strike noon, yet Agatha Beaumont had sent another urgent request for her grandson's presence. Sarah's fingers traced over the crumpled paper. Nick was to dine with his grandmother that very evening. Why then would Mrs. Beaumont send such a plea if there was naught amiss?

Carefully, Sarah refolded the crumpled paper. Had Nick stopped to see his grandmother on his way to the docks? If he had, then all was well, but if he hadn't . . . Sarah thought of dear Rebecca Nurse. She and Nick's grandmother would probably be about the same age. Did Rebecca still languish in the Salem Jail or had the madness reached its end? *'Tis no longer in my power to help you, old friend,* Sarah thought sadly. *There is no way for me to see to your comfort.* Making her decision, Sarah tucked the note into her pocket. She would pay a visit to Mrs. Agatha Beaumont and pray that someone in Salem would see to Rebecca.

The walk was shorter than she had anticipated, but the dampness that hung in the air was oppressive and hinted of rain. Sarah wiped her forehead. If late April air was so warm here, what would the August sun be like? She turned down the walk and stared at the magnificent white house before her. It was not as large as Nick's she thought, noting the windows that spoke of three levels, yet it was grander than any she had ever seen in Salem Village or Salem Town. With a determined step, Sarah continued on.

Her knock was answered by a large, burly man who looked more like a dockhand than a butler. His face was weathered and his thick hair was short and wayward. His dark jacket was a cut too tight and the buttons of his waistcoat strained to be free from their moorings.

"I've come to see Mrs. Agatha Beaumont," Sarah stated calmly. As she stepped into the foyer, her eyes widened with surprise. The walls were painted a dark green, and heavy tapestries blocked the daylight, creating an atmosphere that was both morose and foreboding.

"What be the nature of your call, miss? Mrs. Beaumont be a busy lady and she don't take kindly to strangers at her door."

Sarah ignored the man's intimidating stare. "I beg pardon, but I was under the impression that Mrs. Beaumont was gravely ill."

"Ha." The butler took Sarah's shoulder in his beefy hand and spun her back toward the entrance. "Let me save us both time and aggravation, little lady. Miss Agatha don't take kindly to strangers that's looking for a handout."

"But . . ." Sarah stammered as the man guided her none too gently to the door. "Mr. Beaumont sent me," she gasped. The hand on her shoulder was instantly released, and Sarah struggled to regain her balance.

The burly butler gave her a shrewd look and placed his thick hands on his waist. "State your business, miss."

Sarah smoothed down her apron and skirt and returned the man's steady glare. "My name is Miss Sarah Townsend. I am from the Beaumont household and I have come on behalf of Mr. Beaumont to check on Mrs. Beaumont's health. I have some knowledge in the art of healing and thought I might be of service."

The man's scowl deepened. "I know everyone that works for Master Nick."

Sarah hesitated for only a moment before reaching into her pocket and retrieving the note. "I don't mean to intrude," Sarah said gently. "I merely thought to offer assistance wherever needed." She watched in amazement as the man's abrupt anger drained away and he refolded the note and returned it to her.

"It is I who should beg pardon, miss. But Miss Agatha," he glanced toward the ceiling above them, "today ain't one of her better days. 'Twould be wiser for you to call back tomorrow."

"But if she's ill, perhaps I can help?"

The man shook his head. "She won't let no one near her when she gets into these moods. She wants to see Master Nick and no one else can satisfy."

Sarah's eyes narrowed. "Are you telling me that Mrs. Beaumont is not sick, that she's just throwing a tantrum?"

A loud crash sounded from overhead, immediately followed by a distressed wail. Within moments, a disheveled maid flew down the steps.

"That's it," she cried, tears streaming down her cheeks. "I'll not work in this house a minute longer. She's a vicious old biddy and I'll not take her insults any longer."

"Watch your tongue, Daisy," the large man cautioned. "Besides, you know today be one of her bad days."

"Luther, they're all bad days." Daisy tugged off her apron and shoved it hard at his chest. "I want no part of this house. I'm going home." With a flounce of her stained skirt, Daisy turned and forsaking the servants' entrance, left through the Beaumonts' front door.

Sarah's gentle hand restrained Luther as he started off after the wayward maid. "What truly ails Mrs. Beaumont?" she questioned softly.

Luther gave a final scowl toward the closed door, then turned his attention back to Sarah. "The mistress suffers something terrible from joint knots."

Sarah frowned. "Joint knots?"

Luther held up his large hand and pointed to the knuckles. "The joints are all swollen and knotted. Her legs don't work at all anymore and now the sickness be in her hands, too."

"But her physician—surely he could offer some relief."

Luther shook his head and threaded his fingers through his wayward hair. "He says drink brandy or take laudanum. But when Miss Agatha takes brandy to smooth the edge off, it gives her a sour stomach and foul disposition."

"And the laudanum?" Sarah prompted.

"Won't take it." Luther looked toward the ceiling. "Miss Agatha be well past her seventieth year," he whispered. "I think she's afraid that one day she'll go to sleep and not awake. So," he paused, "you gotta take into account that sometimes Miss Agatha has bad days, and the rest of the time she's just plain mean."

89

Sarah nodded thoughtfully. "Have you a willow tree in the area? One that is not too far away?"

Luther stared at her with a raised brow. "There be a grove of willows just down the meadow."

Sarah smiled. "Good. First I want you to send someone to fetch some bark. Good thick pieces about a hand long. When they come back, set the bark to steep in a large kettle with boiling water. Let me know when that is done." Sarah took a step toward the stairs and then paused. "Which room?"

Luther's face held a look of disbelief. "The large one at the end of the hall toward the front of the house."

Sarah nodded. "It would help if you could get that bark as soon as possible." Turning, she mounted the stairs.

Sarah tapped firmly on the chamber door before releasing the latch. Pushing open the door, she ducked as a saucer sailed past her head to collide with the wall and shatter to the floor.

"Mrs. Beaumont?" Sarah quickly surveyed the darkened room. The walls were painted a deep shade of blue and here, too, the shades had been pulled so that little light could seep in.

"Who the devil are you, and where's Daisy?" a shrill voice commanded.

Sarah stepped further into the shadowy room. On the opposite wall stood the largest tester bed she had ever seen. Richly embroidered linens hung from the bed's frame and in its center, propped by a dozen lace-covered pillows, sat Agatha Beaumont as regal as Queen Mary herself. Sarah resisted the urge to curtsy and stepped closer to the bed.

"I said who the devil are you, girl? Are ye deaf? I want an answer. Luuuther!"

90

Sarah suppressed a smile at the sight before her. Agatha Beaumont, who had all her servants cringing in fear, was but a frail old lady with wispy white hair. "Pray do not find fault with your servant, madame. My name is Sarah Townsend and I am currently Mr. Beaumont's . . . ah . . . housekeeper." Sarah stumbled over her title, thinking of how little she had accomplished that morning. "Upon seeing your note, I thought I might be of assistance."

Agatha's sharp gaze raked Sarah from head to toe. "First, Miss Townsend, or whatever your true name be, let's get one fact perfectly clear. Just because I am momentarily confined to this bed doesn't make me a doddering old fool who will believe every story that reaches my ears. And unless Wadsworth has up and beat me to meet our Maker, you're not the housekeeper in my grandson's home. Besides," Agatha struggled to straighten her wizened body even further, "how did you come to read a private letter sent to my grandson?"

Ignoring Agatha's angry glare, Sarah sighed, pulled a straight-backed chair near the bed, and took a seat. "Put your mind at rest," she started slowly, not sure how to begin her story. "Wadsworth is indeed alive and healthy. And you are right about my not being the housekeeper, for this morning I felt completely useless. Do you know that Mrs. Killingham would not even let me scour the pans? Wadsworth would not allow me to help polish the silver and there was no dust to be found anywhere. So when I came across your note—"

"You decided to come and try to get on my good side," Agatha interrupted. "Well, save your time and get out. I don't have a good side."

"You are in pain," Sarah said gently, noting that

91

Mrs. Beaumont went to great lengths to keep her hands beneath the coverlet. "And I know of a brew that might help."

Agatha's eyes narrowed and she leaned forward. "You are not from around here, are you? Your speech is as strange as that ridiculous dress you are wearing. Tell me, just where did my grandson find you?"

Sarah took a deep breath and decided that since her circumstances were not of her making, there was nothing to lose by sharing them. Quietly she told her story, starting with the sounds that woke her on that dreadful night. She made light of the horrors on the ship, for the memories still made her stomach lurch and her skin crawl. She ended with the meeting between Nick and his attorney, Mr. Danvers.

"So as you can see," Sarah concluded, "I find myself in quite a dilemma. I have no way to get home until the confusion of the papers is put to rest. And I am the housekeeper in a house that needs no keeping."

Agatha stared hard at the girl. She had not become such a success in business by believing every sad tale that came her way, but there was something about the girl that made her want to know more.

"So you've come to me to get the money to sail you back home?"

Sarah quickly shook her head. "No, no. I've an understanding with Mr. Beaumont." She felt her cheeks grow warm as the memory of their time in the garden rushed forth. "He . . . ah . . ." She struggled to clear her throat. "Mr. Beaumont has been kind enough to allow his agent to carry a letter to my family informing them that I am safe. And although I ache to embrace them myself, I am content to see

92

out our arrangement."

Agatha watched Sarah's cheeks bloom with color. *And just what else has my Nicky been kind enough to do?* she thought as she continued to scrutinize the girl.

"Pull back those blasted tapestries so I can get a better look at you, child."

Sarah chuckled, and rose to let the sunlight in. "I passed ten and nine some months ago, Mrs. Beaumont, so I am hardly a child."

But not yet a woman, I'll wager, Agatha thought as she watched Sarah return to her chair. She was pretty enough, with good clear skin and bright eyes, but she had none of the social sophistication that usually marked one of her grandson's consorts. In fact, her clothing placed her just one step beyond the servants, and Agatha knew Nick did not dally with those who worked for him.

"I find your story fascinating," Agatha said after a long silence. "A bit farfetched, but clever and fascinating nonetheless."

Sarah's easy smile faded and she rose stiffly from her chair. "I do not tell falsehoods, Mrs. Beaumont. Regardless of what you or your grandson think of me, I am a good Christian woman. I thought I might be of help, but I can see now that my presence distresses you, so I'll bid you good day."

"You'll bid me nothing of the kind. Now get off that high horse you're riding and sit back down."

Sarah stood firm beside her chair.

Agatha gave an exaggerated sigh. "So much for Christian charity. Here I thought the Lord had finally sent someone who could bring some relief to my pain."

Sarah shifted only slightly. "I shall be happy to

give instructions to your man, Luther."

Agatha pouted. "Luther would just as soon poison me and put us both out of our miseries."

Sarah stood firm, quietly watching Nick's grandmother as she struggled to shift herself on the bed. The old woman smothered a groan as she used her hand to lever herself.

Sarah was instantly at her side. "Here, let me." Her words were soft, and with gentle hands she soon had the woman more comfortably settled.

Agatha glared. "I thought you were leaving." But pain edged her voice and took the sting from her words.

Sarah gave a final pat to the pillow. "I think not." She ignored Agatha's gasp of outrage as she perched on the edge of the bed and took the woman's gnarled hand.

"Don't." Embarrassed by the grotesque sight, Agatha tried to snatch her hand from Sarah's, but the pain had drained her strength.

Sarah traced her fingers over the swollen knuckles and fingers that now resembled twisted claws. "Is there tallow for the candles?"

Agatha snorted and, as Sarah released her hand, she quickly placed it out of sight beneath the covers. "My candles are made of beeswax. I won't have tallow in my house. I can't abide the smell."

"Very well." Sarah rose. "I shall ask Luther to fetch some." She moved to the fire, and despite the heat that already filled the room, stoked the flames higher.

"What are you about, girl?" Agatha snapped, watching Sarah add more wood to the flames. " 'Tis no sense to build a great fire and then have to stand back from it. 'Tis a waste of good wood."

94

A knock sounded and Luther entered, gingerly carrying a hot kettle. Sarah took the kettle and placed it over the flames. Ignoring Agatha's threats, she calmly gave Luther a list of ingredients and sent him on his way.

"My grandson will have your head for this."

"I think he will thank me for seeing to your comfort."

"Ah ha," Agatha snorted, curiously watching Sarah at the hearth. "So you want my Nicky to thank you."

Sarah returned to the bed with a silver sick cup that sported handles on both sides. "In truth, Mrs. Beaumont, I don't care what your grandson thinks of me. Now, try a taste of this, and tell me if it's still too warm." Gently she urged the spouted cup to Agatha's thin lips.

Agatha gave Sarah a long, appraising stare before pulling one of her gnarled hands from the covers. She could not manage the cup on her own but rested her hand against Sarah's to guide the spout to her mouth. She grimaced at the taste, and when she would have pushed the cup away, Sarah gently urged her on. Agatha threatened and complained. Sarah softly cajoled, and by the time Luther returned, the cup was empty.

"That was vile," Agatha shuddered, sticking out her tongue.

"I believe it is an acquired taste," Sarah said gently. "Somewhat like dry sherry." She ignored Agatha's fierce glare and turned to her next task. Carefully she melted the tallow in a shallow pan, then gingerly carried the hot pan to the bed.

"What are you doing?" Agatha's voice was now tinged with fear as well as pain. "You'll not . . ."

Agatha's frail cry echoed in the room as Sarah took her hand and quickly coated it with the hot wax.

"You're hurting me!" Agatha's tears ran freely as she tried to pull her hand away. Luther lurched forward, his eyes wide with surprise, but his steps halted with the gentle sound of Sarah's voice.

"Calm yourself," Sarah soothed as she began to gently massage the wax-coated hand with her own. "There is a sting at first, but can you tell me now that you feel no relief?"

Agatha angrily wiped the tears from her face, then realized that what Sarah said was true. The terrible twisting pain that so often tried to wring her soul from her body was easing. She felt Sarah's fingers firmly rubbing over her own swollen knuckles as if coaxing the pain to leave her. When the procedure was repeated on her other hand, Agatha offered no more than a wince when her hand first touched the hot wax. Again she waited in wonder, and again she felt the pain begin to slip away. She watched the slow, hypnotic motion of Sarah's hands and felt her eyelids grow heavy.

Sarah peeled the last of the cooling wax from Agatha's fingers and then gently soothed her wrinkled skin with a cool cream. Agatha snored on and never noticed when Sarah carefully rose from the bed.

"How did you know to do that?" Luther whispered, eyes still wide from what he had witnessed.

Sarah motioned him from the room. She longed for a moment of privacy to rub the kinks from her back, but Luther stayed at her side.

"My father, although not a doctor, knew much about healing," she said quietly as they made their way down the stairs. "The heat from the tallow soothes the stiffness. But you have to be very, very

96

careful, for if the tallow is allowed to get too hot, you would burn the skin, and that would be worse than the original pain."

"But if it helps . . ."

Sarah placed her hand on Luther's arm. "There is nothing to be gained by trading one pain for another. But it would be my pleasure to teach you or anyone else in the household the technique so Mrs. Beaumont can have what little relief we can offer.

Luther nodded gratefully. "And the bark mixture?"

Sarah paused. "I know not what, but there seems to be something in the willow that helps to ease pain. Not like laudanum, for, in truth, if you wished, you could go up and wake Mrs. Beaumont this very instant." Luther's look clearly said that that was the last thing in his mind. "She is sleeping because the pain has lessened," Sarah continued. "Not because she is drugged. And when she wakes, she should feel better for the rest."

"Then should she have more?"

Sarah shook her head and reached for the front door. "Have a care, Luther, for if used too often, the drink will lose its merit. Now I must be off or Wadsworth will be wondering where I disappeared to."

Luther followed her out onto the marble step and frowned. "Where is your carriage?"

Sarah smiled and looked at the tree-lined lane that led to the house. "I walked over and I shall walk back. 'Tis not a far journey, but one I must start now." Waving good-bye, Sarah started off before Luther could offer protest. He stood silently watching until she cleared the lane. *Lord, things ain't never gonna be the same,* he muttered. *And she walked clean from Master*

Nick's house! Shaking his head, Luther stepped back into the foyer and offered a prayer that Miss Agatha's nap be a long one.

Alone in the garden, Sarah perched on a stone bench and tried to force the thoughts of home from her mind, but the images of Samuel and Elizabeth refused to be banished. *I must be causing them such distress,* she thought. A single tear traced a slow path down her cheek. *They must be frantic and it will be two more weeks at best before they receive my note to know that I am safe.* She clenched her hands in her lap and tried to fight the pain of helplessness that washed over her. Why, she puzzled again and again, had the fates placed her in the hands of Captain Riggins?

The sun slipped from view, leaving shadowy hues of pink and orange to tinge the night sky. But despite the chill that touched the air, Sarah remained lost in thought.

Nick stepped into the garden and spied her still form. Her midnight hair was caught up under a lacy white cap, exposing the delicate curve of her neck. Her hands were clasped in her lap and her head was bowed. At first he thought her deep in prayer, but as his eyes took in the subtle droop of her shoulders, Nick knew something was wrong. Silently he made his way down the stone path. As he came closer, he saw the sparkle of her tears before Sarah heard his steps and quickly wiped her face with the hem of her apron.

Nick said nothing as he joined her on the bench; only the night sounds of crickets and katydids broke the silence. But even as he waited, he felt it. The urge

98

to pull her closer, to run his fingers through the thick satin strands of her hair, to inhale the subtle scent that was so much a part of her. He watched a tear roll down her cheek and pulled his handkerchief from his pocket. Gently he tucked the cloth into her clasped hands.

Mortified that he should find her at such a private moment, Sarah dabbed at her eyes with the snowy white fabric. She knew she should say something, excuse herself and flee to the privacy of her room, but no words would come and her legs refused to budge. Desperately she struggled for control.

Nick reached over and tipped her head up with his finger. Their eyes met. Each felt the jolt. For Sarah the compassion that radiated out toward her was her undoing. The last of her restraint melted away, and when Nick gathered her against his chest, a lifetime of tears poured forth. The tears that Samuel had forbidden her to shed over the death of their parents, tears she had not allowed herself during the terror of her kidnapping, tears for the aging Rebecca locked in the drafty Salem Jail without the smallest comfort — they all poured forth to soak Nick's waistcoat and dampen the white linen of his shirt.

Nick said nothing as she wept in his arms, but his hands rhythmically stroked her back. He hated to see a woman cry, but rarely was he moved by it. Tears were a convenient tool used by the weaker sex to manipulate and control, and he wondered what gift from him she would hint at for having spent the afternoon with his grandmother. When she eventually began to quiet, he continued to hold her close, captured by the delicate scent that was so much a part of her.

"Did my grandmother say something to upset you?"

Sarah sniffed and gave a final wipe of her eyes before reluctantly pulling away from his chest. "Your grandmother is a delightful lady."

"Ha!" Nick's short laughter filled the night. "That is a kind way to describe a tyrant like Agatha. But tell me, if it is not my grandmother, what brought this on?" His thumb brushed aside a stray tear.

Embarrassed, Sarah straightened, and her eyes dropped back to her lap. "Being with your grandmother has made my thoughts dwell too much on my family and the pain they must be feeling."

Nick nodded with understanding. She was striving for sympathy in hopes he'd grace her with a gift to raise her spirits. "Tell me about them," he prompted, thinking two could play well at her game. "You spoke of Samuel Wittfield as your stepbrother, but what of your parents?"

Sarah felt the tears threaten anew, and her head began to pound. "My parents died this past winter."

"So you are alone?"

She shook her head. "I do live alone, but Samuel and his wife Elizabeth are very dear to me."

"Tell me more about Wittfield," Nick commanded, anxious to know more about the man whose name appeared on her bondage papers.

"As a child, I quite adored Samuel. He was so tall and strong." A sad smile touched Sarah's face. "But I think I must have made quite a pest of myself always following him around." Her nimble fingers refolded the handkerchief, and she forced a brighter smile. "Still, he was quite tolerant of me."

Tolerant? Nick's eyes narrowed with thought. She had said tolerant, not kind or caring. "This Samuel, is he older?"

She nodded. "I was but five when my father married Prudence Wittfield. Samuel had already seen twenty and was married to Elizabeth."

"And they lived with you?"

Her nervous fingers began to twist the handkerchief into knots. "My father and I moved into Prudence's house. Samuel and Elizabeth live a short ways over."

And with you out of the way, Nick thought, *if this land you speak of truly exists, then your dear brother Samuel is again the sole heir.*

Her tone grew wistful. "There was so much love . . ." She looked up to the stars that twinkled overhead, surprised to find the hour had grown so late. "I think that is what I have missed the most," she said softly. "My father dearly loved Prudence. But now, with my parents gone, the house has grown so quiet." Her gaze dropped back to her. "I visit Samuel and Elizabeth often, but I try not to intrude." She turned her eyes back to Nick. "They must be so distraught by now. Can you imagine how they must be feeling, to have gone to my house and found me missing? I didn't even have the opportunity to make my bed."

Nick suppressed a chuckle. He could just picture Sarah with her toes peeking out from the hem of her nightrail, requesting her abductors to be patient so she might tidy her room before they carted her off. But his smile faded as he remembered the condition she had been in when Beckett had found her. Again he reached for her hand, noting the redness of her skin.

"Is this from tending to my grandmother this afternoon?" He carried her hand within both of his and brushed his lips across the tender flesh.

Sarah felt the warmth of his lips shoot straight to her heart, radiate down to her toes, only to bounce back and settle deep within her stomach. She had promised herself that he would not touch her again, for the memory of his lips on hers still burned strong. But like a moth drawn to the flame, it was impossible to pull away. " 'Tis not a problem," she stammered, wondering how to reclaim her hand.

Nick raised a brow and his eyes began to twinkle. "But I could do something to make you feel better?"

Sarah nodded and looked pointedly to the hand he still kept captured within his own. She could still feel his breath on her skin, and her heartbeat quickened.

"Ah." Nick smiled. "You'd like a bracelet. Well, you are in luck. I happened by the jeweler's today, and Walter has just finished a new piece." His thumb traced around the circumference of her wrist. "It is gold and is about an inch wide but fashioned of soft links. I think it would fit you nicely. I shall take you there tomorrow."

"Why?" Sarah's brow wrinkled with confusion as Nick's eyes darkened with promise.

"So you can see if the piece pleases you."

Completely bewildered, Sarah stared at Nick as he allowed her to reclaim her hand. How had a conversation about her family turned into a discussion on jewelry? She stood wearily, wishing the ache behind her eyes would lessen. His roundabout thoughts were becoming impossible to follow.

"I'm sorry," she stammered, standing awkwardly before him. "I don't understand."

Nick leaned back and gazed up at her with undisguised passion. "I wish to present you with a gift."

Sarah rubbed at her temples, for nothing was

making sense. "But why would you want to do that?"

Nick's eyes twinkled. "Because you helped my grandmother . . ." he prompted.

Sarah shook her head. How had Agatha become part of this puzzle? "Please," she stammered. "There is no need. And if somehow I have given cause for you to feel that payment was necessary, I humbly beg your forgiveness. After all you have done for me," she sniffed, "you must think me most uncharitable, and for that I beg pardon." Turning, as her eyes again filled with tears, Sarah fled to the safety of her room.

Nick stared with total fascination at her retreating back. Either he was daft or Sarah had just rebuffed his generosity. He rubbed his hand along his jaw. What did she hope to gain by doing that? And if jewelry wasn't her passion, why then had she hinted so pointedly for a bracelet? He went over their conversation in his mind but found no answers. Could she really be the innocent she claimed, he wondered, and did anyone truly care that much for their family? He tried to think of his own parents, but their memories were a vague, unpleasant blur. The only family he had left was his grandmother.

A grin tugged at the corners of his mouth as he thought of Gran. She had arranged for Mrs. Hempsted to prepare all his favorite dishes, then spent the entire evening trying to capture his promise that Sarah could visit on the morrow. Nick's smile bloomed full. How Gran loved a duel of the wits. He hadn't had the heart to tell her that Sarah was free to visit whenever she pleased, so he had played the game, leaving her smug with the thoughts of her victory.

Nick rose and quietly paced the stone path while his mind searched for flaws in Sarah's tale. Gran was nobody's fool and she believed the story completely. He shoved his hands deep within his pockets and found the damp handkerchief. Her tears had certainly seemed genuine, he thought, but he'd wait a bit longer before he'd believe her reason for their cause.

The clouds covered the moon, and Nick stood silent in the darkness. Perhaps on the morrow he would pay a visit to Captain Jenkins. The retired sea captain had once lived in the north before settling in Virginia. And although Nick realized he had never heard the man say a kind thing about his former home, perhaps Captain Jenkins could shed some light on Sarah's way of life. Nick rubbed his hands together against the night chill. But first, he thought, he would deal with Sarah directly, and he knew the perfect way to recapture a woman's smile.

Chapter Eight

Sarah stared down at the delicate gold links that surrounded her wrist and wondered yet again how they had gotten there. Looking up, her eyes settled on Nick as he conversed with the jeweler in the corner of the shop. He had given not a clue to his purpose when he requested she accompany him on his morning errands.

I should have realized a man in his position wouldn't have errands to tend to, she thought, chiding herself for being duped. She looked back to the bracelet. The piece was pleasantly heavy, and the workmanship was exquisite. She closed her eyes in frustration. How was she ever going to be able to reciprocate? She could still see the smile on Nick's face when he had clipped his gift around her wrist, and her knees grew weak from the memory.

Sarah stood before a glass case admiring Walter Johnson's talent as she studied Nick from the corner of her eye. His form-fitting breeches were fawn-colored and his coat a deep emerald. The snowy white lace of his cuffs only seemed to emphasize the honey color of his skin.

Nick looked up and, catching her eye, smiled intently. Sarah felt her heart quicken. *This will never do,* she thought, quickly turning her back to the men lest they witness her reaction. She pressed her hand to her cheek and felt the heat intensify as the bracelet caressed her skin.

Picking up a silver bowl from the wooden counter, she let her fingers trace over the cool, smooth surface as she struggled to find an answer.

"Would you like that also?" Nick's voice sounded close to her ear, and Sarah jumped to find him directly behind her. "I ah . . . no thank you." Her hand trembled as she quickly placed the bowl back on the counter. "I was just admiring the excellent workmanship."

Nick reached around her to touch the rim of the bowl, trapping her body firmly between his and the counter. "Would you not like this to take home with you as a memento of your time in Virginia?"

Sarah's hands clenched at her side as his nearness overwhelmed her. She could feel his body against her back. One hand rested intimately on her shoulder while his other sensuously traced back and forth along the rim of the silver bowl.

Walter Johnson, oblivious to the seduction going on before him, moved behind the counter. "If madame doesn't like the design, I would be most happy to alter it to please her."

Sarah struggled to keep her voice even as the light scent of Nick's cologne invaded her senses. "Oh no, 'tis lovely just as it is."

"Then we'll take it." Nick's breath whispered across her cheek and Sarah could stand no more. With a quick, determined sidestep, she pulled away from the warmth of him.

"No, please," she protested. "You have already gifted me with this lovely bracelet." She watched

106

the jeweler's wide smile begin to fade.

"Would you rather choose something else?" Nick questioned.

"No, no." Sarah's hand clamped over the bracelet as if daring either man to suggest she return it. "The bracelet is most exquisite. I simply do not require a silver bowl as well. One gift is more than generous." Even as she heard her words, Sarah realized she had committed herself to keeping Nick's gift, and inwardly she smiled.

"And if I insist?"

She searched the dark eyes that gazed back at her and wondered how to bring the happy smile back to his features. "You truly wish for me to select a second piece?" she questioned softly.

Nick nodded, more at ease. Now he was back on familiar footing. Sarah had merely wanted to pick out another piece herself. "Choose whatever you wish." He gestured to the grand display of pieces within the shop.

Sarah turned and walked immediately to a glass case on the near wall. "I'd like that one."

Walter Johnson's face bloomed with pleasure as she pointed to a heavy silver necklace. It was one of his finest pieces, and the most costly item in his shop. "What an excellent eye you have madame." Quickly he extracted a tiny key from his waistcoat and unlocked the case. "This is one of my personal favorites." He withdrew the necklace and lovingly passed it to Sarah.

Sarah examined the piece carefully, delighting in the craftsmanship. " 'Tis truly a work of art," she said as she turned her smile to Nick and handed him the necklace. "Is it not most beautiful?"

Nick inspected the necklace and found it excellent. Walter produced only the finest, still, he never would have selected it. It was not the cost that put him off, but the style just didn't suit Sarah. He handed the necklace back to Walter with a nod of his head. "The lady has spoken."

Sarah's smile radiated her pleasure, and Nick felt his own returning. When the transaction was completed, Nick extended the small package toward Sarah. "Would you like to carry it?"

She shook her head and allowed Nick to take her arm as they left the shop. "You are a very generous man." She gazed up at him, her violet eyes dancing with pleasure.

Nick patted her hand, liking the way it felt on his arm. "You are a very beautiful lady." He grinned as the color flared in her cheeks. "But I must admit that you have baffled me."

"How so?" She tipped her head and gave him a questioning stare.

Nick turned them in the direction of the small town. "I would never have guessed you would fancy that particular piece."

Sarah stopped, her violet eyes wide and innocent as she looked up at him. "Oh, but 'tis not for me."

"What?" Nick's voice exploded and he spun her around to face him. His hands clamped on her shoulders preventing her escape. "I've just spent a fortune and you say it is not for you?"

Startled by the tone of his voice, Sarah stammered, "You seemed so intent on purchasing another piece, I thought you wished to aid Mr. Johnson with his business."

"Walter Johnson is one of the most respected craftsmen in the South." Nick's eyes grew dark. "Now tell me, if that silver necklace is not for you, then just what did you plan to do with it?"

"I thought it would suit your grandmother," she

whispered, feeling once again she had blundered, and badly.

Nick's eyes flared wide in disbelief. "Whatever were you hoping to gain?"

Sarah stared down at her shoes in despair. "I misunderstood. I thought you meant to give the man more business."

Nick's hands fell from her shoulders as his mind filled with suspicion. "And now you'll expect me to believe that you didn't hope to get into Gran's good graces by presenting her with a costly gift."

Sarah's head snapped up. "I have no gift for your grandmother. I only thought I was helping you make a selection." Hesitantly, her hand reached out to touch his sleeve. "Would you like me to take it back? Surely I could retrieve your money if I but explained the misunderstanding to Mr. Johnson."

Nick's eyes narrowed as he searched her face for answers. "Are you telling me that you picked out that piece for *me* to give to my grandmother?"

Sarah nodded vigorously, wisps of midnight hair pulling free to curl about her face. "The moment I saw it I thought of her. Don't you think she will be pleased?"

Nick shook his head and tried to make sense of what had just happened. Sarah was right, the necklace would be an excellent gift for Gran, and she'd love the expense of it. But if she hadn't meant to present the gift herself, what had she hoped to gain? His eyes studied her intently.

"Tell me why, when you knew I wanted to get a gift for you, you purposefully chose something for someone else?"

Sarah searched for the words that would return his good mood. "You already gave me a beautiful gift. See . . ." With childlike enthusiasm she extended her arm, and allowed the bracelet to sparkle in the sunlight. " 'Tis the most beautiful thing I have ever owned, and I shall treasure it always." Her face radiated with pleasure. "There was no need for you to give me more. When I realized your determination to purchase another piece, I thought of your grandmother." Her eyes dropped to her feet and her voice grew softer. "I'm sorry if I have displeased you."

Nick raised her chin with a single finger. "You have surprised me yet again," he observed, his dimples winking. "But I doubt that you could ever displease me."

Sarah felt her body grow warm, and suddenly she wished they were anywhere but on a public road in front of the silversmith's shop. Thoughts that should never enter a maiden's head were suddenly foremost in her mind. And for once she did not try to push them aside.

"Nick, Nicholas Beaumont, is that you?" The magic vanished as a throaty female voice called from a carriage across the road. Sarah's eyes grew wide as she watched a tall, stately woman in a scandalous dress descend from the carriage to approach them. Her gown was a shocking shade of lavender, and the low décolletage pressed so tightly, Sarah feared the woman in danger of spilling out of her gown. Unknowingly, she took several steps backward until a wooden fence halted her retreat.

"I'm in a rush as always, but I thought that was you." The woman extended her hand for Nick to kiss. " 'Tis an age and a half since we've seen you and I'm quite put out about it."

Nick executed a courtly bow. "Mrs. Myerson. How have you been keeping and how is that crafty husband of yours? Does he still cheat at cards?"

Sylvia Myerson's laughter rang out. "You always

had a wicked tongue, Nicholas. And when I tell George, he shall insist you spend the evening just to give him a chance to empty your pockets."

"Ah, Sylvia," Nick chuckled. "I fear I would not prove good company, for I'm on to his tricks and it would be George who would come out the loser."

"Then you shan't come, even to dine?" she pouted.

Nick grinned. "I would deem it an honor to break bread at your table."

Sylvia narrowed her eyes. "Just as long as bread is the only thing you and George see fit to break," she admonished. Reaching up, she planted a kiss directly on Nick's mouth. "And the next time I send you an invitation you are to come, do you hear? Now I must be off or I shall be late for my music lesson." Sylvia winked over her fan and retreated as quickly as she had come.

Nick smiled. Sylvia Myerson was a social whirlwind, and one was never quite sure just where she'd set down. He watched the gentle sway of her skirt as she hurried toward her carriage and wondered if anyone could lay claim to a conversation with her that lasted longer than two minutes. But, he acknowledged, even married, Sylvia Myerson was a damn fine-looking woman. Still smiling, Nick turned back to Sarah only to find her skin pale and her eyes wide as saucers.

"Angel, what's wrong?" Nick took several long strides to reach her. "Are you ill? 'Tis probably the sun. I should never have made you walk so far. Stay here and I shall hire a carriage to take us home. I'll only be a moment."

Sarah, who had yet to find her tongue, could not begin to explain that neither the sun nor the length of their morning venture had anything to do with her state. Leaning back against the high fence that bor-

111

dered the silversmith shop, she watched Nick's lengthy stride carry him away. She tried to call to him that she was fine, but he turned the corner and disappeared from view.

Sarah stepped away from the fence and tried to assimilate what she had just seen. Whatever had possessed that poor woman to appear in public in such scandalous attire? In Salem, she would have been publicly mocked and run from the town. Sarah thought of the scene that Samuel had made when poor Sarah Good had crossed his path looking for work. It was not her fault that her husband often disappeared for weeks at a time leaving her to cope with the care and feeding of their large brood of children. But the woman was slovenly and smoked a pipe, and Samuel had preached for hours on the sins of laziness. Sarah shook her head. She had often thought Samuel might fare better if he had read some scripture on charity. But he was older and it was not her place to instruct him. So she had slipped the harried woman a few loaves of her own bread and then prayed soundly for her salvation.

The sun grew warm upon her face as she waited, and Sarah couldn't help but wonder how Nick would have reacted if the pipe-smoking Sarah Good had come knocking at his door. A warm pleasure seeped into her veins as she thought of how gently Nick had just treated his misguided acquaintance. The woman had been most forward, even trying to kiss him, yet, despite his discomfort, Nick had maintained his manners. Sarah smiled and touched the bracelet. Nicholas Beaumont was a very special man.

The sound of a carriage caught her attention. But as Sarah stepped forward, the air was forced from her stomach with a bone-jarring whack and, within a blink, she viewed her surroundings from the ground.

"Gee, lady, I'm really sorry. Are you hurt?"

Sarah turned to see that her assailant was no more than a small, grimy lad with a hoop. "Are you injured?" she gasped, brushing the dirt from her hands and climbing to her knees.

"Naw, I'm fine. I just didn't see you standing there. You ain't gonna tell my ma, are you?"

Sarah reached for the dirty hand that extended toward her. "I don't think we need to involve anyone else in this, Master . . . ?"

"The name is James Thaddeus Richardson." He shook her hand soundly. "But you can call me Jimmy."

Sarah estimated the lad to be about seven years old and, judging from the dirt he carried on his small frame, it was almost that long since his last bath. "Well, Jimmy, you can call me Sarah. Now tell me, are you sure you're not injured?"

Jimmy shook his head, letting his sun-streaked hair flop across his face. "Na, no lady could hurt me. 'Sides, I never cry. I didn't even cry when Bruce Wilson beat me up."

Sarah struggled to keep the smile from her lips. "But why would Bruce Wilson want to fight with you?"

Satisfied there was no damage to his hoop, Jimmy looked back at Sarah. "I won some coins from him when we was throwing the dice. His maw got sore and told him to get the money back. But we needed the money, too, so I said he was just a bad loser. Then he beat me up."

Sarah gasped aloud. "You gamble . . . for money?"

Jimmy wiped his nose on his sleeve. "Nah, not too often."

Sarah placed a hand to still the frantic beating of her heart. He was a mere child. "Well, I am certainly glad to hear that," she replied sternly.

"Yeah, usually I don't got no money, and since I'm better than most, none of the other parents will let their kids play with me."

At a loss for words, Sarah shuddered. It was one thing for an adult to choose the road to damnation, but to allow a child—

"You know," Jimmy's childish voice intruded. "You're real pretty. But why are you wearing such a funny dress?"

Completely taken aback, Sarah's hands paused from brushing the dirt from her gown. "You don't like what I'm wearing?" she questioned as her fingers smoothed over the finest wool she had ever touched.

Jimmy screwed up his face and gave her an appraising stare. "Well, it *is* pretty odd-looking."

They both turned as a carriage pulled to a stop beside them. Nick had taken less than a step down before Jimmy grabbed his hoop and dashed down the street as if his bare feet were dancing on hot coals.

"What happened?" Nick took in the dust that covered her skirt, and his grip on her hands tightened. "Are you injured?"

Sarah tried not to wince from the pressure of his hands on her fingers. "I'm fine," she said. But Nick's look told her he carried a different opinion. Dismayed, she looked down to see her black skirt was filthy.

Pulling her hands from his, she took a step back. *Why can I never do anything right when he's around?* she thought dejectedly. *First I blunder in the jewelry shop and now he finds me playing in the dirt.* "Do you know that boy?" She gestured to the child's retreating form and tried inconspicuously to brush the dust from her skirt.

Nick shaded his eyes with his palm. "That would be the young Richardson boy. I think his name is Jimmy. Why, did he knock you down?"

Sarah quickly shook her head and made a vow to seek out Jimmy's mother as soon as circumstances allowed. "We had a discussion on fashion," she said carefully as Nick helped her into the carriage. "He didn't seem to appreciate my new dress."

Nick's eyes skimmed over the severe neckline that almost reached her chin, then down the tight-fitted sleeves that hid her slender arms. "Smart lad," he muttered before joining her and taking the reins. "Now, let's get you home so you can rest."

Sarah shifted on the smooth leather seat, liking the gentle sway of the carriage. "Why do you think he said that?"

Nick cleared his throat, stalling for time. "Well . . . it *is* a bit unusual," he replied tactfully.

She let her fingers trace over the soft black wool of her sleeve. "But Charlotte did an outstanding job. These seams are the finest I have ever seen. And the quality of the cloth is superb. This gown will last a lifetime."

Nick rolled his eyes. "Thank heaven for that."

Sarah's forehead wrinkled with thought. "I take it that Jimmy comes from rather poor circumstances. He probably has never seen a gown as fine as this before."

"That's it exactly." Nick pounced on her answer and gave her a melting smile. "I would bet on the fact that for James Richardson, the style of your gown was definitely a first."

Sarah continued to frown. "I don't think betting is

115

appropriate under the circumstances."

Nick returned her stare. "What circumstances?"

"Don't you think 'tis scandalous for a child to bet?"

Nick's confusion was now totally complete. "What are you talking about?"

Folding her hands in her lap and looking straight ahead, her words were stiff. "I just don't think it's appropriate for an adult to bet with a child."

"Who's betting with children?"

Sarah gave him a long, pointed stare.

Nick thought for a moment before the light finally dawned. "Angel, I am not going to bet with Jimmy. It was just a figure of speech. Besides," he chuckled, "from what I hear, Jimmy would probably beat me."

"That's not funny!" she gasped.

Nick shook his head sadly. "No, it's not."

For several minutes the carriage rolled in silence, and Nick wondered how things with Sarah always managed to become so confusing. "I'm sorry I didn't introduce you to Sylvia," he said suddenly. "But she never stays long enough in one place to have decent conversation."

"That poor woman." Sarah shook her head. "I must admit, it truly warmed my heart to see how politely you treated her. Most wouldn't have been so kind."

Nick's puzzled look returned. "Why would you say that Sylvia was poor?" he questioned, thinking of the elaborate albeit gaudy Myerson mansion.

Sarah clenched her hands in her lap. "She is married to a man who cheats." Her tone gave hint to the seriousness she placed on the matter. "And to make it worse," she added in a hushed whisper, "it doesn't seem to be a secret. Is that why she is forced to wear such clothing, as a warning of some type?"

Nick speculated on the reaction Charlotte Rousseau would have to hear that one of her most costly gowns had been considered worse than sackcloth and ashes. "Sarah . . ." he began gently, not exactly sure what to say. "I'm sure that Sylvia chose the gown herself and, in fact, probably paid dearly for it."

"The town would make her pay to wear something like that?" Her voice was incredulous.

"No, no." Nick tried to follow the twisted reasoning of her mind but found it impossible. "I'm sure Sylvia didn't pay for the gown herself; her husband George paid for it."

Sarah drew herself more erect on the seat. "Then he's not a very kind man, for 'twas his vice that caused this mess in the first place."

"What vice?" Nick struggled to contain his frustration. "What mess?"

"His gambling," she whispered, looking over her shoulder to be sure none would hear her slander. "That, and the fact he cheats at cards."

Nick tried to decipher the code that would allow him to see the connection between George Myerson being a bad card cheat and the fact that his wife wore gowns that cost a fortune. "I definitely think that you have stood in the sun too long," he said gently. "And as master of the house, I prescribe a cool drink and a long nap when we get home."

Sarah felt herself grow warm from his tone and the way he used the word home, for, in truth, when his grand house came into view, she began to feel as if she *was* returning home. "I thought I might visit your grandmother this afternoon."

Nick helped her out of the carriage, pleased to see that she no longer looked quite as pale. "I have business at the wharf later today. I shall escort you in my carriage and then retrieve you on my return."

"Thank you." Sarah turned to go into the house, but his hand on her arm halted her progress.

"If Gran starts to give you a difficult time, tell Luther to fetch you a carriage. I don't want you walking home as you did yesterday."

"Why should Mrs. Beaumont be difficult? We got on wonderfully yesterday."

Nick looked deep into the violet eyes that stared back at him and wondered what she would do if he gathered her in his arms and suggested that they spend the afternoon together in bed. He knew she was attracted to him, even though she struggled to hide the fact, for he had only to smile at her and her cheeks turned the most delightful shade of pink. But the innocence that filled her eyes plagued him and he fought back his desires.

"Yesterday . . ." he paused to clear the huskiness from his throat, "you saw Gran at her weakest. She'll not appreciate that today. She's a proud, tenacious lady, and it's more than difficult for her to accept the fact that, at her age, she can't keep up with the image of her youth."

Sarah smiled with the thought. "I imagine the young Mrs. Beaumont was quite a force to be reckoned with."

Nick reached around her and opened the front door. "She still is," he chuckled softly. "She still is."

Chapter Nine

A gentle tap sounded on the door, and Agatha looked up. "Go away," she snapped. "I told you I didn't want to be disturbed."

Sarah pushed open the door and peeked around. "I know. Luther was most emphatic, but I didn't think you would mind if I came to speak with you."

"Well, you thought wrong. Now get out."

Pleased to hear that today the voice carried no pain, Sarah edged around the door and closed it behind her. She found Agatha sitting upright by the window. She wore a dress of black lace and had wrapped a shawl of white about her frail shoulders.

"Are you stupid, girl, or just plain insolent?" Agatha shifted on her high-backed, wooden chair and wished yet again that she might move about without assistance. She watched Sarah's continued approach, and her eyes narrowed. "So tell me . . ." she paused for effect. "Are you my grandson's mistress yet, or do you just wish to be?"

Sarah stopped dead, and wondered for the briefest instant if the old woman could read her mind. She felt the color flare in her cheeks and hoped the bracelet was safely tucked under the cuff of her sleeve. *Why am I surprised?* she thought. *Evil thoughts are always found out.* And although she had wished only for a moment that he might kiss her again, she knew she had no right to such a thought.

"Do you love him?" Agatha challenged. "That handsome face and those dark eyes that can look straight into your soul."

Sarah remained silent. How could she admit to Nick's grandmother what she had yet to admit to herself?

"Cat got your tongue?" Agatha taunted. "Or have I hit on the truth?" She turned back toward the window. "Just leave the way you came in."

Sarah pulled her shoulders back. "I thought I explained yesterday that I was Mr. Beaumont's housekeeper."

Agatha rolled her eyes. "Didn't believe it then, don't believe it now. So get out. I want to be alone."

Sarah had taken but a single step backward when Nick's warning flashed through her mind. *She'll not appreciate that you saw her at her weakest . . . she's a proud lady and can't accept the fact she can no longer keep up with the image of her youth.* Sarah watched Agatha stare stubbornly out the window. *You're lonely and too obstinate to admit it,* she thought with sudden clarity. A warm feeling of compassion seeped into Sarah's limbs, and she found herself moving to stand directly before Agatha.

"But if I leave, then you'll miss the treat I've brought for you."

Agatha's eyes narrowed in her wrinkled face.

"What is it?" she demanded, craning her neck to see what Sarah carried in her basket.

"Then you'd like me to stay?"

Agatha flopped back against her chair and folded her thin arms across her flat chest. "I probably won't like it anyway. But suit yourself."

Sarah pulled a stool close and suppressed a smile as she noted how Agatha's eyes never left the basket.

"If it's a cake, I shall hate it. They're always too dry. You might just as well take it back where it came from."

Now Sarah did smile. "It is not a cake."

Agatha thumped the arm of her chair with her gnarled fist, then grimaced in pain. "Are you going to open that damned basket or sit there grinning all day? At the speed you're going I shall be cold in my grave before you decide what to do."

Slowly, Sarah began to peel back the red-and-white checkered cloth. "Wadsworth and I were in the garden today and . . ."

"It's flowers. I knew it." Agatha sagged back in her chair. "I hate flowers, they make me sneeze."

Sarah put on a patient expression. "No, 'tis not flowers. But if you interrupt me again, I shall just conclude that you don't want our gift. And if what Wadsworth tells me is correct, then that truly would be a shame." Agatha turned her face toward the window, but Sarah only smiled and continued to peel back the cloth. The scent of fresh strawberries and chocolate floated from the basket, and Agatha's head snapped back so fast Sarah almost laughed aloud.

"You brought me strawberries?"

Sarah reached into the basket and retrieved a

crystal dish overflowing with chocolate-covered berries. She set the dish gently on Agatha's lap and sat at Agatha's feet. "Much of the first crop is not completely ripe yet, but Wadsworth and I found there were quite a few early bloomers," she said softly.

Grateful that today her fingers worked, her stomach carried no pain, and her teeth didn't ache, Agatha plucked the plumpest red berry from the dish and bit into it. The chocolate melted on her tongue and the juice from the fruit dripped down her chin. It was the most delicious thing she had tasted in months. Greedily, she shoved two more into her mouth before she looked back at Sarah.

"I suppose you feel all proud of yourself now." The words were sharp, but Sarah noted the way Agatha's face filled with pleasure, and took no offense.

"I can claim no credit. It was Wadsworth who remembered, so it is he who gets your praise. I'll be sure to tell him how much you enjoyed his thoughtfulness."

Reluctantly, Agatha offered the dish to Sarah. "Do you want one?"

Still smiling, Sarah shook her head. "I could be noble and say that they were all for you." She gave Agatha a conspiratorial wink. "But the truth of the matter is that while we were fashioning them, I sampled more than my share." She pressed a hand to her stomach and rolled her eyes toward the ceiling.

Agatha cackled at Sarah's memory, then cradling the dish lovingly on her lap, she settled back. "When I was a girl, I couldn't wait for the first strawberry crop to come in. Even though it was never a large one and the berries later in the summer were bigger, there is something to be said for the first of the season." She plucked another from the dish and slowly bit into it. "I remember one summer when my sister and I were still in the schoolroom. I sneaked down to the garden and ate every berry on the vine."

Sarah pressed her hand to her lips. "What happened?"

Agatha shrugged and popped the rest of the berry into her mouth, savoring the combination of dark chocolate and sun-sweetened fruit. "My father was going to take a switch to me, but I was sick all over his shoes." Agatha chuckled from the memory. "I spent nearly a week in my bed from that little escapade."

Fascinated, Sarah stared at Agatha in wonder. She understood her love for the succulent red berries, for she adored them herself. But it was beyond her comprehension that anyone would do something so blatant. She tried to picture Agatha as a bright young girl who thumbed her nose at the rules, but the image wouldn't come.

"You mentioned a sister," Sarah prompted. "Does she live nearby?"

A sad look covered Agatha's face. "She died many years ago," she said quietly. "Besides my husband, she was my dearest companion."

Sarah reached out and took one of Agatha's sticky hands within her own. "I didn't mean to make you sad."

Agatha shook her head. "Helena was very dear to me." She smiled with the memory. "My father always used to say that I got all the energy and vinegar while Hallie got all the goodness."

Sarah pulled her stool closer. "What happened?"

For a long moment Agatha stared out the window as images of her youth sprang painfully to mind, then she turned back to Sarah. "Hallie and my husband both died the same year of the fever." She stared down at hands now twisted and knotted with age. "No one was surprised when Hallie took ill. She'd been sickly all her life, and it was only natural that I would return home to nurse her. I was her favorite, you see, and she'd always take her medicine for me." For several minutes Agatha sat silent, lost within her memories. When she looked up, her eyes were lifeless. "Hallie died, and the day we put her in the ground, a part of me died, too. I thought nothing would ever hurt as much, but I was wrong. Oh, how I was wrong."

Despite the warmth of the afternoon sun that poured through the window, Agatha shivered and pulled her shawl closer about her shoulders. "My husband, Roger, was the next to go." Her voice caught. "Many said that it was my fault, that I was the one who carried the fever home to him from tending to Helena."

Sarah knelt beside her chair. "Surely you don't believe you were responsible. God takes who He sees fit to take." She set the crystal dish aside, and gently placed both her hands over Agatha's. "If we tried to reason the wisdom of his ways, then we'd all go mad, for it's not for man to know."

Agatha gave Sarah a steady look. "I can accept that now, but there were times when I believed the whispers myself. It was too hard not to think that if I had stayed home with my family mayhap the fever would never have found Roger." She shook her head, and the white lace cap that covered her hair bobbed from side to side. "But the worst of it was my son."

"Nick's father?"

Again Agatha nodded. "I was so eaten with grief from losing both my sister and husband that I ended up losing Rupert, too."

"Did he become ill?" Sarah's voice held quiet compassion.

A tear gathered and slowly trickled down Agatha's wrinkled cheek. "He became hateful." She wiped at her eyes with her knuckles. "I was so sure that something was going to happen to him, too, that I became overbearing." She shook her head sadly. "I watched his every move to be sure he was safe, yet I found fault with his every action. He was my only child, and I desperately wanted him to be perfect." Her voice softened. "He would be the image of Roger and all that was good, and when he was grown, he'd take over the shipping business Roger had worked so hard to start. Rupert would be my living monument for the husband I had lost."

"That would be quite a challenge for a young boy." Sarah watched the emotions etch themselves deeper on Agatha's pale face.

"I can see that now." She heaved a weary sigh. "But not then. All I could see was that the harder I pushed, the weaker Rupert became. His backbone disappeared and he believed that the world owed him a living. When I finally realized what he was becoming and refused to give him more money, he left home. I never spoke with him again."

Sarah felt Agatha's body stiffen, whether in regret or anger she did not know.

"But Nick . . ." The smile returned to Agatha's

thin lips. "The only thing of value Rupert and his trollop ever did during their entire worthless marriage was to produce that child. My poor Nicky," Agatha sighed. "Those fools were blessed with a priceless gift from heaven, and both of them were too stupid to realize it." Her cheeks flared with color. "All they could think about was their own selfish pleasures. Rupert drank until he couldn't perform his husbandly duties anymore so she took to the streets. Then my perfect son drank even more to forget the fact that he had married a whore." Agatha shuddered. "But the worst of it all was when they both drank to forget about Nicky —"

"Surely, in their own way, they cared for their son," Sarah interrupted.

Agatha gave her a hard stare. "The only thing Rupert cared about was that the bottle never be empty."

"But the mother —"

"Was a disgrace. The things those two put that child through would make your heart break. And even if it means that I lose my immortal soul, I'll not say I'm sorry that they died." Agatha struggled to control her anger, amazed that even after all this time, the thoughts of her son could still cause such pain. "When the constable came to tell me of the carriage accident that took them both, I wept. Not from sorrow as people thought. My tears were tears of joy. Finally, little Nicky could begin to have a life."

Sarah's hand pressed tight against her middle as if willing a wound to heal. "But how old was he?"

"Nick had yet to see his sixth year." Agatha set her jaw and stared hard at Sarah, as if daring her to challenge her values.

Sarah continued to sit at Agatha's feet, her heart pounding painfully for the child that once was and then stronger still for the man he had become. "He loves you very much," she said quietly, her voice thick with emotion.

Agatha drew herself erect. "We love each other," she declared. "But he can be so obstinate when he does not get his own way."

"Is that why you send him notes that say you are dying?" Agatha had the grace to blush, and Sarah continued. "He is truly distressed when he receives them. I know, I was there once."

"He's not distressed enough to come," Agatha pouted, and again she folded her arms across her chest.

Sarah shook her head. They were two of a kind, grandmother and grandson.

"Pass me that bowl," Agatha commanded, suddenly realizing that her treasure was out of reach.

Sarah placed the bowl back on the woman's lap and smiled as Agatha popped another berry in her mouth. "If you eat too many, you shall make yourself sick," she cautioned.

Agatha looked down her thin nose. "Why should I care? There's a better than even chance that I'll be sick tomorrow even without the berries."

"Why does everyone insist on gambling?" Sarah shifted her position on her stool. "It seems to be a way of life in this town."

"And just who have you seen gambling?" Agatha challenged.

Sarah studied her hands. "Well, no one actually, but everyone is constantly referring to it. Don't they know gambling is a sin?"

"Probably not," Agatha said. "You'll have to enlighten them." She studied Sarah in silence. "You know, you remind me of my sister. Same clear porcelain skin and thick, dark lashes. I always hated Hallie for those lashes."

Sarah sat quietly. She was beginning to realize that in Virginia, what was said often was not what was meant.

"That must be it," Agatha continued as she licked the chocolate from her twisted fingers. "You remind me of my sister. That must be why I feel so melancholy."

"Would you truly like me to leave?"

Agatha, mouth full of strawberry, shook her head, making the lace cap shift about her wispy white hair. "Now that you're here, you might as well stay," she said finally. "You know, I haven't thought about Hallie for the longest time. We used to have such grand adventures together."

"Tell me," Sarah prompted. And Agatha did.

The afternoon sun painted the bedroom with dusty shadows, but neither Agatha nor her guest noticed. Lost in the memories of her youth, Agatha found a captive audience in Sarah. No matter how insignificant the story, to Sarah it was fascinating. She marveled at Agatha's daring and total disregard for the confines of society. And more than once she suppressed a giggle when she thought of Agatha living in Salem. Rebecca would love to hear the stories, but Sarah knew even she would be shocked by Agatha's devil-may-care attitudes. In the midst of a particularly scandalous tale, both women were startled by the rap on the door.

Sarah scrambled awkwardly to her feet as Nick crossed the room.

"And how is my favorite girl?" He gave Agatha's pale cheek a hearty kiss, then turned to gaze at Sarah. Wisps of midnight hair had pulled free from her cap to curl about her delicate features. "I see your visitor is still alive and sports no visible bruises. Can I conclude then that you have had a good day?" His dark-sapphire eyes smiled down at his grandmother, and Sarah felt her knees melt.

Agatha gave his hand a playful swat. "Behave yourself, Nicky. Sarah brought me strawberries."

"She did, did she?" Nick's eyes returned to her, and Sarah felt the heat in the room intensify. "And you saved none for me?" His wounded expression made Agatha smile.

"Not a one," she said smugly.

"Yes, we did," Sarah answered at the same time. She blushed as both grandmother and grandson turned to stare at her. "I had Wadsworth reserve some for your supper tonight."

"Well, well." Nick turned a satisfied smile back to his grandmother. "It seems that someone is watching out for me after all. Thank you, Sarah."

Sarah turned her innocent eyes from one to the other, knowing she had missed something, but not sure what.

"Humph." Agatha's mouth pulled down at the corners. "At least Sarah saw fit to bring me a gift, which is more than I can say for you."

Nick's dark eyes widened with surprise. "You expect me to bring you a gift?"

Agatha shrugged. "That would have been nice. But, as usual, I see you are empty-handed."

"Ah, that I am," Nick teased, placing his arm gently about his grandmother's frail shoulders. "Definitely empty-handed. But that simply makes it easier for me to hug you."

Agatha struggled to hide her smile as she tried to push him away. "I would rather have had a present."

"Ah, Gran." He kissed her cheek, inhaling the rose scent that clung to her clothing. "It just so happens that I have a gift for you, too." He gave Sarah a wink and then reached into his pocket to retrieve the package.

Agatha hesitated a moment, holding the package in the palm of her hand. The sparkle of her eyes spoke of her excitement even as she tried to pout. "I don't know if I should bother—"

"Oh, but 'tis lovely," Sarah interrupted, not knowing this was a game they played each time Nick brought his grandmother a gift. "You must open it."

Agatha raised a brow and gave Nick a searching look. "How is it that Sarah knows about my present?"

Nick shook his head as he read the true question behind Agatha's words. "Why don't you just open it," he said firmly, refusing to rise to her bait.

Without waiting for permission, but knowing that Agatha could never manage the wrapping, Nick unfastened the package and placed it back in her hand so she had only to lift back the paper to view her surprise. Sarah waited with stilled breath as Agatha peeled back the wrapping.

"Oh, Nicky." Agatha beamed as she discarded the brown paper and palmed the necklace. "It is beautiful." She awkwardly held the chain higher to

130

better view the workmanship. "Did Walter Johnson make this?" She peered at the design wishing she had a party to go to where she might show it off. "He probably charged you an arm and a leg for it. His prices are always too dear."

"If you don't care for it, I could take it back," Nick teased.

Agatha bared her teeth and snarled in his direction. "Don't you dare try to take back my lovely present. I declare, Nicky, with one exception, I think this is the nicest thing you have ever given to me."

Nick smiled, genuinely pleased that Gran was happy. "You say that about everything I give you."

Agatha shook her head and pressed the necklace between her knotted hands. "I definitely think that this is the best present ever."

"Sarah picked it out." Even as the words left his mouth, Nick knew he had made a mistake. But he almost laughed out loud at the stunned expressions on both their faces.

"Oh . . ."

A thousand questions echoed in the single word Agatha uttered, and Nick knew it was timely to make his exit. "We have to be going, Gran. But I'll stop by tomorrow."

Agatha watched her grandson turn, and noted the faintest blush that touched his high cheekbones. *Well, well, well,* she thought. *This is an interesting kettle of fish.* "Sarah," she turned to the girl. "The necklace is lovely. You have a keen eye for quality. But tell me, what did Nick give you?"

Not realizing she had just been outwitted, and unused to deception of any type, Sarah immediately stepped forward and extended her arm, allowing the bracelet to slip from beneath her cuff. " 'Tis the most beautiful thing I have ever received," she said, holding forth her arm for Agatha's inspection. Agatha's bent fingers touched the bracelet and she smiled knowingly. Sarah felt a suffocating guilt suddenly surround her. *What am I doing?* she thought frantically. *'Tis bad enough I have accepted such a gift, but now I am flaunting it.* Her cheeks grew hot and, as quickly as she could, she pulled back her arm and tried to tuck the piece back under her sleeve.

"If you do that," Agatha nodded toward her wrist, "no one will be able to see your beautiful gift." She watched the color stain the young girl's cheeks, and the wheels in Agatha's sharp mind spun faster. She turned back to her grandson and found him also captivated by Sarah's sudden discomfort. *Well, well, well,* she repeated to herself. *Just what do we have here?*

"You must stay for dinner, Nick," Agatha commanded in her strongest voice.

Nick smiled but shook his head. He could almost hear his grandmother's thoughts. "I have business later this evening."

"Then leave Sarah to dine with me and fetch her on your return."

Nick touched Sarah's shoulder and motioned her toward the door so she wouldn't be pulled into his grandmother's trap. "Not tonight, Gran. I'll stop in and see you on the morrow."

Agatha folded her arms across her chest, her foot tapping against the hard wood floor. "I think you have more than business on your mind, Nicholas Beaumont."

Nick gave Sarah a gentle nudge out the door before crossing back to place a kiss on his grandmother's head. "I have business in Jamestown tomorrow. I'll stop by on my way to the docks."

Agatha gave him a horrified look. "Nicholas Beaumont, don't you dare call on this house before noon. You know how I hate rushing in the morning."

"Afraid I'll catch you in your nightrail?" he teased, flashing her a devilish grin.

"You come on your way home, that way you can tell me what's going on."

Nick smiled and executed a courtly bow. "I am your servant, madame."

Agatha snorted. "And the day I believe that, pigs will fly." But Nick had already closed the door and her words amused no one but herself. With great effort, Agatha pulled at the heavy brocade drapery to stare out the window. She could see Nick's carriage and, within moments, Nick and Sarah came into view. Agatha watched her grandson hold Sarah's arm to assist her, his laughter ringing in the air.

Well, well, well, she thought again. Neither Nick nor Sarah looked up toward the window where she sat, and neither knew that she stared after them until the carriage was completely out of view.

Agatha let the curtain fall back in place and thought about Nick's visit. He might have come to see *her,* but he hadn't been able to keep his eyes from the girl. *He's in love,* she thought. *He's in love and he hasn't even realized it yet.* A strange, unsettling feeling seeped into her bones, and Agatha suddenly longed for her bed. Nick would marry and then he'd never have time to visit or take a meal with her. He'd want to spent all his time with his new bride. Agatha felt her chest grow tight and her eyelids sting. He'd make a call out of duty now and then, but he'd be too busy with his new family to be really interested in an old woman like herself. She felt tears gather and sniffed hard. Her trembling hand reached for the golden bell to fetch the maids, then she paused.

Perhaps Nick's being in love wouldn't be such a bad thing after all. Sarah was a sweet girl and a grand improvement over Marigold Thurmont. She would be good for Nick, Agatha decided, thinking of the afternoon they had just spent. Agatha pressed her knotted fingers together and rested her chin on her hands. With a little badgering, Sarah would probably urge Nicky to spend even more time with her, she thought, and her spirits began to brighten. *And if Nick gets married,* she realized suddenly, *then I'll get grandbabies.* The image of holding Nick's child on her lap sent joy seeping into every joint of her aching body. The notion of losing her grandson slowly gave way to a plan that would ensure Sarah remained in Virginia.

Agatha worked out the entire scheme in her mind, then rethought her logic the way Roger had always insisted she do with business matters.

"It will work," she declared triumphantly to the empty room. A new sense of purpose made her giddy with excitement as she reached for the bell.

Luther entered, carrying a silver tray with her medicine cup.

"I already fixed the drink, Miss Agatha," he stated proudly. "It's not too hot and just the way Miss Sarah showed me. So you drink it right up now."

Impatiently, Agatha balanced the cup and, to

134

Luther's amazement, drank the potion straight down without a protest.

"Luther," Agatha tried to hide her growing enthusiasm, "I'd like you to arrange for Mr. Danvers to call upon me tomorrow. I have some legal matters I wish to discuss with him."

Luther rubbed his chin and looked confused. "I thought I heard Master Nick say that Mr. Danvers wasn't your attorney no more."

Agatha grinned with satisfaction. "You're absolutely right. Mr. Danvers no longer works for Beaumont Shipping. But I have matters of a personal nature."

"You sure, Miss Agatha? I thought you didn't care for that man."

Agatha smiled and, with some difficulty, rubbed her fingers together. "I can't abide the man. But for what I have in mind, Michael Danvers will be perfect." She looked up, her eyes dancing with mischief. "I'm going to need an ace in the hole for this hand, Luther. And if I have my way Mr. Michael Danvers, attorney-at-law, is going to become my ace."

Luther folded his arms across his massive chest. "And just how is it that I already know that you don't want me to say nothing to Master Nick?"

Agatha gave her servant a conspiratorial wink. "Things are going to be wonderful around here, Luther. You just trust me and wait and see. And Luther . . ." she said as he turned to do her bidding, "make sure that Mr. Danvers calls on me well before noon."

Luther nodded and left the room. Young Ruby entered, gave a curtsy to her mistress, and began to light the tapers to push back the night. But Agatha never noticed. With her shawl pulled tight about her shoulders, she began to gently rock to and fro.

Ruby paused to stare at her mistress. In the three years she had worked for Miss Agatha, she had never heard the woman sing. But now Miss Agatha was humming a lullaby. Fascinated, she watched from the corner of her eye until her task was completed. *Wait until they hear this in the kitchen!* she thought. With a quick curtsy, the girl silently made her exit.

Agatha never noticed. She was completely absorbed with thoughts of holding Nicky's child.

Chapter Ten

"But I want you to have it."

Sarah stared in wonder at the vibrant woolen threads that cascaded over her palm. "Mrs. Beaumont, these are too beautiful to give away."

Agatha shifted against her pillows, then wished she hadn't moved. "What they are is too pretty to keep locked up in that old chest." She smothered a groan, then relented. "Sarah, could you help me?"

Sarah rose from where she knelt beside an ornately carved chest. "You ate too many strawberries yesterday," she scolded, but her hands were gentle as she resettled Agatha in her high tester bed.

"Rubbish, the ache in my bones has nothing to do with strawberries," Agatha huffed.

"No, but the ache in your stomach does." Sarah raised a brow as Agatha began to pout.

"Are you going to finish unpacking that chest or are you going to stand there staring at me all day?" Agatha folded her arms and returned Sarah's glare measure for measure. Sarah smiled, shook her head, and moved back to the chest.

"I meant it when I said I want you to take that yarn." Agatha gestured to the loose bundles that Sarah had just set aside.

Sarah picked up the brightly colored hanks and knew they cost a pretty penny. Indigo, saffron, and a bright cherry-red sparkled in the sunlight while a wide assortment of greens and browns still covered the floor.

"I started to make a set of chair seats, but after making one, I lacked the patience to see it through. Do you see them?" Agatha peered over the foot of the bed. "They should be in there somewhere. Unless they've fallen apart by now."

"Here they are," Sarah cheered triumphantly. She unfolded a large square of heavy linen to reveal an intricate pattern of animals and fruit trees. "Did you do this?" Her fingers traced over the complex stitches and the delicate shading.

Agatha nodded with pride, but her smile faded as she looked down at her gnarled hands. "I always meant to go back and finish those. But now," she sighed deeply, "it's too late. Still," she brightened, "I could have the finished piece made into a pillow. It shouldn't take one of Charlotte's girls too long, and then it would be ready in time for Nick's engagement announcement."

Sarah felt her knees go weak. She sank back to her kneeling position on the floor and held onto the corner of the trunk for support. "Mr. Beaumont is engaged?" She struggled to keep her voice from cracking.

Agatha shook her head, making her lace cap slip from side to side. "He's decided to settle down and start a family, but I don't think he's made a final decision yet as to who the lucky girl will be. Personally, I wish he would hurry and make up his mind. I want to hold my grandson."

"But he hasn't decided who to marry, you say?"

Sarah tried to still the frantic beating of her heart as breath again entered her lungs.

Agatha pleated the bed linen with her bent fingers. "I think he'll make the most beautiful babies, don't you?" From the corner of her eye she watched the color drain from Sarah's face, only to bounce back again, and her voice lowered to a secret whisper. "He might be my grandson, but let me tell you, that Nicholas is one fine specimen of a man. With that thick black wavy hair and those dark sapphire eyes, and strong . . . Why, did you know that Nick can—"

"Would you like a fresh glass of lemonade, Mrs. Beaumont?" Sarah interrupted. "I thought I heard Luther say that Mrs. Killingham had made some special. Why don't I just go down and fetch it for you."

"Don't bother." Agatha struggled not to smile. "I'll just ring for it. Have you ever noticed how well Nick fills out his jacket?"

Sarah snatched the golden bell out of reach and placed it on the dresser. "I'll save Luther the trip," she stammered. "You just rest a moment and I'll be right back."

Agatha watched in amusement as Sarah fled the room. *This is going to be even easier than I thought,* she giggled with satisfaction. And with her hands folded meekly on her lap and an angelic smile on her wrinkled face, Agatha patiently waited for Sarah to reappear.

Sarah stared down at the folded invitation in confusion. Her afternoon with Agatha was slowly turning into a nightmare. First, the woman had gone on for ages about Nick and his virtues until Sarah thought she might go crazy from the images that sprang to mind, and now there was an invitation from people she had never met. "But, Mrs. Beaumont, why should the Bellinghams want me to dine with them?"

"Because they are important friends of mine," Agatha stated calmly. She took in Sarah's confused look and continued. "And since you are the granddaughter of my oldest friend from the North, 'tis only proper that they should invite us to dine. But I am incapacitated, so the invitation is for you and Nicholas."

"Mrs. Beaumont, I'm nobody's granddaughter. My grandparents died before I was born." Sarah's eyes narrowed as she noted the contented smile on Agatha's pale face. "Do you even have a friend in the North?"

Agatha's grin grew wider still. "Not that I'd lay claim to."

"Then they are inviting me under false pretenses."

Agatha shrugged. "It matters not. They want to meet you."

Sarah shook her head and set the folded note back on the bed within Agatha's reach. "It matters to *me*," she said quietly. "You want me to lie, and I cannot do that."

Agatha's smile faded as she snatched back the invitation. "No one is asking you to lie, dear." She struggled to keep the impatience from her words. "Just be a little creative with the truth."

Again Sarah shook her head. "I can't do that." Her voice held disappointment. "You spoke a falsehood to say that you knew my family, and I can't allow it to continue."

"You mean to tell me that you wouldn't enjoy spending a social evening in the company of my grandson? Why, you'd be treated like visiting royalty—a queen. You'd have a romantic carriage ride, the finest food, and company I can guarantee will amuse you." Agatha's sense of anxiety set her stomach to churning again. She had never thought of Sarah as being anything but agreeable. "I'm sure you'll have a glamorous evening," she said, giving an exaggerated wink. "Especially in the company of Nick. He's so handsome. Don't you agree?"

Sarah felt her bracelet caress the sensitive skin of her wrist, and her resolve frayed even more. "Mr. Beaumont is indeed a most handsome man," she stammered, "as you well know. And I would truly enjoy partaking in the evening you described." Sarah took a deep breath to strengthen her convictions. "But not under false pretenses. To lie for the sake of gaining an evening's entertainment would be a travesty."

"Then perhaps it is time for you to leave, since you won't do this simple favor for me." Agatha shifted on her bed, suddenly uncomfortable with the situation.

Sarah gathered the unfinished embroidery. "I would do most anything for you," she said quietly. "But you ask too much when you ask me to lie and deceive for your pleasure."

"Just take the wool and go then." Agatha scowled, looking pointedly toward the door. "I don't need friends who can't be depended on."

Sarah left the room with a heavy heart. Declining Luther's offer to fetch a carriage, she chose to walk home. The afternoon was clear and breezy,

141

and the fresh air felt cool against the warmth of her face.

You really know how to tempt me, don't you, Lord?" she thought as she slowly made her way alongside the road. She had only to close her eyes to feel Nick's arms about her. He had held her so tenderly when she had cried for her family. But tenderness gave way to passion as Sarah relived their kiss in the garden. "What am I going to do?" she cried to the gathering clouds. "In just another few weeks I shall be on my way back home."

"Hey, Miss Sarah, you lost or something?"

Startled from her thoughts, Sarah looked up to find young Jimmy Richardson, hoop in hand, directly before her. Her eyes darted about only to realize that she must have walked well past the road to Nick's house.

"Well, if it isn't Master Richardson."

Jimmy scuffed the dirt with his bare foot and peeked up at her through the sun-streaked hair that hung in his face. "Aww, you can just call me Jimmy. What's you doing out this way? You didn't change your mind and decide to tell my ma that I knocked you down, did you?"

Sarah smiled, and shook her head. "I was taking a walk and I guess I just wasn't watching where I was going. Pretty silly, don't you think?"

Jimmy gave her an appraising look. "It sure is, but then you're a funny lady. You want me to take you back?"

Sarah looked at the shanty that stood off to the side of the road. Smaller than the cookhouse behind Nick's mansion, the door of the shack hung ajar and the boards were in desperate need of paint. A thriving garden filled the side yard. Sarah turned back to Jimmy. "Is that your garden?" she asked, walking toward the rickety fence.

Jimmy climbed on the gate and let his weight swing it open. "Yep, I keep the weeds out myself." A wide-eyed young child with a rag doll hesitantly made her way through the well-tended rows. "Jessie, you get out of those beans."

Before Sarah even registered the mishap, Jimmy Richardson flew from his perch on the gate to rescue the beans from the child.

"This here's Jessie," he said, holding the squirming child for Sarah's approval. "She almost two years old."

Sarah held out her hand. "How do you do, Miss Jessie?" At the sound of Sarah's voice, Jessie stopped her struggles to get down and allowed her brother to hold her.

"Hey, she likes you," Jimmy declared. "Jessie don't stand still for no one, not even Ma."

Sarah took in the dirt-covered clothing worn by both children and wondered if either child had ever been bathed. Jessie had her brother's bright eyes, but her hair, like her brother's, was grimy with dirt.

"Jimmy, is your mother home?" Sarah asked softly, offering her finger for Jessie to grab.

Jimmy's brow pulled into a frown. "I thought you said you wasn't going to tell her."

"Oh, but I'm not," Sarah said quickly, giving him a reassuring smile. "It's just that it would be terribly rude of me to stand at your gate and talk with you and your sister and then completely ignore your mother."

"Well, I don't know . . ."

Jimmy's decision was made for him midstride

when Mrs. Richardson stepped from the house. "Jimmy, who's that at the gate? I thought I told you to stay out of trouble."

Sarah watched a woman not much older than herself walk wearily from the house. Her hair hung in limp strands about her pale face, her gray eyes were flat and lifeless, and her shoulders hunched as if she bore the weight of the world.

"I'm sorry, miss, for whatever he's done. He's a good boy, but sometimes he's just a little too full of life."

Sarah smiled and extended her hand. "No, no," she reassured the woman. "Jimmy hasn't done anything. We met yesterday in town and he was most polite."

Jimmy beamed with relief and turned an innocent smile to his mother.

Mrs. Richardson's look clearly showed she didn't believe a word Sarah said, but she was grateful there was no trouble. "You must be from the North," she said slowly, taking the baby from her son.

Sarah's eyes widened with surprise. "How ever did you guess."

" 'Cause you talk funny," Jimmy answered.

"James!" Mrs. Richardson shifted the baby to her other hip and glared at her son. "Sometimes he says things before he thinks."

Jimmy looked at his mother with confusion. He knew he was in trouble from the tone of her voice, but he wasn't sure why. "But she does, Ma, just listen to her. Go on, Miss Sarah, say something."

"Actually, Jimmy," Sarah gave him a wink. " 'Tis not I who speaks strangely but you." This sent Jimmy into gales of laughter. "My name is Sarah

Townsend," she introduced herself, smiling at the woman, "and I think you most fortunate to have two such beautiful children."

Gracie Richardson's eyes grew wide and heat filled her face. No one had ever complimented her before. She wiped her hand on her dirty apron before hesitantly extending it toward her guest. "I'm Gracie," she stammered. "This here's Jessie. She's my youngest."

Sarah let her finger trace down the child's round cheek and wished for a damp rag to wash it clean. "She's going to be quite a beauty when she grows up."

Gracie studied her daughter thoughtfully. "She'll do fine. But Catherine — now she's the real beauty in the family."

Jessie had discovered Sarah's bracelet and contented herself with trying to untie the links. "And how old is Catherine?" Sarah asked.

"She just turned ten and three." Grace Richardson again shifted the hefty toddler. "Would you like to come in for a cup of cider?" she asked in a hesitant tone. "It's fresh; we just drew it this morning."

Pleased at the invitation, Sarah allowed Jimmy to swing the gate wide so she might enter. She followed Gracie Richardson and her children through the yard and into the house. The inside of the shanty was in the same disrepair as the outside, but obvious attempts had been made there to keep what little the family owned neat and tidy. One large bed filled the corner of the room and, even from a distance, Sarah could see that the coverlets were threadbare. A young girl sat patiently working a butter churn.

"Catherine, this is Miss Townsend." Gracie

looked about the room with embarrassment and wondered what she had been thinking of to invite someone inside. "Will you fetch us some fresh cider?" The girl nodded and Grace turned back to her guest. "Here, you take the chair," she stammered. "I'm used to the stool." She set the baby down and Jimmy plopped on the floor between them.

Sarah placed her bag behind the offered chair and took a seat. "That's quite a garden you have outside," she said, smiling at Gracie. "Jimmy tells me that he helps with the weeding."

Gracie nodded nervously. What was she supposed to say? As long as she could remember, she'd never had anyone in the house except the kids and their father. Was she supposed to offer something from the garden?

"Jimmy's a good boy," she said finally, "when he's not getting himself into trouble."

Sarah accepted the wooden cup the young girl offered and took a deep drink of the tart cider. "This is delicious. Thank you, Catherine." The girl blushed and immediately returned to her churning. "Do you make this yourself?" Sarah asked, taking another drink.

Gracie nodded her head and her hands began to twist in her lap. "We have our own trees down in the far pasture."

"They're not really ours," Jimmy piped in. "Mr. Blanchard really owns them, but we like to pretend they're ours."

"We rent this place and the land from Mr. Blanchard," Gracie added quickly, lest the woman think they were no better than common thieves who stole apples from other folks.

146

"Well, I think your recipe is delicious," Sarah said firmly, setting her cup on the rickety table that stood to her left.

"Jessie, no," Jimmy suddenly screamed. Both women turned to find the baby sitting at their feet completely tangled in yarn.

"Oh, my God," Gracie gasped, falling to her knees and trying to save the threads from the destructive hands of her daughter.

Sarah, too, went to her knees. "I don't think she's hurt." She lifted the child, who immediately wailed at being separated from her new colorful toy.

"Jessie's fine," Gracie gulped, close to tears. "But look, the yarn is so tangled."

Sarah exchanged the screaming child for the tangled skeins of yarn. "I'm sure they can be salvaged. Besides, 'twas my fault for setting my bag on the floor where she could get at it."

"May I help?"

Sarah turned at the soft-spoken words to find Catherine standing just behind her. The girl stared at the tangled yarns as if Sarah held a mound of jewels in her hands. "Are you handy with a needle, Catherine?" she asked.

Gracie handed Jessie to her son. "Jimmy, take her outside for a few minutes so we can hear ourselves think." She prayed desperately that Sarah would not demand restitution for the damage.

Catherine took the threads from Sarah and returned to her churning stool. Placing the strands on her lap, she carefully began to untangle Jessie's creation.

"I'm sure Catherine will be able to put them to rights again," Gracie stammered, cursing herself for inviting Sarah inside. "And if some are damaged," she took a deep breath and pressed a hand to her stomach, "I'll pay for them somehow."

Sarah shook her head. "They look fine. And if Catherine does not mind the chore of untangling them, then I shall be forever grateful. But now I'm afraid I must leave you."

Anxiously, Catherine looked up from her task. "It will take me more than a few minutes."

"Take whatever time you need." Sarah smiled. "Would you bring them to me at Mr. Beaumont's house when you're finished?"

Gracie's hand flew to her heart. "You're a guest of Mr. Beaumont?"

Sarah gathered the linen squares back into her bag. "I work for Mr. Beaumont," she said gently. "Do you know him?"

Color flared in Gracie's pale face. "Everyone in Middle Plantation knows Mr. Beaumont and his grandmother."

"Why, those threads were Mrs. Beaumont's," Sarah said brightly.

Gracie paled even more. "Then Mrs. Beaumont will be the one to collect for the damages."

Sarah shook her head. "No, Mrs. Beaumont gave the threads to me to do with what I wished. And I seek no damages. You gave me a delicious cup of cider, and for that I am grateful. But now I must be off."

"I'll have these untangled by sunup tomorrow," Catherine called softly.

Sarah waved from the doorway. "That will be lovely. And Grace, may I call again?"

Before her better judgment could take over, Grace found herself nodding yes, and then Sarah

148

was out the door. Grace turned to her daughter on shaking legs. "Are many damaged?"

Catherine looked up at her mother with concern. "I can probably save most of them, but look at these." She held up a clump, hopelessly knotted.

Gracie reached for the vivid threads and shook her head. "No wonder Jessie went right to these. I've never seen such pretty colors before, not even in Mr. Jacobs's shop."

Catherine let her fingers run lovingly through the bright strands. "Ma," she said with sudden excitement, "what if I was to take some of the pieces that are too knotted to use and make a gift for Miss Townsend? She could hardly be mad if we gave her a present."

Gracie felt a ray of hope. "I don't know, Catherine. She might not like you using her threads no matter what."

Catherine shook her head, the pattern already forming in her mind. "I don't think she was mad when she left, and she doesn't seem like the others." Her fingers deftly untangled several more strands. "I'm going to do it, Ma," she said with growing excitement. "I'm going to take these ruined threads and make her a gift."

Gracie pressed her hands against the back rungs of their only chair. "Oh, Catherine, what will your father say if he finds out what happened?"

"Ma," Catherine said, looking up from her work. "Pa hasn't been home in more than two months. You don't know where he is or even if he's coming home this time."

Gracie flopped down on the chair and tried to keep the tears of hopelessness from her eyes. "He's got to come home, Catherine. I don't know what will become of us if he don't."

"You did what?"

Agatha cringed from the anger in Nick's voice, but held her ground. "Don't you take that tone with me, young man," she snapped. "Disagree with me if you must, but I will be respected in my own home or you'll be out searching for a hickory switch."

"Gran, what were you thinking of?" Nick sat at the foot of her bed and leaned back against the tester.

Agatha folded her arms across her chest. *My grandchild,* she thought. "Sarah's reputation," she answered. "Nicky, have you given one minute of thought as to what people will say when they learn that Sarah, a young, beautiful, unmarried woman is living as a guest in your home?"

Nick folded his arms and stared back at her, unwilling to admit his grandmother's scheme had once been his own. "She's my housekeeper," he said defiantly.

"And pigs can fly," Agatha snorted. "She's your mistress."

Nick jerked to his feet and began to pace. "She's as pure as new-fallen snow, Gran, and I'd challenge any man or woman who said differently."

Agatha gave her grandson a patient smile. "And how long before you wear down her virtue, Nick?" she asked quietly.

"Whom I bed is not your concern, Gran." He scowled. "It never has been and it never will be."

"It is when it concerns Sarah. Nick, that girl has been gently raised. For the sake of her reputation

150

alone, you must allow her come and live here."
Agatha watched Nick's frown grow deeper and
pressed her advantage. "What good is it to return
her to her home if you've taken her virtue? No
man would take her to wife knowing she'd been
used and discarded. And how can you, a ripe-
blooded man, look at a creature as beautiful as
Sarah and not want to bed her?"

Nick moved to the dresser and poured himself a
brandy. The liquid burned a path down his throat
but did little to melt the knot that was forming in
his stomach. Gran was right, as usual. It was only
a matter of time before someone realized Sarah
lived beneath his roof. And once that fact was out,
the damage would be done.

Reluctantly, he turned back to his grandmother.
"What makes you think that Sarah has a reputation
worth saving?" he challenged stubbornly.

Agatha held back her smile. She was winning
but it would be best not to take any chances.
"Nick," she said patiently. "Can you really believe
that her story is false?" She shook her head. "If
Sarah Townsend is not a puritan from Massachusetts, then I'll give my best kid slippers to the first
person I meet on the street."

Nick settled back on the foot of the bed.
"You're probably right," he said with resignation.
"I'll tell Sarah when I get home and we'll have her
move over in the morning."

"Why not tonight?" Agatha tried to contain her
excitement. "I've already had a room made ready
so it would be no trouble."

Nick stood and looked down at the slight form
of his grandmother. "In the morning.
Now, what about this invitation?"

"I just thought that Sarah's reputation would be better protected if I was to say that she was the granddaughter of a dear friend from the North."

Nick shook his head and rubbed at his jaw. "Gran, you don't even know where the North is, let alone have a friend there."

Agatha's eyes narrowed. "Don't get fresh with me, young man. Every fool knows that north is up there somewhere." Her arm gestured widely. "And for the sake of little Sarah's reputation, I don't mind claiming a distant friend. It seems the least I can do under the circumstances."

"And Sarah agreed to this?"

Agatha shifted uncomfortably on her pillows. "I don't think that I quite explained everything . . ." Her voice trailed off. "It would probably be best for you to tell her the plan."

"In other words, you started to tell her and she got upset?"

Agatha rolled her eyes. "Well, Nicky, you know how puritanical those Puritans are."

Nick took a deep breath. After spending the afternoon with Captain Jenkins, he had all too clear an idea. "Damn boring, those Puritans," the man had declared. "Don't believe in a friendly game of cards, never even heard of bowling. Hell, those people think that a harpsichord is an instrument of the devil." But what bothered Nick most was that, despite knowing what he did, he still wanted her. He had only to think of her violet eyes sparkling up at him and his pulse began to race.

"Why not take her for a nice stroll in the garden and explain the situation to her?" Agatha offered.

"I know what needs to be done, Gran." He leaned over to kiss her cheek. "I'll bring Sarah tomorrow after we break the fast."

As Agatha watched Nick leave, she clapped her gnarled fingers together. "Thank you, God," she breathed a prayer. "I'm one step closer to my grandson."

Nick waited until Wadsworth had served the first course of their supper before broaching the subject. As he watched Sarah's violet eyes fill with confusion he knew he had not done well with it.

"How have I displeased you?" she questioned anxiously. Her stomach tied itself into a knot. Was Agatha that upset at not getting her own way? Sarah's mind scattered in all directions searching for a clue. But it couldn't have been Agatha she had wronged, she thought, for it was to Agatha that he wanted to give her. *What have I done wrong?* she screamed silently. *Tell me so I might right it.*

You please me too well, Nick thought as his grandmother's warning played through his mind. "You've done nothing wrong, Sarah," he stated firmly. "But I think you would fare better at my grandmother's house until my agent has returned from Salem."

"But why?" She watched his dark eyes grow stormy and knew this wasn't a man used to explaining himself. "I'm sorry," she stammered. "I should not question your decisions. You've been nothing but kind."

Nick tried to be patient. "Trust me when I say that this decision does not come lightly, Sarah. I simply feel you would fare better at Gran's."

Sarah stared at her hands, folded primly in her lap. His words might declare her innocent, but she

153

had not missed the irritation in his voice or the anger that glittered in his dark eyes. *He has no use for me,* she thought miserably. *He knows I spent my time idly, visiting with his grandmother.* Her stomach clenched tighter and her own eyes felt hot and prickly. "I would do whatever you wish."

Nick watched her chin start to tremble and his anger grew. He didn't want her to leave; their parting would come soon enough. But as he watched her bowed head, the thoughts of scandal being heaped on her delicate shoulders was more than he could bear. "Then it's settled. I'll take you to Agatha's in the morning."

Sarah felt her words of protest choke in her throat. *I'll try harder to find some useful task,* she cried silently. But to Nick she only nodded her head in compliance.

The note arrived before they had finished the evening meal, and for Sarah it was a godsend. After Nick made his declaration, her food had tasted like sawdust, and each swallow had become a major chore. Nick read the ivory-colored paper, then tossed it onto the table faceup. Sarah immediately recognized the scratchy hand as Agatha's.

"Your grandmother?"

Nick nodded as he closed his eyes in frustration and rubbed a hand across his face.

Sarah was out of her chair in an instant. "Just let me fetch my shawl and I'll be ready."

Nick braced his hands on the table's edge and gave her a searching look. "Luther told me that when you left Gran this afternoon, you were upset. What did she say to you?"

Sarah shrugged. " 'Twas of no importance. We had a small disagreement."

154

"Enough of a disagreement for you to walk home, even though I specifically told you I wanted you to use the carriage?"

"It was a beautiful day," she defended.

Nick's look said he didn't believe her for a minute. "And after all she put you through today, you would still wish to drop everything and rush to her side?"

Sarah nodded, surprised that Nick felt there was a choice to be made.

"You know she's not truly ill," he continued. "She just wants the company."

Sarah stood awkwardly behind her chair. "But what if she isn't looking for attention? What if she really *is* ill this time?"

Nick rose and flipped his linen napkin down beside his plate. "She isn't. But if you're determined, we'll go."

Sarah tapped gently and opened the door. Dozens of candles flickered about the room creating a false illusion of daylight, but Agatha was not to be seen. Sarah entered quietly and approached the grand tester bed. At first she thought the bed lay empty, then she realized that Agatha's reed-thin body appeared as only a slight wrinkle in the coverlet. The woman's eyes were closed and her skin was as pale as the linens on which she rested.

"Mrs. Beaumont," Sarah whispered gently, not wanting to wake her if she slept.

Agatha's eyes fluttered open. "Sarah, is that you?"

From the foot of the bed, Nick rolled his eyes at

155

the scene before him. No wonder she wants Sarah to stay with her, he thought. She's found a completely gullible listener. He watched Sarah competently help his grandmother to sit, propping her with the dozen pillows that cluttered the bed. He noted the gentle way she handled the woman, and was suddenly, darkly envious of Sarah's devotion.

"Nick . . ." Agatha's call was feeble. "Would you come closer so I might see you, too."

Nick heaved an impatient sigh but moved to the side of the bed. "Gran, you can see me just fine. Why, there's a month's supply of candles being burned at this very minute. In fact, with all these candles, I'm surprised that those eagle eyes of yours missed that large dust ball that Emily left under the dresser."

"Where?" Sarah turned.

"Where?" Agatha sat straighter in her bed and cranked her neck for a better look. "That child is so lazy that it's a miracle that this house hasn't fallen over from the dirt she's ignored."

Pleased to note that his grandmother's voice was back to full strength and as tart as ever, Nick smiled and perched on the edge of her bed. Gently, he took one of her gnarled hands within his own. "Why did you send for us?"

Agatha smiled up at him. "I need to speak with Sarah, and I didn't want to wait until the morrow. Did you tell her?" she asked expectantly.

Nick looked at Sarah and realized the joy had again left her face. "Sarah has agreed with me that it would be best for all concerned if she was to move in with you tomorrow morning."

"But why not just let her stay now?" Agatha asked, her steel-gray eyes widening innocently.

Nick set her hand back on the coverlet and stood. "Because I said she will come tomorrow. Now, if you are settled for the evening, we'll make our departure."

"Might I have a private word with Sarah before you go, Nick?" Agatha called to his retreating back. "It will only take a moment."

Nick looked from one to the other. "I'll be down in the carriage, Sarah." His voice was hard and clipped. "Don't be long. Gran, I'll see you in the morning." Then, contrary to his harsh tone, Nick crossed the room and placed a kiss on his grandmother's cheek before leaving.

"Sarah," Agatha called, "come and sit." She patted the edge of the bed. Feeling numb from Nick's rejection, Sarah approached the bed. There was nothing Agatha could say that would make her feel worse, she thought. She was wrong.

"Sarah . . ." Agatha began sternly. "It distressed me greatly that you are acting so selfishly in this matter."

Her eyes flew to Agatha's face. "What have I done?"

"Can't you see how difficult this is for Nick? Why, any other man wouldn't care a wit about your feelings, but not my Nicky. And it distresses me to no end that you are not the least bit sensitive to his situation."

"But what have I done?" Sarah asked again. "I asked Mr. Beaumont, but he would tell me nothing."

"Well, of course not," Agatha admonished, "he's a gentleman through and through. And what gentleman is going to speak to a lady about his reputation." Agatha watched Sarah try to absorb

157

the story and her excitement grew. Her scheme was going to work after all. "You are a beautiful, but unmarried lady, Sarah," she continued gently. "If you continue to live under my grandson's roof and word got about town, Nick's reputation would be ruined."

Sarah's eyes grew wide in horror. "That's terrible," she gasped. "But surely people would be reassured once they found out that I was just the housekeeper."

Agatha slowly shook her head. "Sarah, no one would believe that of one as pretty as you." Agatha waited for Sarah's understanding, but none came. Suddenly for Agatha, the truth dawned. Sarah had no idea of what a striking beauty she was. "Sarah," she continued, even more pleased with her choice, "haven't you ever seen yourself in the mirror?"

Sarah blushed. "Actually I have. There is one almost as big as myself in the room Mr. Beaumont has lent me."

"And do you like what you see?" Agatha prompted.

"Mirrors make me uncomfortable," she said, not sure what Agatha was hinting at. "It's like watching a person who's watching me."

"Then you'll just have to take my word for it when I tell you that you are beautiful. Now, I ask you, what decent father is going to let Nick come to call when he finds that Nick has a beautiful, unmarried woman living under his roof? I know that there is nothing between you and my grandson, and you know that there is nothing there, but how are you going to make a caring father believe what already strains the imagination?"

Sarah felt the lump again settle in her stomach.

"Why didn't Mr. Beaumont tell me that my presence was causing such a problem?" she whispered in anguish.

Agatha hushed her and patted her hand. "He's too much of a gentleman to speak of his own feelings about the matter," she said softly. "And I know that you'll agree with me when I say that since he won't put himself first, the task is up to us even if it means doing things that we find uncomfortable."

Sarah's eyes narrowed. "What sort of things?"

"I'd never ask you to tell a lie for my grandson," Agatha said firmly. "But if Nick should tell the story that you are related to a friend of the Beaumont family, in order to protect his good name, I would hope that you would not embarrass him by demanding to share the truth."

Completely taken aback that she had caused Nick such hardship, Sarah struggled to find a way to make amends.

"And it might become necessary for you to accompany Nick to social functions," Agatha continued. "As a friend of the family and living under my roof, society would think less of my Nicholas if he wasn't to provide you with proper escort. It wouldn't have to be often," Agatha hastened to add. "Only enough to reassure those who would wish to question."

For a long moment Sarah sat in silence, trying to find a way around Agatha's words. But the more she thought, the more the soundness of the woman's reasoning rang out. Nick Beaumont's reputation rested in her hands, and if it meant turning a blind eye to the truth, then she'd do it. The man had saved her life, she owed him at least that much.

"So you now understand my concern?" Agatha prompted.

Sarah stood and straightened her shoulders to settle her new burden. "You may depend on me," she said firmly.

Chapter Eleven

Sarah awoke to the sound of songbirds outside her window. Their cheerful notes chipped away the darkness, allowing the first rays of the morning sun to spread their beauty across the Virginia sky. For a heartbeat she lay motionless. Then, as her senses registered the thick feather softness of her bed and the smooth pillow beneath her cheek, a deep, contented smile curved her lips and she stretched.

"Nicholas Beaumont," she whispered to the empty room. Sarah flipped over onto her back and pulled the covers to her chin. She had been at Agatha's for a full week, yet thoughts of Nick were still the first to greet her when she rose to face the day, and memories of him were always the last to leave before she surrendered to sleep at night. Sarah tossed back the covers. She shivered as her bare feet danced over the cold floor, for it was still too early for the maidservant to bring the fire. She could have lingered, warm beneath the quilts, but today Nick was coming.

Quickly, she poured cold water from the porcelain pitcher into the bowl and washed the sleep from her eyes. She rubbed a crushed mint leaf over her teeth, then, using the new tortoise shell comb that Nick had given her, Sarah unbraided her hair and made short work of the tangles. Ignoring the looking glass that stood to the side of the dresser, she retwisted her ebony locks atop her head, secured it with her pins, then replaced her lace cap.

A woolen jacket and skirt of deep orchid had been carefully laid over the chest at the foot of her bed. And as Sarah stepped into the skirt and pulled it up over her nightrail, she couldn't help but think that the fabric was too fine to wear for everyday purposes.

But this isn't everyday, her mind sang as she slipped her arms into the long, fitted sleeves of the jacket. *Nick is coming today.* She pinned the bib of her white apron into place, then with nimble fingers tied the laces in the back. Her hand smoothed down the front of her skirt, and her smile grew as she noticed the delicate lace that now graced the apron's edge. *Dear Madame Rousseau,* she thought with affection. *You always strive to do something extra.*

Turning back to the bed, Sarah tidied the coverlets and fluffed the pillow. By the time Tanzy appeared bearing hot coals to rekindle the fire, the room had been straightened and Sarah was on her way downstairs. She loved these early hours of the morning, for they belonged to her alone. Agatha's servants were already about their tasks, and as Sarah strolled through the herb garden, she could listen to the low, sweet song of Mrs. Hempsted as she prepared the morning meal or the rhythmic thump of the axe as Oscar split logs for firewood. Birds sang from the treetops, and as the sun broke through to officially claim the day, Sarah felt enveloped by a peace she had never known. But her peace was short-lived as memories of Salem intruded.

I do so long to be home, she had told herself over

and over, for thoughts of Samuel and Elizabeth worrying about her had grown to the point that they were almost more than she could bear. *But once they know I'm safe* . . . Sarah thought about the home that she had grown up in. Even with the lean-to addition her father had so skillfully added off the kitchen, her house was not much larger than the brick cook house that stood in Agatha's backyard. Her vegetable and herb garden might be small by Virginia standards, but it depended upon her alone to tend it.

Sarah breathed deeply of the fresh, dewy air. She wanted to be back among her own things, to listen to people that said what they truly meant, not more or less, to walk down the road, wave to a neighbor, and not see clothing that would have shocked the devil himself. Yes, she definitely wanted to be home. But why then, she wondered, did the realization that she would soon be returning to Salem bring no comfort?

Her steps slowed as she strolled the brick path around the hedges. To her relief, the dinner invitation with the Bellinghams had been politely turned down, yet her days and nights were more than full. Where at Nick's she had been idle, Agatha had constant needs. Sarah plucked a spring rose, breathed its scent, and thought of Agatha. She had become the grandmother she had never known. Full of complaints and absurd notions, the old woman had wormed her way into Sarah's affections and now firmly commanded a corner of her heart. How she would manage to say good-bye was a question she could no longer answer. And Nick . . . Her chest drew tight. Would she ever be able to face the day knowing that Nicholas Beaumont would not be part of it?

Never had she met a man so fascinating. Witty

and well read, he had been to places she had never even heard of. He came to visit his grandmother often, and Sarah found herself constantly watching the clock and listening for the sounds of his rich voice in the foyer; then her heart would skip a beat as his footsteps sounded up the stairs.

Always, he would go straight to Agatha and place a kiss on her cheek. But when he turned and their eyes met in greeting, her stomach would fill with butterflies.

"Miss Sarah, you out here?"

Sarah turned to the sound of Mrs. Hempsted's voice. "Yes, I'm coming," she called.

Mrs. Hempsted stood in the open door to the cookhouse, scowling at the rising sun. Her hair was covered by a bright-red bandana and her face was already shiny from the heat of the morning fire. "Do you think you'll be wanting some chicken to go with that ham and beef for this afternoon?"

Puzzled, Sarah looked at the woman. Nick's grandmother was the one who set the meals. "Did you wish me to ask Mrs. Beaumont when she rises?"

Mrs. Hempsted placed her hands on her ample hips. "If I wanted to know what Miss Agatha wanted, I would ask Miss Agatha. Now since Mr. Nick isn't here I thought I would ask you."

Sarah felt her heart leap. Nick must be coming earlier than usual. "Mr. Beaumont is dining with us this afternoon?"

Mrs. Hempsted heaved a great sigh, then eyed Sarah with a critical stare. "Mr. Nick asked me to ready him a basket for an afternoon picnic. And since I can't see him carting Miss Agatha clear across country, you must be the one he's taking. So do you want some nice roasted chicken to go with the ham and beef? I've made my special buttermilk muffins

that Mr. Nick is partial to, and there's pickled asparagus, and cabbage with onions. The chicken soup
will be ready shortly, and I cut some thick wedges of
Mr. Nick's favorite cheeses." She counted the items
on her fingers and found them wanting. "We also
have apple fritters and a nice boiled pudding, and I
think some good stewed calf's feet would be pleasing. Then for a sweet, I've got fresh macaroons and
my special butter pound cake. That's a favorite with
Mr. Nick," she confided. "There are some oranges
left from the batch he had sent up from the docks,
and I'll put in a good selection of his favorite jellies."

Sarah struggled to keep her mouth from gaping
open. She would never become accustomed to the
grand displays of foods that were served at each
meal. "All that for one afternoon?" her voice
squeaked.

Mrs. Hempsted brushed her hands against her
apron. "Mr. Nick's got to keep his strength up. He's
a hard-working man. So what shall it be, a little
roasted chicken to round it out?"

Sarah could only shake her head and wonder how
many other people Mrs. Hempsted had rounded out
besides herself. "You really think that much food is
necessary?"

The cook folded her arms across her generous
bosom. "Maybe more but not a drop less," she
stated. "Miss Sarah, I mean you no disrespect, but
you gotta learn how to care proper for a southern
gentleman. They get real testy if you don't feed them
right."

Sarah's heart raced with the thoughts of caring for
one southern gentleman in particular. And if Mrs.
Hempsted was right, he was coming to fetch her for
a picnic. *Now,* she thought desperately, *if I can just
find out what a picnic is before Nick arrives.*

* * *

A picnic, Sarah learned a short while later, was an excursion with food. But exactly why people would want to take their meal and eat it out of doors when there was a perfectly good table to sit at inside remained a mystery. Excited and relieved at the same time, her hands trembled as she placed Agatha's breakfast tray over her lap and smoothed the covers into place.

The hall clocked chimed the hour of noon Agatha stared at her grandson. "I want to go, too," she pouted.

"Maybe next time, Gran," Nick said, grinning at his fragile grandmother and the huge tray of food before her. "Besides, I would have thought that the very idea of a bumpy carriage ride would be enough to make you shudder."

Agatha poured molasses, thick and dark, over her waffles and then speared one of the pieces Sarah had already cut. "Go ahead then." She chewed noisily. "Leave an old woman like me alone to her own devices. I'm sure I'll not find the afternoon too boring with no one to talk to but myself. You just go ahead and have a good time. Don't give me a thought. It truly doesn't matter that I'll probably never see the river again before I die. You two young people just go off by yourselves and enjoy the peace of the afternoon. Don't even think that I might be lying dead in my bed before you return. You just go and have a good time."

Torn between desire and responsibility, Sarah took a step toward the bed and gave Nick a beseeching look. "Mr. Beaumont, I think we should go another day."

Nick took in the good color of his grandmother's

cheeks. His mind was made up. He'd been looking forward to this interlude alone with Sarah ever since he had conceived the idea.

"I'm sure you'll live through the afternoon." He placed a kiss on top of her snow-white hair. "If for no other reason than to question Sarah when she returns. Sarah," Nick reached for her hand. "Come."

Agatha struggled to hide her glee. The sparks between them were almost visible. She gave an exaggerated sigh. "You go, Sarah." Her voice was faint. "It's enough for me to know that you would have stayed with me if you could have."

"Mr. Beaumont . . ." Sarah turned to stand her ground. She knew Agatha wasn't dying, but regardless of what anyone thought, the woman was ill. "I think we should . . ." Her words never finished, for as she turned, Sarah was sure she saw Agatha conceal a smile.

Completely confused, she made no protest when Nick touched her arm and motioned her to the door. *She wants us to go,* Sarah thought as she made her way down the stairs, *but for some reason she doesn't want us to know that.* For long moments she pondered the situation, but the answer continued to evade her.

Feeling absurdly pleased with himself, Nick maneuvered the carriage off the main road and established a leisurely pace for the horses. He had hoped sending Sarah to his grandmother's would be a good idea, but never would he have guessed the magnitude of her effect on Gran's household. "Joyous" Luther had called her, and now everyone at his grandmother's walked with a lighter step and seemed surprisingly pleased with themselves. While at his own home, Wadsworth's chin was in constant danger of scraping the floor and Mrs. Killingham, who had been with him for more than fifteen years, suddenly couldn't remember his likes in food. Twice in the seven days that Sarah had been gone, the woman had served him shirred calves' brains.

The sun grew warm upon his back, and Nick flexed his broad shoulders. He had never anticipated that seeing Sarah alone would become such an impossible task. As the days had slowly dragged by, he realized he was becoming jealous of an old woman too frail to climb from her bed without aid. He shook his head and flicked the reins. *Well, no more,* he thought. *This afternoon is ours and I plan to make the most of it.*

Sarah sat beside Nick on the driver's seat and enjoyed the bright splashes of yellow and pink wildflowers that dotted the roadside. The sun had passed its zenith and blazed down in all its glory. But the massive oak and pecan trees that lined the road lent shade, and a gentle spring breeze refreshed them as the carriage continued on its way.

When they reached the stream, Nick drew the carriage to a halt. "I have a surprise for you." He reached into the deep pocket of his coat and withdrew a small package.

Sarah accepted the gift with a quizzical smile. "Why have you done this?"

Nick took in the sparkling color of her eyes and wished his answer might be different. "It is not from me."

Carefully, Sarah peeled back the paper to reveal a hand-stitched brooch about the size of a shilling. "Mr. Beaumont!" she gasped with delight. " 'Tis beautiful. Look at this delicate stitching."

Nick's smile deepened at her pleasure. "Catherine

Richardson made it for you. Wadsworth found her hovering at the back door this morning."

To Sarah the value of the brooch increased tenfold. "She made it herself? I thought she might be clever with a needle, but I had no idea the girl possessed such talent." Carefully she pinned the brooch onto the high neckline of her gown. "Do you know anything of the Richardsons?" She turned to Nick. "The children seem so nice, but their needs are many."

Nick shook his head. "I think they live down near the Blanchard's orchard, but I'm not certain. As for Mr. Richardson, I don't believe I've ever met the man."

Sarah considered this bit of information and silently resolved to look into the matter more closely.

Nick soaked in the tranquility of their surroundings. "I'm glad I thought of this." Water rippled gently in the background to mingle with the constant melodies of the birds.

"I can understand why you would want to come here. Oh, look," Sarah whispered. Eyes wide with excitement, she extended her arm toward a shadowy glen where a doe stood guard while her wobbly fawn approached the stream to drink. For a long moment all was still, then the doe turned in their direction and froze. Sarah watched with disappointment as mother and baby quickly darted back into the bushes.

"I thought we would eat here." Nick descended from the carriage, then reached back to help her down.

Sarah tried to stem the trembling that intensified each time he touched her, but to no avail. Feeling her cheeks grow warm with color, she turned away. "I must confess I've never been on a picnic before, so I'm not sure what you want me to do." She continued to study the water intently.

Nick smiled at her stiff back and reached into the carriage for the blanket and one of the many hampers Mrs. Hempsted had prepared. "Do you mean to tell me that you never had a gentleman call on you before?"

Startled, Sarah spun about to find Nick spreading the blanket at the base of a pecan tree. Did this event mean he was courting her? Her mind whirled. *It can't be,* reason argued. *I'm going home soon.* "Are you teasing me?" she challenged.

Nick said nothing, but his smile was slow and lazy.

She fought back a surge of excitement and watched silently as he opened the food hamper. He extracted two delicate crystal goblets, then filled each one with wine and extended a glass. Their eyes met, his warm and full of invitation, hers wary and unsure. She accepted the offered glass, then sank to her knees on the corner of the blanket. Nick leaned back to lie on his side. He touched his glass to hers and then, never taking his eyes from her, took a deep drink.

Sarah raised the glass to her lips and wondered why her chest had grown so tight. She welcomed the mellow bite of the wine, but her hand trembled.

"I'm glad you're here with me." Nick kept her eyes trapped with his own.

Sarah blinked, but found she could not look away. "Why?" she stammered.

Nick's smile deepened as he watched the sun play over her creamy complexion revealing all too clearly the glowing innocence in her eyes. She wasn't searching for compliments, he realized, and briefly he wondered if even in childhood he had ever been that innocent, that naive.

"I wanted to be alone with you," he said finally. "You're the most beautiful woman I've ever seen and I want to spend some time with you."

Sarah felt her heart begin to pound, sending riotous color to her cheeks. Her wildest dream was coming true, and she didn't have the vaguest clue as to what to do next.

"You've the most enchanting smile," he continued. "Your eyes sparkle like precious gems and your lips invite a man to taste their sweetness."

Now she did respond, and her laughter rang out sweet and full and tinged with relief. "Now I know you are teasing," she chuckled.

Nick watched her intently as she finished her wine. She wasn't flirting, returning his love talk with clever lines as he was accustomed. And it suddenly dawned on him that she really believed he was teasing. His smile vanished completely as he sat up. He plucked the empty glass from her fingers and edged closer. For a long moment they sat knee to knee in silence, and Nick wondered how she'd react if he simply pulled her to the ground and covered her with his body.

For Sarah the silence was anything but comfortable. *Don't expect too much from me,* his eyes seemed to warn, even while they hinted at the ecstasy of the unknown.

His hand reached forward tracing the smoothness of her cheek and her eyes fluttered closed.

"Open your eyes, Sarah." His breath fanned her face even as his finger outlined the contours of her mouth.

Sarah struggled to obey his command. He was so close she could smell the soap he used for shaving, and suddenly she wanted to reach up and place her palm against his smooth cheek. She felt so queer, sleepy and excited at the same time.

As his finger caressed her full bottom lip, new sensations invaded her body. She wanted to close her eyes and bask in the warmth he was creating, but his gaze held hers captive. His hand moved to her eyes, stroking the delicate slant of each brow.

"You're so beautiful," he whispered, his breath warm against her face. "You have eyes that can look beyond and capture a man's soul."

For an instant, panic filled her. She didn't want to capture anyone's soul. But her body was mesmerized by his touch and his eyes refused to let her look away.

Nick saw her anxiety and leaned forward to press a kiss against her hot cheek. He reveled in the taste of her and, as his senses heightened, he realized she would be even more intoxicating as a lover than he had first thought. His fingertips threaded through the silky softness of her hair, knocking her small lace cap to the ground. He caressed the edge of her ear, then his fingers skimmed back to her face leaving fiery traces in their wake.

Still holding her eyes captive, Nick let his finger wander down her cheek to her throat. He felt her pulse leap frantically at the base of her neck and his finger continued its journey. Her eyes grew wide as his hand slowly moved from neck to shoulder and then lower. Her breath quickened, but like a small animal caught in a trap, she couldn't move, and the thought to simply say Stop or to push his hand away never entered her mind.

Slowly, ever so slowly, she felt his finger continue its lazy pattern, each time inching lower, each time retreating until frustration and desire raced through her veins.

"Please," she whispered.

His smile deepened and the promise in his eyes intensified. "Please what?" he teased. "Please stop?" His finger moved back up toward her shoulder. "Or please continue?" This time when his hand dipped lower, it found its goal. Slowly, purposefully, his finger circled her feminine peak, and when his thumb brushed over her hardened nipple, Sarah felt an arrow of exquisite desire akin to pain shoot through her. Her eyes fluttered closed, and deep within her soul her womanhood blossomed for the first time. She felt the warm damp rush as his hand closed over her breast and his lips began to feast on her neck.

"Say my name," he commanded as his teeth raked down her throat. "You always call me Mr. Beaumont." His hand moved to her other breast, finding the tip hard and aching for his touch. "I want to taste my name on your lips."

Sarah struggled to find her wits, but as his mouth hovered a breath above hers, their eyes again met in passion. "Nicholas," she whispered. "Nicholas Beaumont."

He took possession then, his lips moving purposefully over hers. His tongue traced the contours of her mouth, then urged her lips to part. She tasted of wine and passion and madness, and he drank to quench an insatiable thirst. A small sound, perhaps a sigh, escaped their lips and Nick took the kiss deeper. Like a starving man presented with a banquet, like a pauper presented with wealth, there was a strange desperation stirring within him. And suddenly he realized that no matter how much he took, he would never have enough of her.

Slowly raising his head, he studied her upturned face. Her eyes were closed, her thick lashes dark streaks across her pale skin, skin that glowed with the luster of satin. He could feel the frantic pounding of her heart beneath his hand. Then her eyes fluttered open, and in their smoky violet depths he found what he had created: yearning, desire, confusion. But in the fleeting instant before her eyes closed again, Nick saw the innocence that was the very core of her being.

She was his now, he knew from the way her body arched toward him. But the triumph was missing, replaced instead with an aching desire to cherish and protect. His hand was unsteady as it rose to brush a stray curl from her heated face. *Why am I doing this?* His conscience picked at his brain. *Have I become so jaded with easy women that now I am reduced to seducing innocents?* The honeyed taste in his mouth turned suddenly bitter.

Sarah felt Nick's withdrawal and her eyes flew open. One minute he had been tempting the very soul from her body and now he sat on the opposite end of the blanket. Her passion-laden eyes filled with confusion as she watched him set out the dishes Mrs. Hempsted had prepared. What had happened? What had she done? Her tongue touched lips that were suddenly parched.

Nick looked up and took her gaze like a kick to the stomach. *You don't know what you ask for, my sweet,* he thought silently. *There's nothing I'd like more than to lose myself within your honeyed sweetness, but you're worth so much more. Much, much more than I could ever give you.*

"Are you hungry?" He kept his tone light and forced a smile.

Sarah straightened and felt the heat in her veins turn to ice. How could he sit there and act so calm when her heart still threatened to leap from her chest? He refilled her wineglass and extended the offering, but as their fingers brushed, Nick instantly

174

withdrew.

Insight dawned with painful clarity. *I've disgusted him*. Sarah fought back the tremors that started deep within her soul. *I let him touch me and never uttered a protest*. Her breast still throbbed with unsated desire and her mortification grew.

Nick filled a plate with the tasty delicacies and handed it to her. This time Sarah was aware of the subtle way he kept their fingers from touching and her eyes grew hot and stingy. Her hands tightly gripped the china plate as she fought for control of her senses. With eyes huge and wary, she watched Nick fill his own plate, then turn his gaze toward the stream as he began to eat. *He doesn't even want to look at me*. She felt the tears gather but blinked them away. She'd not shame herself further by crying.

With slow deliberate movements she speared a stem of asparagus and carefully placed it in her mouth. The vegetable turned into a huge chunk of wood as she struggled to chew.

"So," he said finally, keeping his eyes fixed on the stream before them. "Do you plan to marry when you return home?"

Sarah felt the few bites she had managed to swallow threaten to come up, and desperately she struggled for composure. Her hand pressed hard against her stomach to quell its churning. With quiet dignity she set her plate aside. *If I mean nothing to him, then he'll mean nothing to me,* she thought, wondering how long it would take her brain to convince her heart of the rightness of her decision.

Her eyes settled on the sparkling water, and it was easy to blame the sun's glare for the tears that gathered but refused to fall. "I think that it shall be my fate to remain a spinster," she said quietly. "In Salem, marriages are rarely completed without a dowry."

Frowning, Nick turned to face her. "What of the land you spoke of? Surely there is someone who would profit from its acquisition and as such would take you to wife."

Sarah shook her head, but refused to meet his gaze. She'd not give him the satisfaction of knowing her heart was being torn asunder. "I've never wanted the land, and its ownership has caused me nothing but heartache." She managed to keep her voice calm and sure. "My stepbrother Samuel covets that ground and so I've come to the conclusion it must be his. He and Elizabeth will put it to good use." For several moments she remained silent, her hands clenched tightly in her lap. "Samuel has never come right out and asked me, you realize, but in my heart I know this will bring him peace."

"That land was meant as a gift for your husband," Nick argued, uneasy with the quiet determination of her voice.

"That is not to be."

"You could still take a husband." Nick leaned forward. "Remember, I promised to settle five hundred pounds on you when I return you to your home."

"I can't take your money." Her eyes grew dark from the insult of his words. Did he really think his coin could ease the burden of their parting?

Nick smiled. "But you must. It is the answer to your needs, and I would think a very tempting dowry indeed." He watched her delicate brow arch in dispute. "Just consider it a gift," he added quickly. "A gift from me to you for services rendered."

Sarah felt the pain of his words slice through her like a cut that for a heartbeat refuses to bleed. He considered her a harlot, a woman with no pride, someone to be paid for her favors.

"Surely," Nick continued, "there is some gentleman who you would consider."

Sarah shook her head, determined he would never know the source of her pain. "There was a man once . . ." Her words were soft and strained. "I imagined myself his wife and cared for him greatly in my mind . . . but he did not return my feelings." She looked up and found Nick's eyes cold and angry. Not understanding why, she shrugged her shoulders, then stared down at her hands. "I could never be married and know that my heart would always belong to another."

Nick frowned at her quiet stance. Had she been thinking of someone else when their lips had met? Had she allowed his caress so she could pretend it belonged to another? He looked down at his plate and had the sudden wish to throw it, food and all, into the river.

"Mr. Beaumont," her voice stammered.

"Nick!" he shouted. "Why do you find it so impossible to say my name? It's Nick!"

Sarah felt the tremors that had lingered just under the surface begin to rise again. "Nick . . ." she hesitated. "How long does a picnic have to last?"

He jerked to his feet with angry motions. "If you're finished," he gestured to her full plate, "we could go back now."

Sarah nodded gratefully and, dumping the food Mrs. Hempsted had so carefully prepared, handed back the empty plate. With quick, efficient motions Nick repacked the hamper. The blanket was clenched into a bundle against his chest and he motioned her to the carriage.

Sarah struggled to maintain her composure. *He can't wait to be rid of me,* she thought, watching him carelessly toss the blanket into the back of the carriage. *He can't wait to get home and have me off his hands.*

They rode in stormy silence and with each rock of the carriage, Sarah felt shame wash over her in huge, consuming waves. *No wonder he thinks of me as a harlot.* She struggled not to cry. *I played the part well.* But the worst, she realized as Nick left her at his grandmother's front door, was that given the chance, she'd let him do it all again.

Chapter Twelve

Irate that the picnic had not produced the desired results, Agatha stewed in her bed. She had questioned Sarah at length but had learned nothing. The girl would go on forever with descriptions of southern wildflowers and then conclude that the afternoon had been most wonderful. But to Agatha any fool with one good eye could see that Sarah was miserable. Her face no longer sparkled when Nick's name was mentioned. And as the afternoon drew to a close each day, Agatha watched Sarah watch the clock. Always, just before Nick was due to arrive, she would suddenly remember some urgent task and beg her leave.

Agatha folded her arms across her flat chest. *They think that because my legs don't work I'm a senile old woman,* she grumbled. *Well, there's more than one way to gain information.*

Mrs. Hempsted was only to happy to vent her frustration that none of her good food had been touched. "What's wrong with those two young people?" she demanded of Agatha. "The weather was perfect, they had a feast fit for a king, yet they come high-tailing back home before a body even realizes they're gone? I tell you, Mrs. Beaumont. In our day, you wouldn't find two youngsters that didn't know what to do with an afternoon of privacy and a basket of good food." Giving a huff and muttering about how youth was wasted on the young, the cook left the bedroom.

As Agatha assimilated this new information her determination intensified. "Luther!" Her bellow belied the fragile body that emitted it. Within moments the butler was standing at the foot of her bed. "I want you to fetch Michael Danvers for me."

"Again, Miss Agatha?" Luther shifted nervously. "Miss Agatha, you know that man ain't no good."

Agatha narrowed her eyes and set her jaw. "Luther, everyone is good for something. You go and see Michael Danvers. Tell him to call on me tomorrow, and to be here before noon."

Luther shook his head, but he'd been with Miss Agatha too long to miss the steely determination in her eye. He'd do what she asked, like it or not, but he was going to keep a close watch on the man.

Sarah paced near the side of the house and waited for Nick to finish with his grandmother. Her heart raced within her chest and her nerves urged her to flee, but she was determined to see it through. *'Tis not fair to Mrs. Beaumont,* she concluded. *I am the cause and I must take the responsibility.*

She heard the door open, then Nick was standing on the top step. Clad completely in black, with tight breeches and a long, fitted coat, the image he presented took her breath away. For a long moment she could only stare as he spoke with Luther, then

180

the door closed and he was bounding down the steps to his horse.

It would have been so easy not to move, hidden as she was by a massive juniper bush, but as Nick turned his horse to go, Sarah stepped forward and called his name.

Nick smiled, delighting in the sight of her as she rounded the bush. But his smile faded with the memory of how carefully she had avoided him during the past week.

His black stallion sidestepped nervously as Sarah approached and Nick tightened the rein. "Well, to what do I owe this honor?" The sarcasm in his voice was unmistakable and Sarah felt her legs begin to tremble.

Gathering the last of her shredded pride, she stepped closer to the imposing horse. "I wish to apologize to you." She took a deep breath and looked directly into Nick's dark-sapphire eyes.

He quirked a brow. "Really? For what?"

She had known it wouldn't be easy, but then things of value rarely were. Squaring her shoulders, she refused to lower her gaze. "My behavior on the day of our picnic was inexcusable. I was forward and wanton. For that I humbly beg your pardon."

Weary of their game of cat and mouse, Nick looked up toward the gathering clouds and wondered if he would ever come to understand her. He was tired, tired of trying to replace her face in his thoughts with that of another, tired of trying to find the taste of her on the lips of other. Feeling far older than his years, Nick swung down from the saddle.

For a long, silent moment he stared. Like a man too long without water he let his senses drink in the sight of her. The midnight hair, porcelain skin, even the smudges under her eyes. He reached out with his thumb to gently caress the discolored skin.

"Did I cause this?" he whispered, bringing his lips down to touch her brow. "For if your lack of sleep is over me, then 'tis I who must beg pardon."

"But I . . ."

Nick placed his finger across her lips. "I did the unforgivable," he said gently. "You are so enchanting that for a space of time, I actually forgot who you were."

Sarah stepped back as the pain of his words sliced through her. "I see." She struggled to keep her voice calm and, determined to say her piece, she held her ground. "Regardless of your thoughts of me, I implore you not to forget your grandmother."

This time Nick stepped back. "What are you talking about?"

Sarah took a deep breath, refusing to be cowed by his towering form. "Before our . . ." she stammered, unsure of what to call their fiasco, "before . . . you came to see Mrs. Beaumont every day."

Nick placed his hands on his hips and his eyes narrowed dangerously. "And?"

"And since that afternoon, you've only been to see your grandmother three times." Cautiously, she placed her hand on his arm. "She misses you desperately when you don't come, Mr. Beaumont. Please don't let the embarrassment I've created cause you to forgo your visits."

Impatiently, Nick's boot began to tap on the lowest step. "Has my grandmother put this ridiculous notion in your head or did you manage to discover it all by yourself?"

Sarah drew herself erect. She'd made her apology, but she wasn't going to let him throw it back in her face. He had been just as eager on that blanket as she herself. "I'm simply asking you not to let my presence influence your visits to your grandmother."

Nick laughed out loud, caught her close in a fierce hug, and swung her about in a circle. Still laughing, he put her on the step so they stood almost eye to eye. "First," he brushed his fingertips over her cheek, "you did nothing wrong at the picnic. I took advantage of your gentle nature, and that was unforgivable. Second," again he touched his finger to her lips, "I've had urgent business in Jamestown this week." He tilted his head to the side and gave her a long, appraising stare. "Did you really think that I had stayed away because of you?"

Sarah blushed to the roots of her hair. "I wasn't sure," she stammered, wishing she understood his moods better. "You were so angry on our return."

He tied his horse back to the post, then turned and extended his hand. "Walk with me." Sarah reached for his hand without a second thought and let Nick direct her around the side of the house toward the winding paths that led to the gardens. For a long while they walked in silence, but when he turned toward the maze, Sarah hesitated.

Nick stopped at the entrance. "You've never been inside before." His voice was warm and coaxing. "There is a fountain at the center I'd like you to see."

Still, Sarah hung back. "I've seen it from the parlor window. It's lovely, but I think I should return to Mrs. Beaumont."

183

"Nonsense." Nick gave her an impatient look. "My grandmother has you all the time. Grant me these few more minutes. I would speak with you about something of importance and wish to do so in private."

"Then we should go back into the house." Sarah tried to turn, but Nick refused to release her hand.

"Are you afraid of the hedge?" he asked with sudden insight.

Sarah looked up at the green wall of leaves that towered over her. "Don't be ridiculous. Why should I be afraid of a bush?" She reached out and rubbed one of the waxy leaves between her fingers.

"Do you trust me?"

Her eyes darted to his face. The gentle understanding that radiated from his smile wrapped her in warmth.

Nick's smile bloomed fully. "You have nothing to fear," he said gently. "I've played in this maze since I was a child and could walk its paths blindfolded. Won't you come with me?"

Sarah could only nod. The heat that ran from his hand into hers had traveled straight to her heart. And as they started off into the maze there was no longer any hesitation to her step.

When they reached the center, Sarah was delighted to find the fountain was even grander than it appeared from the window.

"This has always been a special place for me." Nick dropped her hand and moved to sit on the structure's outer stone ring. "After my parents died and I came here to live, Gran and I had more than our share of unpleasant moments." He looked around at the walls of green that surrounded them. "I used to run away and hide here." A fleeting smile crossed his lips. "I used to imagine Gran would think I had been captured by a press gang in search of able-bodied seamen to complete their crew. I would be gone and then she'd be sorry. Other times I'd pretend I'd run away with a fierce band of pirates." Glancing to the ground, he spied a branch to his liking and within a blink had scooped it up, stripped it clean, and leaped to the fountain's edge. Removing his coat, he tossed it in her direction. "En garde," he challenged.

Amazed by his agile moves and playful stance, Sarah caught the garment and laughed aloud. "You do cut a dashing image, but why-ever would you want to be a pirate? Are they not evil creatures who steal?"

Nick hopped down from the fountain to stand before her. "Where is your imagination? I would have been brave and strong and only a little wicked." He gave her a lecherous grin.

Sarah studied him carefully. His breeches fit like a second skin and his waistcoat hugged his lean middle. His shoulders were wide, his muscles obvious, and his smile had turned more than a little tempting.

"Is it possible for a pirate to be good?" She smiled up at him. "I would have thought that if you weren't completely evil, then you wouldn't be a true pirate."

Nick flopped down on the bench next to her. "Have you no imagination at all?" he challenged. "Did you never play as a child?"

"I don't think so," she said thoughtfully. "I'm sure I must have, but there was always so much to do."

"Surely in your free time you did something."

Sarah gave a faint smile. "Mr. Beaumont . . ." His eyes narrowed dangerously. "Nick," she corrected. "I have had more free time since I've been in Virginia than I have had in my entire life."

Nick thought of the countless hours she spent tending to his grandmother and wondered how that could possibly be true. He watched shadows briefly cloud her eyes and knew she thought of her family. Determined to return her good mood, he glanced about and spied what he needed. Placing the stick firmly in her hand, he pulled her to her feet and then was off to pluck another weapon from the ground. Again, he hopped up to balance on the edge of the fountain.

"I've had enough of your insolence, wench," he said, wiggling his eyebrows. "And when I've finished with you, you're going to walk the plank."

Sarah, stick dangling limply from her hand, laughed again. But her laughter stopped abruptly as Nick advanced one measured step at a time. She felt her heartbeat quicken. "What am I to do?" she asked. Unable to stand the intensity of his stare, she began to edge away.

"Defend yourself, you land lover."

Sarah looked from Nick's menacing form to the branch in her hand and back again as her violet eyes grew round. "You want me to hit you with a stick?"

" 'Tis a well-honed sword, m'lady, and you'd better learn how to use it or you're going to become my prisoner."

Growing more nervous by the moment, Sarah continued to retreat step for step as Nick advanced. Suddenly she looked past his shoulder and her eyes filled with fear. "Mr. Beaumont," she cried. "Quick, behind you."

Responding to the panic in her voice, Nick spun about with his branch at the ready only to face a wall of green. Nothing was there. Stunned, he turned back to see a glimpse of Sarah's skirts as she darted into the maze. A deep smile touched his lips. "You'll never best me," he called. "And when I capture you, there'll be a stiff penance to pay." Then with a leap, he, too, was off into the maze.

From her chair beside the upstairs parlor window, Agatha watched their game for only a moment before turning back to her guest.

"I appreciate your enthusiasm, Mr. Danvers," she said sharply. "But when I give instructions, I expect you to arrive at the appointed time."

Danvers shifted to the edge of his seat. "But Mrs. Beaumont . . ."

Agatha silenced him with a glare. "Don't make me lose my patience, young man," she cautioned.

"No, madam," Danvers stammered, hating the very sight of her. How dare she speak to him like some errant child. He was an attorney!

"Now, do you understand what I require of you this time?" she pressed.

"Yes, madam, as you wish, Mrs. Beaumont." Danvers nodded his head and swallowed bitterly. He needed the money and the old hag knew it.

"Good, now leave quickly. And Danvers . . ." she proclaimed as he reached the door. "Don't ever think you can outwit me."

Michael Danvers wiped the perspiration from his face with a stained handkerchief as he descended the wide staircase. Since word had gotten about that he was no longer employed by Beaumont Shipping, he had lost his three largest clients.

187

Angrily, he shoved the cloth into his pocket. Did the old woman think that he was so hard on his luck that he'd be grateful to become her lackey? Ignoring Luther, he stormed out the front door. The old hag might pay well, but since she wouldn't allow him to say that he worked for her, he still couldn't regain his former standing.

Jerking his reins from the post, Danvers yanked his horse closer to the step. Nick's black stallion tossed back his head and whinnied. Danvers paused. Beaumont was still on the property. Maybe he'd just stay long enough to let the man see him. He chuckled to himself. That would certainly give Mrs. Beaumont something to explain. But even as the idea came, Danvers looked back to see Luther standing on the porch. His burly arms were folded across his wide chest and his scowl was more than threatening.

"You have a good day, Mr. Danvers," the servant called.

Danvers swallowed hard. *Don't do anything rash,* he counseled himself silently. *Your time and place will come. Just be patient.*

He tried to mount, but the horse, sensing its rider's nerves, shied and sidestepped. Danvers muttered under his breath and yanked the horse close again. Again he missed. Sweat dripped from his pale face as he swore in humiliation, for he was sure he could hear Luther's low chuckle from the step. Finally he managed to mount and, giving the horse a vicious crack with his crop, they were gone.

Luther watched from the top step until Danvers was no longer in sight, then, stepping down, he fed the anxious stallion a carrot. "Mrs. Agatha's making a mistake in trusting that one with her business." He spoke in a low and soothing tone to the nervous animal. "Ain't no good ever gonna come of her dealing with that man." The stallion nudged Luther's shoulder in search of another treat. "You mark my word on it." He gave the horse's nose a final rub, then turned back to the house.

Exhausted and laughing, Sarah flopped down on the stone bench before the fountain and began pulling the leaves and twigs from her hair. "You are a menace to polite society," she declared with conviction.

The pleasure on her face took the barb from her words as Nick flopped down on the ground beside her and rested his arms on the bench. "Well, you might not have played as a child, but you certainly learned how to run." His breath was uneven, and Sarah felt satisfaction soar through her.

"Your grandmother is going to think that I've been rolling on the ground." She plucked another leaf from her hair.

"Here, lean over."

Sarah bent forward, and their eyes met as Nick's long fingers removed the foliage from her hair. Her mouth went dry as she inhaled the male scent of him.

"There, that's the last of them," he said reluctantly.

Slowly, Sarah sat up. "I really should be going back in." Desperately she searched for a reason to tarry longer.

Nick swung his body onto the bench beside her. "In three days, I have to travel inland. The sister of a friend of mine is to be married. Would you like to accompany me?"

Sarah tried to contain her pleasure. "You'd like me to attend a wedding with you?"

Nick stood and again extended his hand. "Christopher and his family live on one of the larger plantations. Julie is the baby of the family so there's sure to be even more than the usual entertainment."

Sarah's eyes grew wide. "Entertainment . . . at a wedding?"

Nick laughed at her stunned expression. "Some things are better experienced than explained," he said as they walked slowly through the maze. "But I think I can guarantee you'll have a good time."

Sarah smiled as they stood at the maze's entranceway. "Then I'd love to accompany you."

Nick nodded with satisfaction. "Luther will dig out one of Gran's trunks for you."

Sarah gave him a puzzled look. "Why do I need a trunk?"

"To take your things?" he offered hopefully.

Totally befuddled, she questioned him. "Why do I need to take things to a wedding? "What things would I take?"

Nick smacked his forehead with his hand. "I'm sorry," he said, taking her hand and walking her toward the back door. "I didn't mention that we'd be staying for a few days." He watched her eyes grow skeptical and hastened on. "It will take most of the first day just to get there," he explained. "The wedding will take place at noon and then the celebrations will conclude the next day."

"It sounds wonderful," Sarah's smile grew wistful, "but do you think it wise to leave Mrs. Beaumont for so long?"

Nick relaxed. "Gran adores the Carlsons, but in her condition the strain of a trip that long would be pure torture for her. Still . . ." He cocked his head to the side and gave Sarah a long appraising stare. "If you truly wish to make her feel a part of the festivities, why not let her help you decide what to take? You know how she enjoys telling people what to do."

Sarah nodded, and since she had no idea where to even begin, the idea sounded wonderful. With Agatha planning things, she thought, everything would turn out fine.

Chapter Thirteen

"Surely you can't mean for me to wear this?" Sarah stared down in horror as Charlotte Rousseau tied the final bow and tucked the ribbon drawstrings out of sight.

Ignoring the comment, Charlotte stood back to admire the sight of her creation. The form-fitting bodice was stiff-boned, perfectly accentuating the delicate proportions of Sarah's tiny waist and hinting of cleavage that lay just below the gown's low, square-cut neckline. The magnificently embroidered skirt was windowed back to reveal a tiered petticoat edged with additional embroidery and lace. The sleeves were tight to the elbow, then flared into tiny pleats. Soft lace, of deep midnight blue, gathered under the pleats and fell in delicate folds to the wrist. It was a masterpiece, Charlotte thought, enjoying the rush of pride. But best of all, the rich sapphire color made Sarah look like royalty. *She'll be the envy of every woman there,* Charlotte mused, *and not just because she's on the arm of Nicholas Beaumont.*

"Now, I know this is not what you're accustomed to," Charlotte cajoled, taking Sarah's hand and

MORE PASSION AND ADVENTURE AWAIT... YOUR TRIP TO A BIG ADVENTUROUS WORLD BEGINS WHEN YOU ACCEPT YOUR FIRST 4 NOVELS ABSOLUTELY *FREE* (AN $18.00 VALUE)

Accept your Free gift and start to experience more of the passion and adventure you like in a historical romance novel. Each Zebra novel is filled with proud men, spirited women and tempestuous love that you'll remember long after you turn the last page.

Zebra Historical Romances are the finest novels of their kind. They are written by authors who really know how to weave tales of romance and adventure in the historical settings you love. You'll feel like you've actually gone back in time with the thrilling stories that each Zebra novel offers.

GET YOUR FREE GIFT WITH THE START OF YOUR HOME SUBSCRIPTION

Our readers tell us that these books sell out very fast in book stores and often they miss the newest titles. So Zebra has made arrangements for you to receive the four newest novels published each month.

You'll be guaranteed that you'll never miss a title, and home delivery is so convenient. And to show you just how easy it is to get Zebra Historical Romances, we'll send you your first 4 books absolutely FREE! Our gift to you just for trying our home subscription service.

BIG SAVINGS AND FREE HOME DELIVERY

Each month, you'll receive the four newest titles as soon as they are published. You'll probably receive them even before the bookstores do. What's more, you may preview these exciting novels free for 10 days. If you like them as much as we think you will, just pay the low preferred subscriber's price of just $3.75 each. *You'll save $3.00 each month off the publisher's price.* AND, your savings are even greater because there are never any shipping, handling or other hidden charges—FREE Home Delivery. Of course you can return any shipment within 10 days for full credit, no questions asked. There is no minimum number of books you must buy.

urging her forward. "So let's let Mrs. Beaumont give her opinion."

Sarah allowed the dressmaker to direct her down the hallway, but her face turned a fiery red when they passed Luther coming out of Agatha's room.

He stopped dead in his tracks and his eyes grew round as saucers before a huge grin split his weathered face. "Why, Miss Sarah," he beamed. "You sure do look pretty in that fine dress. Why, you gonna be the grandest lady there, including the bride." He whistled his appreciation between his teeth, then turned back to his business. "My oh my," he muttered, descending the stairs. "Wait until Master Nick gets a look at that."

Certain that Nick's grandmother would object to the indecency of her costume, Sarah stood in total embarrassment at the foot of the bed.

Agatha smiled with delight. "Charlotte, my dear, you are a wonder. The color is perfect, just as you said."

Sarah stiffened slowly. Surely they were just teasing. Wasn't Nick always telling her she misunderstood what was said? She folded her arms and tapped her foot, anxious to be out of the scandalous outfit.

"Turn around, Sarah," the old woman commanded. "Let me see the full effect."

Sarah played their game as long as she could. Finally she could stand no more. "You don't really think for me to wear this, do you?"

Agatha's eyes narrowed at the tone in Sarah's voice. "If I hadn't meant for you to wear it, I would never have picked it from Charlotte's sketches, let alone paid the exorbitant fee she is charging me."

193

Sarah felt the blood drain from her body. "You actually want me to wear this dress? In public?" Feeling totally betrayed, and realizing for the first time that the joke was on her, she struggled to keep her knees from shaking. She had trusted Agatha to know what was right, but instead they had made a mockery of her. Her senses clamored with confusion. Did Agatha realize the intensity of her feelings for Nick? Was that why she had Charlotte dress her in such a provocative manner?

Agatha watched the tears gather in Sarah's eyes. "What's wrong with the gown?" she demanded. "Do you not like the color?"

Sarah shook her head and discreetly tried to wipe her eyes with her hand. "The color is beautiful and the fabric exquisite."

"Then why are you crying?" Agatha snapped. "I cannot read your thoughts. If something distresses you, tell me."

Sarah drew herself erect. "Look . . ." She held up her hand. The lace flopped back revealing the slender curve of her arm. "My skin shows."

Charlotte watched Agatha struggling to maintain her patience and stepped between the two. *"Ma petite . . ."* She took Sarah's hands within her own. "You have skin as fine as porcelain and such lovely arms. What is the harm in it?"

Sarah turned a beseeching look to the dressmaker. " 'Tis a sin for a woman to bare her arms in public. And look here . . ." She gestured to the low cut of the neckline. "You can almost see," her face glowed brighter, "you can almost see my chest."

Agatha straightened as much as she dared in her bed. "Now you listen to me, young woman," she snapped. "Up there in that godforsaken place you live in, people might have the ridiculous notion that showing an arm is harmful, but you're not in the North. You're in Virginia. Charlotte Rousseau dresses the wealthiest women in this county and I'll not have you insult her in this manner."

Eyes wide with confusion, Sarah spun about to face the seamstress. "I never meant—" she stammered.

"Of course you didn't," Agatha interrupted. "Now, sit down and look through those sketches."

Gingerly, Sarah perched on Agatha's sick chair and accepted the packet of drawings Charlotte handed her.

"Do you see a single gown like the ones you wear at home?" Agatha demanded as Sarah turned the pages. "Of course you don't, because you're not in the North. You're in Virginia. And I'll not sit by and have you insult the good God-fearing women of my town because they have a flair for fashion."

Stunned, Sarah handed the packet back to Charlotte. "I never meant to cause offense."

"Then we'll hear no more about the gown," Agatha scolded.

Mortified that she had placed her piety above others, Sarah felt a lump grow in her throat.

"There, there." Charlotte handed her a small lace handkerchief. "No harm is done. You simply didn't understand. I had the same problem with my eldest girl, Claudette. I send her to England to see what the Royals are wearing and then I let her travel on to France. When she returns, it's the French this and the French that. To her young mind, if the style wasn't French then it was useless, a rag, not worthy of her time. I had to make her see that different styles appeal to different people. And in Virginia," she tipped Sarah's chin up, "it's the style to wear the very latest in fashion. No one is trying to embarrass you or compromise your values. We simply wanted you to look your best so you would have a good time."

"I see," Sarah said quietly. "Then I must humbly beg your pardon."

Charlotte shook her head and laughed, relieved that the tension had passed. "Not to worry, *chère amie*," she said easily. "Children are allowed to make mistakes. It is only when they refuse to learn from them that we adults have the right to find fault. Do you not agree, Mrs. Beaumont?"

Agatha folded her arms across her chest and gave Sarah a threatening stare. "So are you going to wear the gown or have I paid good money for naught?"

Sarah smiled back at the wizened old woman. "Thank you for your generosity. But I shall go and take this off now so nothing happens to it."

With the grace of youth, Sarah glided from the room, anxious to seek a moment's privacy to contemplate the situation.

"She is certainly beautiful, is she not, madame?" Charlotte sighed, leaning against the bedpost, thinking of how Sarah's raven-black hair and pale skin so perfectly complemented the deep sapphire shades of the gown.

Agatha smiled with satisfaction. "She can be damn stubborn at times, but then I like backbone in a person. She'll be good for my Nicky."

Charlotte straightened slowly and swallowed hard. "Then it is official? They are to be wed?"

Agatha shook her head. "Nick's not ready to

make the announcement yet," she said with regret. "But I can tell you this, it will be soon, and if I have my way, it will be the grandest wedding Virginia has ever seen." Delighting in the way her plan was progressing, Agatha missed the pain that for a brief moment flashed in Charlotte's eyes. "And Charlotte . . ." she whispered, motioning the woman closer to the bed. "I want you to start on the wedding dress. I want you to design the most beautiful wedding dress that ever existed. Something that a queen might wear for her king."

Charlotte's pride rose to the surface and she placed a smile on her face. "I design nothing less than the best, madame," she declared solemnly, "as you well know."

Still wearing the dress and lost in thought, Sarah was startled when a light tap sounded at her door. "Oh, I thought you were Ruby," she sighed as the dressmaker entered. "I can't figure out how to undo the back laces."

Charlotte smiled. "I do often wonder myself why I create styles that are so impossible to get in and out of."

Sarah reached out to touch Charlotte's arm. "I truly am sorry that I offended you." She looked down at her gown, and when she raised her head, her eyes were clear and determined. "I would never want you to think me ungrateful for all you have done for me."

"Hush, hush," Charlotte scolded. "We'll have no more of that." But instead of undoing the back laces, the dressmaker's brow wrinkled in thought as she moved slowly around the girl.

"I was thinking . . ." Charlotte reached for Sarah's arm and held it out. "This is the part that makes you uncomfortable, is it not? The way the lace flops back to reveal your forearm?" She watched the color singe Sarah's cheeks and had her answer. For several moments she stood silent and Sarah, afraid to cause further offense, stood with her arm extended forward.

Suddenly, a knowing smile touched the dressmaker's face and she bent to rout through her bag on the floor. "What if I thread ribbon through the lace here at the cuff," she said excitedly. Her fingers nimbly worked the ribbon until it encircled Sarah's slender wrist. "If we tie it into a bow, then when you raise your hand, *voilà!* Our arm stays covered. Would that suit you better?" She looked up to see tears of gratitude in the girl's eyes.

"Thank you, madame," Sarah whispered. "You are more than just a clever person, you are also a kind one."

Charlotte felt her own tears threaten, and willed them away. "And the neckline, that troubles you, too?"

Sarah slowly nodded her head.

"Then what if I sent over a scarf of the very finest gossamer." Charlotte tapped a finger against her cheek. "If I am not mistaken, I have the perfect shade of blue to enhance the gown. Then, if you were to pull it around your shoulders like so and fasten it with a brooch, the gentlemen would only get a hint of the charms you possess."

"You would do that for me?" Sarah's heart swelled with appreciation.

Charlotte winked. "If you cringe in the corner all night, then who will see my beautiful gown?"

"But will Mrs. Beaumont be offended?"

Charlotte shook her head. "The changes will only enhance the style. Why, I'll bet that within two weeks, half the dressmakers in town will be trying to copy our new sleeve."

Sarah bit her lip and told herself again that Charlotte didn't really indulge in gambling, that it was only a figure of speech. But why couldn't people speak plain and say what they meant? she wondered. There were so many things to remember.

"Sarah, do you hear me?"

She blinked and turned to see Charlotte standing near the dresser holding her brooch.

"I asked, *mon amie,* if you were the one who created this?"

Sarah shook her head and stepped out of the fancy skirt. "Catherine Richardson made that as a gift. Is it not clever?"

"The fingers that stitched this piece were more than clever, *mon amie,* they are very talented. But who is this Catherine Richardson?"

Sarah felt a prick of excitement start at her toes and slowly work its way upward. "Catherine is a young girl in search of employment." She carefully folded the skirt and placed it on the bed, then untied the drawstrings for the underskirt. "Do you think you might have a use for someone of her talent?"

Charlotte eyed the brooch critically. "It is better that she work for me rather than my competition. When you return from the wedding, you bring her to my shop and introduce us, no?"

Sarah beamed with pleasure. "Definitely yes."

"Then all is well." Charlotte retrieved her bag as she watched Sarah gently fold the underskirt and placed it, too, on the bed. *"Chère amie . . ."* Her voice was hesitant. "Is there something more? Your eyes still hold a shadow."

Sarah pulled on her woolen skirt, then hastily slipped her arms into the jacket. "All is well, madame."

Charlotte halted Sarah's hands as she clumsily tried to tie the drawstrings. "You can trust me to keep your confidence."

Sarah sank on the corner of her bed. " 'Tis not right," she said, her eyes sparkling with unshed tears. "I am to attend a wedding, an event of joy and love. And I'm so excited that I can hardly wait."

Charlotte sat and placed her arm about Sarah's trembling shoulders. "These are not tears of happiness, *chèrie*. Even in the South we can tell the difference," she teased.

Sarah shook her head and wiped her eyes with the hem of her apron. "My family must be consumed with worry. Can you not imagine how you would feel if one day your daughter just disappeared?"

Charlotte shuddered. "I would be frantic."

"Exactly." Sarah sniffed. "It doesn't seem just for me to be having such a grand time."

For a long moment, Charlotte sat deep in thought. Then she rose and again gathered her belongings. "I think you are wrong, *ma petite enfant*. If Claudette was to suddenly be missing, my worry would be immense until I knew she was safe. But, if after I had her home again, I found she had been gently cared for, then I would be more than grateful. I think you are wrong to imagine that because your family suffers, they would wish you to suffer, too."

Sarah smiled in thanks, but long after the dressmaker had gone, she still wondered if Samuel and Elizabeth would share Madame Rousseau's opinion.

Chapter Fourteen

June 1692 — Salem, Massachusetts

"I wish Samuel were here." Elizabeth shivered as she gazed about the crowded room. She and the Widow Tate had arrived as early as they dared to witness the procedures. But now that she sat in the same room as the accused witches, Elizabeth felt a sickly feeling deep in her stomach and she longed for the comforting presence of her husband. "I don't think we should have come without him."

"Samuel told you he had to go to the docks today," Ann hissed. "Now be quiet, I want to hear what is said." She craned her neck for a better view as the aging Rebecca Nurse was brought to stand before the magistrates.

"Goody Nurse, you have been accused of causing mischief and practicing witchcraft. How do you plead?" The magistrate's voice boomed through the room.

Rebecca Nurse, lame and ill, swayed against the bar but said nothing.

"See," Ann whispered. "The devil tells her to hold her tongue in the presence of those who fear God."

"She cannot hear," called one of Rebecca's sisters.

Ann turned and glared at the woman until Elizabeth pinched her arm smartly. "Do not draw attention to ourselves," Elizabeth snapped. "Do you want everyone to remember that Sarah, too, has been labeled a witch when Samuel is not here to protect us?"

Angered at being publicly chastised, Ann tightened her shawl and gave Elizabeth a withering look. "Don't you mean to protect you? 'Tis not my family that harbors a witch."

Elizabeth gasped and pressed a hand to her pounding heart, but before she could speak, screams and moans the likes of which she'd never heard before pulled the attention of both women back to the front of the room.

Abigail Williams, niece of the Reverend Mr. Parris, rolled about on the floor in fits of agony. "Goody Nurse hurts me," she shrieked. "Make her stop! Make her stop!" Within moments all of Abigail's young companions had joined her on the floor to roll about in a most grievous fashion.

"I am innocent," Rebecca's frail voice rang out, and the meeting room grew silent. "I never hurt no child." All who watched and heard the words of the pious old woman suddenly found it hard to believe that a woman too ill to leave her bed would direct her specter to dance about the countryside and cause harm to children. "I am innocent, I say." Rebecca's voice rang true. "As God as my witness, I am as innocent as the child unborn."

Abigail Williams glanced nervously about the room, her eyes narrowing. "But you cut me just this morning," she wailed, holding up a bloodied hand for all to see. "I fought with you, and here's the knife to prove it."

The congregation gasped in horror at the sight

of the child's wounded hand and the witch's knife she held as proof.

Feeling the sympathy again directed toward her, Abigail continued. "Two weeks ago you stole into my room at night and bid me fly with you on your broom. When I refused, you bade me dance with the devil and drink his blood. Again I refused. This morning you said you had come to punish me. You used your knife."

"That's a lie!" A young man stepped forward and, giving Abigail a harsh look, took the knife-blade from her fingers. Ignoring her threatening stare, he turned toward the magistrates. "This blade is from my knife," he said easily. "I broke it only yesterday when Abigail and I were walking down by the stream. She must have taken the piece when I wasn't looking." He held forth his knife and fitted the broken blade into place. A rumble of disapproval ran through the crowd.

"Abigail Williams, you keep your story to the truth," the magistrate warned. "You need not tell lies to have us believe you."

Uncertain of how to proceed, Abigail did what she did best; she fell onto the floor in a fit of moaning. Mercy Lewis quickly followed the example of her friend.

" 'Tis the witch," she cried in pitiful sobs. "Her eyes burn us. Make her stop!"

The crowd stood and edged forward to better view the spectacle, for no one had seen a witch use her eyes before. One magistrate whispered to another and a black cloth was quickly tied about the eyes of Rebecca Nurse. Instantly both girls relaxed their torments and were able to be eased back on their chairs.

"We need no further proof," the magistrate declared solemnly. "Goody Nurse, I find you guilty of witchcraft and sentence you to remain in Salem Prison until you can be taken out and hung by the neck until you are dead." His gavel pounded the sentence.

Elizabeth clutched Ann's hand tighter. "Let us leave this place," she said, swaying. "I feel not at all well."

Ann took in her friend's pale complexion and grudgingly rose from her seat. "I wanted to see who would be the next accused," she complained, "but you do look poorly."

Outside in the spring air, Elizabeth took several steadying breaths. "It became so warm in there," she said, fanning herself as they started their long walk. "I found it difficult to breathe."

Ann turned a critical eye to her neighbor. "Do you think that Sarah is close by? Do you think that she was trying to steal your breath?"

Elizabeth nervously scanned the sides of the road. "We have not seen the cat since the day Sarah disappeared and took its shape. Samuel wants to burn her house down to rid our property of any evils that may still linger there. But I am not convinced. I think the devil might covet the thoughts of a fire."

Ann scrunched her narrow face. "Don't you know anything?" she challenged. "Fire is the only way to truly kill a witch. Fire or a hanging. And I think Samuel is right. If you burn Sarah's house, mayhap she will not return to haunt you."

Nearly an hour later when they reached Elizabeth's house, the women paused at the gate. Samuel's wagon, still hitched to the horse, sat in the yard.

"I thought you said Samuel would be gone all

day," Ann complained. "If I had known he was home, he could have come to fetch us from the trials."

Elizabeth felt a dreadful premonition wash over her, and her body started to tremble. "He said he would not return until evening." Hesitantly, the two entered the house.

Elizabeth found her husband seated at the table with his head resting on his hands. "Samuel?" she questioned, rushing to his side. "Husband, what is wrong?"

Samuel Wittfield looked up, his eyes red from the quantity of drink he'd consumed. "I met a man at the docks today." His voice was slurred with anger and brandy. "It seems that all these weeks we've spent in constant worry, our little Sarah is safe."

Ann pulled out a chair and leaned close. "Sarah is here?" she questioned, remembering how Elizabeth had suddenly found it hard to breathe in the crowded meeting house.

Samuel shook his head. "Little Sarah," he sneered, "little innocent Sarah is living in sin with a man in Virginia."

"Virginia?" Ann and Elizabeth gasped in unison. "But how did she get to Virginia?" Elizabeth's voice quivered with fear.

Samuel rose and began to pace before the hearth. "The man was reluctant to impart much information. But if you ask me," he turned back to the anxiously waiting women, "I would think that Sarah traveled in the manner of all witches. I think she flew."

Chapter Fifteen

Sarah awoke to find the room full of dusty shadows. For the briefest moment she lay in panic, not knowing where she was. But as she moved to sit, her stiff muscles brought back instant awareness. The carriage ride had taken nearly six hours over the bumpiest roads she had ever traveled. And although Nick had had the driver stop often for her comfort, she had arrived at the plantation exhausted. Mrs. Carlson had taken one sympathetic look in her direction, glared at Nick, then whisked her away from the hectic preparations.

Realizing she must have slept away the remainder of the afternoon, Sarah rose and peered out the window. Formal gardens filled with blue and pink larkspur wound around the side of the house, while beyond, green fields of tobacco stretched as far as the eye could see. The sun slipped from view and the sky flared with brilliant shades of fuchsia and gold. As the katydids began their evening song, Sarah basked in the beauty laid out before her.

"You were more than bountiful when you created Virginia, Lord," she whispered, then watched a hawk circle lazily overhead until it disappeared from view in the swaying tops of the distant trees.

The evening breeze turned chilly, and Sarah reluctantly moved from the window. Her stomach grumbled noisily as she slipped back into her black velvet gown and tidied her hair. *I've got to find Nick,* she thought. Her lips curved into a smile. *And then I need food.*

With excitement soaring through her veins, Sarah descended the grand curving staircase that led to the main hall. A massive crystal chandelier hung from the ceiling, its candles sprinkling light like diamonds in all directions. Bowers of thick green hung everywhere and the scent of spring flowers rose to greet her.

"So, Sleeping Beauty awakes at last."

Sarah looked down to find a dashing man leaning lazily against the newel post at the foot of the stairs. Her eyes grew wide, for she had never seen a gentleman dressed completely in white before and she wondered briefly why anyone would choose such an impractical outfit. His hair was blond and sun-streaked, his eyes the clearest blue she had ever seen, and his smile, infectious.

"Did you have a good rest?"

"Mr. Carlson?" she questioned.

"Christopher Carlson at your service, madam." He executed a perfect bow.

Sarah fought back her nerves and continued down the steps, wishing Nick was somewhere in sight. "My name is Sarah Townsend," she said softly. "I came with Mr. Beaumont."

"Nick said you were a treasure." Christopher extended his hand as she reached the bottom step and saw the faint blush that touched her cheeks. "Now I see for myself that he was right."

Mrs. Carlson flew out of the parlor and cast a fleeting look in their direction as she sailed by. "I hope you had a nice rest, Sarah. Chris, go put on your wig and then take Sarah in to Nick so he'll stop scowling. I think he's already frightened more than half the maids and I still have much to see to."

"And the other half?" Chris called to his mother's retreating form.

"Drooling on his boots as usual," came the faint reply. "Don't forget your wig."

Sarah anxiously reached back to touched her own hair, hoping it was still well tucked beneath her lace cap, but Christopher merely laughed.

"Mothers," he sighed. "I have thoughts that even when I'm old and gray, mine will be scurrying around and scolding me for tracking mud on the floor. Now, you tell me," he said, taking her hand and tucking it over his arm, "do you think I need to wear a wig?"

Sarah tilted her head to the side and gave him a quizzical look. She had come to realize that except for Nick, all of the men she had come in contact with wore a hairpiece of one type or another. Oscar had even kept his on when he was chopping wood. "Don't you care for them?" she questioned.

Christopher gave an exaggerated grimace. "Pure torture, if you ask me. I'd like to shoot the damn fool that invented them."

A bemused expression touched her lips. "Mr. Beaumont doesn't seem to care for them, either."

Christopher grinned and turned toward the salon. "I'll tell you a secret," he whispered. "When we were in Eton, Nick and I made a vow never to wear the blasted things. And once, when we were full of mischief and smuggled brandy, we sneaked into the headmaster's house and stole the lot of them." His eyes grew bright with laughter. "We were just innocent youths," he defended. "We had no way of knowing that most of the masters had shaved off their own hair."

"What happened?" she gasped.

Chris's dimples twinkled with mischief. "The next morning at breakfast all hell broke loose. Never have I seen so many naked heads at one time," he chuckled.

"Did you get in trouble?"

Chris heard the worry in her voice and his smile deepened. "We were caned soundly before the entire school, and then the prefects shaved our heads. I think they were sorry they hadn't thought of the scheme," he confided, threading his fingers through his thick blond locks.

Sarah tried to imagine Nick without his curly black hair tied back in a queue, but the image wouldn't come. Instead she could only picture a small boy being viciously beaten before an entire school. Her heart wrenched from the pain he must have suffered. "That must have been horrible."

Christopher patted her hand where it rested on his arm. "We did have to take our meals standing for quite a few days." He looked down at her face and saw the innocence that Nick found so appealing. "Don't fret," he soothed. "It wasn't as bad as it could have been. Besides," he whispered, "Nick somehow managed to turn our bald heads into a symbol of bravery and courage. By the end of the

210

week we were the envy of the class." At her skeptical look, Chris laughed out loud and placed his hand over his heart. " 'Tis all true, I swear. We kept our heads bare for the rest of the semester."

Sarah gave him a dubious grin. "Now that must have been quite a sight."

Chris shook his head as he led her into the salon. "Agatha nearly fainted when she saw us. She cried buckets and then threatened to beat us all over again."

"And your mother?"

Chris's white teeth sparkled as he smiled down at her. "After seeing the reaction Nick got from his grandmother, I took the way of the coward and stayed there for a few weeks until my hair started to grow back."

Sarah's laughter bubbled forth. "You are teasing me, aren't you?"

Chris winked. "Just ask Nick why all the girls found him so fascinating that year and see if he doesn't tell the same story."

Sarah barely heard his words, for at that moment, her eyes located Nick as he held court on the opposite side of the room. He leaned insolently against the wall surrounded by a group of women.

"Would you like to go outside first and find a good stick?" Chris whispered in her ear.

Sarah blinked and pulled her attention away from the man who was making her heart race. "I'm sorry, what did you say?"

Chris struggled to conceal his grin. "Would you like to go outside and fetch a stick?" He nearly laughed at the frown that wrinkled her brow. "To fight off the ladies," he teased. Then he laughed out loud at her startled expression.

" 'Tis not polite to scowl, Nick," Julie Carlson pouted as she walked her fingers up his arm.

Nick tore his eyes from Sarah and looked down at the petite young woman who stood before him. "And you shouldn't be flirting on the eve of your wedding."

Julie shrugged and tossed her blond ringlets over her shoulder in a gesture she had perfected at the age of five. "I'm not married yet. Besides, the only one I'm talking to is you." She batted her lashes.

Nick's eyes narrowed as he bent close to her ear. "You're playing with fire."

Julie felt his breath on her neck and her knees turned to jelly. Determined to make the most of what might be her last opportunity, she stepped closer, allowing the fullness of her skirt to press intimately against him. "And what if I said that I'm cold and need a little fire to warm me?" Coyly she gazed up at him.

"I'd say you're a little girl looking for trouble."

Julie stomped her foot in frustration at his amused expression. "I am not a little girl." She leaned forward to touch a button on his waistcoat, giving him an enticing view of her charms in the process. "Just in case you haven't noticed," she whispered smugly, "I'm all grown up."

Nick's smile turned dangerous and his eyes threatened. "If I took you up on your invitation, you'd run faster than the time Chris chased you with that black snake."

Julie felt her heart pound in her chest and her breath was uneven. "And what if I don't run this time?"

Nick cocked a brow. "Then your husband should give you a good spanking, my dear."

She gasped and felt heat stain her cheeks. "Clarence won't arrive until the ceremony tomorrow."

"So you'd like me to give you a spanking?" he challenged.

Their eyes locked, his in amusement for the little sister of his best friend, hers with desire for the man she had longed for since she was twelve.

She tossed down the challenge. "It could prove to be interesting. I guess it would depend if you were man enough to do it."

Frowning, Nick straightened and Julie nervously stepped back only to realize that his gaze didn't center on her. Frustrated, she turned to see Sarah smiling up at her brother. Julie looked back at Nick and jealousy filled her, for never had she seen his eyes so possessive.

"It looks like your new lady friend is quite taken with my big brother," she purred.

Nick's gaze never wavered. "Sarah's a friend of the family," he said easily. "Her grandmother and Gran were best friends or some such nonsense."

"And nonsense it is if you expect me to believe that," Julie snapped. "Agatha's never traveled to the North and you know it."

Nick narrowed his eyes and looked down at her. "And how is it in your brief years of ten and six that you have recorded every event in the life of a grand lady who is past seventy?"

Julie fought the urge to retreat, for never had

she heard such a hard edge in Nick's voice. With every ounce of willpower she possessed she forced herself to inch closer, take Nick's arm, and lean against his side. "Look at them," she sighed dreamily. "Don't you think they make a lovely couple? Even in that absurd dress, you must admit that she looks good on Christopher's arm."

Nick was having the same thoughts and found them not at all to his liking. "Excuse me, Julie, I need to speak with your brother for a moment."

She halted him with a hand on his arm. "I'm not fickle like some are," she said, glancing in Sarah's direction. "I'll be in the barn later tonight," she whispered, as she gave him her most smoldering look. "I'll wait for you at midnight." Then as her skirts swished, she turned and crossed the room to greet her newest guest.

Christopher Carlson liked watching people, and Nick Beaumont was always one of his favorite subjects. From the day they had first met on the ship to England, he'd been fascinated with Nick's intensity. And although more than a score of years had passed, he'd yet to meet another with Nick's relentless drive. Now, as he watched his friend from across the room, he couldn't help but chuckle.

Nick's amused, knowing smile had all but disappeared, and when Sarah chatted and laughed with one of the neighbors, Chris watched his friend's scowl grow steadily darker. Even Julie hadn't been able to break his concentration. Chris glanced about the room, and breathed a sigh of relief that their mother was not in sight. Julie had always flirted when Nick came to visit, but tonight her seductive ways would have set a lesser heart to blaze. He smiled in sympathy as his little sister stormed past and offered a prayer that she was past the age of brewing mischief.

You're hooked, old friend, Chris thought with satisfaction as he watched Nick help Sarah fill her plate from the food-laden table. *You've never lacked a beautiful woman for your arm, but you've also never truly cared where their eyes wandered or with whom they danced. And now,* Chris rubbed his hands together in delight. *I think you care more than you know.*

The hour was just past midnight before Nick was able to extract himself and Sarah from the festivities. Mrs. Carlson had insisted that he and Chris were the only ones sober enough to finish hanging the garland. And when she failed to complain that neither man had yet to don his wig, Nick knew she was truly desperate. So for hours he had stood trapped atop the ladder. At first, Sarah too, had offered help, handing him bows of twisted greens. But whereas she had no reservation in enlisting Nick's assistance, Mrs. Carlson's social conscience wouldn't let Sarah, as a guest, help also. She had whisked the girl away and deposited her with a group of neighbors who had arrived early to enjoy the festivities to the fullest.

Nick's first inclination had been to climb down from his ladder and rescue her; then his heart had swelled with pride as he watched the smiles grow around her. Chris, perched atop his own ladder, had given him their special thumbs-up sign, and Nick decided that his best course of action was to get the task completed as quickly as possible.

He worked like a demon, causing Chris to scramble to keep up, but, despite his hectic pace, he was careful to keep Sarah constantly in view. He smiled when he heard the delightful sound of her soft laughter and struggled to conceal his frown when the men seemed to spend too much time trying to impress her. But each time he was tempted to climb down, she would look up at him. As if reading his thoughts, she would glance at the hung garland and nod her head in approval.

They had been on the last piece when he had watched Julie take Sarah aside. She had looked up at him twice as Julie spoke to her, her violet eyes searching his for answers. And as Julie turned and left, he realized that Sarah's smile had vanished.

In his haste to be done, Nick smashed his thumb soundly with the hammer. His hearty curse rang out at the exact moment the musicians decided to stop practice. All heads turned in his direction and he clamped his jaw hard to remain silent as pain soared through him.

Relieved that her garland was finished, Mrs. Carlson had insisted Nick come down from the ladder immediately so she could inspect the damage. His thumb, already turning blue, was the least of his worries. Brushing aside the motherly attention, Nick navigated the crowded room with Sarah in tow, leaving Chris to contend with his mother and any other chore she deemed must be completed before morning.

Nick guided Sarah through a maze of rooms until they reached the privacy of the back porch. He watched her shiver in the moonlight and silently doffed his coat to place it about her shoulders.

"You really should do something about your finger," she said softly. But her head stayed bowed and her eyes refused to meet his.

Nick stopped, leaned back against the railing, then turned Sarah to stand before him. "It's not my thumb I'm worried about." His injured hand reached up to touch her chin, raising her eyes to his. "What did she say to you?" He watched a single luminous tear gather.

For a moment he thought she would remain silent, then, taking a deep breath and gazing past his shoulder, her words tumbled forth. "I didn't mean to shame you." Her eyes darted to his then away again. "And I have a new dress for tomorrow, but I never thought that tonight would be considered part of the celebration."

Nick frowned. "What makes you think you have shamed me? I considered myself most fortunate. In case you didn't notice, you were the most beautiful woman in the room." Even in the moonlight he could see the color bloom in her pale cheeks.

"It's just so hard to remember," she continued, daring to look at him. "At home this dress would be considered too grand to wear except for the most special of occasions. And even then I would be setting myself apart from my neighbors. But here . . ." she gestured about them. "Here I am dressed like a housekeeper."

"Sarah . . ." his voice was tender. "I don't care what clothing you wear."

Her smile was slow in coming. Did he think she hadn't noticed the questioning looks or heard the chuckles behind her back? Agatha had been right—unless she dressed the part, she was going

217

to cause Nick nothing but embarrassment.

Nick gave her a leering grin. "In fact, I think I would like it best if you wore none at all."

Sarah's laughter rang out at the absurdity of his thoughts, and suddenly she realized that, like her father, Nick possessed the ability to utter a few simple words and her world became right again. "I do have a grand dress for tomorrow," she assured him as the heat from his smile began to penetrate. "Your grandmother spent a fortune on it."

Nick's smile deepened and he edged her closer between his legs. "Why didn't you dance this evening? I noticed you were never in want of company."

"That's because you never stopped watching me." She tilted her head and raised a brow. "Were you afraid that I'd do something wrong?"

Nick rested his hands on her waist and ignored her pointed look that said he should remove them. "Do you not know how to dance? I could teach you if you'd like."

Sarah folded her arms across her chest and tried to ignore the tremors his thumbs caused as they reached up to brush back and forth across the velvet nap at her ribs. "I can dance just fine, thank you." She tried to keep her voice calm, but his nearness was making it impossible.

"Then why didn't you?" he challenged, squeezing her waist ever so slightly.

Sarah fought back the lump that was growing in her throat. "We don't believe in instruments," she said quickly, hating the breathy sound of her words. "The ministers say they are the voice of the devil."

Nick's eyes mirrored his astonishment. "But

you sing. I've heard you. What harm can there be in an instrument that plays a tune?"

Sarah shook her head. "I don't know. It's never made sense to me. Once, many years ago, a man came through Salem with a lyre." Her questioning eyes looked up at Nick and she instinctively leaned closer. "His songs were so sweet that they could bring a tear to your eye. I thought it grand, for you know that David once played a lyre for King Saul." Her voice faded off and Nick edged her closer still.

"What happened?" he whispered. When she turned her face up to his, the light of the full moon danced on her pale cheeks and Nick felt his breath leave his body.

"The ministers ran him out of town." She paused in thought. "I don't think he minded leaving until they broke his lyre." Her body trembled and again her eyes sought his. "Why do you think they did that? He had already agreed to go. Why did they have to break his lyre?" Again Nick felt the tremors run through her. "That was the first time I ever saw a grown man cry," she stammered.

Lost in the beauty of her, Nick struggled to find words that might offer comfort, but finding none, he simply pulled her close and enfolded her in his arms.

Sarah luxuriated in the warmth of his body. The clean, manly scent of him permeated her being and she felt her insides begin to melt. "I should be going," she whispered as her cheek rubbed against his muscular shoulder.

Reluctant to let her go, Nick's mind scrambled. "Not until you prove to me that you can dance."

Sarah stepped back, her eyes full of laughter.

"You don't believe me." Nick shook his head, moved several steps away from her, and began to hum a tune that had been played often that evening. He executed a deep bow and extended his hand.

Sarah felt her blood race and wondered how her mind would ever function, but her feet moved of their own accord as she dipped into a curtsy and reached for his hand. Their fingers touched and each felt the heat and desire of the other. Their eyes met and held in longing. As the tune continued they stepped close, only to back away again as the dance dictated.

She stepped lightly around him, flirting, enticing, and as Nick repeated the motion, each step, each movement, took on new meaning as they courted each other. Drawing close, Nick's arm encircled her waist as they stepped about, and the desire that blazed in her eyes was almost his undoing. As they broke apart Sarah stepped back to execute a number of complicated moves, but when they drew together again and his arm encircled her waist, Nick's tune stopped. For the longest moment they stood pressed tightly together, exulting in feelings that could not be openly acknowledged. Then his head lowered and his lips touched hers. For Nick the waiting had been too long, and as his mouth moved hungrily over hers, he thought he might die from the wanting.

Sarah pressed closer still as her arms reached up to encircle his neck. His lips drew everything from her, then returned the feelings a hundredfold. She tasted the dark, mysterious flavor of him and wondered if her thirst would ever be sated. His heart pounded against her breast and her body

220

ached for the touch of his hands. But even so it was she who broke the kiss and stood on legs that threatened to crumple.

"Don't ask this of me," her voice trembled. "I have not the strength to tell you no." She watched passion flare in his eyes but as Nick stepped forward, she stepped back. "I wish I could be closer to you than your clothing when you've been caught in a spring rain, but I know for us this cannot be. I have no defenses against the desires you stir in me, so the responsibility to know what is right must belong to you." As she turned to go, Nick's coat slipped from her shoulders. "If left to me," she whispered, "I would throw caution to the wind and then we would both be lost."

Christopher smiled as he strolled by the back porch. He could hear the soft, rich baritone of Nick's voice as he watched the shadowy couple twirl about. And as his steps took him from their view, he couldn't help but envy Nick for finding Sarah first. His feet moved soundlessly down the well-trod path to the barn, and he wondered what great emergency awaited him there. Nick had gone so far as to extract a promise that he would see to it, and a promise was something they rarely demanded of the other.

He entered the barn and heard the muffled weeping even before he lit the lantern.

"Julie?" he called, recognizing the sound of his sister's sobs as he climbed the ladder to the loft.

"Nick, is that you?"

So that's the way of it, Chris thought as he swung over the last step. In the lanternlight he found his little sister propped against a bale of hay, her eyes swollen and red from crying. His chest swelled in sympathy as he crossed over to her. "Oh, little one," he soothed, pulling her close to cry on his shoulder. "When are you ever going to learn?"

"Where is Nick?" she demanded with a sniff. "Did you tell him to stay away from me? Is that why he didn't come?"

Chris brushed her tears with his thumb. "Julie, you are being married tomorrow. What are you thinking of?"

"He told me he would come," she whined.

Chris stared up at the ceiling and prayed for divine inspiration. "Dear heart, Nick never told you he'd meet you here."

"But I'm in love with him."

"You might be in love with Nick, but Nick is in love with Sarah."

Julie pushed herself away from her brother's shoulder so she might see his face. "Did he tell you that? Did he say those exact words. Did he say *I am in love with Sarah?*"

Chris pulled his handkerchief from his pocket and handed it to her. "My sweet, you have only to look at them to see. Have you ever known Nick to care if his lady danced with another? Have you ever watched him scowl if she but laughed at another's joke? He's in love, and if my guess is not mistaken, Sarah's in love with him, too."

Julie scrubbed the handkerchief across her face and soundly blew her nose. "But it's not fair," she pouted. "I'd be better for him than she would. She doesn't even know how to dress. Tonight she could have been one of the servants."

Chris gave her curls a playful tug. "And did you see that to Nick it mattered not in the slightest?"

Still frowning, Julie pulled her knees up and wrapped her arms about them. "I think He's making a mistake."

Chris hugged her shoulder. "I think you are the one who might be making the mistake. Why are you crying over Nick when you've promised your heart to Clarence?"

She shrugged and stared into the shadowy corners of the loft. "I thought I could force Nick's hand."

Chris swore softly under his breath. "But if you don't love Clarence, you should call the wedding off."

"What, and return all those glorious wedding presents?"

"The presents aren't going to keep you warm on a cold night when you're married to a man you don't love."

Julie pulled herself to her feet and gave her brother a haughty stare. "Unlike some people," she paused, "Clarence worships the ground I walk on. I don't think he'll have any trouble keeping me warm. And Mr. Nicholas Beaumont can just put that thought in his pipe and smoke it." With the dignity of a queen and the stubbornness of a willful child, Julie flipped her leg over the ladder and left the loft.

"Is she all right?" Nick questioned from his perch on the back step.

Chris reached the porch and nodded wearily. "She brings it on herself, you know, but still one

223

can't help feeling sorry for her. Our parents spoiled her so much when she was little that now she just doesn't understand when she can't have everything she wants."

Nick stood and stretched. "And what of tomorrow?"

Chris shrugged. "She'll be fine, as radiant as always. Her pride will allow her no less."

"What of her husband? Is he going to make her happy?"

Chris snorted. "If giving in to her every whim will make her happy, then Clarence Morgan is the right man. Julie can wrap him around her little finger."

Nick shook his head. "Julie is a sweet child, but she's going to make them both miserable."

"Just as long as she does it at home. Her new home, that is . . . Where is Sarah?"

"She's gone to her room." Nick's voice was tight as he struggled to keep his thoughts from imagining Sarah snuggled beneath the covers.

Never one to mince words, Chris looked Nick straight in the eye. "And are you going to tell me how you two really met or are you going to stick to that nonsensical story of her being the granddaughter of a friend of Agatha's?"

For a long moment Nick was silent; then he turned and nodded toward the woods. "Does that creek still run along the northern border?"

Chris's grin turned devilish. "Deep enough to dive and cold enough to freeze your privates off."

Nick reached for the top buttons of his waistcoat and began to pull them open. "Let's go," he challenged, hoping an icy bath would cool the fire that burned in his loins and threatened him with tossing caution to the wind. "And I'll wager a keg of my finest brandy that you turn blue a full lap before me."

Chris's laughter rang out as he tossed his own coat over the railing. "Brandy be hanged. Let's make it interesting. The winner gets to partner Sarah at dinner tomorrow."

Nick nodded. "It's a bet."

Chapter Sixteen

The morning of the wedding bloomed bright and clear. As Sarah entered the grand salon, she couldn't believe the transformation. Roses, in every shade of pink, had been artfully woven into the garlands of green that Nick and Chris had hung the night before. Their fresh scent filled the room, and Sarah realized that their full glory would be revealed as the heat of the day coaxed their petals to open. Delicate chains of white paper scalloped the garlands and huge white paper bows filled the corners. The effect was magnificent and Sarah could only wonder if Mrs. Carlson had seen her bed at all the night before.

Carefully she ventured further into the room. The musicians had left their instruments resting on the chairs that had been provided for them in the far corner, but Sarah resisted the urge to inspect them at close range. In her mind she could still hear the melodies they had created the night before, and although she found the situation not at all unpleasant, the teaching of her ministers ran deep.

Crossing the room, she saw a long table covered with white linen. In its center rested the most splendid cake she had ever seen. It stood four tiers tall and the white icing that covered it formed flowers and lattices of the most delicate nature. Two maids laden with heavy silver trays entered the room and immediately crossed over to her. They smiled shyly in her direction, then set about assembling a grand pyramid of sweets on either side of the cake.

Mrs. Carlson bustled in carrying yet another immense tray. Sarah rushed to assist her. "Are you expecting many for the ceremony?" she asked, amazed at the quantity of food being set forth.

The woman sighed gratefully, allowing Sarah to take the weight of the tray. "Since the weather has held I think we should have just under two hundred."

"Two hundred people?" Sarah could not contain her amazement.

"Yes. Except for the Thermonts and the Fitzwaters who sent their regrets, I think everyone else is expected." Mrs. Carlson shifted the tray and frowned. "Where are those boys?" She added an additional jelly to the pyramid on the right. "They're never nearby when you need them. And God forbid I should get them to wear their wigs today like proper gentlemen."

"Are you looking for Mr. Beaumont and Master Chris?" the youngest maid questioned. "They're down by the woodpile. That's what all the cheering is about."

"At the woodpile?" Mrs. Carlson and Sarah spoke in unison.

The girl nodded. "They made a bet with each other as to who could split a cord of wood the fastest."

Mrs. Carlson rolled her eyes toward heaven. "What next?" she muttered.

"Oh, it is all right," the maid added hastily. "Mr. Carlson is holding the money."

Sarah couldn't believe what she was hearing, but she offered no resistance when Mrs. Carlson took her hand and announced they were going to see for themselves.

"So who do you think will win?" Mrs. Carlson winked as they reached the edge of the crowd that had gathered. Slaves stood with house servants, and wedding guests in all their finery circled Nick and Chris as their axes rose and fell with startling speed.

Mrs. Carlson stepped to the front of the circle and clapped her hands smartly. "Chris, Nick, stop this immediately." Amid the groans of protest from the crowd, the two axes fell silent. "Christopher Carlson, what can you be thinking of? Your sister is getting married today. And you," she turned on her husband. "You're as bad as these two scalliwags. I have chores that need tending and a wedding to see to, and I can't accomplish anything if the help is in the yard. Now, just how long is this going to take?"

Nick straightened and wiped the sweat from his brow. Like Chris, his jacket and waistcoat hung from a nearby fencepost and his once-white shirt was completely pulled from his breeches. He glanced at the stack of wood already chopped. "I say we chop for thirty minutes more, then call the contest ended."

Mrs. Carlson eyed her son and the growing crowd, then looked at the small timepiece she wore pinned to her gown. "One half hour and not a minute longer and then I expect everyone to help make up for this lost time. Is that understood?"

"Yes, madam," Chris and Nick said in unison, exchanging grins.

"Then stop standing there resting and get on with it," she commanded. "Mr. Carlson, I place five pounds of my egg money on Christopher." The crowd cheered, but she raised her hand for silence. "And I want to place five pounds of my house money on Nicholas." The roar of the crowd doubled and both men bowed in her direction.

Nick spit in his hands and rubbed them together briskly. Blisters were already forming, but he was not put off, for he had looked up to find Sarah standing directly before him on the inner edge of the growing circle.

Chris saw Sarah, too, and his smile turned devilish. He rubbed his own sore hands on the sides of his breeches. "Same odds as last night?" He gave Nick a challenging wink.

Nick returned the grin. "You're a glutton for punishment, my friend."

Chris glanced again in Sarah's direction, then to the hoots of the men and squeals from the ladies, he pulled his shirt off over his head and tossed it to the ground. His well-defined shoulder muscles glistened in the sunlight. "You might be a fish, Beaumont, but then, fish don't do very well on land, do they?"

Nick's eyes flashed his own determination and his shirt followed suit. But instead of dropping it to the ground, he tossed the damp garment in Sarah's direction and smiled when she reached to catch it. "Hold that for me, would you?" he called. "I won't be but a minute."

Chris flexed his muscles and raised his axe. "It's thirty of them, and you'd better be ready."

Nick threw back his head, laughed at the sky, then took his position. A pistol sounded and Sarah jumped as the contest began anew.

Sarah didn't even realize she pressed Nick's shirt close to her heart as she watched the axes rise and fall. Never in her life had she seen a naked chest, and now two stood displayed boldly before her. Transfixed, she watched the blue veins on Nick's powerful forearms trace a pattern up his inner arm. The fluid motion of his axe whistled as it sliced through the air to land again and again. His broad shoulders were soon covered with sweat and they glistened as they flexed and stretched in the sunlight. The muscles of his chest revealed hidden strength, and Sarah could not stop her eyes from following the dark hair that curled down the center of that flat, broad expanse to disappear into the waistband of his snug breeches.

Her mouth went dry and her head grew light as she watched each well-placed stroke of his axe. And when the sudden thought of lying naked within the circle of his arms struck her soul, Sarah felt her insides melt.

The gun sounded again, and Sarah blinked with a start. Could a half hour have truly passed so quickly? Then she realized that beneath her gown her chemise was soaked with perspiration from standing unprotected in the blazing sun. Blinking against the sudden glare, she watched the two men shake hands, then lean back on their axe handles. Chris joked good-naturedly with the crowd as his own wood was stacked and measured. But Nick's smile didn't return until his pile was declared higher and he was officially proclaimed the winner. Even then his expression was more of satisfaction than pleasure.

Two buckets of icy water were hauled from the stream and Sarah gasped along with Nick as one was dumped over him. He shivered and shook his head, reminding her of a dog caught in the rain as he sent water droplets flying.

Chris retrieved his shirt from the ground and slapped it against his thigh to remove the dust before wiping it down his chest. "The next time I'll not let you beat me so easily," he teased, trying to catch his breath.

Sarah tried to ignore the money changing hands all around her as she hesitantly stepped forward to hand Nick his shirt. "That was quite a contest," she said as the crowd melted away to find cooler entertainment. "I had no idea that you two were so . . ."

"Competitive?" Nick offered, glaring at Chris's exposed chest while his own heaved with each breath.

"Heavily muscled?" Chris winked, holding the stitch in his side.

"Athletic," Sarah stated firmly, looking from one to the other. "Whatever made you do such a madcap stunt."

Chris flung his arm around Nick's shoulder. "You'd never know it, but usually I can beat this clown."

"And pigs can fly," Nick snorted, pulling his damp shirt on over his head.

"But why do it at all?" she questioned, trying not to stare at the wet cloth as it clung to his chest.

231

"Usually for the fun of it." Chris laughed painfully. "But today the stakes were too rich to pass up."

Sarah shook her head as she studied them. "But neither of you have need for money."

Chris shrugged and threaded his fingers through his hair. "Sometimes money is not the answer." He glanced at Nick and despite the pain in his side, his eyes began to twinkle. "I would not put my body through this torture for a mere handful of coins."

"Are you trying to tell me that you did this," she waved toward the towering stacks of wood, "just for the folly of it?"

Both stood sheepishly and refused to meet her gaze.

Sarah folded her arms across her chest, her eyes narrowing. "Then tell me, just what is this magnificent prize that would make two grown men chop wood until they practically collapse?"

Chris flipped his shirt around his neck and let his hands hang on the ends. "Why you, my sweet." Then giving a wink, he trotted off toward the house, leaving Sarah to stare at Nick with eyes full of wonder.

The grandfather clock in the hallway struck midday and the wedding proceeded exactly as planned. Julie, dressed in the palest of pink, joined her young man to speak their vows before friends and family in the grand salon. Then all the guests were herded out onto the lawn where huge tables had been arranged.

Clad in her new gown of sapphire, and feeling

uncomfortably aware of herself, Sarah sat beside Nick on one of the long benches. Chris sat across from them and kept the entire table of twenty amused with his anecdotes. The sun was about to set when the last course was finally served, and Sarah felt she would not be able to eat another bite for days.

"I shall have to add gluttony to my list of sins," she sighed, leaning back from the table.

Nick turned to watch her. The idea that anyone, save the clergy, would care enough to keep track of their sins amazed him. Yet as he viewed the sincerity on her delicate features he was struck again by the vast differences in their life-styles. She could dance with the grace of a feather in a gentle breeze, yet instruments made her uneasy. He absently kneaded the growing stiffness in his shoulder and wondered if she'd run in fright to find that he owned a harpsichord and was quite accomplished at its keyboard.

They could hear the call of the French horn from the house and the violins being tuned, and soon the lilting sounds of a minuet drifted down the lawn, compelling many of the guests to retreat to the salon in hopes of dancing off the grand meal they had just consumed.

Nick took Sarah's arm and helped her from the bench. "Have I told you how lovely you look in your new gown?" His eyes were dark and unfathomable when she looked up at him.

"Madame Rousseau made it," she stammered, unable to forget the sight of his bare chest.

"Actually I find it doesn't matter what you wear," he said, taking her arm and steering her toward the house. "You would still be the most beautiful woman here."

Sarah turned and smiled at him as they reached the steps. "And you are well in your cups if you think that," she said easily. "Everyone knows that the rule clearly states that the bride be the most comely one at a wedding."

Nick leaned closer. "And do you always follow the rules?"

Startled by his intensity, Sarah took a step back. "I have to go in," she said quickly while her heart pounded loudly in her throat. "I promised Mrs. Carlson I would lend a hand. Why don't you go to the salon and join in the dancing?"

Nick propped his foot on the step and rested his hand on his knee. "I'll come looking for you later," he stated solemnly. "I want you with me for the bedding ceremony."

Eyes wide, Sarah couldn't begin to voice an answer. Feeling the heat again stain her cheeks, she fled into the house.

Nick watched until her skirt disappeared into the doorway before he turned away. He didn't know what hurt more, the aching muscles in his back and chest or the constant throb of his manhood. He tried to flex his shoulders and bit back a groan. He had been a fool to let Chris goad him into that insane contest. But he had been an even bigger fool the night before with Sarah. How neatly she had tossed things back in his lap, insisting he make the decisions for the both of them. The responsibility weighed heavily on his sore shoulders and he dreaded the decision he knew he must make. Never before had desperation entered into one of his liaisons. His women were always more than willing and eager to please. They knew his wants and serviced him well; he, in turn, returned the pleasure. But now all he could think of was Sarah. Desire filled his veins, making him throb with want and hard with need. Deciding there was no hope for it, Nick turned his step toward the stream in search of another freezing swim. If his body was numb, perhaps his mind could find some answers.

At Mrs. Carlson's insistence, Sarah joined with the other unattached girls as they led Julie to the special chamber that had been prepared for her first night of marriage. Huge bouquets of baby's breath and pink carnations filled the corners of the room, and candles flicked shadows on the walls. Julie's elaborate white wig was carefully removed and returned to its stand on the dresser. Fascinated, Sarah watched as Julie perched on a padded stool and allowed two companions to draw down her braids and brush her hair until it hung about her shoulders like a glowing golden cloak. Embarrassed by the lack of privacy afforded the new bride, Sarah stayed quietly on the edge of the merriment as Julie was helped from her wedding dress and into the lacy nightrail in which she would meet her husband. The diaphanous gown drew sighs of envy, and as Julie waved aside the outer dressing robe, the room filled with giggles and advice on how to pleasure a man. Julie was placed in bed, and all but a few candles were extinguished. Anticipation became a tangible force. But Sarah stared in confusion when skirts were raised and stockings were lowered.

"Sarah, hurry," Julie commanded from her lofty perch. "Take your stocking down. The men will be

here any moment. And you don't want them to see
your legs." Julie stretched immodestly, pressing herself against the lacy front of her gown. "Or maybe
that is why you tarry—you do want them to see
what's hidden beneath your skirt."

At a loss to what was happening, and completely
unnerved as center of attention, Sarah felt her skin
grow hot. Not wanting to cause Julie further embarrassment, she complied as quickly as she dared,
then stood awkwardly with one bare foot tucked in
her shoe.

Riotous laughter floated up the stairs and down
the hall; then the door to Julie's chamber flew
open. Sarah's eyes went round as saucers and her
breath stopped completely as she watched a rowdy
host of gentlemen with Chris in the lead carry
Clarence Morgan on their shoulders. And when she
realized that Mr. Morgan's feet were bare and he
wore only his nightshirt, Sarah felt her skin turn to
flame. What could these people be thinking of?
she wondered. Had they no respect for Julie's sen-
sitivities in such a delicate matter? Then a more
shocking thought occurred. Surely they would not
be expected to stay and watch. Inconspicuously, she
tried to edge to the back of the group, but the
room was now crowded with well-wishers and
Sarah found she could hardly move. Horrified, she
watched as Clarence Morgan was neatly tucked
under the covers beside his bride. The jokes grew
more risqué and the advice more bawdy, and
Sarah, embarrassed beyond her wildest imagination, desperately hoped the floor would open to
swallow her.

Chris turned, and, spying her for the first time,
smiled with anticipation. "Stockings," he called.

"Ladies first. Let's not be shy, my dears. Which one of you lovelies is going to be the next?"

Sarah watched as each girl stood at the foot of the bed and tossed a stocking over her shoulder toward the married couple. Cheers filled the room again and again until her head ached from the consuming noise. Her own stocking fell like a stone in her hand and nervously she tried again to edge her way to the back of the room. But Chris would have none of it and, as he tugged on her arm, she reluctantly let him move her into place at the foot of the bed. Deciding there could be no harm in the game, and desperate to have it done with, she was ready to toss it when her eyes met Nick's. He smiled knowingly, and she felt her stomach turn to butterflies. With a flick of her wrist, Sarah sent the stocking sailing. The roar in the room turned deafening, and Sarah spun about to see Julie dangling her stocking from one finger.

"Yours landed the closest to Julie," Chris explained, planting a smacking kiss on her forehead. "That means you'll be the next to marry."

Sarah felt her smile freeze in place and she wondered desperately what would happen if she were to snatch her stocking back. Unable to move, she watched without breathing as each man tossed a stocking toward Clarence Morgan. Cheers went up when Chris's stocking covered the most distance on the counterpane. But when Nick threw and passed Chris's marker by the breadth of two fingers, Sarah lost her courage and fled the room.

Nick had seen Sarah's eyes grow wide with panic as he tossed, and when he heard the cheers, he knew that he had hit the mark. Smiling with satisfaction, he accepted the bottle of Brown Betty wine that was his prize, then retrieved both stockings from the impatient couple as the room began to clear. Leaning over, he placed a chaste kiss on Julie's forehead. "Be happy, little sister," he whispered. Nick turned and never saw how Julie's eyes filled with tears as they followed him to the door.

Nick felt his impatience growing. It was well past midnight and Sarah was nowhere to be found. He had searched the salon, still filled with dancers, then the library. He had even crept up the stairs like a thief to sneak a peek into her bedroom. The windows had been opened wide, her trunk sat primly at the foot of the bed, but the room was empty. Walking slowly down the stairs, he heard bawdy laughter from the back hallway. He had bypassed the three gaming rooms, for he knew her aversion to dice and gambling. Now, pausing in the foyer, Nick wondered if he should have checked the gaming tables after all.

He felt a touch on his back and knew it was Sarah before he even turned around. Helpless to erase the wide grin that covered his face, he stood silent and smiled at her.

Sarah looked up into his dark eyes and her determination grew. "Will you come with me?" she questioned softly, extending her hand.

Like a dreamer afraid of waking, Nick said nothing, but allowed her to take his gloved hand. He remained silent when she led him out the door and through the gardens at the back of the house. But when her steps took the path to the barn, Nick felt his pulse quicken. Had she changed her mind? Was the decision no longer his alone?

"Do you know where you are going?" he asked, willing it not to be a mistake.

"I know." Her smile was gentle and full of promise as they continued silently.

Nick paused once more at the barn's great red door. "Are you sure this is where you want to be?"

For a long moment she seemed to be studying him, and Nick found his breath caught in his throat like a green lad with his first woman — eager, impatient, and desperate not to be found wanting.

"Do you trust me?" she challenged softly, her eyes shadowed by the darkness of the night.

"With my life," he answered, more surprised than she by the conviction of his words.

Silently she turned and beckoned for him to follow. With a sure step she picked her way through the barn's shadowy interior, around bales of hay and sacks of grain. The sweet smell of fresh-cut grass tickled his nose. Then he saw it. A lantern set on a low stool illuminated the interior of the far stall. Coming closer, he realized that the ground had been raked clean and then covered with fresh straw. A dark blanket spread over the straw completed the pallet. Nick felt his heart stop at the sight, then the blood raced so fast that his head grew light. Determined to let her set the pace, he waited, waited while every nerve in his body clamored for release, waited while his mind took on the clarity of a fog-laden field. He could not have moved if his life had depended on it, for it had become suddenly difficult to remember to draw breath.

"Will you take your coat off?" she coaxed, with a gentleness reserved for children.

Dumbly he nodded. Simple words like "yes" now seemed completely beyond his vocabulary. But as he reached back to let the jacket slip from him, his muscles sang in protest from his morning's folly. Instinctively she stepped behind and eased the garment from his stiff shoulders.

She guided him into the stall and directed him to kneel on the blanket. Moving to stand before him, she drew his gloves off his hands and gasped at the torn blisters that covered his palms.

"Oh, Nick." His name on her lips sent chills of anticipation coursing through his veins. She cradled one injured hand between her own and brought it to her cheek.

For Nick, the world beyond the barn ceased to be. He would have wished the softest of linen and a wide feather bed on which to take her, but now his only desire was to feel the warmth of her damp flesh pressed close to his.

"Why did you do this to yourself?" she whispered, her voice filled with pain.

His eyes said that was the most ridiculous question he had ever heard. She only shook her head. "How foolish to try to win what you already have," she scolded gently. "Would you take off your shirt?"

His eyes never left hers as he slowly dragged his shirt from the waistband of his breeches. But when he would have pulled the garment over his head, her hands brushed his away. "Let me," she said softly. And then he was naked to the waist before her.

It took every ounce of willpower he possessed not to reach out and run his hand down the cool porcelain skin of her cheek. But he resolved to let her see it through. He'd be ready when she faltered, but until then . . .

Gracefully she rose and moved to stand behind

him, making her shadow flicker on the rough-hewed walls of the stall. Nick inhaled a pungent tang, but his befuddled mind failed to register its source until the bite of the horse liniment hit his shoulders.

Chapter Seventeen

"What in hell . . ." Nick tried to turn and rise, but Sarah's hands were firm on his sore shoulders.

"Be still," she scolded. "And don't curse at me. Your shoulders pain you yet you're too stubborn to see to this yourself."

Nick's protest died on his lips as her hands began to rub in earnest. They didn't glide over his flesh, as one might expect from a genteel lady, but probed deeply, searching out each sore muscle and eliminating the stiffness. His body began to relax, and when she coaxed him to sit on the blanket so she might reach better, he complied without protest. The horse stall was small, and within minutes the tangy odor of the liniment nearly took his breath away. But as her fingers continued their magic, Nick decided breathing was not that important. His eyelids lost their moorings to flutter closed, and soon his muscles began to ease beneath her hands.

Using her sleeve, Sarah wiped the tears that streamed down her face from the strong fumes of the liniment. Never had she encountered such an odious liquid. She had begged the Carlson's head groom for his best, and when the little man had barred her from the tackroom while he mixed the potion, she had had her doubts. But now, judging from the slump of Nick's shoulders, the wicked concoction had done its job well.

She had thought him asleep when his contented sigh broke the silence. "Wherever did you learn to do this?" he questioned as his neck rolled limply on his shoulders.

Sarah replaced the cork on the jug and wiped the moisture from her eyes again. "Does it please you?" She knew only too well that it pleased *her.* His flesh was firm and lean beneath her hands, and the breadth of his shoulders and the depth of his muscles fascinated her. Having grown up among a people who shunned open displays of affection and touched only when necessary, she luxuriated in the opportunity to feel her hands on his bare flesh.

Nick flexed his shoulders and stretched. "I almost feel human again. You are a miracle worker."

She continued to massage the muscles of his right shoulder blade. "It takes only common sense to know that if liniment will soothe the sore muscles on a horse, it should also work on a jackass."

Nick straightened and within a heartbeat had a stunned Sarah sitting captive in his lap. "Jackass, is it now?"

"Mr. Beaumont," she gasped, wiping the odious liquid off her hands. "Let me up this instant."

From the outrage in her voice he might have let her go, but in the lanternlight he had seen the cost of her caring. Her eyes were red and wet with tears from the fumes, yet she had uttered not a word of complaint as she had worked the liniment into his flesh. His heart turned over in his chest, and he knew before the night was out that he had to make her his.

"Put your shirt on," she gasped as he pulled her close. "Your muscles will tighten up again if left uncovered." Sarah struggled against his unyielding grip and strove to keep her voice from betraying her inner turmoil. This morning in the sunlight, she had wanted nothing more than to touch his bare chest. Now, if she but turned her head she could kiss it.

Nick glanced around and saw a second blanket folded neatly to the side. Keeping her firmly in place with one arm, he reached for the blanket and dragged it about his shoulders. The heat from the liniment had penetrated deep, and now it was the growing ache in his loins that demanded attention.

"You've soothed me," he said, his voice low and husky. "It's only fair that I return the favor." His strong fingers began to rub sensuous patterns around her collarbone, touching the bare flesh exposed by Charlotte's daring neckline, and Sarah felt her resistance begin to melt. Then, because it seemed as natural as breathing, when he lowered his head, she raised her lips for his kiss.

At first, his touch was feather-light, brushing against her lips like the dance of a butterfly in search of nectar. And when her lips parted to admit his seeking tongue, Nick thought he might die from the pleasure of it. Wondering if his lust for her would ever be sated, he eased her to the blanket and followed her down with his body. His fingers threaded through the silky softness of her midnight hair while his lips brushed against her fine-boned features — nose, cheek, chin — to sprinkle kisses with abandon. His bare chest moved gently across her breast and the sound of rustling taffeta only enflamed him more.

She made no move to escape from his arms, but instead threaded her own fingers through his hair to pull his lips back to hers, enticing him to take the kiss deeper. Her body arched against his when his knee slipped between her legs, and her sigh of pleasure was swallowed by his kiss.

When his hand reached for the hem of her gown, Nick waited for her protest. None came. Closing his eyes and pressing his lips to the side of her neck, he savored the feel of her silken flesh as his palm traveled up the gentle curve of her leg. Layers of petticoats brushed against his wrist as his hand moved to her inner thigh. He heard her breath stop, even while her heart pounded furiously beneath him. His wide palm rested intimately on the warm, soft core of her femininity. And still, her silence bid him continue.

Nick shuddered with arousal, and scattered kisses about her face and throat. His fingers brushed against her delicate flesh and she turned her face into his neck even as her legs hesitantly moved further apart to grant him access.

Sarah gasped with pleasure as his hand stroked her softly. Ecstasy beckoned, and a consuming pressure began to build within her. She felt his hand move to cover that secret part of her. When she realized exactly how he meant to touch her, her heartbeat doubled from the intimacy of the thought.

Nick felt her tremble beneath him and wondered how such a slight and untutored girl should be able to grant him such pleasure. Raising his head, he gazed down at her in the lanternlight, wanting to capture forever in his mind the pleasure on her face. But in that pause, with satisfaction but a heartbeat away, Sarah opened her eyes and smiled at him.

Nick felt his blood begin to cool. The violet eyes that gazed up at him pleading for release held complete trust. She believed in him to do the right thing. "I have not the strength to tell you no," she had whispered. And as he gazed down at her, he was suddenly consumed by the fear that one night with her might not be enough. Would the act he had contemplated since the first time he laid eyes on her, ever truly be completed or would his mind continue to ache for her even after his body was sated? His heart pounded with want, his body throbbed with need, and Sarah lay beneath him waiting . . . waiting for him to bring a release to the tension he had created within her . . . waiting for his decision. Nick closed his eyes and let his forehead rest against hers, their breaths mingled and in his heart he knew he would never be able to take her if he meant to send her home. His hand slid unsteadily to her knee.

"Did I do something wrong?" The slight tremor in her voice tempted him to throw caution to the wind. But the trust in her eyes brought his sanity racing back. Slowly, he pressed a warm kiss upon her lips, even as his hand was smoothing her skirt back into place.

"Never take a man to a barn at night unless he is your husband," Nick said slowly. "Barns can become very dangerous places." Sitting up, he reached for his shirt and pulled it on over his head. "We should be getting back to the house. You need your sleep, for we've a long day tomorrow."

Sarah sat up and wrapped her arms about her

knees, wondering how she had come so close to touching heaven only to be pulled back to earth with such a bone-jarring fall. "Nick . . ." she hesitated, tasting the sound of his name on her tongue. "What happened?"

What can I tell you? his mind challenged. *Would you still look at me in want if I made you realize how close I came to using you to satisfy my own pleasure without once giving thought to your future?* Nick stood and reached for his jacket.

"You just gave me the best back rub I've ever had." He helped her to stand but avoided her eyes, afraid to see the pain his actions had already caused her. Pain for which he had no remedy. With quick, efficient movements, he folded the horse blankets and tossed them over the wall. The silence between them grew, forcing Nick to turn and watch her slowly brush the wrinkles from her skirt. Frantically, he searched for a way to restore her smile. Then, with an exaggerated bow, he leaned forward and sniffed. "Positively the most unusual scent of the season. Tell me, Miss Townsend, is it a secret family potion or did you have it imported from France?"

Reeling with confusion and the desperate need to cry, Sarah fought back her tears and gratefully accepted his attempt at humor. "I'm not sure what you mean, Mr. Beaumont." She struggled to keep her voice light and carefree. "Isn't this scent, this eau de horse, what all the young ladies are wearing this season?"

Despite her efforts, he heard the unmistakable pain in her voice, and guilt gnawed like a giant rat in his belly. "If I've done the right thing, then damn it why don't I feel good about it?" he muttered.

Sarah turned for the lantern. "I'm sorry, what did you say?"

Nick took the lantern, but when he would have reached for her arm, she carefully sidestepped him and kept her face averted. "We'd better get back to the house," he sighed. "We leave early tomorrow, so you'll want to get a good night's rest."

What I want is a night in your arms, she thought, *and to understand what really happened here.* But the words never left her lips and, side by side yet never touching, the two left the barn to spend the night in turmoil.

The sun had yet to make its presence known when Sarah left the snoring women in her room and tiptoed down the rear stairs to seek solitude in the back gardens. The early-morning air was brisk and she pulled her shawl more firmly about her shoulders as she restlessly paced the garden's meandering paths. Why didn't he want her? she puzzled. First the picnic and now this. True, she had asked him to the barn, but it had been Nick who had pulled her to his lap and started the fires burning.

"Lord," she whispered to the morning stars, "why does this have to be so difficult? Why do I care so much for a man I must leave? And why is it that with but one kiss, he can make me forget all that I am about? I wasn't raised to be wanton, but he looks at me and I burn." Her fingers rubbed at her temples as she tried to clear the confusion from her mind and recapture the serenity she always strove to maintain. In her heart, she knew Nick had made the right decision for them, just as she had asked him to. Why then was she finding it so hard to accept? She watched the first hint of daylight touch the darkness of the night and lifted her face into the breeze that stirred the magnolia blossoms around her. Her silent tears were over, but they'd left a dry, achy lump deep in her heart, and a knot now seemed permanently lodged in her throat.

"You're certainly up early."

Sarah spun about to find Chris leaning beside a gnarled oak tree. Her hand flew to her lips as she gasped in fright.

"I didn't mean to startle you," he said gently, reaching to take her arm and urging her to sit on the nearby bench.

Sarah shook her head and tried to calm the frantic beating of her heart. "I'm sorry," she gasped hoarsely. "I didn't hear you approach."

Chris tipped her chin up with his forefinger and scowled. "Are you all right? Did something happen?"

Sarah jerked away before she could stop herself. "I'm fine." She forced a smile. "I just couldn't sleep."

He sat beside her on the bench and braced his arm on the edge behind her. "I know what you mean. Tell me, does Bertha still snore?"

Sarah's eyes grew wide in amazement. "How do you know that?"

Chris chuckled and leaned closer. "Julie had to share a room with her once when we went to a wedding at the Attwater's. The next morning she told anyone who would listen and most who would not that Bertha Adkins was an elephant who hogged the bed and snored like a damaged brass horn."

Sarah felt the beginnings of a smile and took a grateful breath of the dew-laden air. "Well, since it's not a secret," she confided, "Mrs. Adkins does indeed snore, but I'll not comment as to her resemblance to an animal."

For a moment they sat in comfortable silence, then as the sky began to blossom with streaks of color and the songbirds started their chatter, Chris reached over and took her hand. "Are you anxious to be home?" he questioned.

Sarah felt her nerves begin to tighten again. "I find I miss my family more than I would ever have thought possible."

Chris smiled down at her but refused to release her hand. "I know about the kidnapping, Sarah," he said gently. "Nick told me the afternoon you arrived."

She stared down at her feet and prayed that her tears were indeed over.

He watched her shudder and placed his arm about her slender shoulders. "It's all right. I'll not betray your confidence. But I must admit, after seeing you and Nick together, it truly makes one want to believe in fate."

She turned her questioning eyes to him. "What do you mean?"

Chris shrugged. "I've known Nick for more than twenty years and never have I seen him as happy as he is when he's with you. Then he tells me the circumstances of your meeting and—*voilà!* Fate."

Sarah shook her head and turned back to watch the symphony of colors that now streaked the sky. "I think you are mistaken," she said sadly, thinking of the final moments in the barn and how quickly Nick had rushed her back to her room after. "Mr.

Beaumont has been more than gracious to me, but I return home knowing only too well that he harbors no regret to see the last of me."

"You can't really believe that nonsense. He's in love with you. And if I'm not mistaken, you more than return his feelings."

Sarah felt her tears threaten anew. "You *are* mistaken," she said slowly. "I care for Mr. Beaumont very deeply, but the feelings are not returned. Besides," she straightened on the bench, "it's probably just as well, for I shall be leaving for Salem in but a few more weeks."

"But if you love him, how can you just walk away?" Chris challenged angrily.

Sarah shrugged from his grasp and stood. "I did not say that I loved him. I said I am going home."

"You can't. You and Nick are perfect for each other."

"I must," she said slowly, needing to believe the words. "Our lives are too different. In Salem, women have much to see to. I'm used to hard work and simple pleasures."

Chris wondered as to her point, for his mother was the hardest working person he knew. Did Sarah actually think that people in the South didn't labor long and hard for their bounty?

"I have four baskets of wool waiting for me to return home," she continued. "They need to be carded and spun so I can be ready to weave. Do you know," she paused, "that before coming here, I'd never worn a piece of clothing that was not made by either my mother or myself?"

"Sarah . . ." Chris said with exasperation, "as much I would wish it, clothing doesn't grow on trees here. My mother made the very shirt I am wearing. Wherever did you get such foolish notions?"

"At home I have a garden," she rushed on. "I like the responsibility. I enjoy being able to taste the fruits of my labor. Here in the South, things move at a different speed. I have no chores to claim my time or my talents. I have nothing but leisure time. And even then I don't know what dress I should wear." She gestured sadly. " 'Tis best that I return to the world from which I come."

"This is the silliest thing I have ever heard of," Chris snorted. "You're a guest here. You can't expect the very people who offer you their hospitality to hand you a list of chores to see to. We just don't do things that way."

"Exactly," she said sadly. "Your way is too different from my way."

Chris stood and grasped her shoulders. "And how will Nick survive when you leave and take his heart back to Salem? Do you think he cares a hoot what gown you choose when the mere sight of you makes him light up like a bonfire?"

Sarah felt a spark of hope, then fought it back. "He's said nothing to make me think what you say is true," she stated calmly.

Chris urged her to sit again. "Let me tell you a story," he said gently, "of a little boy who was raised by his grandmother . . ."

When he finished, Sarah's face was again wet with tears. "I just don't understand how parents could be that cruel," she sniffed. "But Mrs. Beaumont loves him, I know that she does."

Chris nodded. "Aye, she does at that. But in the beginning, it was a love with conditions. It depended on how well he bent to her wishes and to

252

what extent he succeeded. Agatha meant well, but she made the same mistake with Nick that she did with his father. She tried to mold him into the husband she lost."

"But Nick isn't anything like his father," Sarah gasped, remembering Agatha's horrible stories of the drunken lout. "Besides, how could you know this if you didn't meet Nick until you went to England?"

"We didn't always live on the plantation," Chris said calmly. "There was a period when my father worked out here with the slaves and my mother and I lived above the King's Tavern. The first time I ever saw Nick we were both in knee pants. His father had passed out on the front steps and Nick was trying to help him home. I don't think I'll ever forget the look on Nick's face when he saw me at the window."

"But you didn't meet again until school?"

Chris nodded. "I recognized him immediately, and he I, but in all these years we've never spoken of it."

"Then why bring it up now?"

Chris reached over and again took her hand. "Because even as close as we are, Nick still keeps a distance between us. He keeps a distance between himself and everyone, including his grandmother. He's too strong-willed to allow himself to become vulnerable again. Yet despite it all, his eyes dance when he turns and looks at you. So something whispers to me from deep inside that you are the person Nick might let in. And . . ." Chris paused to capture her eyes, "I think you love him."

Sarah shook her head and tried to rise, but Chris held tight to her hand.

"We both know that with his financial standing, Nick could crook his finger and get any girl he wanted. But in all the years I've known him, the only time I've ever seen him truly happy has been this time he's spent here with you."

"You're wrong," she gasped, pulling her hands from his. "Dear God, you must be wrong. I can't bear the thought of causing him more pain, but for my own salvation I must go home."

Chris stood, but made no move to touch her. "If you think hard on the matter, Sarah, you'll find that there are very few things in life that you *must* do." He paused. "Many that you choose to do, but few that you really must do." Then, turning, Chris walked quickly down the path toward the house.

Sarah sat back down on the brick bench and tried to gather her thoughts. If Chris spoke the truth, then why had Nick refused her last night? Did he not realize she was willing? Her face flamed with the memory of his touch. Never had she allowed a man such liberties with her body. Even the thoughts of his hand on her flesh brought goosebumps to the surface.

Sarah rubbed her arms briskly. "This is becoming too complicated, Lord," she whispered. "I feel like I've joined a game the rules of which I do not know." As her steps carried her slowly back to the house, Sarah offered a prayer that begged for guidance.

Chapter Eighteen

The sun had almost completed its downward path before the carriage turned onto the tree-lined road that led to the Beaumont estate. Having endured six hours of bone-jarring torture in stormy silence, Sarah was weary beyond belief. She had played Christopher's words over and over in her mind, but they just didn't fit the proud, intimidating man who sat before her. Now as the carriage pulled to a stop, she wanted nothing more than to find her bed. But as she thought of Agatha, anxiously awaiting their arrival, she knew her bid for sleep would have to wait.

Her composure was firmly in place when Nick took her arm to help her from the carriage.

"Sarah . . ."

She stopped more from the tone in his voice than the pressure on her arm.

"You were right last night." He gazed down at her, his eyes dark. "Sometimes I am a complete jackass."

She knew he waited for her smile, but her pain was still too fresh and her smile wouldn't come. "Yes, you are. But stay," she said softly. "Mrs. Beaumont will be waiting for us. Why don't you come in for a few minutes and share a cup."

Nick felt her rejection more keenly than he would ever have thought possible. Had he been noble only to lose her completely? *But you're sending her home,* his mind argued. *You never really had her in the first place.* His hand tightened on her arm. "I am sorry."

"I am, too." Her eyes mirrored her regret. "Let's go find your grandmother. She's probably been driving Luther mad these last days."

Deciding she couldn't hate him more than she already did, Nick pulled her close and hugged her shoulders to his side. "Jackass, is it?"

"Yes, Mr. Beaumont. And I'm sure your grandmother would agree."

For the briefest moment, a worried look crossed his face. Surely she wasn't planning on telling Gran about their disaster in the barn.

She punched his arm and laughed out loud. "Jackass," she declared firmly, smiling up at him for the first time that day as they entered the house.

"Well, you two certainly took your own sweet time in coming!"

Nick turned to Sarah and shook his head. "Some things never change," he whispered.

But to Sarah, things had changed and not for the better. At first she thought the candles not bright enough, for Agatha had no color in her pale cheeks. Then, as she approached the bed, she felt her anxiety grow. Never had she seen Agatha look so frail: She sat propped against the pillows, new lines ringing her eyes and mouth. Sarah could hardly believe the transformation. It was as if the

256

woman was wasting away before her very eyes. She turned to Nick, but he had already moved to sit on the bed beside her.

"So how are you, Gran? I was hoping to see you up and in your chair."

Agatha shrugged her thin shoulders. "My arm's been aching. Besides, with you and Sarah gone, there was nothing to get up for. Now tell me, how was the wedding? Did you give my best to Mrs. Carlson and that rascal husband of hers?"

Nick turned to Sarah. "Gran is especially fond of Mr. Carlson because of his outrageous behavior. He flirts with her constantly."

Agatha snorted at the expression on Sarah's face. "Oh, don't worry," she said, rolling her eyes. "We never did anything. Not that the man didn't invite me down to the barn a time or two."

Nick had the grace to cough and Sarah blushed, but Agatha's once-sharp eyes never noticed. "I don't think I ever had as much fun as that summer in '74. Do you remember that, Nicky?" she questioned. "The time right after you and Chris finished school."

Nick smiled and nodded. "If I remember correctly, you enjoyed yourself because you and Mrs. Carlson played whist for twenty-four hours straight."

"Ah, those were the days," Agatha sighed. "Tell me, did they set up a room for gaming this time?"

"Three rooms," Sarah stated primly, her voice full of censure.

Nick looked from Sarah's stiff form back to his grandmother. "I don't think Sarah quite approved."

"Bah," Agatha waved a hand. "There's no sin in

a good game of whist. Now, dice—that's another thing entirely."

Nick's rich laughter filled the room. "That's because you always lose at dice," he chuckled. He turned to see Sarah leaning wearily against the bedpost. "Gran . . ." he bent to kiss her cheek. "I'm going to leave now. Sarah is exhausted and you look like you could use some rest as well."

Agatha sighed. As much as she hated to see him go, she was tired, and lately it was becoming more difficult to catch her breath. But now that she knew they were home, maybe she'd sleep better. "You'll come for breakfast tomorrow," she stated firmly, giving him a look that dared contradiction.

Nick shook his head. "I've been away for three days, and I'll need to be at the docks all the earlier. I'll stop by on my return, but it might be late."

Agatha huffed. "When are you ever going to come when I want you to?" she challenged.

Nick dropped a kiss on her snowy white head. "Maybe when you ask instead of giving me a command." He rose to go, and Sarah straightened.

"I'll see Mr. Beaumont to the door and be right back," she said softly.

"He knows where the door is," Agatha snapped, "and I want to hear all the gossip from the wedding."

"I'll only be a moment." Sarah smiled, then, turning, she left the room with Nick, pulling him away from Agatha's door. "I think you should call the doctor. She looks terrible."

Nick's smile was full of compassion, and he gently patted her hand. "I do see that," he said, "but it's not really that bad."

"Not really that bad!" Sarah gasped in a hushed whisper. "How can you say that? Luther said she's been off her food. Can you not see how poorly she's become. She practically emaciated."

"What I meant was I understand your surprise." Nick took her hand. "The first time I had to make a trip after Gran took ill, I returned to find her at death's door, or so I thought. The household was in an uproar. Gran hadn't eaten since I left, they told me. Well I went to the cookhouse to have a talk with Mrs. Hempsted to see what she could prepare to tempt Gran's appetite. Only I found Mrs. Hempsted in a tizzy because someone was stealing food. Gran walked with a cane then and it didn't take much work to find that the old faker had been refusing the meals in her room and then sneaking into her own cookhouse by night and raiding the larder.

"But now she can't even leave her bed without assistance."

Nick smiled. "And can you really be that sure that she hasn't bribed a maid to bring her a snack? A coin here or there will buy you almost anything, including silence."

Sarah shook her head, not ready to give in. "But she looks so . . ."

"Old?" Nick said quietly.

"Yes!" she gasped. "I don't remember her looking so fragile, and we've only been gone three days."

Again Nick nodded. "In the beginning, each time I went away for a few days, I was startled at her appearance when I returned. How could a person age before my eyes, I would think."

"That's it exactly."

"Then as the months turned to years, I began to realize that that was how Gran really looked. The longer you're around her, her fiery temper and wicked disposition make you forget that, beneath it all, she's still an old woman. So to return home and see her thus was indeed a shock. Trust me, by tomorrow, you'll think she's improved, and within a few days she'll seem just like always."

Sarah's brow wrinkled with thought. "You might be right, but I'm still not sure. I think I'll keep a close watch anyway."

Before she could object, Nick raised her hand and placed a kiss on her palm. "Thank you for caring about her," he whispered as he closed her hand around the kiss. "I'll be back late tomorrow. You try to get some rest and don't let Gran run you ragged."

Sarah smiled and clenched her fist tighter. "Until tomorrow," she whispered to his retreating back.

"So . . ." Agatha challenged when Sarah entered her room. "Did you get him to kiss you good-bye?"

Sarah held her fist tight and slipped it into the deep pocket of her skirt. "Now, Mrs. Beaumont," she chastised, "what ever would make you think that?"

Agatha chuckled. "Just because my legs don't work, don't be foolish enough to think my mind doesn't. I can see the way Nicky looks at you. Now tell me, what did you think of Julie?"

Sarah perched on the corner of the bed and leaned her back gratefully against the bedpost. "She was lovely. Her gown was the most delicate shade of pink and covered with lace and beads.

260

She sparkled like a jewel every time she made a move. But her wig . . ." Sarah's eyes grew wide from the memory. "Mrs. Beaumont, never in all my life have I seen such a creation. It was nearly this tall." She gestured with her hands above her head. "It was pure white and decorated with pearls and the tiniest pink ribbons. All in all it was quite beautiful."

"But . . ." Agatha prompted as her eyes began to sparkle.

Sarah gave a tired sigh. "I can't imagine how she managed to walk around all day with such a huge thing on her head. If you ask my opinion," she glanced over her shoulder as if assuring their privacy, "I think it would have done better as a centerpiece."

Agatha chuckled and clapped her gnarled hands together. "That child always was spoiled rotten. Was she up to mischief as usual?"

Already feeling guilty for her comment on the wig, Sarah could bring herself to say no more. Carefully she smoothed her skirt and folded her hands. "She made a beautiful bride."

Agatha winced from the sudden twinge in her arm. "Damn these old bones," she swore. "Did you get to meet Marigold?"

Sarah's brow wrinkled in thought as she tried to remember all the names and faces of the past two days. "I don't think so. Did you expect her to be there?"

Agatha snorted. "Wherever my Nicky goes, you can just bet that Marigold Thurmont will be there, sniffing at his heels."

Sarah shook her head. "I'm sure I would have remembered a name as lovely as Marigold."

"Bah," Agatha sneezed loudly. "Lovely isn't the word for it. Marigold has hair the color of mud and a voice that's just as pleasant."

Sarah smiled despite herself. "No, I don't remember seeing any mud, on the ground or otherwise."

"Good." Agatha folded her hands on the coverlet. "Maybe her parents have finally pounded some sense in her head. Now, tell me, what did people think of your new dress?"

Sarah stretched and tried to settle more comfortably. "Thanks to you, I was a complete success. I actually lost count of how many asked me where it came from."

"And what did you say?"

Sarah smiled and suppressed a yawn. "Why, I told them it had been designed by Madame Rousseau, the best dressmaker in town."

Agatha's pale eyes began to sparkle. "You know, I think if I play my cards right, I might make a profit at this after all." She grinned at Sarah's confused expression. "I made Charlotte promise me a slight commission from any referrals that came from that dress. It cost a fortune, so it's the least she could do."

Sarah's eyes grew wide. "You are terrible," she chuckled, wondering why she had ever imagined Agatha to be failing. The woman might be old, but she was still sharper than a tack.

"Not terrible," Agatha's expression was smug. "Just a clever businesswoman."

"Speaking of business . . ." Sarah sat up straighter. "I have some to attend to myself. I

262

promised Madame Rousseau that I would bring Catherine to meet her."

"Catherine who?" Agatha demanded with a frown. "I know no Catherine."

"Catherine Richardson," Sarah said slowly, removing her brooch. "She made this." She placed the brooch in Agatha's palm. "Look at how delicate the stitches are. Isn't she talented?"

" 'Tis indeed good work." Agatha examined the piece closely. "I wouldn't mind having one myself. Is she going to sell these to Charlotte?"

"I really couldn't say." Sarah tucked the brooch back into her pocket. "Catherine and her family live near the end of the south road. They are in desperate want of common necessities, and if Catherine could get employment with Madame Rousseau, her family would benefit greatly."

"And what is your profit in this arrangement?" Agatha challenged.

Sarah's eyes filled with surprise. "Why, nothing."

Agatha shook her head. "Sarah, Sarah, Sarah," she said slowly. "When are you ever going to learn? There is always a profit to be made. The trick is to find out how to make it yours."

Sarah looked confused. "But why should I expect a profit from Catherine's labor? I'm not doing any of the work."

"No, but you *are* presenting her with the opportunity, are you not?" Sarah nodded slowly. "Then you should be compensated."

"But I'm not even sure that things will work out."

Agatha gestured toward the brooch. "Charlotte is a businesswoman even if you are not. She'll not be

263

so foolish as to turn down the fingers that hold this talent."

Sarah clapped her hands together. "I do hope you are right. But I must ask a favor of you."

Agatha's eyes rounded with surprise, for in all the weeks Sarah had been with her, never once had she asked for a thing. "What do you need?"

"I would like to borrow a few pounds." She spoke quickly as her enthusiasm grew. "I would return it to you as soon as I reach home."

Agatha waved her hand. "That's not the point. What do you need it for?"

Sarah edged closer on the bed. "If someone came to you seeking employment and their clothes spoke of desperate circumstances, you would hire them. But you would feel as if you were doing them a favor, so any wage offered would seem grand."

Agatha nodded silently.

"But if the same person came to you with skills you could use and looked as if they didn't need your employment, you might be tempted to offer more to entice them to work for you, am I not correct?"

A slow smile crossed Agatha's wrinkled face. "And this little Catherine you spoke of, her circumstances are that desperate?"

Sarah shuddered. "I don't know how the family is managing to make ends meet."

"And you wish to buy her a new frock for when she meets Charlotte so she'll be offered higher wages." Sarah nodded and Agatha cackled in glee. "After all that Charlotte has done for you, you'd do that to her?"

Sarah looked down and smiled. "Did you not say that business is business?"

Agatha's cackle turned to a full belly laugh that brought tears to her eyes. "My dear, I think I might have underestimated you."

Catherine, who had hardly spoken at all all morning, now chatted like a magpie as they reached the broken gate to her yard.

"Ma, Jimmy, come quick," she cried with excitement. And before she and Sarah could enter, Gracie Richardson, with baby Jessie on her hip and Jimmy at her side, came tumbling out of the shack. "I gotta job," Catherine shouted to the sky before reaching to give her mother and sister a fierce hug. "I'm gonna start tomorrow. Can you believe it? She thinks I have talent. She's gonna let me start with hems and then I get to work up to inside seams, and soon she promised she'd teach me to do the fancy beadwork. I just can't believe it." Catherine reached for Jimmy and swung him around in a circle.

Gracie turned to Sarah with eyes wide. "Is this true? It really worked out like you said?"

Sarah, who had not stopped smiling since they had left the shop, nodded with pleasure. "Madame Rousseau asked Catherine to do a seam for her while we waited and then she asked her to stitch a flower. You should have seen her, Gracie," Sarah beamed with pride. "Madame said she had never seen such straight stitching from one so young. She is willing to let Catherine work with her and learn the trade."

265

"Catherine ain't gonna have to move there, is she?" Jimmy questioned.

"No," Sarah said smiling. "I know in most apprenticeships that is common, but Catherine may come home each evening. That way she can still lend a hand here."

"And she's gonna really make money?" Jimmy's eyes were now wide with the same excitement as his sister's.

Sarah named an amount that made Gracie stagger and almost drop Jessie. "They want to pay her that much?"

"You should have heard Miss Sarah, Ma, she was wonderful."

Sarah blushed. "I just pointed out to Madame Rousseau that since she usually has to house and shelter the apprentices she takes in, it would be only fair to apply at least part of that money to Catherine's wage since she would be coming home at night."

"I just can't believe it." Gracie felt the tears on her cheeks but could do nothing to stop them.

"Now stop that," Sarah commanded softly. "We still have more business to discuss."

"We do?" Gracie sniffed, wiping her nose on her sleeve and setting the baby down.

"Yes. I would like to make you a proposition," Sarah said. "I have arranged to extend you a line of credit in Mr. Wilkins's store. Catherine will need at least another skirt and apron like the one we purchased this morning. Also, it will be a full month before Madame will pay Catherine anything. So if you need to make any other purchases, Mr. Wilkins will run a tab. Catherine will pay him one shilling each month starting two months from now until the account is free and clear. Does this sound agreeable to you?"

Again Gracie could only nod her head as tears coursed down her cheeks.

"Does this mean I can get a peppermint stick, Ma?" Jimmy asked excitedly.

Gracie looked to Sarah with questioning eyes. "I would think that a peppermint stick every two weeks as payment for keeping the garden clear of weeds should be a fee that your mother and sister could agree to."

"Whoooeeeee." Jimmy hopped and danced around, then stopped suddenly. "Hey, Miss Sarah, do you think you could find a job for me, too? he asked. "You know, one where they would pay me with real money."

Sarah smiled. "I'll see what I can do, but for now I think your mother could really use your help around here."

Gracie looked at the shack and then back to Sarah. "Mr. Wilkins will really extend credit?"

"Ma . . ." Catherine grabbed her mother's hands with excitement. "What if we were to get a bucket of paint and maybe a few nails?"

"I'm real good with nails," Jimmy piped in.

"We could . . . Hey, who's that?"

The group turned to see Ruby clutching her heart and running down the road as fast as her thick legs would carry her.

"Miz Sarah," she cried, gasping for breath. "Miz Sarah, you gotta come quick." The maid stopped and almost doubled over from the pain in her side. "It's Mrs. Beaumont," she gasped. "I think she's *re-*

ally dying this time and she didn't even write no note."

"Dear God." Sarah grasped the woman's hands and tried to calm her. "What happened, Ruby? Where is Luther? Did he go to fetch Mr. Beaumont?"

Ruby shook her head and struggled for air. "Luther had to go down to Jamestown this morning. He's not gonna be back till supper."

"Did you send anyone to fetch Mr. Beaumont?" Sarah tried to keep the panic from her voice as she watched Ruby nod her head.

"Oscar took the wagon. But Miz Sarah, Oscar, he don't know the docks like Luther does and I don't know if he's even gonna be able to find Master Nick." Tears ran freely down the woman's face.

"Catherine, run in the house and fetch Miss Ruby some cider," Gracie said, shifting anxiously from foot to foot, not knowing how to help.

"Did you send for the doctor?" Sarah questioned.

Ruby shook her head as her hands twisted her skirt in distress. "Mrs. Beaumont, she said no doctors. She said she just wanted you and Master Nick. Miz Sarah, we didn't know what to do. I ran to the dressmaker shop and then all the way here. Mrs. Beaumont, she ain't never been so bad before." Ruby gratefully accepted the cup of cider and took a gulp.

Sarah turned to Jimmy. "Can you run fast?"

"I sure can." His chest popped with pride. "You just watch me."

"Then I want you to run to the doctor's as fast as you can. Tell him to get over to Mrs. Beaumont's."

"Yes ma'am." Jimmy saluted, then was off like a shot.

"Ruby, you stay here until you catch your breath. Gracie, get Catherine to the store for the things she'll need for tomorrow. Mr. Wilkins is expecting you. I'll see you again as soon as I can." Turning, Sarah hiked her skirt past her knees and ran down the lane as if the devil himself were chasing her.

It seemed like a lifetime before she reached Agatha's front steps, and Tanzy yanked the door open before Sarah's hand even touched the knob. "Thank God you're back Miss Sarah. Miss Agatha is so sick."

"Who is with her?" Sarah took a deep breath and started up the stairs, Tanzy close on her heels.

"Why, no one would dare go in without Miss Agatha's permission," she whined. "It's just so awful."

Sarah bit back the reply about common sense that rested on her tongue. "Fetch me hot and cold water, a basin, and some clean cloths," she snapped, "and get them now." Tanzy nodded and scurried back down the stairs.

Taking only a second to calm her breathing, Sarah turned the knob and entered the room where the feared Agatha Beaumont lay all alone and dying. She found Agatha flat on her back, struggling for breath, and nearly blue from the effort.

"It's going to be all right," she soothed, gathering the old woman in her arms and gently easing her into a sitting position. "Just be calm. You're not alone anymore. I'm here now."

Agatha's gnarled hand clamped onto Sarah's arm

like a claw. "Sarah?" she gasped.

"Don't try to talk. Just concentrate on breathing deep, easy breaths." With a firm hand, she kept Agatha's shoulders braced and began to rub with a slow, steady motion on the woman's back. As Agatha's breathing eased slightly, Sarah let her relax back against the pillows that she had propped into place. "You'll breathe better if you're not flat." She struggled to keep her voice calm, for Agatha was clearly terrified. "Just relax and take slow, even breaths."

Tanzy knocked timidly and entered with a tray and a steaming kettle. "Tanzy . . ." Sarah's voice was soft and even, "when the doctor arrives, be sure to bring him right up."

"No doctor," Agatha pleaded with a pitiful cry.

"There, there." Sarah took Agatha's hands within her own. I'm not going to leave you, but you must try to stay calm." She turned back to find Tanzy beside the bed, her eyes wide in horror. If Agatha hadn't known she was sick, one look on the maid's face would have placed her six feet under. "Set down the tray and then you may go," she said firmly, giving the girl a threatening stare. "And close the door behind you."

Sarah sat quietly and watched Agatha's eyes flutter open. "Can you tell me what happened?" she asked gently, taking a damp cloth and wiping the perspiration from the woman's face. "Are you in pain?"

Agatha nodded. "The worst seems to be over now," she wheezed. "But when it happened, it felt like some giant fist was trying to rip my heart from my chest." Tears began to gather and Sarah blotted

270

them gently with the cool cloth.

"Sarah, I'm so afraid of dying." Her tears came faster and Sarah could only blink back her own. "I'm going to die and Nick isn't going to come in time."

"Hush," Sarah scolded. "You're alive now and shall stay that way until Nick arrives."

Regretfully, Agatha shook her head back and forth on the pillow. "He won't, you know." Her voice was frail and haggard and her eyes drifted closed. "But the fault is my own. I've sent for him so many times when naught was amiss that now he'll not know the difference."

"Oscar will find him," Sarah promised desperately. "Agatha, open your eyes and look at me." She counted the heartbeats until Agatha's eyes opened again. "I want you to look at me. I've never lied to you and I know that if we both have faith, Nick will get here in time."

Agatha blinked and for an instant her eyes grew clearer. "Sarah?" she questioned.

"I'm right here." Sarah pressed gently on the woman's hands. "I'll not leave you."

Agatha struggled to sit a little straighter. "Why, you're different. Why did I never notice that before?"

"Just hold my hands and hang on for Nick."

Agatha smiled and felt a gentle peace seep into her aging bones. "It's all right," she whispered hoarsely, "I don't seem to be afraid anymore. Do you know how much you look like my little sister, Helena." She gave Sarah a quizzical look. "You do, you know."

Sarah struggled to keep her tears at bay. "Agatha, you have to stay for Nick."

Agatha eyes began to flutter. "Never going to forgive himself for not being here." She struggled to keep her eyes open. "Promise me you'll help him. Take his pain like you took my fear," she gasped.

Sarah swallowed hard against the knot in her throat. "Please just hold on."

"No," Agatha's voice grew stronger. "It's my time. But I can't go if Nicky . . . if Nicky suffers. Promise me you'll be with him tonight. Promise you'll give him comfort."

Sarah nodded, unable to see for the tears in her eyes.

"Good, pull the pillows away . . . lay me flat."

"But you can't breathe that way." Sarah sniffed, praying that any minute she'd hear the front door open and Nick's steps flying up the stairs.

"Won't die sitting up," Agatha said firmly. "Spare you the horror of breaking my bones."

Sarah struggled to stay calm. "Darling, no one is going to break any of your bones, but you have to sit up to breathe."

Agatha weakly shook her head. "When Hallie died . . . she froze in place. Doctor couldn't get . . . her body to straighten . . . had to break her bones." Agatha shuddered from the memory. "Hardest thing . . . I ever did. Let me . . . spare you that."

"Agatha, please."

"My time . . . Sarah." Agatha's voice was the barest whisper, but her thin lips smiled. "You . . . you know . . . better than I . . ."

"Agatha, think of Nick, please, just a few minutes more."

Agatha's eyes brightened. "Nick has you now. . . . Please, Sarah . . . Hallie needs me. Don't . . . make me wait . . . Let me go home."

With tear-filled eyes and hands that trembled, Sarah eased the pillows from beneath Agatha's frail head. She watched the woman heave a great sigh as if a giant burden had been lifted.

"Remember . . . promise to Nick," she whispered. "Oh, Sarah . . . look . . ." Her voice grew weaker. "There's . . . my darling . . . Roger."

Sarah watched Agatha's eyes flutter closed on the name of her husband and knew she had truly started her journey home.

Chapter Nineteen

Numb with grief, Sarah slipped to the side of the bed to offer a prayer for the swift delivery of Agatha's soul into heaven. Then, still clutching the gnarled fingers, she pressed her face against the coverlet and wept.

Her tears were nearly spent when she heard the front door open. Pulling swiftly to her feet, she met Nick at the head of the stairs.

"Is she . . ." Nick never said the word; the tears that streaked Sarah's face were his answer. Turning, he flopped down to sit on the top step. "How long?"

Dropping to her knees behind him, Sarah hesitated only a heartbeat before wrapping her arms about his shoulders. Pain radiated from his body, but in that pain she found her strength, and her voice was steady when she spoke.

"She had an easy passing."

Nick shuddered within her arms. "I should have been here."

Sarah pressed her cheek against his shoulder. "You were here to bring joy to her life, and you did," she said slowly, searching for words that might grant him comfort. "In her last minutes, she had nothing but praise for the love you gifted her. And although she would have given anything to have seen you one last time, had it been in her power to do so, she would not have exchanged a lifetime of happiness for a final word of parting. You gave her too many special memories and she cherished them deeply."

"Was she in pain?" His voice was hoarse, and for the first time in her life, Sarah Townsend willfully told a lie.

"No . . . she wasn't. I think she was more annoyed that the time couldn't be of her choosing."

Nick gave a painful chuckle. "That sounds like Gran. She'd thumb her nose at the devil himself."

"Nick . . ." Sarah hesitated and then pressed on. "At the very end she seemed more than relieved to be going. It was almost as if she was excited. I think she saw her husband, for she smiled and spoke his name with her last breath."

Nick shuddered again and then straightened and took a deep, cleansing breath. "She loved Roger very much. When I was little, she'd sit me on her lap and tell the most outrageous stories. Grandfather was always the hero. He could command a ship, win at cards, deal in business—there was nothing that he couldn't do."

Sarah smiled against his back. "He sounds just like you."

Nick shook his head. "I always thought it unfair that he was taken from her so early in life," he sighed. "Gran lost so many people who were dear to her."

"She had you to love her, Nick," Sarah said gently. "Some go through their entire life and never have that."

Nick eased out of her arms and stood unsteadily on the step for a moment. His knuckles were white where he gripped the banister, and Sarah was startled to see how much color had drained from his face when he turned to her.

"I shall always harbor the wish to have been with her at the end," he said quietly. "But since I wasn't, I can only take comfort that she was not alone. She probably never spoke of it, but I know for a fact that during these past weeks Gran had grown to love you very much."

Sarah felt her own tears threaten anew and fought them back. "Thank you," she whispered. "She was a truly extraordinary person."

Nick wiped his hand across his face, erasing the last of his weakness. "And now, I need to say good-bye."

Sarah nodded and stepped aside, but as Nick reached his grandmother's door, he hesitated. "Would you come with me?"

In that moment, Sarah saw the vulnerable young boy Chris had spoken of, and knew she would have walked over hot coals if he had asked. She reached for his hand and led him into the room where Agatha Beaumont had once reigned supreme.

Sarah would forever be amazed at the hours that followed Agatha's death, for as news spread, it was as if the town itself had been cast into mourning. Shops closed and business in Middle Plantation came to a standstill.

Ezra Hawkins, the cabinetmaker, had been the first to arrive and he carried a fine coffin of cedar in the back of his wagon. "For a final thank you to Mrs. Beaumont," he said solemnly. But when Nick offered payment, the man heartily refused. "Long time back, my shop was damaged bad in a fire. Mrs. Beaumont was a spry young filly then. Showed up on my doorstep one morning and handed me the money to get back on my feet again. She let me repay the principal, but she wouldn't take no interest, said neighbors owed each other and that was that. Then she made me swear on all things holy not to tell a soul what she did. Well, I kept my promise these past twenty-seven years, but I also made a promise to myself that day." Hawkins had watched with hat in hand and tears in his eyes as Luther and Oscar unloaded his gift. Then, without another word, the man climbed into his wagon and pulled away.

Charlotte Rousseau and Gracie Richardson had arrived next. They chatted together easily as Charlotte fashioned a pillow for the casket from some of her finest satin and Gracie stitched black bands of mourning onto shirtsleeves. No one seemed to care that one dressed in the height of fashion and the other didn't.

And so the afternoon continued. Walter Johnson arrived to affix ornate silver fasteners on the coffin and he, too, refused payment, leaving Nick to stand in wonder about the unknown generosity of the woman he had called Gran. She had touched so many lives, yet she had made each promise secrecy. *Why,* he wondered, *did you not share this with me?*

Black wreaths appeared on the front door, and food began to arrive with each tick of the clock. By the time the sun had set, Agatha rested in the parlor like a queen in her casket, and three more

277

tables had been added to the dining room to hold all the cakes, custard tarts, and fancy jellies brought by neighbors.

The hands of the clock edged past midnight as Sarah extinguished the last candle and slowly made her way up the darkened staircase. Less than an hour before, an exhausted Nick had retired to the room he had occupied as a boy, and Sarah couldn't help but wonder what thoughts filled his mind as the night settled in around them. Agatha's words echoed over and over in her heart. *He'll never forgive himself for not being here . . . promise me you'll take his pain . . . promise me you'll stay with him tonight.*

Oh, Agatha, she thought, entering her chambers and securing the door behind her, *do you have any idea what you ask of me?* But even as her mind spun with confusion, her hands were removing her lace cap and reaching for the pins that held her hair.

Lost in thought, Nick rested in bed and watched the moonlight filter through his opened window. Toy soldiers lined the top of his desk, but tonight their imagined battles were far from his mind.

"Why did you never tell me, Gran?" he challenged the silence of the room, for in truth he still could feel her presence. "Did you think me incapable of keeping your secret? Did you think I would find fault with the fact that you cared for our neighbors, that you were willing to share your wealth? Did you think I would beg you to save it for me?" A silent tear escaped to trace down his lean cheek. "We were supposed to be so close, yet you never spoke a word of it." Nick felt the achy lump in his chest begin to swell and he swallowed hard. "And damn it, why didn't you wait to tell me good-bye? Why didn't I come early today like you asked?"

"Because regardless of our wants, it was not meant to be."

Nick jerked upright on the bed and turned to see a shadowy figure standing in the doorway. "Sarah?" His voice was hesitant. "What are you doing here?"

He heard the latch slip into place, then watched as she glided across the room to stand in the glow of the moonlight. He could see the gentle curve of her hip through the thin fabric of her nightrail and briefly he wondered if his grief was causing him to hallucinate.

"Please don't send me away." Her voice trembled but from what, he knew not. "I learned an important lesson today, and I would share it with you."

Nick drew his knees up under the sheet and rested his arms on them. "Sarah, you shouldn't be here. Go back to your own room. We can talk of this in the morning."

Her fingers shook as she reached for the bow at the throat of her gown, for even in her dreams she had never gone this far. Her nerves stretched to the limit. Would she have to undress completely? She had no experience on which to draw, and as her trembling increased, only a deep unrelenting need to be with him kept her from fleeing. "Please let me stay." She hesitated, then took a step closer. "I've been alone for such a long time. Please don't make me be alone tonight."

Nick watched in amazement as his hand reached for her. He hadn't meant to do that. He had wanted her to go back to her own room where she

279

would be safe, but his hand closed around hers and all sanity fled. Gently, purposefully, he pulled her the last remaining step to the bed. Her hand touched his wrist when he reached for the ribbon around her throat, but it did not bid him cease. Instead, her fingertips caressed the sensitive flesh of his inner arm, and Nick felt his heart beat all the harder.

Her forehead touched his, their breath mingled, and his hands glided up her rib cage to close over her breast. Through the thin fabric of her gown he felt her nipples harden against his palms as he gently aroused her. Silently, he wished she would make him stop, desperately he prayed she'd let him continue. He felt her frantic heartbeat and his arms slipped around her to pull her close, wanting to reassure and comfort, needing to possess. He leaned back, and Sarah tumbled with him onto the bed.

Their lips met, desperate, hot, seeking. Then her gown was gone and the sheet pulled aside. Each gasped as flesh seared flesh.

"Let me stay with you tonight," she whispered against his throat, loving the feel of his skin beneath her fingers. "Please let me stay."

The sound of her plea raced along his skin, tantalizing, enticing, beckoning, and his need to possess her increased tenfold. "The devil himself couldn't take you from this bed tonight," he breathed against her lips. "Tonight you're mine."

The devil himself might have put me here, she thought. Then Nick's lips closed over her breast and all reasoning was gone. A fire started deep within her and its flames reached outward sensitizing every inch of her flesh. His lips tugged at her nipple even as his hand traced back to that secret place it had touched but once before.

This time there was no hesitation, and when his seeking fingers entered to caress, Sarah arched in pleasure sweeter than she had ever imagined.

Go slowly, his brain cautioned again and again. *Go slowly.* But her hands were touching, her legs caressing, and when the heel of her foot journeyed up the back of his calf, Nick could wait no longer. She was tight and hot and unbelievably wonderful as her flesh resisted, then stretched to admit him. Fearing he'd crush her with his weight, his hands braced against the bed, levering his chest from hers as he pressed deeper and deeper into the heart of her. Her body closed around him. Somewhere in his brain he knew he must be hurting her, but she offered no protest and even tried to move with him. Her futile efforts were his undoing.

Sarah gasped in pain as his body invaded hers— white-hot pain that robbed her joy and obliterated her pleasure. She tried to move to relieve the pressure, but each motion only planted him deeper, and, finally, fighting tears, she bit her lip and prayed that it would be soon be over.

Nick gathered her close and tried to bring her pleasure, but his own needs refused to be placed aside and, holding her tightly to his body, he lost himself within her and collapsed.

Boneless with exhaustion, Nick wondered if he'd ever find the words that might describe his feelings for her at that moment. She had given him a touch of heaven and erased the burning ache that had lodged deep within his chest. But his eyes refused to open, even though his greatest wish was to see her face. "I'm sorry . . . Sarah." His words were hot against her skin. "It w-went . . . too fast. Next time . . ."

Sarah's limp arm reached up to touch the quivering muscles of his back. "Hush," she whispered softly. "Sleep now."

Nick mumbled something against her throat, but his thoughts remained a mystery, for within seconds his deep, even breathing told her he slept.

She let her tears come then: silent tears of mourning for the loss of Agatha, bitter tears of disappointment for what they had shared. Her head ached and her body still throbbed from the turbulence of his possession. Was it possible that without the bonds of marriage there could be no pleasure, she wondered?

Gently, so as not to wake him, Sarah eased herself from beneath him. Nick mumbled again and stretched languidly, pulling the pillow close. For just a moment, she allowed herself the luxury of gazing upon his lean, muscular body—the broad back that tapered to his narrow waist, his firm buttocks, and those endless legs. Gooseflesh ran up her arms, and despite the warm night air, she shivered. Quickly, she located her discarded gown and pulled it on.

"I wish it could have been different," she whispered to his sleeping form. "For I love you with all my heart." She untangled the sheet and carefully flipped it over him. "But you don't love me, and somehow I must learn to face that fact."

Sarah rose with the sun, her aching muscles a silent reminder of the night before. Sleep had not been hers after leaving Nick, and for hours she had tossed and turned on her bed, struggling with emotions that would grant her no peace.

How could you have fallen in love with a man who only wishes carnal knowledge of you? her mind challenged. *He does care for me,* her heart would reply. *He's kind and gentle and he took me into his home . . . But he's never said he loves you,* her conscience taunted. *Well, I've never said it, either.* Over and over her mind argued with her heart until Sarah could stand no more. Wearily, she dressed, knowing there was no hope of rest and that the day would be more than full. The household was just coming to life when she tiptoed down the hall, taking great satisfaction that the door to Nick's room was still closed. Instinctively, she knew he still slept and her step grew lighter.

Downstairs, Sarah went directly into the parlor where Agatha rested and reslanted the wooden blinds. She lit the candles that surrounded the casket, then, reaching over, carefully removed the netting that had draped the casket for the night. Gently she smoothed the satin blanket that covered Agatha's legs and feet.

"I'm not repentant for last night," she whispered to the still form. "I know to lie with a man outside the bonds of marriage is a sin, but I feel no remorse." Sarah looked down at her shoes. "I can't ask for forgiveness knowing the choice was mine and willingly made." Her eyes looked up to the lifeless form that rested before her. "I know how much you loved Nick. You even took me into your home to protect his reputation. But last night he needed me, we needed each other."

For a moment she stood in silence, fighting the knot of tears that lodged in her throat. "If I stay, I can only offer temptation for that which is not holy." Her soft voice quivered in pain as she gazed about the parlor with its dark-blue walls and brocade draperies, then back to the coffin. "My heart will remain in Virginia, but I'll leave your grandson free to make a good marriage without a hint of scandal to mar his name." Sarah touched Agatha's cold hand in a final good-bye then slipped a small brooch into the pocket of Agatha's gown. "This is very dear to me," she whispered. "Catherine made it for me and 'tis the only thing I possess that has not come from you or Nick." Taking a shaky step, she moved back from the casket. "When I'm home and memories of this misadventure grow dim with age, know that in my heart, I shall never forget you."

The day moved slowly. Neighbors and friends began arriving hours before noon and soon the house was filled with people. Sarah busied herself helping Luther at the door, greeting those who came to offer condolences as well as those who came only for a look inside the grand Beaumont house. Food was consumed at an alarming speed, and by midafternoon Sarah was grateful for the abundance that had been prepared the day before. She monitored the dining room and kept Tanzy and Ruby busy with constant trips to the cookhouse.

Nick kept vigil by the parlor door doing his best to console those who had come to comfort him; families he had known since childhood, officials from Jamestown, and merchants he hadn't even realized Agatha knew. He didn't miss the looks of question directed toward Sarah, but he offered no comment. Chairs had been arranged about the room for those who wished to linger, either in prayer or in memory, but Nick kept his distance from those who would have wished more.

He watched Sarah move gracefully about the room, and the shadows beneath her eyes were a constant reminder of their time together and how badly he had treated her. Her virginity had stained his sheets and he hadn't even given her tenderness. His hand rubbed over his jaw in disgust. He had fallen asleep like a selfish swine, never giving a single thought to her feelings. And of all the days to sleep late . . . he stormed silently, for there had not been a private moment he might share with her since rising. *Just grant me another chance,* he pleaded with fate. *Tonight, after everyone is gone and the house is quiet, give me the opportunity to show her how much I care.*

The Reverend Jeffers launched into another mournful prayer, and Sarah wondered why the man didn't offer comfort and hope instead of taking the opportunity to preach on the miseries of hell. She ached to go and stand at Nick's side or take his hand within her own to give comfort, for the lines of strain by his mouth etched deeper with each passing hour. But thoughts of him trying to explain away the night before was something she wasn't yet ready to face.

More than a hundred strong they had followed the wagon that carried Agatha Beaumont to her final resting place. The earth had been cleared away next to her husband's grave and Nick stood in silence as the ropes were lowered and spades of dirt were passed. His eyes touched briefly on the graves of his parents, but his grief went completely to the grandmother he'd laid to rest.

The sun had long since disappeared from the sky before the trying day was over. Wearily, Nick closed the door behind the last mourner, but, despite his exhaustion, he felt a curious weight lift from his shoulders as he stretched. Pulling his stock free and unbuttoning his waistcoat, he entered the parlor to find Luther setting the last of the chairs back into place. The braces on which the casket had rested had already been removed and the room looked neat and tidy as always.

"You did a fine job today, Luther," Nick said, walking to the side bar and pouring two brandies. "Come," he extended the glass, "I think we both deserve this."

Luther hesitantly reached for the glass. "Miss Agatha, she don't fancy the staff drinking." He sniffed the amber liquid, then took a healthy swallow and sighed with appreciation. "Damn but that's good. You think Miss Agatha would mind?"

Nick downed his own, enjoying the drink's fiery path and the warmth that settled in his stomach. Reaching for the decanter, he poured them each another. "Luther, if Gran is in heaven tonight and peering over a cloud to watch what's going on . . ." He swirled the liquid in his glass then looked up at the servant. "I'd say she must be feeling damn proud of how you and Oscar and the others handled everything today."

Luther's weathered face broke into a sad grin. "Thank you, sir. But most of the credit gotta go to Miss Sarah. She was the one that kept things moving. Between greeting people in here with you and

286

seeing to the platters in the dining room, why, I don't think she sat down once today."

Nick stretched again and set his glass back on the tray. "And just where did Miss Sarah disappear to? I haven't seen her since the minister left."

Luther savored his last swallow of the fine brandy. "Mrs. Hempsted made Tanzy take her up to bed about thirty minutes ago. Poor little thing was almost asleep on her feet." Luther replaced his own glass and picked up the tray. "If you don't need me now, Master Nick, I'll just see to these glasses."

Nick nodded. "Luther, you and the others have a good rest tomorrow. After today, you deserve it."

"Thank you, sir." Luther started for the doorway, but his step was slow.

"Is there something else?" Nick questioned.

Luther shifted nervously from foot to foot. "Master Nick, this probably isn't the time to speak of it, but we, the staff and me, we was wondering just what's gonna happen to us. We know you can't use all of us over at your house. Wadsworth would have a fit."

Nick crossed the room and placed a comforting hand on Luther's shoulder. "I haven't a clue as to what we shall do with the house yet, but you can reassure all the servants that everyone who wishes to stay will keep his employment. You served my grandmother well, and I'll not forget it."

"Thank you, sir." Relief flooded the man's face.

Nick reached over and pinched out the final candle, then followed Luther into the hall. "I'm going home tonight and I'll take Miss Sarah with me. You make sure you and the others have that rest tomorrow. I'll be back the day after with some decisions and we'll talk then."

"Thank you again, sir," Luther stammered, looking close to tears. "You want me to have Tanzy fetch Miss Sarah?"

Nick paused at the foot of the stairs. "I want you to find your bed. You look exhausted. I'll see you the day after tomorrow."

A knowing grin brightened Luther's troubled features as he watched Master Nick purposefully climb the stairs. *Maybe things is gonna be all right after all,* he thought.

Sarah awoke to the click of the latch on her door. "Tanzy, is that you?" she called wearily. "I told you I didn't want any supper."

"Good, then you'll not mind that I didn't bring any."

Sleep fled completely at the sound of Nick's voice. "What are you doing here," she gasped, sitting up and pulling the covers to her chin. Her eyes adjusted to the darkness, and in the hazy moonlight she could see Nick's tall form standing just inside the doorway.

"I'm tired and I'm going home," he said.

She felt her pulse quicken with dread. He was going to tell her now. He'd say the words that would make the night before an absurd folly caused by the strain of Agatha's death. But Nick said nothing. He crossed the room and, taking her hand, pulled her gently from the bed.

Before Sarah could gather her wits, his lips were on hers. Stunned by the onslaught of sensations, her arms reached up to circle his neck. His tongue brushed across her own and she pressed closer still, feeling her breasts flatten against the hard muscles of his chest.

Reluctantly, Nick broke the kiss and gazed down at her. "I've wanted to do that all day," he sighed against her lips. "Each time I looked up and saw you from across the room, I wanted to scream for everyone to leave so I could hold you."

Her fingers gently touched the lines at the corners of his eyes. "You need your bed." He captured her hand, placed a kiss in its palm. The sensation shot to her toes.

"That's exactly where I am going." Reaching behind her, he tugged a blanket from the bed, then flipped it around her shoulders like a cape.

"What are you doing?" she gasped as he scooped her into his arms and opened the door.

"I told you, I'm going home."

"But . . ."

Nick stopped at the top of the stairs, his eyes dark and intense as he gazed down at her. "I'm going home, and your place is with me."

He hesitated for the briefest moment, and Sarah knew she was being given a choice. It would take only one word and she would be back in her solitary bed to spend the night alone. But her needs were too great to do what she thought was right, and as her arms crept up to encircle his neck, her body snuggled closer to the warmth of his chest. "Take me home, Nick," she whispered, and both knew she wasn't referring to Salem.

He had held her close to his side during the ride home, urging the horses to maintain a fast clip as the stars winked down on them in the open carriage. The cool night air tugged at her hair and touched her hot cheeks, yet did nothing to extinguish the flames that burned beneath her skin. Her anticipation heightened, but with it came uncertainty.

Sarah could only stare in wonder when Nick placed her gently in the center of his bed. His eyes fixed on hers as he shed his coat and waistcoat, then tugged his white shirt over his head to join the growing pile on the floor. The bed dipped with his weight as shoes and stockings were pulled off, and still his gaze held hers captive.

Hesitantly, Sarah reached out and let her fingers trace down the lean muscles of his side. His flesh jumped, his eyes darkened, and a heady satisfaction seeped into her nervous limbs. But when he rose and his hands moved to the buttons on his breeches, Sarah jerked to a sitting position and tore her eyes from his as she reached to extinguish the single candle.

Nick caught her hand and brought her fingers to his lips. "I didn't see you last night." His words sent shivers up her spine, leaving goosebumps in their wake. "Tonight I want to see you." He watched color flare in her cheeks and again was touched by her innocence.

Carefully he sat on the edge of the bed, feeling the tremors that flowed from her fingers as he held her hand within his own and silently he cursed himself for blundering the night before. His thumb rubbed gently over her palm, needing to soothe, then skimmed inside the sleeve of her gown, needing to excite.

Sarah felt her bones turn to water as his fingertips worked their magic. They traced up her arms

290

then paused to pull her hair free from the blanket. His hands slid into her hair, and when he inched her closer she melted against him like winter snow in a spring thaw. "You are so beautiful," he whispered, his breath warm on her throat. "And you belong to me."

Sarah's heart soared with the sound of his words. He loved her! His hand palmed the back of her head, bringing her slowly closer for his kiss, and in that simple gesture came more sweetness than she could ever have imagined. Her heart sang, *he loves me,* and her soul filled with joy. She twisted off the bed, shedding the blanket and her caution in the process. Hitching her nightrail past her knees, she straddled Nick's lap, startling them both with her boldness. For Sarah, her newfound joy could not be contained, and when the heat in Nick's eyes grew brighter, she let her arms rest on his shoulders as her bare legs encircled his hips.

"I wanted to touch you so badly today," she whispered, as her fingers toyed with the hair at the back of his neck.

Nick slid his hands about her waist and pulled her closer still, wondering what had caused the sudden transformation. "It's a good thing you didn't or I might have taken you right there on the floor."

Her hands gently touched the lines of strain that still lingered at the corners of his mouth. "You looked so sad and I desperately wanted to make you smile again."

He felt his heartbeat quicken. "What would you have done?"

Her violet eyes paused in thought, then sparkled as her imagination took hold. Her lips hovered a breath from his. "I would have smoothed away the heartache." Her voice was husky with passion as the tip of her tongue reached out to trace the faint lines at the corners of his mouth.

He struggled to let her maintain the pace, for he could feel the joy that radiated from her, even as his own body screamed for release. "Is that all?" he demanded. "Would you tempt me and then offer no sustenance?" His gaze dropped to the rounded peaks of her breast pressing against her gown.

Looking up, he again watched her cheeks bloom with color. His palms rested on her bare thighs and she offered no protest when they slid slowly up and around the curve of her hip to her ribs, taking the gown with it. Their eyes met in question and he felt her breath lock in her chest as she reached down between them, then pulled the gown over her head.

Completely naked, Sarah sat as one made of stone, astonished she could display herself so wantonly before him. *He loves you,* her heart counseled gently, and although she could feel her flesh grow hot from his gaze, she made no move to cover herself. *Let him find me pleasing,* she wished silently. *Let me share my love with him.*

Nick reached for the gift she offered, and his hands gently covered her. Her eyes grew misty as he caressed her flesh, molding and stroking. And when he leaned forward to capture her nipple with his lips, he felt her arch closer and his sanity fled.

Sarah flopped back over his arm as Nick suckled at her breast. The gentle tug of his lips sent circles of rapture rippling through her, and when he drank deeper, she felt she might die from the pleasure of it. Ecstasy filled her, surrounding her with soft

292

cries of delight until she floated in a sea of warmth.

Nick watched her struggle to open her eyes and her smile sent arrows of passion straight to his heart. Holding her close, he tumbled backward with her, luxuriating in the soft curtain of hair that fell about his neck and face. Her skin was flushed, her eyes filled with promise, and Nick could wait no more. Within the blink of an eye she was beneath him. His knee pressed high at the juncture of her thighs, and tenderly he gathered her close.

"It won't hurt this time," he promised, caressing her gently, arousing her pliant flesh.

Sarah pressed kisses along his shoulder and jaw. "It wouldn't matter if it did."

His lips met hers, open, wet, and wonderful. He tasted of power and sorrow and she drank it all. She gasped when she felt him enter, but her flesh was ready and her heart accepted him. Willingly she surrounded him with her love.

Nick sank into her and felt he had surely died and reached heaven. Her velvety muscles sheathed and caressed him and her quiet sigh of acceptance sent him soaring. Moving gently, he wedged his hand between them, then watched her through hazy eyes as her body arched in triumph and she reached the stars.

Sarah shuddered in the aftermath of passion. She hadn't been prepared for the intensity of his love. Never had she felt so cherished. Her eyes met his, then grew wide as she realized he still rested within her.

Nick laughed at her stunned expression and rocked her close.

"I thought it was over," she whispered as if sharing some great secret, then blushed bewitchingly. "I don't really have much experience with this sort of thing."

He flexed his body and watched her eyes glaze over. "I wouldn't think so," he teased. "But if you're tired, we could always stop."

Fearful he do just that, Sarah shifted and locked her legs around his waist. "I'm not tired at all," she said, her voice shivering with pleasure.

Nick's breath caught in his throat as her muscles gripped him tighter, then he was moving with her in the motion older than time itself. Higher and higher he took her until her cry of release triggered his own.

Reluctant to move but fearing he would crush her, Nick rolled to his back taking her with him. She felt so fragile. Her head rested on his shoulder, her arm draped limply across his chest, and their legs entwined. His mind spun about in all directions trying to decide which thought to follow first, but reasoning was hard to find with her flesh still quivering against him. He hadn't known a woman could make him weak. And the realization did not sit easy. She shivered, and he untangled the sheet to cover them.

Sarah snuggled closer. Nick had wrapped her in love so soft and compelling, that her eyes refused to open. She felt his hands gently rub her back, and it seemed perfectly reasonable to spend the rest of her life in his arms. Somewhere in the back of her mind she realized he had yet to say the actual words, but her heart was too content to care.

Nick knew by her even breathing that she slept, and his arms tightened instinctively. How was it that she was so different? he wondered. He had

had his share of ladies, but none had touched his heart like Sarah. She had given joy as well as passion, and his body still ached in want of her. He rubbed his chin on the top of her head and considered waking her with kisses, but remained content to simply hold her. *You've brought peace to my life,* he thought. *How am I ever going to be able to face the day when you are gone?*

Chapter Twenty

Snug and content, Sarah counted the deep, resonant chimes from the hall clock, but as the eighth chime echoed through the house she jerked upright, and her eyes darted about the darkened room in confusion.

A hand glided up her bare spine and gently kneaded the back of her neck. "Is something amiss?" Nick's deep rich voice turned her flesh to jelly.

Clutching the blanket to her chest, Sarah looked back at him. His head still rested on the pillow they had shared and his smile was doing strange things to her insides.

" 'Tis eight o'clock," she gasped, noticing for the first time how effective the heavy draperies were at blocking the sunlight.

"Yes, I imagine it is." His hand smoothed down the tangles of her hair, luxuriating in the heavy weight of it and the glimpse of porcelain flesh it revealed.

"But we're still in bed." Her voice held disbelief, and his smile deepened.

"We certainly are." Tugging her hair gently, Nick pulled until she flopped back to her place on his shoulder, her soft curves molding perfectly to the hard planes of his body.

"Nick . . ." Her hand rested on his heart and her voice was a velvet purr. " 'Tis way past morning. We can't stay in bed. There is too much to do."

Nick tipped her face up for his kiss. "You are right, as usual." His touch was feather-light as he traced the soft fullness of her lips, then his mouth closed hungrily over hers. Their legs entwined, caressing, enticing, and heartbeats grew faster. "As for me," he nibbled her bottom lip. "I think I shall start right here."

Sarah pressed closer to the heat of his body. "I think it's going to be a long morning," she sighed against his throat as he stoked the flames of passion higher.

Nick flipped them both over and saw the undisguised love that filled her violet eyes. "A very, very long morning." Then capturing her lips, he sealed his promise.

Sarah floated down the stairs in a ray of sunlight to find Wadsworth standing at the bottom.

"Mr. Beaumont is waiting for you in the dining room, miss." The butler's tone was formal, but the knowing smile in his eyes undid her. Despite her resolve, Sarah felt her cheeks grow hot.

"Thank you, Wadsworth," she stammered, trying to hide her discomfort.

"And, Miss Sarah . . ." She watched in amazement as his rigid face broke into a rich smile. "Might I say how glad we all are to have you home again?"

Embarrassment drained away to be instantly replaced with deep contentment. "Thank you, Wadsworth." Her voice was filled with gratitude. "It truly does feel like home."

Still smiling, Sarah joined Nick in the dining room. The warmth in his eyes echoed in his voice.

"Did you sleep well?" he asked, grinning.

The rosy blush on her cheeks turned a darker hue, but her eyes met his squarely. " 'Twas the best night abed I've had in weeks." She moved to her chair and smiled over her shoulder. "And I hope to repeat it often."

Nick's rich laughter filled the dining room. How she had changed, he mused. Her polite reserve had all but vanished and the bewitching smiles she sent his way were making his blood boil.

Although the hands of the clock had long passed noon, they had yet to finish their meal when Wadsworth entered.

"Sir, Mr. Webster has arrived."

Reluctantly Nick wiped his mouth, then tossed his napkin on the table. "Show the man to my study and offer him some refreshment, Wadsworth. You can say that I'll be along directly." He reached for Sarah's hand, letting his thumb rub against the sensitive flesh of her inner wrist. "Webster has brought Gran's will," he explained. "I already know the contents, so this is just a formality that I thought best to have over and done with." Nick rose and helped Sarah from her chair. "I shouldn't be long. Why don't you wait for me in the garden?"

Sarah smiled and, checking to be sure the butler was no longer about, rose up on her tiptoes to

298

place a fleeting kiss against his lips.

Nick sighed in frustration as his arm clamped about her waist. "Did I teach you nothing last night? That was not a kiss. *This* is a kiss." His hand cradled the back of her head, and his lips stole the very breath from her body. Both were shaken when it ended. Sarah kept her arms locked around his neck, and her eyes sparkled with mischief.

"I think I need more practice," she whispered. "Sometimes, when I'm slow to catch on, it helps if I do it over and over until I get it right."

Nick eased her from his arms, knowing if he did not do so immediately, he'd carry her off to his room again. "You're a temptress, Miss Townsend. Get thee to the garden before I toss up your skirts and take you here and now."

Sarah sidestepped quickly from his reach and laughed with pleasure. "Don't be too long."

Nick entered his study and his good mood fled. Mangus Webster stood deep in conversation with Michael Danvers. "What the devil are you doing here?" Nick snapped at Danvers. "You no longer have any business with either my company or myself."

"Nick . . ." Mangus hastily stepped forward and extended his hand. "Danvers is here because I asked him to be. It seems there is a new version of your grandmother's will."

Nick's eyes mirrored his displeasure as he sat behind his desk and motioned for the attorneys to be seated. "Now, just what is this ridiculous story of yours, Danvers?"

* * *

Sarah strolled the well-tended paths that wound behind the house. The roses swayed softly in the gentle breeze, lending their fragrance to nature's heady perfume. She took the clippers from her basket and plucked several tight buds of the palest pink. Surrounded by the delicate baby's breath that already filled her basket, she thought they would be the perfect complement for the black vase that stood in the hall. But as she turned to retrace her steps to the house, the wind tugged at her skirts and she looked up to find the sky full of angry black clouds.

"Miss Sarah!" Wadsworth waved to catch her attention, then holding his coat against the growing wind, quickly covered the path to reach her. "Mr. Beaumont wishes you to join him in the study if you would." He took the basket of flowers from her arm and scowled at the darkening sky.

Sarah clutched at her skirts as the wind plastered them to her legs. "I think we're in for a good dousing." Her words were punctuated by fat raindrops that dotted the brick path. Running the last few steps, she and the aging butler reached the back porch just as the sky opened in earnest. Sarah laughed and shook the moisture from her hair. "Oh, Wadsworth," she sighed. "Don't you just love the fresh smell of a summer rain?"

But Wadsworth wasn't smiling. " 'Taint no ordinary rain, Miss Sarah. Look . . ." His thin arm raised and pointed toward the carriage house. Above the roof hung the blackest clouds Sarah had ever seen. Wadsworth set down the basket of flowers. "I don't know why," he said, "but whenever the storm comes from that direction," he nodded toward the back of the property, "it's a fierce one. And the way it came up so sudden like, I'll wager more than a few shingles will be missing by morning."

Sarah shivered, for the wind now carried a sharp bite, and the image of Gracie Richardson's dilapidated shack had sprung to mind. She doubted it could withstand much abuse from the weather. The rains came harder, and within seconds the carriage house was obliterated from view.

"I'd better see to the upstairs windows." Wadsworth pulled open the back door. "And Mr. Beaumont is waiting for you in the study."

She nodded and picked up her basket but made no move to join him in the doorway. "You go on, I'll just be a minute." Sarah turned her attention back to the growing storm and took a deep breath of the moisture-filled air. It was alive with energy, she could feel it in her bones. The hair on her arms prickled and she felt the power of nature close at hand.

"In truth we do need the rain, Father," she whispered. "But I think this might be a tad too much." Lightning flashed, filling the darkened sky with terror, and Sarah jumped and laughed with a start as thunder crashed around her. "Send as much rain as you wish," she shouted above the howling wind. "Just don't be angry when it's not appreciated."

Slipping into the house, Sarah tidied her hair, but avoided the looking glass in the hallway. She knocked lightly, then entered the study as the three men rose to greet her.

She smiled, crossing the room to the attorney

with her hand extended. "Mr. Danvers, how nice to see you again," she said.

The man's expression was more smirk than smile and, releasing his hand, Sarah turned to Nick. " 'Tis raining something fierce. You wished to see me?"

Nick's eyes had grown as dark as the storm-filled sky, but he gestured for her to sit. "This is Mangus Webster, my attorney. It seems you already know Danvers. He is an acquaintance of yours?"

Sarah's brow wrinkled in confusion at the tone in his voice. She took a chair on the opposite side of the desk. "We met here in this very room. Do you not remember?"

" 'Tis of no importance," Nick brushed her words aside, and turned to the older attorney. "She's here now, Webster, so let's get on with it."

Mangus Webster straightened his crimson waistcoat over his wide belly and stood. Wire-rimmed glasses perched low on his nose, and his wig was elaborate with chestnut curls that fell in great coils about his shoulders. "I understand you spent a great deal of time with Mrs. Beaumont before she died. Is that correct?"

Sarah turned to Nick but found him scowling at Danvers, who leaned insolently against the mantel. "That's right," she said, returning her gaze to Webster. "I lived with Mrs. Beaumont for several weeks."

"And are you aware that Mrs. Beaumont wrote a codicil to her existing will?"

"No," Sarah said, shifting nervously. She could feel Nick's impatience from across the room.

Danvers straightened and withdrew a folded document from his coat pocket. As his voice droned on, Sarah's eyes moved from man to man. Webster paced nervously, and, despite the chill that had claimed the room, wiped perspiration from his ruddy forehead. Danvers, who stood by the cold fireplace as he read, resembled a fox amid a flock of sheep. Only Nick seemed completely unmoved by his grandmother's newest edict. Reclined in his chair, his chin rested on steepled fingers.

Lightning flashed, followed by an ominous roll of thunder, and Sarah felt the house absorb the impact of the storm. Suddenly she remembered all too clearly the first night she had been in this room . . . cold, soaked, petrified. Her skin turned clammy, and she wished the men would leave so she could return to the security of Nick's arms. She suppressed a shiver, and clenched her hands tightly together in her lap. Perhaps Wadsworth would take it into his head to serve hot cider and not that vile dark coffee Nick was so fond of.

"So you see," Danvers taunted. "Your grandmother left you not a penny. I guess the old woman just didn't like you, Beaumont."

Sarah heard only the last sentence and her eyes flashed with anger. "How dare you make such a statement?" she snapped.

Nick's smile turned dangerous. He rose to his feet and gained the satisfaction of watching Danvers hastily step backward. "It's all right, Sarah," Nick said, his voice held none of the tension that coursed through his veins.

"So you can see, Miss Townsend," Webster cleared his voice, "you are a very wealthy woman."

Sarah's eyes flashed with impatience. "Whatever

303

do you mean?"

"You now own all of Mrs. Agatha Beaumont's possessions," Danvers sneered, looking at Nick. "As of this moment you own half of Beaumont Shipping."

Sarah flopped back on her chair as the strength of her anger drained away. "I don't believe it. What cruel hoax are you trying to play—"

"It is no hoax," Webster interrupted. "I've checked the signatures. This document is completely in order."

"But Beaumont Shipping belongs to Mr. Beaumont," Sarah said.

Nick circled the desk and took her hand in his. "And will again, darling," he said smoothly. "As soon as we are married, the business will revert back to me."

Sarah felt her heart beat so loudly she wondered if the others could hear. "Married?" she stammered, almost afraid to hope for such a miracle.

"Married?" Danvers gasped. He had known the will stipulated marriage in order for Nick to reclaim the business, but he had hoped for more outrage. Surely the man wasn't going to let himself become shackled to an indentured servant. Where was the anger at being so manipulated? Beaumont's temper was legendary, yet now he blithely accepted marriage to a servant. Disappointment marred Danver's features as he watched Webster refold the document.

"Married," Nick said pleasantly. "Today, if possible. Mangus, do you think you could get a special dispensation that would allow us to forgo the posting of banns?"

Relieved that Nick had accepted the news so well, the older attorney cleared his throat. Nick had a nasty temper that he himself had witnessed on more than one occasion, and he in no way wanted it turned in his direction. "A good attorney always tries to anticipate his clients' needs, Mr. Beaumont. And when I learned of the new will this morning, I took it upon myself to speak with both the magistrates and the minister. The courts are aware of your fine standing in the community and the reverend Jeffers was also more than willing to comply. If you wish, I can arrange for the ceremony to take place at my office this evening."

Nick nodded. "Do it then."

"Nick," Sarah gasped. "You truly want to marry me?"

His smile was dark and sensuous. "Don't you think that we should after . . ." His voice trailed off and he watched her cheeks turn pink.

"I love you," she said softly, not caring that two others were witness to her declaration. "I love you with all my heart."

Nick brushed a fleeting kiss against her forehead. "And within just a few hours, you are going to be my wife."

"Gentlemen." His arm remained possessively clamped around Sarah's waist. "As you can see, both the lady and I are more than ready. So Webster, if you would see to the arrangements I would appreciate your haste in the matter."

Webster beamed. "It shall be done immediately. And may I be the first to offer my congratulations?"

"Just see to it," Nick said pleasantly.

305

Sarah watched in amazement as Danver's smile fled. "You would really marry her?" he questioned.

"Without a second's hesitation," Nick declared solemnly.

Danver's eyes glinted with frustration. "Then you will have fulfilled the conditions of the codicil and after the ceremony, Beaumont Shipping will belong to you again."

Nick released his grip on Sarah and moved to open the door. "There was never any doubt in my mind. Gentlemen, I bid you good day," he replied easily as the attorneys departed.

For Sarah, the afternoon passed in a haze. Nick had offered to send for Charlotte, but her conscience would not allow it. The storm was too fierce to make Charlotte venture out for the sake of a new dress. Giving a shrug of his shoulders, Nick had offered no other suggestions, but closeted himself in his study declaring he had much that demanded his attention.

Sarah bathed, then stood in her shift as she pondered what to wear to her wedding. Her nerves jangled and her fingers trembled as she contemplated the possibilities. The sapphire gown she had worn to Julie Carlson's wedding seemed the perfect choice, but it, along with the rest of her clothing, was still at Agatha's. Rain beat in torrents against her window, and Sarah knew she could not ask one of the servants to fetch it for her. Besides, she thought, mourning for Agatha dictated she wear black.

Pushing aside her disappointment, Sarah quickly

donned her black velvet skirt and jacket. "I'm getting married," she hummed, trying to restore her good mood. Nick's bracelet slipped around her wrist and for the first time she didn't tuck it under her sleeve. She brushed her hair until it glistened in the candlelight, then perched on the corner of her bed to wait.

Sarah clung to the window strap to brace herself as the carriage bumped down the road toward home. Rain continued to drench the countryside making the roads slick and travel difficult.

How strange, she thought as the carriage tipped and swayed. There had been no guests, only Webster and his wife and Michael Danvers to act as witnesses. The minister had read his piece and she and Nick had repeated their vows. A plain gold band was slipped on her finger, then it was over. There was no wedding supper to share in camaraderie with friends, or even a cake to mark the occasion. They had signed the minister's documents and then, after hasty words of congratulations, Nick had bustled her back into the carriage.

In the faint light of the lantern, Sarah could see his features as he sat opposite her on the seat. His arms were folded over his chest and his smile had long since disappeared. She ached to crawl onto his lap and share his warmth, for she felt chilled to the bone. But he made no overtures and she was suddenly too shy to initiate them. *This isn't the way it's supposed to be,* she thought desperately as the carriage pulled to a stop.

Nick swung the carriage door open and stepped

out then turned back to help her descend.

Sarah frowned with confusion as she looked up through the rain, for they stood at Agatha's front door.

"Why did we stop here?" She turned to Nick and found his features contorted with black rage. "What is wrong?"

Nick pulled his arm from her touch with a vicious jerk. "I thought you would like to spend the night in your new house. You certainly worked hard enough for it."

"What?" Sarah cried, suddenly afraid as he towered over her.

Nick threw back his head and laughed ironically at the sky. Rain beat against his skin, and he reveled in the sting of it. "You got what you wanted," he shouted. "You wanted security, and you have it. Consider my grandmother's house yours. But as for me, and future funds, I'm afraid you and Danvers calculated wrongly. You'll carry my name," he taunted, "but you'll not get so much as a good day from me in the future. And if you know what is good for you, I advise you to stay out of my sight."

Nick turned to go, but Sarah grabbed his arm. "I do not understand," she said, her voice quaking with fear. "It was your wish to be married."

Nick gave her a hard, appraising stare meant to humiliate, and it did. "A man will do a lot to get back what is his," he said quietly. "As to love, I think not. Get your friend Danvers to share your bed and keep you warm. You two deserve each other." His voice echoed his disgust.

"But I don't even know the man," Sarah cried as

308

her tears mixed with the rain to wash down her face. "Why are you saying this?"

Nick reached into the carriage and plucked a thick gray envelope from the floor. "Here. He gave you this right after the ceremony. Did you think I didn't notice?" He jammed the paper into her hand. "We wouldn't want you to lose it. It might contain the time and place for your next meeting."

Sarah clutched the envelope and felt a sickening dread wash over her. "You don't love me?" Her voice was barely a whisper, but Nick heard and shook his head.

"Did I ever say I did?" He watched her face pale. "I like my women to be women," his tone was insulting. "I prefer experience to the fumbling of the inadequate."

"Then why did you take me?" came her anguished wail.

Nick shrugged and turned back to the carriage. "Because you offered," he replied easily. "What man wouldn't?" Then he was in the carriage and the door closed behind him.

Numb with shock, Sarah stood in the pouring rain until the carriage was out of sight, then, falling to her knees, she retched. An hour later, Luther found her huddled on the front step soaked to the skin and colder than ice. Her lips were blue and her eyes were wide and haunted. He tried to help her into the house, but it was difficult, for Sarah refused to allow anyone to get near to her.

Luther himself braved the storm to fetch Master Nick, but when he returned, he was alone. In strained silence Agatha's servants watched Sarah huddle in a corner. Through gentle coaxing they had convinced her to pull a blanket about her shoulders. But they could only stand by and watch as great tremors consumed her body.

The news spread quickly through the household. Miss Agatha had left all her money to Miss Sarah, and Master Nick had married her to get it back. They watched until Sarah finally collapsed completely, then it was Luther who gently carried her up to bed and Mrs. Hempsted who eased her out of her wet clothing.

"Something's not right here," Luther sighed as they closed the door to Sarah's room, leaving Tanzy to sit with her.

"I just can't imagine Master Nick doing something like this." Mrs. Hempsted's voice was thick with tears as they descended the stairs. "Doesn't he know how good she was to Miss Agatha?"

"I tried to tell him." Luther shook his head. "But all he'd say was Miss Sarah owned this house now and he wanted no more to do with her."

"But he married her!"

Luther's tired head nodded. "That he did. But he sure don't want to see her."

"Luther, why do you think Miz Agatha did such a fool thing?"

Luther threaded his fingers through his wiry hair. "I sure don't know. I knew when she started having that Danvers person come to call she was up to no good. But I just can't believe that after all Miss Sarah did for her, she would wish her such heartache."

Mrs. Hempsted paused at the bottom step. "Once, when I was a young girl, I saw a master take after a slave with his whip. He like to

310

slice that poor fool's skin clean off." She paused to look back up the stairs. "But you know, I still don't think I've ever seen a body hurt worse than Miss Sarah."

Luther placed a comforting hand on her shoulder and heaved another great sigh. "Miss Sarah is stronger than she looks. Maybe tomorrow when the storm is gone, things will seem brighter."

Lightning flashed and the house trembled in protest as the thunder crashed around them. Mrs. Hempsted shivered and, holding a hand to protect the candle's flame, turned to Luther. "Mayhap I should go back up and sit with her. There's no telling what she'll be like if the storm wakes her."

"Tanzy is with her."

"Tanzy is a sweet child, Luther, but she's got the sense of a nanny goat."

"Then we'll both sit with her." Lightning filled the foyer with its eerie light and Mrs. Hempsted paused.

"Luther, what do you think Miss Sarah is gonna do if she finds out we are married?" Luther gathered the cook's ample body close to his and pressed his face to her neck. She always smelled of vanilla and he'd loved her since the first day they had met. "Things will work out, my sweet. Miss Sarah is a good person. Despite what Master Nick says, we both know that."

Mrs. Hempsted trembled. "But Luther, Master Nick is so smart, what if he is right and we are wrong? Miss Agatha didn't care that I'm black and you're white, but Miss Sarah's from the North and she sure has some strange notions about things. What if she snitches on us? If it got out, there

311

could be all kinds of trouble."

Luther had already considered that. "We're not going to say anything at all for a few days," he told her as they quietly climbed the stairs. "We'll wait until we see for ourselves what Miss Sarah is going to do, and then if the time is right, we'll tell her."

"And if the time isn't right?"

Luther pulled her close and pressed his lips to hers. "Then we'll just leave."

Mrs. Hempsted dropped her head to her husband's chest. "But we've been here all our lives."

Luther rubbed his chin over the top of her bandana. "Nigh on to forty years." Lightning flashed again and thunder cracked so loudly they thought it surely had hit them. They broke apart as Tanzy flew out of the doorway.

"Miss Sarah is awake," she gasped, "and she says she's gotta go out. She says it's a matter of life and death and she's getting dressed."

Much to Tanzy's relief, Mrs. Hempsted brushed by her to hurry into the room.

Chapter Twenty-one

"Miss Sarah!" Mrs. Hempsted rushed into the room. "What are you doing, child? You need to be back in your bed."

Sarah turned and finished tying the drawstrings of her skirt. Her eyes were calm as she reached for the matching jacket. "Would you see if Luther is awake, Mrs. Hempsted. I need to go out."

"Luther is awake, Miss Sarah, but there's a terrible storm tonight. Why don't you just crawl back into bed? I'll fetch some nice hot bricks to warm your feet. And tomorrow, after a good night's sleep, if you still feel the need to go out, Luther will take you anywhere you want to go."

Luther entered the room as the thunder rumbled ominously and the windows rattled in their casings. "Miss Sarah, please." He stepped forward, but Sarah stepped back. Sitting on the edge of the bed, she pulled on her slippers. "You don't want to see Master Nick tonight. It can wait for morning."

Her face grew paler than the sheets on which she sat, but her words were calm and sure. "Luther, Mr. Beaumont has nothing to do with this. Do you know where the Blanchard orchard is?"

Warily, the man nodded.

313

"Well I need to get there. Is it safe enough to take a wagon or should we walk?"

"Miss Sarah, why do you wanna go way out there at this time of night?" Mrs. Hempsted asked.

"Do you remember Gracie Richardson?" Sarah tucked her hair under her cap. "Well, she's out in that storm tonight with three young children. They live in a shack that Luther could topple with one good sneeze."

Mrs. Hempsted crossed herself. "Lord have mercy, what are we waiting for? Miss Sarah, you stay here. Let Luther and the men go fetch that woman and her kids."

Grateful for the help, Sarah tried to smile, but it wouldn't come. "I know where to look and Luther doesn't. I'll go with him. Mayhap you could warm up something hot for them to eat when we return?"

"Consider it done. Luther, you keep her out of the rain as much as possible." Mrs. Hempsted wagged a finger, for in truth Sarah looked frail enough to keel over at any moment. Understanding the silent command from his wife, Luther turned to take Sarah's arm.

Instinctively she stepped away. "Don't touch me, Luther." Her skin was the color of parchment and her voice as cold as stone. "I don't want anyone to ever touch me again."

The two servants exchanged nervous glances, but Sarah had already left the room and Luther had no choice but to hurry after.

Nearly three hours later, Luther stopped the wagon at Agatha's back door. Gracie Richardson tumbled out clutching little Jessie tightly, while

Sarah helped Catherine and Jimmy. They were soaked to the skin, covered with mud but grateful to be alive. Luther led the sodden group into the back parlor where Ruby and Tanzy waited with a roaring fire and piles of warm blankets. Mrs. Hempsted ladled hot soup and Sarah helped Gracie get the children into dry clothing.

The shack had already started to collapse, Luther whispered to his wife. And it had been Sarah who had crawled in under the rubble to find them while he and the others kept the roof from falling completely.

Mrs. Hempsted took a hard look at his pale face. "It was close?" she asked.

Warm in his dry clothing and clutching a hot mug of cider, Luther shut his eyes. "I could hear the Lord clearing his throat to call my name. We no sooner got the last of them out and pulled Miss Sarah free when lightning struck and the whole thing went up in flames." Luther shuddered. "If Miss Sarah hadn't insisted we go and fetch them, those babies would be dead right now."

Mrs. Hempsted placed a comforting hand on his shoulder and looked over at Sarah. She looked pale as a ghost, and ready to drop, yet she still managed a soothing word to little Jessie as she combed the tangles from the child's hair. "There's something special about that girl, Luther. I can feel it in my bones."

Luther shifted ever so slightly so his shoulder pressed against his wife. "I feel it, too. And after tonight, I think things are going to work out for us just fine."

By morning the storm had run its course and

315

Agatha Beaumont's grand house resembled an army barracks. The storm had been violent, just as Wadsworth had predicted. Trees had toppled and lightning fires had been plentiful. Houses in the south of town had been the hardest hit, and many of the shacks were no longer standing. Sarah offered the Beaumont house as shelter for any who needed it, and within hours, the place was filled with the laughter of children as they ran through the hallways. Tanzy and Ruby were detailed to entertain the younger ones, and Mrs. Hempsted accepted help in her cookhouse for the first time. When the sun broke through the clouds at midday, Luther and Sarah had organized the comings and goings, and plans were already underway for reconstruction.

As the hours passed, Luther waited patiently for Master Nick to arrive, for news of Miss Sarah's exploits were all over town. But the only knock that sounded at the grand oak door came from more poor folks looking for food and a place to stay for the night.

Charlotte Rousseau arrived the next morning, anxious to see if Catherine was all right, and when Jimmy recounted the story of their daring rescue, she felt herself grow faint.

"Miss Townsend is a hero, is she not?" Charlotte flopped on a chair and tried to calm her nerves.

Jimmy had scrunched up his face and rubbed his nose hard. "Well, her name is Mrs. Beaumont now, but I guess she's still a hero."

"Beaumont?" Charlotte stammered.

"Yep." Jimmy grinned. "You should have seen the mud. Miss Sarah had more on her than me and little Jessie combined."

Standing on legs that trembled, Charlotte thanked Jimmy and went in search of Sarah. She found her in the back, hanging blankets out to dry.

"Chèr amie, what ever are you doing?" Charlotte asked, but as Sarah reached for another blanket, Charlotte took the other end in assistance without waiting for her answer.

"One of the babies was ill last night," she said easily. "And they are so busy inside . . ." Her words faded as she smoothed the blanket over the makeshift wire line Oscar had erected, then reached for another in the basket at her feet.

"So the lady of the house is reduced to doing the laundry?"

Sarah didn't smile. "It needs to be done," she said simply.

Charlotte stayed to help for several hours, amazed at the order Sarah had created amidst the chaos. She had learned by listening that Nick had indeed married Sarah, then in the middle of the storm, he had deposited her at his grandmother's house for the night. But what bothered her most was the cool indifference that etched Sarah's face. According to Tanzy, Miss Sarah barely slept and was running them ragged. *Oh, Nicholas,* Charlotte thought as her weary steps carried her back to her shop, *you are such a fool.*

The storm was three days past when Nick looked up to find Christopher Carlson at the door to his study. They embraced silently in memory of Agatha, then Nick poured them each a drink.

317

"You look like hell," Chris said easily, enjoying the bite of the fiery liquid. He took in Nick's unshaven chin and the dark circles that lined his eyes. "Decided to grow a beard?"

Nick's face mirrored surprise as his hand touched his chin. "I've been busy," he said stiffly. "The storm caused a great deal of damage down at the docks."

Chris leaned back in his chair. "I can imagine. The roads are a mess. We left as soon as we heard about Agatha, but then the storm hit. More than once I thought we'd have to turn back. I tell you, friend, hell is being in a carriage with your mother and sister for three days."

Nick gave a weary grin. "You brought Julie with you?"

Chris groaned and poured himself another brandy. "Clarence Morgan has more success getting grass to grow than he does with my little sister. She's making them both miserable. Spends more time at our house than she does at her own. When she found out that Mother and I were coming to town, she threw a fit until Morgan sent her here with his blessings. I've decided to never forgive the man."

Nick shook his head and drained his glass. "Where are they now?"

"I secured their rooms at the tavern and then dumped them both. I told them I was sure they wouldn't want you to see them looking like such hags from the travel," he said with a wink. "Julie immediately opted to take a nap. I think she's convinced herself that sleep will cure any ailment from a hangnail to crow's-feet."

318

Chris noted the way Nick's smile never reached his eyes and he downed the last of his brandy. "So, what is this I hear that you and Sarah have married?"

Nick pulled up short. "How long have you been in town?"

Chris shrugged. "I can't say I'm surprised. Not after seeing you with her at Julie's wedding. But what does surprise me is that you're allowing her to live in a different house. I thought that the advantage of marriage," he teased, "was a permanent bed partner."

Nick rose and stood at the window, keeping his back to his friend. "I don't want to talk about her. I believed in her and she turned out to be no different from all the rest."

"The rest of what?" Chris questioned, suddenly afraid of where the conversation was going. "Sarah wasn't like anyone *I'd* ever met."

Nick turned back. His eyes were full of anger and regret. "She had Agatha rewrite her will. Gran left all her shares of Beaumont Shipping to Sarah."

"She did what?" Chris shot out of his chair.

"She persuaded Gran to leave everything to her," Nick said quietly, for the idea still gnawed at him. "While we were falling for Sarah's story, she was manipulating my grandmother."

"Damn . . ." Chris expelled a long breath. "I can't believe it. I was so taken by her."

"We all were." Nick's voice was tight. "I thought her the most generous, caring woman I had ever met."

"And instead she turns into a calculating bitch. Damn, I need another drink."

Nick turned back to gaze out the window. "Ruthless and selfish, just like my mother. Isn't that how the story goes? A man always wants a wife who's just like his mother. Well, I sure got one and I didn't even see it coming."

Christopher's eyes grew wide, for never had he heard Nick refer to his parents. He had no idea how to respond.

Nick turned from the window. His smile was ironic. "Have I rendered you speechless?"

Chris took another swallow of brandy. "You've never spoken of your parents before."

Nick shrugged. "They were never worthy of a memory. They still aren't."

"Then, damn it all, there must be a way to have your marriage dissolved."

Nick sat back at his desk and propped his chin on his hands. "And what would I say to the magistrate? Oh, excuse me, Your Excellency, but I married this girl to obtain the property she owns, and now that it belongs to me again, I'd like to return her. Well, yes, she is slightly used, but who's to know?"

Chris shook his head. "That makes you sound as calculating as Sarah."

Nick rose and began to pace. *As calculating as Sarah,* he thought. The words did not ring true. "There is something wrong here, Chris." His eyes darkened with painful memories. "When I think of my mother, even now I remember how utterly clever and vindictive she was. I can't call forth a single time with her that was pleasant. I can't remember one time when she put my needs before her own, or even remembered I existed."

Fascinated, Chris nodded and refilled his glass. "Go on."

"Well . . ." Nick paused and his expression grew lighter. "When I think of Sarah, the only memories I have are good ones. Just to look at her made your day brighter. She always had a smile or a kind word. And not just for me. Even Luther noticed it. He called her 'joyful.' "

"What are you trying to say?"

Nick continued to pace. "Chris, Sarah wasn't calculating. She couldn't even bring herself to tell that absurd story Gran made up about her being a friend of the family."

"Maybe that was when she was at her best. Maybe she was just pretending to be uncomfortable."

Nick shook his head. "I don't think so. Something's been there gnawing at the back of my mind since the beginning of this farce, but I've been too wrapped up in my own grief to think it through."

"What are you trying to say?" he asked again. "Do you think her innocent?"

Nick rubbed at his temples. "If Sarah had been living a lie all this time, there would have been some sign, no matter how small. There would still be some little thing that I could look back on and say, *yes I should have noticed that.*" Nick's eyes were haunted when he turned back to his friend. "I can't find a single reason to call Sarah guilty."

Chris sipped the amber liquid and tried to puzzle through the facts. "Then you believe the kidnapping story? You don't think it was merely a hoax meant to gain your sympathy?"

Nick returned to sit behind his desk. "That's the one thing I'm sure of. She was half frozen and scared to death when Beckett found her. And I've seen her longing for her family in those private moments when she thought no one was about. No, Sarah Townsend was kidnapped from her home in Salem, of that I am sure."

Chris briskly rubbed his hands together. "I think we'd better get to the bottom of this, Nick, and soon." He paused in thought. "Something's very wrong here, and if what you think is true, there is going to be hell to pay."

The knock at the door made both men turn. Wadsworth stood in the doorway. "Sir, excuse me for interrupting," he said. "But Luther is here and insists on speaking with you. Also Peter Beckett has arrived. The *Lady May* has just returned from Salem."

Nick turned to Chris. "Now we'll get some answers, I trust. Wadsworth, send Beckett in and ask Luther to wait."

The butler nodded and left, but it was Luther who immediately entered the study.

"You have to excuse me, Mr. Beaumont," he said, his voice vibrating with anger. "I know you ain't interested in what's going on over at your grandmother's house and I ain't come to tell you anyway." He paused to take a breath. "I just thought since you've always claimed to be a fair man, you might be interested in this." He flipped a gray envelope onto Nick's desk.

Nick recoiled, recognizing it as the one Danvers had given to Sarah. "I don't appreciate your attitude, Luther," Nick snapped.

Luther's meaty fist crashed down on the desk. "I don't give a damn, sir. You hurt Miss Sarah more than a body's got a right to. But if there's any justice in this world, you'll hurt just as bad once you read this." He shoved the envelope forward on the desk.

"Did Sarah send you with this?" Nick reached for the paper and felt his heartbeat quicken.

"No, sir," Luther said with quiet dignity. "I don't even think Miss Sarah has had time to read it. She's been too busy looking out for other folks. Now if you'll excuse me, I know you're a busy man." Luther turned and left the room.

Chris looked back at Nick. "She has certainly won him over. In all the years I've known Luther, I don't think I've ever heard him raise his voice."

Nick's fingers ran the length of the stiff paper. It still carried the water stains and mud from that fateful night. Slowly, he extracted the folded letter. He recognized the handwriting instantly and, as the words burned into his brain, he felt his heart constrict in agony.

"Dear God, Chris, what have I done?"

Chris pulled the letter from Nick's limp fingers and scanned the contents. "You've just tossed away the best woman in the county."

Nick's head dropped forward to rest in his hands. "Why didn't I see it? Gran was always trying to manipulate things to suit her moods. Why did I never question her part in this? Why was I so ready to blame Sarah?"

Chris tossed the note back on the desk. "If Agatha were alive, hers would have been the first name on your lips. But with death, we

323

try to remember only the good."

Nick straightened, his eyes filled with reproach for himself. "I hurt her, Chris. You heard what Luther said. She'll never forgive me."

"Are you going to just give up? If you are, I'll tell you plain here and now that I'll be on her doorstep with ring in hand before the sun sets."

The despair in Nick's eyes turned dangerous. "Tread gently, friend," his voice was cold. "That is my wife you speak of."

Chris grinned. "Then just what are you going to do to win her back?"

Nick rose and went to the study door. "First I am going to get my answers from Beckett and then I am going to see my wife. You are welcome to join me for the first, but not the latter."

The two men sat in stunned silence as Beckett stood before them and told of the happenings in Salem. "The entire village is in chaos," he said. "Neighbors feeding off the fear of neighbors . . . never have I seen such madness."

"Then you think there really is something to this witchcraft?" Chris gasped.

Beckett shook his head. His hands twisted his knit cap as he searched to find the words to describe the horror he had witnessed. "Have ye ever seen a woman go hysterical, sir?" he asked finally. "One that's been so taken with grief or fear that she can't even think anymore, and much as ye don't want to, ye need to slap her to bring her round again? Well, Salem Village is like that, so consumed with its fear about witches that it's hysterical."

324

"I could believe it of a few," Nick said slowly. "But an entire village? Surely there is someone there with common sense."

Beckett nodded. "I met a well-learned man from Topsfield. Being from the next town over, he came out of curiosity to see the trials. For, like yourselves, he couldn't believe an entire village could be so taken in."

"And . . . ?" Chris prompted.

Beckett looked down at his feet. "We sat together at the hearings, and like I said, he was a real learned gentleman. He saw the trials for the mockery they were, and later that night he voiced his opinion at the tavern where we stayed. Said that those girls weren't bewitched, just in need of a good paddling."

"Did anyone listen?"

"Aye, sir, they listened, and good. Arrested him the next day and put him in jail."

"But why?" Chris gasped, unable to comprehend the full meaning of what he was hearing.

Beckett took a deep breath. "In Salem, sir, if you speak against the witchcraft trials, then ye must be a supporter of witchcraft, and therefore ye are accused and found guilty by yer own words. For they believe that only those in league with the devil would try to deny it exists."

"This is madness," Nick snapped in anger.

"Aye, sir, but there's more. Miss Sarah's been accused."

"Of witchcraft?" Nick and Chris spoke in unison.

Beckett nodded slowly. "Aye, sir. Seems that some old biddy in town claims to have seen her turn into a cat. They think that's why she's not there anymore, that she's off roaming the countryside looking for mischief to do for the devil."

"But surely her family doesn't believe such a ridiculous tale." Nick jerked to his feet and began to pace. "Did you give them Sarah's letter?"

Beckett's face grew sad and his eyes pleaded for understanding as he pulled Sarah's letter from the leather pouch at his side. "I know what ye told me to do, sir." He handed the unopened letter back to Nick. "But when I seen how things was up there, well I just think ye should know that the old woman isn't alone with her accusation. Miss Sarah's sister-in-law also claims to have witnessed the transformation. They've burned her house to the ground and her stepbrother, Samuel Wittfield, has reclaimed his family land."

"I don't believe it. Her own family?"

Beckett nodded. "Aye. When I seen how the winds were blowing, I grew afeared for Miss Sarah. Not knowing what her letter said, I feared she might have said exactly where she was living. Sir, I think it was Samuel that sold her to Riggins in the first place. I didn't think ye would want the man to know where Miss Sarah was."

"Did you tell them anything?" Nick's voice contained the anger he was holding on to by threads.

Beckett shifted nervously. "Only that I knew she was safe and in Virginia. I thought if I was wrong, her family would be grateful for the information. But, sir, I don't think I be wrong."

"My God," Chris flopped back in his chair.

"Beckett, were you able to get any information

326

on Sarah's friend, Rebecca Nurse?"

Nick watched the man's ruddy face go pale. "They found her guilty of witchcraft, sir. I watched as they hung her."

Nick braced his arms against the mantel and stared at the cold ashes. "This news is going to break her completely. After what I've done to her, to hear that her old friend is dead and her family has used and abandoned her—I just don't know how much more she can bear."

"Sir?" Beckett pulled another letter from his pocket. "When I spoke to Samuel Wittfield and told him I was going to travel south again, he gave me this letter to take to Miss Sarah. But I think you should have it."

Nick turned and reached for the folded paper. "There's no seal." He sat at his desk and looked up at his agent. "He gave it to you like this?"

Beckett nodded. "I think the man wanted it to be read, and not just by Miss Sarah. Read it, sir, and ye will see what I mean."

Nick's eyes ran down the paper. When he looked up, his face was filled with rage.

"What is it?" Chris demanded. "Do they tell her her friend had been killed?"

Nick shook his head, wishing he could plant his fist in the face of Samuel Wittfield. "Her brother expresses his sorrow that Sarah was the victim of such a hideous crime. He states how relieved he and his wife are to learn that she is safe, and then the son of a bitch begs her to return home with great haste, for they miss her dearly."

"What?" Chris gasped. "And he doesn't mention that she's been accused of witchcraft?"

Nick tossed the letter to his desk. "Not a damn word—"

"Begging pardon, sir," Beckett interrupted. "I know the letter asks Miss Sarah to come home. But, sir, I'd lay a year's wages that she'd be in jail before the sun could set."

Nick rested his hand on Beckett's shoulder. "You've done a good job, Peter, and I thank you for it. But I need your silence in this matter until I can see it settled."

Beckett straightened. "Ain't nobody should have to go through what Miss Sarah did—being sold in the dead of night, and by the very ones ye hold dear. Ye have my word none shall hear of this by my lips. But the crew was in Salem, too. They witnessed the madness and are sure to talk."

"Did they know you inquired after Sarah?"

"No, sir, I was very discreet."

Nick nodded. "Then the crew would have no reason to place Sarah in connection with the madness."

Beckett smiled for the first time. "No, sir, they surely wouldn't."

"Good. Now I want you to stop out back and see Mrs. Killingham. If my nose hasn't betrayed me, she's been baking cherry pies today and I know they're your favorite."

Beckett's face beamed with pleasure. "Thank ye, sir."

Nick held a tight rein on his anger until the study door closed. "That son of a bitch," he snarled, snatching the letter from his desk. "What man would sell his own sister into bondage and then beg her to come home where he knows she could be killed?"

Chris shook his head sadly. "Sarah spoke about her friend Rebecca. And for the life of me I cannot fathom how a village of God-fearing people could stand by and watch a frail old woman be hung." He looked at Nick through eyes filled with confusion. "What are you going to do?"

Nick tossed Samuel's letter back onto his desk with disgust. "I need to go down to Jamestown for a few hours and see to the *Lady May*. Then I shall pay an overdue visit to my wife."

"Mother and Julie will expect to come for dinner this evening," Chris reminded him.

Nick picked up his gloves. "You are all welcome. Do you wish to join me in Jamestown?"

Chris smiled and rose from his chair. "I wouldn't miss it for the world. That will give me an hour down and an hour back to question you on how you plan to win Sarah back."

Despite his foul temper, a smile tugged at the corners of Nick's mouth. "You think I will share that with you?"

Chris gave Nick an exaggerated wink. "I know you're legendary with the ladies. And now that you are an old married man, it seems only fitting that you should pass on the secret of your success."

Nick chuckled and shook his head, amazed at the contentment he found in being labeled an old married man. "Let's go," he admonished. "Time is fleeting, and I would have my business done so I can reclaim my wife."

"Then why not see Sarah first?" Chris asked as they reached the front door.

Nick shook his head. "I would still need to go to

Jamestown. No, I'll have the business over and done with and then I can turn all my attentions to where they really matter."

"To Sarah?"

Nick smiled. "To my wife."

Chapter Twenty-two

Julie Morgan dismissed the carriage driver and gazed longingly at the grand white house that stood before her. *You should have chosen me, Nick,* she thought, walking slowly up the brick path. Pausing at the entrance, she patted her long blond curls and pinched color into her cheeks before raising the knocker. Her most dazzling smile was firmly in place when Wadsworth opened the door.

"Mrs. Morgan to see Mr. Beaumont," she stated formally, brushing past the butler to step into the foyer.

"Why, Miss Julie, is that you?" Wadsworth's face lit with recognition. "Why, I haven't seen you since you were just a little thing."

Julie gave the butler a withering stare. "It's Mrs. Clarence Morgan now, Wadsworth. Would you please tell Mr. Beaumont that I'm here."

Unruffled, Wadsworth continued to smile. "I'm afraid I can't do that, Mrs. Morgan. Mr. Beaumont has gone with your brother down to the docks in Jamestown."

Julie's face mirrored her disappointment. "Then tell Mrs. Beau . . . Beaumont," she stumbled over the name, "tell Sarah that I am here and wish to see her."

Wadsworth shook his head. "Can't do that, either, Miss Julie. She's over at Mrs. Beaumont's old house. We had a bad storm a few days back and lots of folks were left without a place to live. Miss Sarah's been helping them out a bit."

Julie rolled her eyes. "How very noble." She glanced about the sunny foyer. How she loved this house, with its crisp white walls, bright airy windows, and sinfully expensive paintings. She sighed wistfully at the opulence of it all. "Wadsworth, I've decided I'll wait. Would you bring me a julep, please?"

Wadsworth's smile turned dubious. "It might be a long time, Miss Julie. Are you sure you wouldn't want me to fetch a carriage to carry you back to town?"

Julie pulled her shoulders back and gave Wadsworth her haughtiest stare. "I shall wait in the study. I'm sure Nick won't mind if I amuse myself with one of his volumes until he and my brother return."

"If that's what you wish, miss. It's right through here."

Julie brushed past the butler. "I know where it is, Wadsworth," she sighed. "Now will you get me that drink, or am I going to have to tell Mr. Beaumont you were rude to me?"

Wadsworth's face turned to stone. "As you wish, madam."

Julie waited until the study door was closed before dancing across the room and flopping down in the chair behind Nick's desk. Her fingers rubbed against the smooth grain of the wood as her eyes scanned the book-filled room. *What a waste,* she thought, noting the leather-bound first editions that claimed a special shelf. *You don't know how to spend your money, Nicky. You've squandered so much of it on useless paper. Now, if I were spending it . . .* Julie sat up straight and frowned. A small black vase rested on the corner of Nick's desk but its pink roses were days past their prime and petals had already started to fall.

She clucked her tongue with disgust. "I'd never let the servants get away with such sloppy housekeeping," she said to the empty room. Plucking the wilted roses from the vase, she crossed the room and dropped them into the ashcan.

"There," she said firmly, dusting off her hands. "Now, things are as they should be." She returned to the desk and tugged at the knobs, only to find all the drawers locked. Her fingers ran down the spine of Nick's quill and she fancied him penning her an amorous letter. Then she saw it. Hastily tucked within the pages of his book, the folded note beckoned her to look closer. Without a moment's hesitation, Julie reached for the volume and withdrew the paper. She scanned the contents and her eyes began to sparkle as a devilish smile tugged at her lips.

"Well, well, well," she said softly. "Little Sarah's family misses her." Her mind clicked at a furious speed and her brow wrinkled. Why wasn't the letter with Sarah, she wondered. Could it be that Nick was so possessive he begrudged her a trip home? She imagined Nick's dark eyes smiling down at her. "I want you always at my side, Julie," he would declare solemnly. She felt her heart begin to flutter. "I would never leave you, my darling," she whispered. Julie straightened and scanned the letter again. I *would never leave,* she thought, *but Sarah would, or Nick wouldn't have kept this from her.*

The study door edged open. Julie jumped to her feet, shoving the letter into her reticule in the process. "Wadsworth," she gasped. "You gave me a start."

"Sorry, madam." His tone was clipped and formal. "I am just bringing the refreshment you requested."

Julie shook her head, making her blond curls dance about her shoulders. "I've changed my mind, Wadsworth," she said lightly. "You may fetch me a carriage. I don't feel like waiting after all."

Wadsworth frowned and glanced down at the silver tray he carried. "Do you not wish your drink, madam?"

Julie breezed across the room, whisked the glass from the tray, and took a dainty sip. "There . . ." She returned the drink. "Now if you are satisfied . . ." She looked down her nose. "You may fetch me a carriage."

Wadsworth glanced about the room. Something was amiss, he could feel it in his bones. "As you wish, madam. I shall call you directly."

"Oh, pooh," she said, dancing by him. "I shall wait on the porch so do hurry."

Wadsworth gave a curt nod and left to do her bidding.

Julie found Sarah folding children's clothing in

334

Agatha's back parlor. "My goodness, you look terrible," she said, taking in the dark circles that ringed Sarah's eyes. "What on earth have you done to yourself?"

Sarah smiled in greeting but didn't stop her chore. "Julie, how nice to see you again. I didn't know you were coming for a visit so soon."

Julie pulled a chair near, dusted its clean surface with her handkerchief, then sat down. "Chris brought Mother and me when we heard of Agatha's death. The families have always been extremely close, you know."

Sarah nodded but remained silent.

Julie looked about the room. The heavy draperies had been pulled back to let the sunlight in, but she wrinkled her nose at the dark-colored walls. "Why are you doing that?" she grimaced at the wicker basket that sat at Sarah's feet. "Why isn't one of your servants taking care of it?"

"Everyone is already busy," Sarah said easily.

Julie rolled her eyes. "Sarah," she said in an impatient tone. "Servants are never busy. Oh, they'll tell you they are, but they're really not." She picked the child's smock from Sarah's lap with two fingers and dropped it back into the basket. "You're going to have to learn how to give orders if you are going to have a successful marriage. Why, you should be home right now seeing to Nick's dinner party."

Sarah felt her chest tighten. He had said she'd get not even a good morning, but she hadn't realized it could hurt so much. She hadn't known that just the mention of his name would bring back the lump in her throat and make her eyes hot and stingy. Her hand trembled as she reached down to

335

retrieve the smock. "Julie, I appreciate your advice . . . but circumstances have been a little hectic of late—"

"Oh, I know," Julie interrupted. "We heard all about the storm and how you've taken folks in. But Sarah, Nick is not going to be at all impressed if tonight's dinner doesn't go well."

Sarah struggled to keep her voice even. "I'm sure Mrs. Killingham has everything under control. She's been with Mr. Beaumont for years."

Julie watched Sarah's pale face grow paler still, and a flicker of excitement stirred within her. Something was definitely wrong between the newly wed couple. Could it be that Nick had found marriage as confining as she had? Or was he just asserting his will as Clarence had tried so hard to do?

"You know, now that you're married, you really shouldn't let Nick get the upper hand," she counseled. "I don't care how many times he says he loves you, you've got to learn to be strong to get your own way."

Sarah swallowed hard. *But he never said he loved me,* her mind screamed with pain. *I offered him my very soul and he left in the rain.* She tried to speak, but couldn't find her voice.

"I will never let Clarence have control over me," Julie continued primly. "I don't care what the law says about him being the master of the house. I'm going to do what I want. You should, too."

Sarah tilted her head in confusion. "What would you have me do?"

"Well, if I were you and I wanted to go home for a visit," Julie leaned forward, "then I would go

336

and I wouldn't care what Nick said to the contrary."

Sarah's eyes turned wistful. "I would love to see my family again."

"How long have you been visiting in Virginia?" Julie tried to keep her voice casual as her excitement grew.

Sarah paused. "It's been over three months," she said slowly. Three months longing for her family . . . waiting for word . . . losing her heart . .

"More than three months! Then, Sarah, why are you letting Nick keep you here?"

Sarah shook her head slowly. "That is not the case."

Julie reached for her hand. "Please don't think me too personal, but I feel we women must stick together in matters such as these. Tell me, do you know of your brother's letter?"

Sarah's eyes grew wide. "A letter from Samuel?"

Julie nodded and slowly tugged the drawstrings on her bag. "I thought as much. Look, I found this in Nick's desk." She handed Sarah the letter.

"But . . ."

"Now don't go getting all stuffy about how I shouldn't have taken it. It was sitting right out on his desk, and when I realized it was for you, I simply thought I'd bring it. Besides," she patted Sarah's trembling hands, "as much as I adore Nick, I think he's wrong to keep you from going to your family if that's what you want to do."

Sarah's eyes scanned the letter for a second time. "Samuel wants me to return home immediately," her voice was dazed. "What am I going to do?"

Julie smiled. "Well, when Clarence didn't want

337

me to make this trip with Mother and Chris, I just threw a tantrum until he gave in."

"A tantrum?"

"Never mind," she said, patting Sarah's hand. "You'd never be convincing anyhow. But, tell me, do you really want to go back to Salem?"

Sarah nodded. "More than anything else in the world."

"Then you're going to go." Julie stood and her mind clicked into action. "And today, if we can find a boat."

Totally overwhelmed, Sarah stopped as Julie tried to tug her from the room. "I can't go today. There is too much to do here."

Julie forced her scowl into an expression of concern. "Why, Sarah, I'd be happy to lend a hand here in your absence." Her eyes glanced down at the basket of laundry. *I'd have these servants whipped into shape in no time,* she thought. "I know there is much to do, but I'm sure I could manage it."

Sarah smiled in gratitude but shook her head. "That is so kind of you," she said softly. "But what would I use for fare? How would I book a passage?"

Julie waved aside her protest. "You go upstairs and pack your things. Take little with you so no one notices what you are doing. I still have my carriage outside and I will lend you the money for passage."

Sarah paled. "You want me to leave and not even say good-bye? Julie, I can't do that. These people are very dear to me."

"They might be dear to you," Julie huffed, "but

338

I tell you true that they are loyal to Nick. If you go running around saying good-bye, Nick will be here within minutes and he'll be madder than a wet hen."

He's already that mad, Sarah thought as she turned to the stairs. And briefly she wondered if he wouldn't be relieved to find her gone. With a heavy heart, Sarah went to her room and looked at the multitude of things she had accumulated: the lovely sapphire dress Charlotte had so skillfully created, the many gowns Nick had ordered . . . These she folded carefully and left on the end of her bed. They would never do in Salem.

Taking the bag Agatha had once loaned her, Sarah placed a clean nightrail and shift inside, along with her black velvet gown. Her packing completed, she turned to the small desk in the corner of her room and quickly penned a good-bye note to Luther and Mrs. Hempsted. But her eyes swam with tears as she sealed the final one, to Nick.

Rising, she looked about the room. Agatha had been so generous, she thought. Taking in a stranger and treating her as family. *Someday, I shall return the kindness to someone else,* she thought, *and I shall remember you always.* She crossed to the dresser with her letters and saw the tortoiseshell comb Nick had given her. With hands that were far from steady, she propped her notes against it. Then, looking down, she touched the golden links that spanned her wrist.

Clutching the bracelet to her chest, Sarah's eyes pressed closed with pain. "Do I take you for the memories," she whispered, "or do I leave you here with my heart?" Slowly she opened her eyes. She unhooked the catch with trembling fingers and placed the bracelet on the dresser. For a full minute she stood silent, then, taking a deep breath, Sarah picked up her bag and bid a silent farewell to Agatha's household.

The sun slipped from view as Nick climbed back into the carriage at his grandmother's house. "I don't understand it," he said to Christopher. "Sarah isn't here. Luther said she left with Julie this afternoon. Julie told him they were going into town to shop and not to expect Sarah until very late."

"That sounds like my sister." Chris stretched. "Mayhap when they finished, she persuaded Sarah to return to your house for dinner tonight. After all, she doesn't know any of the details concerning your marriage, and Sarah doesn't strike me as the type who would easily share her problems. I'll wager Julie assumed Sarah would return home with her tonight and Sarah was too embarrassed to say otherwise."

Nick signaled the driver. "You're probably right. With any luck, she's at home right now chatting with your mother."

"Who is going to skin us alive for being so late," Chris warned.

As he predicted, Mrs. Carlson stormed from the parlor when she heard them enter. "Nicholas, I was so sorry to hear about Agatha. But would someone please tell me what is going on?"

"It's wonderful to see you again, Mrs. Carlson." Nick kissed her cheek, then handed his hat to

340

Wadsworth. "Have Sarah and Julie returned?"

"No, they haven't," Mrs. Carlson replied impatiently. "And I want to know what is happening. First I wake to find that Julie has gone on without me, then I arrive at your house at the appointed hour and no one is here to greet me."

Chris placed an arm about his mother's shoulders and led her back into the parlor. "I'm sorry we are late. But it was all Nick's fault."

Mrs. Carlson slapped her son's arm away and shook her head. "When are you two going to grow up? I had hopes when I heard you were married, Nick, but now I'm beginning to wonder." The teasing smile in her eyes took the sting from her words.

Nick poured them each a drink. "We stopped by Agatha's on our way home only to find that Sarah and Julie had gone shopping."

Mrs. Carlson accepted her drink and perched on the edge of a gold settee. "Then there is no telling how long they will be. I am famished and those two are probably knee-deep in sketches at Madame Rousseau's."

Nick started to object, but Mrs. Carlson pressed on. "Nick, I would swear that's where they are. Ever since the wedding Julie has been raving about that lovely sapphire gown Sarah wore. I'm telling you, I know my daughter. She has persuaded Sarah to take her there and she won't be satisfied until she owns every gown in the shop."

"Sir, do you wish me to continue to hold dinner?" Wadsworth questioned.

"No!" Mrs. Carlson rose abruptly to her feet and placed her hand on Nick's arm. "Nicholas, I know

I am being extremely forward, and I know you wish Sarah here to join us, but I am starving! Please let us eat, and then you and Chris can go and fetch them."

Chris took in the lines of strain on his mother's face and realized the taxing journey had been harder on her than she was willing to admit. "Nick, I think Mother is right." He turned and caught Nick's eye. "If Julie and Sarah wish to be late, then let them suffer the consequences."

Reluctantly, Nick agreed, silently telling himself that another hour would make little difference between him and Sarah, while, as a host, he did have a duty to the Carlsons.

"Wadsworth, you can inform Mrs. Killingham that we are ready to dine. We've decided not to wait for Julie or Mrs. Beaumont." For the barest moment Nick stood silent, realizing he had referred to Sarah as Mrs. Beaumont for the first time and that the tight knot in his chest was finally starting to ease.

The trio was seated in the dining room when Chris brought up the subject of Salem. "Nick, perhaps Mother would have some ideas of how you might broach the matter with Sarah."

Mrs. Carlson looked up from her plate of peanut soup. "What's the matter?" She gave Nick a sympathetic smile. "Is Sarah homesick already?"

Nick shifted uncomfortably. He hadn't meant to share the news, but perhaps Chris was right. "There are trying times in Salem Village, where Sarah is from," he said hesitantly. "Sarah is desperate to return for a visit, but I fear it is unsafe for her to do so."

"Are the Indians that unsettled?" Mrs. Carlson smiled as Wadsworth removed her plate and replaced it with a delicate poached fish in lemon sauce. "I didn't realize that the North was still having such problems."

"The problem is not with Indians, Mother," Chris said quietly. "It is with witches."

Mrs. Carlson's eyebrows drew together. "Christopher, I thought you beyond those childish imaginings."

"They're not imaginings, Mrs. Carlson," Nick said slowly. "A madness has taken over the village and the townsfolk fear that witches walk among them."

"That's dreadful," she gasped, setting aside her fork.

"What is dreadful?" Julie breezed into the room. "Oh, bother, you've started without me." Deliberately she took the seat meant for Sarah at the foot of the table. "That wasn't very civilized."

"Is Sarah with you?" Chris asked, noting the dark look Nick was sending his sister.

Julie shook her head and all but snatched the plate of soup from Wadsworth's fingers. "No, she's too occupied at the moment to return." Aware that Nick watched her intently, she tried to be genteel as she spooned the savory soup into her mouth, but her stomach demanded more, and she desperately wished she could just pick up the damn plate and drink it as she so often did when she was home. "Now, what were we talking about?" She smiled as Wadsworth removed her empty dish.

Nick started to rise, but Chris stopped him. "Finish your dinner and then go and fetch her.

She's safe enough at Agatha's. Luther won't let any harm come to her. After all, it's not as if she were in Salem."

Julie frowned as she bit into her fish. "What's wrong with Salem? Isn't that where Sarah's family is from?"

"It seems there are witches in Salem." Mrs. Carlson looked down at her steaming plate of vegetables and found her appetite had disappeared.

Julie looked at her mother and laughed. "That's absurd. There are no such things as witches."

Chris set down his own fork. "It seems that in Salem there might be. According to what Beckett told us this morning, they've already hung several women who have been accused."

"Dear God!" Mrs. Carlson's hand flew to her throat. "They've really gone that far? Where are the magistrates? Why haven't they put a stop to it?"

Nick wearily shook his head. "They, too, have been caught up in the madness. The cry of witchcraft has become an easy scapegoat for many."

Chris nodded. "If my cow's gone dry, what better than to blame it on my neighbor and claim foul play. Perhaps I can even demand restitution for the deed."

Mrs. Carlson watched her daughter go completely still. "Are you feeling ill, Julie? You've gone whiter than the table linen."

Julie struggled to keep the terror from her voice. "What does all this have to do with Sarah?"

Chris, too, took in his sister's pale complexion. "Nick was telling us that Sarah is homesick and wants to return to Salem to see her family. But with things as unstable as they are, it could be dangerous. I asked Mother if she might have some advice as to how to ease Sarah's plight."

"And they've really hung someone?" Julie's voice quivered in fear.

"One of Sarah's closest friends, an old woman called Rebecca Nurse."

Julie felt her fear begin to grow. "Oh, Mama, I've done something wrong. But I didn't mean any harm, I just didn't know. Now everyone is going to blame me, and it wasn't my fault."

Nick felt a sickening dread seep into his body. His muscles grew tight and his heart stopped beating. "Julie, what did you say to Sarah?"

Julie shrank back against her chair. "I just told her she shouldn't let you be such a tyrant."

Nick's look became menacing. "What else did you say?"

"I just told her that if she wanted to go home for a visit she should go."

"You *what?*" Nick exploded.

Julie shrugged her shoulders and tried to gather her courage. "When she saw her brother's letter, she was desperate to return. I just told her I thought she should."

"You stole a letter from my desk and gave it to Sarah?"

"Well, it was her letter from her brother," Julie defended. "You had no right to keep it from her—"

"It's going to be all right," Mrs. Carlson's calm voice broke in. "Julie, you were wrong to take that letter no matter how noble your intentions were. But Nicholas, you are making far too much of this. Sarah hasn't gone anywhere. And if you calm yourself, I'm sure you'll find the words to help her understand your reasons for keeping it from her. Sarah isn't a foolish girl, and once she knows the truth, I'm sure she'll agree with you. You can simply point out that her family wouldn't want her to come until things are more settled—"

"But you're wrong, Mama," Julie interrupted. "Sarah's brother is desperate to have her home again. His letter said so. That's why Sarah is so anxious to return."

Chris looked from Nick to his mother and back again. "I think you had better tell them everything."

Nick took a deep breath and tried to remain calm, but the gnawing fear in his stomach refused to be banished. "Sarah has been accused of witchcraft," he said slowly, watching their faces fill with disbelief. "My agent believes that Sarah's family might be behind the accusations."

"Dear God, but why?" Mrs. Carlson could not keep the horror from her voice.

Nick tried to stem the frantic beating of his heart. "With the death of her parents, Sarah inherited five hundred acres of prime land. Her step-brother wants it back."

"Oh, no!" Julie carefully set down her wineglass, for her fingers had begun to shake too much to hold it. "But his letter . . ."

"Was probably meant to entice her home again," Chris said tightly. "And how do you tell someone who is aching to return home that her very family has betrayed her?"

Julie looked down the table at Nick and cringed,

for every muscle in his face was etched with anger. "Nick, Sarah isn't at Agatha's old house," her voice trembled. "We didn't go shopping this afternoon like I said. We took a carriage and went to Jamestown." Nick jerked to his feet and took a menacing step forward. "She said she wanted to go home," Julie rushed on. "I didn't know it was going to be dangerous so I gave her the money for passage."

Nick's eyes grew wide. "You did *what?*"

Julie felt the tears slowly drip down her cheeks and hoped he noticed. "I gave her the fare. Sarah is on a ship called the *Good Providence*. It left for the Massachusetts Bay Colony this afternoon."

"Oh, my God," Chris gasped.

Julie took in the three angry faces that glared in her direction. Unable to bear their censure, she decided to escape in the way she knew best and, giving in to the terror of the situation, she fainted.

Ignoring her daughter's limp body, Mrs. Carlson rose from the table and went to Nick, taking his hand. "You have to do something, Nicholas," she said calmly. "You have to go and get Sarah back, for she doesn't know the danger she is in."

Nick struggled to maintain his temper. Sarah needed him and he needed a clear head. "The *Good Providence* is one of my own ships," he said ironically. "She's smooth on the waters, but not my fastest."

"Then let's go."

He turned to Chris as they entered the foyer. "This will not be a short venture."

Chris shrugged and reached for his hat. "My sister was directly to blame. If you'll agree to let Mother and Julie stay here where I know they shall be safe, I would be honored to sail at your side."

Nick nodded and placed a fleeting kiss on Mrs. Carlson's pale cheek. "Wadsworth will see to your needs, you have only to ask. And Julie—" His voice grew tight.

"Is in dire need of a good paddling," Mrs. Carlson interrupted. "And this time I shall see to it myself. Now off with you both. You have my prayers to find Sarah quickly."

"Then let us be off," Chris said, giving his mother a reassuring hug. "We've a ship to catch and a lady to rescue."

Chapter Twenty-three

Sarah sat on her narrow bunk with her arms locked around her knees. "We did not make a good choice, Julie," she whispered to the empty cabin. " 'Tis a cargo ship on which I sail and I am the only passenger . . . the only woman." Weak with exhaustion, for she was too frightened to sleep, she struggled with memories from the past. Each dip and sway of the boat dredged forth the horrors of her last sea voyage. And although the captain had assured her she was free to move about on the deck, she had only to close her eyes to feel the ropes that had once bound her hands and feet. Twice, a knock had sounded at her door, making her heart pound in fright, but each time the cook had brought her food, her stomach had protested violently from the mere smell of it. A suffocating darkness threatened to consume her every time she closed her eyes, so she sat, watching the sway of the small lantern that hung from the beams overhead.

"What have I done, Nick?" she cried silently, for her tears were long since spent. She tried to think of her home in Salem, of how happy Samuel and Elizabeth would be to have her back. She tried to mentally list the chores that would command her attention. Would she weed her garden first or walk over to Samuel's to retrieve her cow and goat. His letter had said they were at his farm now so he could better care for them. She thought about sleeping in her own bed, but found no comfort, for, as always, her mind returned to Nick.

Sarah's head dropped to her knees. Was he relieved she had departed? Had he found the golden bracelet and her note of farewell? She remembered the way his dark eyes would dance in amusement when she misunderstood a local expression and how patient he had been in explaining. She could feel his arms about her and the gentle way he had held her . . . touched her. "How am I going to live without your smile?" she pleaded brokenly.

"You won't ever have to."

Sarah's head snapped up. She hadn't heard the door to her cabin open, but the rich male voice was very real. Her eyes focused and her heartbeat tripled. "Nick . . . ?" her voice was hesitant, for in truth she had imagined him standing there too many times to count. "Are you real?"

His heart ached at the sight she presented, huddled in the corner of her bunk, clearly terrified of everything that was happening. Relief washed through him, then turned to anger that she had taken such a chance. "If you wish, madam, I would be more than happy to throw up your skirts and paddle your bare backside for pulling this ridiculous stunt. Then you'd know how very real I am."

She would have risen to meet him halfway, but she hadn't eaten since coming aboard and she was afraid she'd fall at his feet. So she opened

350

her arms and beckoned him closer.

Nick needed no invitation as he dropped beside her on the bunk and pulled her roughly onto his lap. They stared at each other in wonder and then they were locked in an embrace. For long, satisfying minutes they rocked together. Nick pressed his face to her neck, feeling the silky softness of her hair brush against his cheek. She had always been of slight form, but now she felt positively frail within his arms and silently he cursed himself for the pain he had caused her. *Never again,* he vowed, pulling her closer still.

"I love you," he said against her hair. "I love you more than life itself. When I realized you had gone, it was as if a piece of me had been cut away."

Sarah luxuriated in the sound of his words. The words she had so longed to hear. Burrowed close against him she felt the warmth of his body and the strength of his arms. Her fingers touched the corded muscles of his neck and she felt the violent pounding of his heart against her breast. Her lips curved into a smile when she realized it matched her own.

"I love you, too," she whispered against his throat. "You bring the sunlight to my day and the smile to my heart, but how did you get here? How ever did you find me?"

"Julie told us what she had done." As Sarah felt him shudder, her arms tightened about him.

"Don't be cross with Julie," she said gently. "She was trying so hard to help me." Reluctantly, Sarah pulled back so she could better see his face. "But how did you get here? We've been almost three days at sea?"

An ironic smile touched his lips. "You had the good sense to run away on one of my own ships," he said, placing light kisses across her forehead and reserving his judgment of Julie for another time. "I am the one who charted the course, so there was a hope we could overtake you. But when I think of all that could have gone wrong . . . You must promise me you'll never do this again."

Sarah smiled and shook her head. "I'm so sorry . . ." Nick placed a finger across her lips to still her words.

"I was wrong to think that you had tried to manipulate Gran, and I said things in anger that hurt you deeply. Now, I can only beg your forgiveness."

"You already have it." Sarah ran her trembling fingers across the troubled brow of her proud husband. "Nick, don't be angry with Agatha. Whatever she did, she did out of love."

Nick reached into his pocket and withdrew the water-stained letter. "Did you ever read this?" he questioned. "The letter Danvers handed to you right after we were wed?"

Sarah shook her head.

Nick opened the paper and placed it in her hand. "It's from Gran," he said quietly.

Sarah's eyes scanned the wrinkled paper, and her eyes welled with tears when she looked back up at Nick. "She wanted me to be your wife," she said in amazement.

Nick smiled. "Gran thought I was moving too slowly and decided to speed up the process. This was her way of forcing my hand."

Sarah looked down at her lap. "I know you didn't want to marry me, but . . ."

"Sarah Townsend Beaumont," he said, gently

352

brushing strands of hair from her pale face. "Will you do me the honor of truly becoming my wife?"

For Sarah a ray of hope blossomed. "I would give you all the shares without marriage," she said solemnly.

Nick took a deep breath. "I know that now. But I find the only thing I truly want is to have you for my wife."

If she could have loved him more it would have been in that moment. Sarah reached up and her palm touched his unshaven cheek. "I love you." Her voice was soft, but clear. "Know that I will never lie to you. Although you won't always wish to hear it, my lips will never willingly tell you a falsehood."

He pressed a kiss to her palm, then gazed deep into her violet eyes. "But I must confess to a falsehood. The night of the storm, when I said I took you without love, I lied. You have been deep in my heart from the first moment I watched you pull the weeds from my garden. You are my wife, my heart, my soul." His voice quivered. "I want you in my life to share my life because I can't imagine living without you."

Sarah closed her eyes and pressed her body to the warmth of his. "I love you with every breath of my being," she said simply. When their lips met again, their kiss was flavored with the salt of her tears.

"No more of this," Nick chided gently, using his thumb to trace the pale skin under her eyes. "You're with me now and you're safe."

"Nick . . ." Sarah's voice trembled. "Would you take me home to see my family? I know it's far and I know you're busy. But my need to see them face-to-face is great. I want them to meet you, to see the man who has claimed my heart. Also, as my husband . . ." She tasted the word on her tongue. "As my husband, you would need to put your name on the land I own."

Nick thought of all the dangers that might await them, but the look on her face was one he could not deny. "If I agree," he said slowly, "it can only be for a day or two at most."

Sarah's eyes brightened. "I don't care if it's only for an hour," she sighed. "I just need to hug them both and let them know how happy I am so they will cease their worry."

Nick felt his heart constrict and wondered how he was ever going to tell her that they suspected her of witchcraft. "If we're going all the way to Salem," he challenged, "you are going to need to get your strength back."

Sarah flung her arms about his neck. "Thank you, thank you," she cried, scattering kisses about his face.

Nick's body ached to take her, but he knew he must wait. "The captain tells me you haven't been able to eat anything." His voice was tender, and Sarah felt a deep contentment wrap around her. "Have you been sick as well?"

She nodded slowly, ashamed to admit her weakness. Nick placed a kiss upon her brow and then rose from the bunk with her in his arms. "I'm taking you up on deck," he explained. "The fresh air will do you good, and once we get some food into you, you'll feel much better." Nick paused in the threshold of her cabin looking down at her and his eyes grew intense. "If I didn't think you would collapse, I'd take you here and now. But sometimes the deed is all the sweeter with the waiting." He placed a chaste kiss on her lips.

"You're a wicked man, Nicholas Beaumont," she said smiling.

"And tonight I'll prove that for sure, Mrs. Beaumont," he promised.

Up on deck, Sarah was relieved to find that Nick had been right. The motion of the ship seemed less pronounced and the fresh air revived her. She was delighted to find Chris aboard, then embarrassed to be the center of so much attention. Nick rarely left her side and she had only to look as if she was in need for someone to come to her aid. A pallet was made for her so she might sit in the sunlight, then a blanket appeared to cover her legs. She managed to eat a mug of soup, and was delighted when her stomach seemed pleased with the offering.

The sun slipped below the horizon and Nick carried her back to their cabin, but she was asleep before he could place her in the bunk. Undaunted, Nick eased the clothing from her body and then joined her under the covers in the narrow space. Pulling her close against him so her head rested on his shoulder, he marveled at the rightness of it all. "I've spent nights in passion and found not half the satisfaction I feel just to hold you in my arms," he whispered to her sleeping form. "It has always been difficult for me to let people get close to me, but I never realized how alone I was until you came and filled my life and then left me. If it was meant to be, so that I might have you, I know now that my lifetime of searching has been more than rewarded. Never will I turn from you. And when my time on earth is ended, yours shall be the name

355

that comes with my last breath." His declaration complete, Nick closed his eyes and joined Sarah in sleep.

The days aboard the ship soon established a comfortable pattern. Sarah rested and under Nick's watchful eye, soon regained her strength. Long naps in the sun and constant food to tempt her appetite soon had the color back in her cheeks. But the nights of passion that she shared with Nick in their narrow bunk were the true reason for the smile that never left her lips.

More than a week had passed before Nick sat her down on a secluded part of the deck and, with Chris at his side, told her of the happenings in Salem. She had remained wide-eyed and silent. Her tears didn't start until he spoke of the death of her friend.

"But Rebecca was so frail," she sobbed against her husband's chest. "Why would anyone say such terrible things about one so pure of heart? How could they do that to a woman of God?"

Nick held her close as she cried, but his eyes met Chris's over her head. He had decided nothing could be gained by telling her Beckett's fears concerning her family and he was more than grateful when Chris agreed.

They had laid their plan carefully. Nick would get rooms for them in the ordinary while Chris traveled to the Village. Once there, he would entice Sarah's brother to return with him without mentioning Sarah's name. Sarah would have her meeting, then, with any luck, they would soon be back at sea.

They hand-selected men from the *Merry Weather* to join them on the *Good Providence,* while the captain of the *Merry Weather* was instructed to sail nearby but not to dock at Salem Harbor. If their plans went awry, his ship would be their backup. Information was passed in hushed whispers, and all but Sarah knew the plan.

On the last day of August, Salem Harbor came into view. Sarah hugged the rail as excitement raced through her. It seemed to take so long to cover the last bit of ocean and her patience threatened to snap as she watched the ship slowly maneuver itself closer to the dock.

Nick stood at her side on the quarterdeck as they waited for the ropes to be secured. Her face glowed with anticipation as she held his arm. Before them lay the confusion of the marketplace. Carts filled with oranges and apples stood between barrels of cargo. Local fishermen unloaded their day's catch, and the air about them grew ripe. Undaunted, Sarah's smile never wavered. She had pushed the news of Rebecca's death to the far corner of her mind and suddenly she couldn't wait to be home again. And now, when thoughts of spending the night in her own bed pressed forward, they brought a contented smile to her lips.

"Better be careful, madam," Nick said, taking her arm and indicating it was time for them to leave the ship. "If you continue to look at me like that, I shall postpone our departure until I can have my way with you below decks."

When they reached the boarding plank, Sarah turned to gaze at her husband. Her hand reached up to cover his heart. "I know you did not want to bring me here," she said quietly. "But that you would put my wants above your own . . ." Her voice shook with emotion, but she was determined not to cry on such a joyous occasion. "I will spend my life trying to think of ways to thank you."

Nick placed his large palm over hers and pressed tightly. "You are my wife. Your welfare comes before my own, and no thanks are necessary. Still, if you truly wished to please me . . ." He bent close and whispered desires that made Sarah's cheeks grow bright with color.

"People do that?" she replied in awe as he turned her back to the boarding plank.

Nick's laughter rang out and did much to relieve the tension of the crew. "I'll show you tonight," he promised with a wink. Then they were standing on the pier of Salem Harbor.

"The village is about a two-hour ride inland," she said. "But I'm afraid I don't know where the livery is." Her eyes scanned the ordered chaos that surrounded them as they walked.

Chris stepped close to Nick's side. "I don't like this," he said. His words were for Nick alone as he gestured toward the docks. An unusual silence permeated the air. No shouts came from impatient captains anxious to be at sea, though many hands moved about loading cargo. No merchant called, enticing the buyer to sample his wares, yet many were about. Only the rats seemed impervious to the strained atmosphere, and their scurry and squeal could be heard as they fought over each scrap carelessly tossed to the ground.

Nick's eyes took in the unnatural scene and he was glad to have Chris firmly planted on Sarah's other side. Instinctively his hand tightened on hers.

"Captain Beaumont?"

Startled to hear his name called in the murky silence, Nick paused, stepping slightly ahead of Sarah. Chris moved to his side, effectively blocking Sarah from view as they watched a tall, well-dressed seaman cross over to them.

"Forgive me for interrupting your passage, but are you not Nicholas Beaumont?"

Nick nodded slowly, and then it dawned. "Sebastian . . . ?" He hesitated. "Sebastian Hawthorne?"

"Yes, you old seadog," the man pumped his hand vigorously.

Nick stepped aside and urged a confused Sarah forward. "My sweet, this is Sebastian Hawthorne. He was one of the best captains who ever worked for Beaumont Shipping. Sebastian, may I present my wife, Sarah Beaumont, and our friend, Christopher Carlson."

Sarah smiled as the men shook hands. "Captain Hawthorne, you no longer work for Beaumont Shipping?"

Hawthorne tipped his hat and smiled. "No, madam. Thanks to your husband's clever mind for business, I was able to make my fortune. I have two ships of my own now that sail out of Salisbury."

"And is it business or pleasure that brings you to Salem, sir?" Chris asked.

They watched in amazement as the captain's face turned pale. "I have one last matter of business to settle and then I shall leave Salem forever." His voice was as cold as stone. "A madness has gripped this town, Nicholas. Look closely to those you hold dear."

Chris glanced about and realized that many on the docks had stopped their business and were now standing, watching them.

"The children from the village of Salem were here just this morning searching for more witches," Hawthorne said softly. "Goings-on the likes you've never seen before. And when the absurd spectacle was over, another fifteen were arrested."

"Oh, no," Sarah cried, pressing her hand to her lips.

"But what of the magistrates?" Nick demanded. "Do they just stand by and allow such madness to happen?"

Hawthorne slowly nodded his head. "Even now, adults from the village are sniffing through the streets searching for any of the children they might have missed." He looked over his shoulder and immediately grew uneasy from the attention they were getting. "I have rooms at the ordinary but three streets over," he said quietly. "Let us retire there where we can speak more freely."

Nick gave a slight nod of agreement. He, too, had sensed the growing undercurrent of tension. They had taken only a few steps when they were approached by a very nervous harbormaster.

"State your name and your business," he demanded sharply.

"Nicholas Beaumont of Beaumont Shipping in the Virginia Colony," Nick replied easily. "My wife," he nodded toward Sarah, "and my business associate, Christopher Carlson."

The man relaxed slightly, for the name of Beaumont Shipping was well known along the waterfront. "And you, sir?"

"Captain Sebastian Hawthorne. I work for Mr.

Beaumont."

Sarah's head snapped up with surprise, but she remained silent. Why had the man lied, she wondered? Did he not want the harbormaster to know of his own good fortune, or had his words to her been the lie?

She looked up at her husband. His eyes were dark and blank, but neither he or Chris offered words to contradict the captain's story.

The harbormaster waved them on their way and Sarah felt the tension relax slightly in Nick's body as they followed Captain Hawthorne from the docks. Her own excitement grew as they traveled down streets that carried names she remembered. It mattered not that nothing else was familiar; she was almost home now, and that fact alone made her step grow light.

The ordinary was in view when a shrill scream pierced the air causing Sarah to clutch Nick's arm with a start. Turning, she found her sister-in-law, Elizabeth Wittfield, descending from a horse-drawn cart.

Sarah's heart swelled with joy. She had thought it would be another day at best before she would see her home, her family. But the fates had delivered Elizabeth to her here and now. Before Nick could even realize what was happening, Sarah had darted across the street to greet her sister.

"Elizabeth," Sarah cried with excitement. "I'm home!"

Elizabeth screamed again, a bone-chilling scream that compelled everyone within earshot to come running.

An arm's length away from embracing, Sarah

stopped short. Elizabeth was cowering away from her, pressed back against the cart and shaking in fear.

"Elizabeth," she said gently. " 'Tis I, Sarah. Didn't you get the message I sent?"

Elizabeth shook her head wildly. Her eyes scanned the crowd, coming to settle on the magistrates who had rushed to her aid. "She's a witch," she screamed, pointing her long, thin finger at Sarah.

The crowd about the two women drew closer, effectively blocking Nick. Fear ate at him as he struggled to get to Sarah. But Captain Hawthorne grabbed his arm and pulled him back. "Wait," the man hissed. "The magistrates are there. Be still or we shall all be arrested."

Nick struggled to remain calm, while his heart demanded he rush in and save her. "What will they do?"

"Watch," Hawthorne whispered. "Watch, but say nothing."

"Elizabeth . . ." Sarah's voice began to tremble. "Don't you remember me? 'Tis Sarah."

"I know you well, you whore of Satan!" Elizabeth screamed. "You're a spawn of the devil, and a murderer besides."

Sarah shook her head in confusion. "Elizabeth, I never killed anyone. I was kidnapped from my bed. I was thrown into a ship and sold into bondage."

"Murderer," Elizabeth shrieked. "Sold into bondage, you say, when you wear a dress like that?"

Sarah looked down at her plain black velvet gown and knew she had erred greatly. She had completely forgotten how quick her Puritan neighbors were to condemn the unusual. "Elizabeth, 'tis the way they dress in Virginia."

"Virginia, or hell, what be the difference?" Elizabeth's voice gained conviction. "You practice sorcery and killed your own brother."

Sarah felt her knees grow weak. "Samuel is dead?" she stammered as her heart pounded loudly in her ears. "It can't be."

"This is enough," Nick spat. "She doesn't need to listen to this. Chris, get back to the ship and tell them to be ready to weigh anchor."

"No," Hawthorne demanded, causing Chris to halt midstride. "I've seen it before and you'll lose her forever if you follow that plan. Trust me, I know what I am about."

Nick gritted his teeth. Every nerve in his body was taut with anger. But he stilled his motion and prayed Hawthorne was right.

Elizabeth's tortured laugh ended on a sob. "You killed him as sure as I am standing here. You took the shape of a sleek black cat, and when Samuel went to tie you in a sack, you bit him. Your body might have landed in the river, but not before you sank your poison into him."

"Elizabeth, I loved Samuel. I would never do anything to hurt him."

"He was tortured by your evil presence," Elizabeth hissed. "His skin burned with fever and his mind saw you at every turn. Yours was the name he cursed, Sarah Townsend," she screamed hysterically. "Yours was the name he finally called from his deathbed."

"But he was my brother. I loved him," Sarah cried softly, unable to contain her tears.

"Love," Elizabeth spat. "You know not the meaning of the word. We took you into our hearts and home and you repaid us by giving my babies to the devil and killing your own brother. I condemn you, Sarah Townsend. You are a witch from the blackest part of hell and I'll have no part of you. You should be hung."

"That's right, I saw it, too."

Stunned by the news of her stepbrother's death and the vicious words that had been heaped on her, Sarah turned mutely toward her second accuser.

Ann Tate, their widowed neighbor, slipped closer to the shaking Elizabeth. "I heard Samuel Wittfield condemn her with his dying breath. And I was there when she turned into a cat for the first time so many months ago. While her brother and this good woman prayed for her safe return, she's been flitting about the countryside doing the devil's business."

"No," Sarah insisted, shaking her head as tears coursed down her pale cheeks. "I was kidnapped and taken to Virginia." Desperately her eyes searched the crowd for Nick.

" 'Tis of no consequence," Ann spat. "With my own eyes I watched you change into a cat, and with my own ears I heard your name on your dying brother's lips. Thomas Hawkins, did you not just tell me this morning that your cow's been acting queer?"

The man took a tentative step closer. "That it has."

"And you Jacob Potter," Ann called. "Did you not say that just yesterday the gate to your yard broke when you pushed it open?"

"Aye, that it did," came the reply.

"Then who do you think has been doing this evil mischief?" Ann challenged, feeling the hysteria building, feeling the power of control. "You are a witch, Sarah Townsend, unfit to breathe the same air as good, God-fearing people."

"Hang the witch," the shout began. "Take her to the gallows now."

The magistrates quickly stepped forward, and two grabbed Sarah's arms. "There'll be no haste in this matter. She'll have a trial like all the rest."

"Hang her" came the chant. "Burn the devil's mistress."

Nick turned to the captain. "I don't care what you say, this madness has gone too far. I'm getting Sarah out of there right now." He never saw the meaty fist that connected with his jaw, and as his legs gave way and he crumpled to the ground, a blinding light filled his head until the darkness came to consume him.

Sebastian Hawthorne hoisted Nick easily over his shoulder and turned to Chris, who stood with his mouth still agape. "He would have rushed in and only succeeded in being arrested. I'll take him aboard my ship, the *Fleetwood*. You follow them," he gestured to the magistrates that now tugged at Sarah's arms. "Follow from a distance and don't speak to anyone. When you know which jail they put her in, join us as quickly as you can."

Chris could do more than nod, for the captain had already turned and was striding down the street with Nick's limp body dangling from his shoulder while the crowd, with Sarah at its center moved in the opposite direction.

Sarah's eyes frantically searched the growing sea of people. Her heart pounded with fear more terrifying than she could have ever imagined. "Nick!" she screamed desperately as they pulled her roughly down the street. "Nick!" But in the multitude before her, the face of her husband was nowhere to be found.

Nick woke to mind-shattering pain and the memory of Sarah in danger. Valiantly he tried to sit, but the ground beneath him swayed with a sickening motion.

"Easy, friend, easy." A hand braced behind his back gave him support, and Nick grimaced with pain as his body shifted upright. He was not on the ground after all, but on the deck of a ship, he realized as his eyes began to focus. His head throbbed, his jaw ached, and when he saw Sebastian Hawthorne kneeling beside him, he remembered all.

"You bastard." Nick pulled away and tried to find his feet. "You let those bloody fanatics take my wife." He stood too quickly and, as his head spun, he lost his balance and crashed to the deck again.

"They have my wife, too," Hawthorne said quietly. "I plan to get her out and sail on the morning tide, but I need your help. If we work together, they can both be saved; if not, then we gamble with the lives of those we hold most dear. I'll be in my cabin if you'd care to talk." He tossed down a leather flask that Nick managed to catch. " 'Tis brandy" was all he said before turning away.

Nick pulled himself against the rail and this time when he managed to stand, he did so slowly and his head stayed attached. The fiery bite of the brandy seared his throat, burned a path clear to his stomach, and did much to ease the painful throbbing in his head. He took one tentative step and then another. Fierce determination seeped into his being and he straightened his body further. Sarah was in jeopardy and she needed him, but first he needed answers. An air of danger surrounded him as he slowly made his way to Hawthorne's cabin.

Hawthorne looked up when Nick flung the door open. "Come in," he invited. "I apologize for striking you so hard. My mate was a bit overzealous with the nine pin."

"And were such theatrics necessary?" Nick snapped angrily, touching the lump that had already formed at the back on his head and then gingerly rubbing his aching jaw.

Hawthorne nodded toward a chair and then made a grand show of lighting his clay pipe. A faint cloud of blue-gray smoke haloed his head and his eyes scrunched against the sting. "More than necessary," he said quietly. "Your life depended on it. As I told Carlson, if you had rushed forth and tried to take your wife by force, the magistrates would have arrested you, too."

"Surely I could have reasoned with them."

"No, damn it." Hawthorne jerked to his feet and began to pace. "You couldn't have. What must I do to make you understand that there is no reasoning with these people? They see witches at every turn. Don't you see? They are not struggling to find the truth. Damn it, man, they don't even *want* to hear the truth."

Nick took the offered chair and pulled it closer to the small table. His anger had turned to fear for Sarah's safety and he knew he'd not rest until he had her back again. "You said they took your wife, too?"

He watched Hawthorne's face contort with pain. " 'Tis been over a month since they took my Jenny." The man slumped back in his chair and drank deeply from his mug. "When I saw you this morning, I knew you were my last hope."

Nick leaned forward. "Tell me everything, that I might understand better."

Hawthorne looked into his mug and saw the bright, laughing eyes of his wife and his own eyes filled with tears. "At first I thought it a grievous mistake. My Jenny was no witch, and we'd been at sea for nigh on two months." Unashamed, he let the tears well in his eyes. "We had landed only that morning. Jenny pleaded with me to take her off the ship for a while, and she's always such a sweet little thing, I couldn't refuse her. We were standing near the blacksmiths admiring a crate of oranges when a cart full of children careens around the corner. I think their pony has run off with them so I rush to stop the cart. A crowd follows and within minutes one of the children has pointed to my Jenny and screamed she was a witch. Jenny was snatched away and taken to jail."

Nick felt a cold dread coil deep within his middle. "Could you do nothing?"

Hawthorne stood and began to pace again. "I went to the harbormaster, but he sent me to the locals. I found where they had taken her and asked to see the charges leveled against her. My God, they filled three pages. I explained as calmly as I could that there must be some error. We had just arrived that morning. For a while I thought the magistrates on my side. If there was a misunderstanding, they wished to get to the bottom of it. They produced a girl, Abigail Williams, the minister's niece. When they asked her how it was possible that my Jenny could be guilty of the crimes listed against her when she'd been with me at sea, the girl faltered not one second. She turned her eyes on me and said clear as day that my Jenny's specter did the damage and was I trying to cover for the works of the devil. I waited for the magistrates to set her down and then tell me that Jenny was free." Hawthorne rubbed the tears from his eyes. "But it never happened. They believed the child. They believed that my kind, sweet Jenny traveled about the countryside, as a spirit of all things, doing the devil's mischief and I wasn't aware of it. It didn't take long to see that whatever the child said those in authority took as gospel, and any who disputed them were standing in the way of justice. So I came back to my ship alone.

"Each day I go to the trials hoping to find some flaw, some error that can be called forth to free my love. But the days go by and I find nothing."

Nick placed his hand on Hawthorne's shoulder and squeezed hard. "Have you seen her at all? Does she fare well?"

Hawthorne sniffed and tried to regain his composure. "They've let me visit her twice, for just a few minutes each time. It breaks my heart to see her in that squalor they call a jail, and they've cast her in irons. They've cast all the supposed witches in irons." He turned to Nick with desperation shining in his eyes. "You have to help me. I'll go mad if they do anything more to her. And I don't know how to get her out."

"Where is Christopher?"

Captain Hawthorne drew himself erect and wiped the last tear from his face. "I sent him to follow your wife. I've seen it happen enough times—the crowd will follow her to one of three jails. Tomorrow or the next day, she'll be brought before the magistrates and accused of her crimes. They'll ask for her plea." Hawthorne laughed hoarsely. "If she claims to be guilty and offers to repent, they'll set her free."

"What?" Nick gasped.

Hawthorne nodded. "But if she professes her innocence, she'll be cast in irons and taken back to jail to await her trial." The man shuddered. "Too many have already lost their lives at Gallows Hill. I'll not let my Jenny be one of them."

Nick rubbed his hand across his aching forehead. "But if we could get word to her to plead guilty, then all would be saved."

Hawthorne smiled sadly. "You're not of the Puritan faith, are you?" he asked. Nick shook his head and the man continued. "I had the same thought," he said slowly. "But when I begged Jenny, she would hear none of it. 'I am innocent and I'll not say elsewise. I'll not admit to seeking the devil's company, Sebastian,' she said. 'I'm a good Christian woman and I'll not denounce God to save my mortal life, so speak no more of it.'" Hawthorne shuddered visibly. "So now you know the problem, tell me Nicholas Beaumont, how are we going to find a solution?"

Chapter Twenty-four

"In here, witch." The rough shove sent Sarah reeling. She fell to her knees on the hard floor. "Tomorrow, the good women of Salem will come to strip you naked. They'll search every inch of your body to find your witch's tit. Then you'll be brought before the magistrates for your examination. By the time you return, the blacksmith will be ready with your chains."

Sarah struggled to her feet. "You speak as if I will be found guilty."

"You will," the jailer sneered.

"But I have done nothing." She tried to keep the panic from her voice, for she knew if she gave in to the fear that threatened, she would be lost forever.

"That's what they all say." The younger of the two men stepped forward and grabbed her roughly by the hair. Her lace cap had been lost in the scuffle with the crowd and now he held a thick handful of hair, pulling sharply until tears came to her eyes. "If you know what's good for you, you'll not cause any mischief tonight. Do you understand?"

Sarah watched the other man strike his palm smartly with his staff and understood perfectly. It was a warning. They would not hesitate to beat her if they felt they had a reason.

The grip on her hair tightened. "Do you understand, witch?" Painfully she nodded. "Good, now get away from this door and stay away."

Sarah found herself again thrust forward to land hard on her hands and knees. Her breath caught in her throat, for the air was thick with the sweet stench of humanity. Gingerly she again climbed to her feet and, as her eyes adjusted to the faint light, she nearly gasped aloud from the sight before her. More than fifty accused huddled together in a room not much larger than Agatha's parlor. Straw had been scattered about on the floor, but it had long since lost its freshness. There were no tables or chairs on which to sit. And as she moved about the room she felt the despair from those who surrounded her.

"Is there water?" Sarah knelt beside a frail woman who looked up with vacant eyes and pointed to a bucket that rested on a high shelf on the far wall.

Carefully, Sarah navigated around the bodies that huddled on the floor. Never had she seen such misery. Using the single cup that hung by a string, she dipped a small sip of water. But the odious liquid had no more than touched her lips when she spit it out.

"Won't be any fresh water until tomorrow." Sarah turned to find a young woman of about twenty watching her with sad, knowing eyes. "They only bring water every other day."

"They say we waste it," came another voice.

"This is madness," Sarah snapped. "One bucket

372

of water for all these people?"

"It takes a while, but you'll get used to it" came another voice.

Sarah felt their fear and desperation, and it moved her. She snatched the bucket roughly from the shelf and stepped to the door. "Is there someone to hear me if I call?"

"Don't" came the panicked reply. "They don't like it when we cause trouble."

"You're not causing trouble," she said firmly. "*I* am." Sarah used her fist to beat against the thick wooden door. "Jailer," she called. "Come quickly." Again and again she pounded until she knew her flesh would carry bruises. But at last she could hear the sounds of movement on the other side. Quickly she stepped back as the massive door swung open.

"What's going on in here?" came the fierce snarl.

Despite the frantic beating of her heart and her trembling knees, Sarah stood her ground. "Sir, there is no water in the bucket. Might we have more? I would be happy to fetch it to save you the effort."

"You! I might have known." The water bucket was snatched from her hands. "So there's no water?" the man snapped. "Then what do you call this?"

Sarah jerked back, but the foul water still caught her in the face. Instinctively her hands flew to her eyes, and they caught the vicious blow from the cane. Curled on the muddied ground for protection, Sarah whimpered in pain. She felt the man's boot nudge her middle but she couldn't move.

"Some of you just take longer to learn than

373

others," he taunted. "Ain't it a shame."

Sarah heard his feet move, but her breath refused to come until she heard the door close behind him. Rolling over to sit, she tried to flex her fingers, but pain speared through then, making her gasp aloud.

"Are you hurt bad?" The young woman's chain rattled as she moved to sit beside her. "You were lucky if all he got was your fingers." Gently she took Sarah's hands in hers. The knuckles were already swelling. Her touch was light, but Sarah still cried out in pain when the woman curled them into a fist. "Well, you can bend them with no bones poppin' out, so don't think anything is broken. Still, they're going to give you some trouble for a while. I think you'd best . . ."

Her words were never finished, for at that moment they heard footsteps outside the door. Quickly the girl pushed Sarah flat and moved away.

The jailer entered and dropped the bucket to the floor. "What's a matter, witch, cat got your tongue?"

Sarah slowly turned and her violet eyes locked on the jailer. "Be careful," she warned softly. "For the book says, do unto others as you would have done unto you."

The man took a slow step back as her icy words caused his flesh to chill. No one in his jail had dared to defy him, and now this little piece of fluff had challenged him twice. His eyes turned to the fresh bucket of water he had just carried in when her voice sounded again. "Don't even think of it."

He took a deep breath and immediately began to choke on the foul air. "Damn," he swore, backing away, careful to avoid bumping the bucket. "This one might really be a witch."

The door closed and the heavy bar dropped into place. Sarah began to tremble with relief. Never had she been so frightened. She drew up her knees and dropped her forehead on them.

"Are you all right?" A hand gently touched her shoulder. "How ever did you get the nerve to speak to him that way?"

Sarah raised her face and tried to still the frantic beating of her heart. "I can't talk," she gasped. "I can't seem to stop shaking." The girl moved, returning with a cup of fresh water. She held Sarah's hand to help her drink. The cool water tasted better than the finest wine on her parched lips, and the tremors soon began to ease.

Sarah drew a shaky breath. "I was just so angry that he would take such advantage." She scrambled to her feet and looked at the squalor that surrounded her. "People shouldn't have to live like this."

"But we're the accused," came a weary voice. "This is our lot in life."

Sarah flexed her fingers again and tried to ignore the pain. "Your lot in life is to make the best of whatever you have," she said slowly. She grimaced from the weight of the bucket and the young girl was instantly there to take it from her.

"My name is Jenny," she said shyly, carrying the bucket as they moved about the room to offer water.

Nick fought to hold his tongue as they left the courtroom. Never had he seen such a travesty of justice. Hawthorne had insisted they attend, and now Nick understood why. In the face of fear, reason had fled completely. Hawthorne was right when he said they would rather find witches than the truth. When they were again on the *Good Providence,* Nick let loose.

"Damn them all to hell," he spat, pacing about the small cabin, feeling the desperate need to strike something. "Those madmen have my Sarah."

"And my Jenny," Hawthorne said quietly. He poured three brandies and joined Chris at the table. "There is no reasoning with these people. They believe whatever madness those children propagate."

Chris took a deep drink, for the sights he had witnessed disturbed him deeply. "But why did they make that poor woman touch them?" he questioned. "I don't understand."

Hawthorne shook his head and an ironic smile touched his face. "That, my friends, is a test for witchcraft. If the child is afflicted and she is touched by the witch, then the diabolical fluid is passed back into the witch. Thus the affliction is momentarily stopped."

"And that is used as proof?" Chris's voice held disbelief.

Hawthorne nodded. "I could go and claim you to be a wizard. If I throw myself on the floor and twitch about, say that I saw you with the devil and that you bade me sign the devil's book, they would come and arrest you. For proof I have only to twitch about until they place your hand on me. If I stop, I've just proved you to be a wizard."

"My God," Chris sighed.

376

"God isn't in Salem, if you ask me," Hawthorne said, looking from one to the other. "If he was, he wouldn't have let them take my Jenny."

Nick pulled out a chair and joined them at the table. His eyes glittered with dangerous lights. "God might not be in Salem," he said quietly, "but we are. And I have a plan."

Bone-weary, Sarah awaited the coming of the dawn. Her gown reeked from the rancid water that had doused her and her fingers, now stiff and swollen, throbbed constantly. *Nick, come and get me,* her mind cried again and again.

The room slumbered peacefully, but Sarah knew she would not sleep, for now she held the truth. She had spent the night moving quietly among the prisoners, trying to give comfort or restore faith that had deserted. And as their stories poured forth, she had listened. It hadn't taken long for the pattern to appear, and as each piece of the puzzle fit into place her outrage grew. These people weren't witches, but the victims of Church politics and bitter land disputes. How was it that no one had noticed before? she wondered. Five of the afflicted came from two families. They lived to the west of the meeting house and had been in favor of the Reverend Mr. Parris. The accused lived east of the meeting house. Again and again she listed the names and circumstances in her mind. Of the church committee members twenty families had been against hiring Parris, and of those seventeen had now been arrested for witchcraft. Her head dropped to her knees. *Nick, where are you?* she cried. *I need you.*

She felt the warmth before she saw it, that first beam of sunlight that filtered through the space in the high window. It touched her and she gloried in its heat.

"I know what I am about now," she whispered. "I have found the answer to the madness." The ray of sunlight grew brighter, haloing her with its brilliance. Sarah heard those behind her begin to stir. "Give me strength," she prayed, kneeling in the light. "Give me the words to make the governor understand."

The door to the jail crashed open, and Sarah flew to her feet. The others, snatched from their sleep, cowered in fear, for in their minds it was the jailer returned and that always meant trouble. Blankets were pulled over heads, and those in the corners huddled more to the shadows hoping not to be noticed.

Sarah knew she stood, but she was sure she must be dreaming, for when she looked up, Nick was standing before her looking every bit the pirate. He wore a sash over one eye and a thick black wig that reached low on his shoulders and covered much of his face.

"You," he pointed with a long sword. "Out."

She resisted the urge to fling herself into his arms as relief flooded through her. An instant later she was dangling over Chris's shoulder as Nick stood guard at the door. He, too, sported a gigantic wig, and as he stepped from the jail, the wind pushed it against her nose, making her sneeze repeatedly.

"Will you be quiet?" Chris hissed, setting her

quickly in the wagon. Hawthorne captured his prize, and within minutes the wagon was full and flying down the roadway.

In what seemed like a lifetime but in reality was less than an hour, they had bid farewell to Captain Hawthorne and his wife, and both the *Good Providence* and the *Fleetwood* had weighed anchor.

Sarah stood on the quarterdeck and watched the last of Salem Harbor fade from view. When Nick moved to stand behind her, she leaned back against him.

"You shouldn't be up here without a cloak," he said gently, folding his arms about her.

"I need to bathe first," she said. "I fear I smell something fierce."

Nick sniffed her hair and chuckled. "That you do. You've been through a trying ordeal, my dear, and it's only fitting that I should help you."

She smiled and locked her arms over his. "Nick, I need to ask a great favor of you." She felt his body stiffen behind her.

"I'm not taking you back there," he said. "When that crowd carried you off, I almost lost my heart. I'll not willingly go through that again. Don't ask that of me."

Sarah turned in his arms. "Would you take me to Boston to speak with Governor Phips?"

Nick scowled down at her. "Why?"

Quietly she told of her night in the prison, recounting the tales and drawing the pattern of names. "I think I can persuade him to put an end to it," she said desperately. "Please let me try."

Nick rubbed his forehead against hers. "We have no choice," he said quietly, emphasizing the word

379

we. "We can't stand by and let this madness continue. I will do everything in my power to help you as long as you are not put in danger. I will not risk that again for all the wealth in Virginia."

Sarah felt her heart swell with pride. "Have I told you lately that I love you, Mr. Beaumont?" she whispered.

"Not often enough, Mrs. Beaumont," he sighed against her lips. "Not nearly often enough."

Chapter Twenty-five

The stone bench on which she sat was cold, but Sarah made no move to rise. Fall had moved through Virginia, painting the leaves a fiery red and brilliant orange. With sad eyes she gazed about the garden. The last of the summer blossoms were gone, but then, so many things that had once filled her life were gone: the whimsical stories of Rebecca Nurse stilled forever by the hangman's noose, her stepbrother Samuel dead, her house in the village burned to the ground. She shivered as much from the memories as from the bite of the wind. Leaves, dried and brittle, snapped free from their moorings to swirl about, and the gentle rustling sound of their flight filled the air.

She gazed down at the official document she clasped in her hand, and though it carried the seal of the governor, her eyes again filled with sorrow. Such a waste, she thought bitterly. Such a tragic waste. The sun left its hiding place in the gray, cloud-filled sky and Sarah basked in its warmth.

"Why are you sad, my daughter?" came the gentle words to her mind.

Sarah's eyes welled with tears. "I failed," she

whispered to the wind. "I know now I was sent to stop the witch trials, but I failed."

"The hangings are done. No more will find their death at Gallows Hill. The tree has been cut down . . . the witch hunt is over."

"But there were no witches in Salem, and twenty innocent people lost their lives. Nineteen taken from their homes, their loved ones, and poor Giles Corey . . ." Sarah's tears began to course down her pale cheeks. "Giles Corey pressed to death because he would not denounce his faith. What madness makes decent people do such things to one another?"

"Greed and the want of power. It overshadowed their faith . . . that same faith they strove so hard to profess."

Sarah turned her troubled face to the sky. "Why wasn't I able to do more?"

"You brought the madness to an end."

Sarah shook her head. "I spoke to the governor and he did nothing."

For a moment the wind swirled in an angry gust around her. "You must have faith, my child" came the gentle rebuff. "Oftimes the heart hears what the mind denies. Yours were the words that took the clouds of doubt from the governor's eyes. Spoken from the heart, you reached him where others failed. The document you hold that stops the killings was the result of your intervention. I will hear no more self-reproach. You have done well."

Sarah turned her face to the sun, and its warmth dried her tears. The light intensified, surrounding her with its brightness, and a light, airy feeling seeped into her awareness. She felt as carefree as the leaves that glided with abandon on the whims of the wind. And suddenly she remembered a time past when there was no time . . . and her body grew lighter still. For an instant she felt free of her earthly bonds . . . and in that moment she remembered the reality of her being.

"Do you wish me home now, Father?" Her eyes pressed closed dreading the answer, for she couldn't bear the thought of leaving Nick.

The sunlight intensified, growing warm on her face, cloaking her in peace and tranquility. "You have always been one of my favorites, Sarah, but alas, your task on earth is not yet completed," came the gentle voice.

Sarah looked up with desperate hope in her eyes.

"Do not be distressed, my child. I know that Nicholas Beaumont now claims your heart. But the love you share is pure, Sarah, and in that you give me glory. It will be your great-grandsons that help to form this new land." The sunlight started to slip away and Sarah blinked rapidly. "Be at peace, my child," the wind seemed to whisper.

Sarah looked down at the document signed by the governor and felt contentment. There would always be a part of her that would ache for those now gone, but with memories they'd never be forgotten and with faith the horrors would never occur again. Taking a deep breath of the crisp fall air, she gazed about with new eyes. *This is my home,* she thought with startling clarity. And as the words echoed again in her mind, her hand pressed to her stomach in wonder. "I'm going to carry Nick's baby," she thought. Heady sensations washed through her, erasing doubts and the pain of the past. She tried to imagine holding a child and her face took on a wistful, dreamlike stare.

Nicholas Beaumont rounded the corner of the house to find his wife sitting alone in the garden. Her face radiated a beauty that startled him with its intensity. For so much of his life he had been alone; now he had Sarah. He shuddered to think how close he had come to losing her. *But we're home,* he thought, and his step quickened as he moved to join her.

"You received the news," he observed, smiling down at her and taking the document from her fingers. "Have I told you how proud I am of you?" He pulled her gently to her feet and enfolded her in his arms.

Sarah blushed and gazed up at him. *I shall never tire of looking at this face,* she thought, *and when I am old in years and feeble in mind, I shall still find comfort with this man.*

"I love you," he said quietly, touching his forehead to hers. "You are my heart, my life, my soul."

Sarah felt a yearning deep within her. "Make me the mother of your children," she whispered.

Nick's smile intensified. Scooping her up in his arms, he turned toward the house. "With pleasure, Mrs. Beaumont."